ACCLAIM FOR JAME

"In *All Things Bright and Strange*, James Markert melds the ordinary and the extraordinary to create a compelling tale. Can miracles be trusted? Are the dead really gone? Can we be undone by what we wish for most? The citizens of Markert's Bellhaven must confront these questions and more, with their fates and the existence of their entire town at stake."

—GREER MACALLISTER,
BESTSELLING AUTHOR OF
*THE MAGICIAN'S LIE* AND
*GIRL IN DISGUISE*

"Mysterious, gritty and a bit mystical, Markert's entertaining new novel inspires the question of "What if?" Many characters are nicely multilayered, providing a good balance of intrigue and realism. The fascinating glimpse into the process of distilling bourbon—and the effect of the Prohibition on Kentucky and its bourbon families—adds another layer to the story."

—*RT BOOK REVIEWS*, 3 STARS
ON *THE ANGELS' SHARE*

"Folksy charm, an undercurrent of menace, and an aura of hope permeate this ultimately inspirational tale."

—*BOOKLIST* ON *THE ANGELS' SHARE*

"Distinguished by complex ideas and a foreboding tone, Markert's enthralling novel (*A White Wind Blew*) captures a dark time and a people desperate for hope."

—*LIBRARY JOURNAL*

"Markert displays great imagination in describing the rivalries, friendships, and intense relationships among the often quirky and cranky terminally ill, and the way that a diagnosis, or even a cure, can upset delicate dynamics."

—PUBLISHERS WEEKLY ON
A WHITE WIND BLEW

"The author's ability to weigh competing views against each other, and the all-too-real human complications are presented with a remarkable understanding of conflicting ideas that makes even villains human eventually. The author writes well and reads easily; you'll finish this book in a day or two and wish for a sequel."

—BOOKPAGE ON A WHITE WIND BLEW

"A tuberculosis epidemic, as seen through the eyes of a sanatorium doctor driven by his love of God and music."

—KIRKUS REVIEWS ON A
WHITE WIND BLEW

"[Markert's] debut novel, A White Wind Blew is set in Waverly Hills, that massive Gothic structure that is said to be one of the most haunted places on earth."

—RONNA KAPLAN FOR THE
HUFFINGTON POST

"The book is at its best when Pike, McVain and their eclectic band of musicians are beating the odds, whether against tuberculosis or against stifling institutional mores."

—CHERYL TRUMAN, KENTUCKY
HERALD-LEADER

"Markert has interwoven three seemingly unrelated subjects—tuberculosis, music, and racism—into a hauntingly lyrical narrative with operatic overtones."

—BOOKLIST ON A WHITE
WIND BLEW

# All Things Bright
# and Strange

## ALSO BY JAMES MARKERT

*The Angels' Share*

# All Things

# Bright
## AND
# Strange

*JAMES MARKERT*

THOMAS NELSON
Since 1798

Published in Nashville, Tennessee, by Thomas Nelson. Thomas Nelson is a registered trademark of HarperCollins Christian Publishing, Inc.

Thomas Nelson titles may be purchased in bulk for educational, business, fund-raising, or sales promotional use. For information, please e-mail SpecialMarkets@ThomasNelson.com.

Publisher's Note: This novel is a work of fiction. Names, characters, places, and incidents are either products of the author's imagination or used fictitiously. All characters are fictional, and any similarity to people living or dead is purely coincidental.

**Library of Congress Cataloging-in-Publication Data**

Names: Markert, James, 1974- author.
Title: All things bright and strange / James Markert, James Markert.
Description: Nashville : Thomas Nelson, 2018.
Identifiers: LCCN 2017039713 | ISBN 9780718090289 (softcover)
Subjects: LCSH: City and town life—Fiction. | Good and evil—Fiction. |
  GSAFD: Christian fiction.
Classification: LCC PS3613.A75379 A79 2018 | DDC 813/.6—dc23 LC record available at https://lccn.loc.gov/2017039713

*Printed in the United States of America*

18 19 20 21 22 LSC 5 4 3 2 1

*Can humanity stand the universe without its supernatural?*

*I don't know.*

PROTESTANT MINISTER, 1920S

*For my parents*
*It would be impossible to create a fictional pair who*
*could rival the pure goodness of the real thing.*
*Thank you.*

# PROLOGUE

1917

The boy shuffled his feet in the dark basement.

His momma had told him not to stomp—only to *pretend* to dance.

They'd been warned not to make noise. Couldn't risk being found yet. The lady had risked her life for them. And two days wasn't long to wait, even in the dark.

But the piano music above was so loud the boy couldn't help but groove and hoof. He wasn't much of a dancer. His gift was different—a gift his momma said had finally put them on the lam. But not being good at something had never stopped him before. Their dance floor above was his ceiling below. Light crept through the floorboard cracks. Shadows moved in accordance with their rhythms and gyrations up there. All of them in glad rags, smoked on giggle juice, having them a swell time just like the lady said they always did.

And come to think, she said next time they'd be able to join in. *"This town is different. You'll be welcomed here."*

The boy ate a corn bread muffin from a basket the lady had

sneaked to them before the party started. He'd already eaten three, but his stomach still felt empty. The wagon trip had been a long one with no food, and by the looks of his thin arms he knew he'd lost weight.

He wiped his hands of the crumbs and silent-shuffled with his thumbs hooked in his trouser pockets. String instruments started above. A violin and something deeper that made his heart thrum warm.

Two wooden crates rested under the stairs. He stacked one atop the other and climbed up like he'd done a few times during the day when there was no risk of being noticed. Up near the ceiling under the first step was a patch where the boards didn't line up flush, an opening just big enough to see the floorboards above.

His momma would tan his hide if someone noticed his eyes lurking. She turned her back in defiance but a minute later was next to him, holding the crates so they wouldn't topple.

"Well?"

The boy squinted, bent his knees for a better angle, and now saw people instead of just shoes and boots and bare feet. Hundred folks if there was twenty.

"You're grinnin' like some fool," she whispered. "What is it, boy?"

"There's some like us in there, Momma." He kept grinning, eyes large. "Blacks and whites in the same place, carryin' on together. One man hambonin' next to a white lady dancin'."

His momma waved that notion away. "Always said you had a good imagination."

The boy rubbed his eyes, but when he looked again, nothing changed. "There's even a black man with a star badge and a fancy topper."

"Like a sheriff?"

"In uniform to the nines."

"Black sheriff in a white town? Hush now, boy."

"Strike me down if I'm lyin'."

She waited. Nothing happened. "Mayhap she told us the truth after all. Mayhap this place is different."

He didn't tell his momma what he saw in the open window *behind* the dancing lady—the cardinal bird on the windowsill. Looked like the same one that used to visit the tree outside their cabin back home.

"What is it?" she asked. "What else you see?"

"Nothin'. That's the crop, Momma. Just like I said."

Momma didn't need to know everything. Like what he'd seen in the woods last night when the lady hurried them out from under the tarp—hundreds of cardinal birds circling. And then in the woods before she hurried them underground—*Cardinal birds clustered in the form of a man? Pinch me.* Just a bunch of redbirds in a low bundle, like a leaf tornado. But tornados didn't have arms and legs and a head. And the lady *had* said these woods were magical, with all those sprawling live oaks and that clinging moss.

Then again, he *did* have a good imagination.

He closed his eyes, remembered how the gust of wind dispersed those birds right before he and Momma had gone underground. The cardinal man gone in a snap.

The boy's smile abandoned him. He looked down from his box perch. "Momma, what is this place?"

"Far as I recall, she jus' say we in Bellhaven."

"Why she say they paint some of the trees yellow?"

She shrugged. "I'm long past dwellin' on the whys of the white mind, boy."

*But I'm not.* He could smell the ocean from here. Saltwater marshes and tidal swamps. *Lady said something about the Charleston peninsula and two rivers.* "I've never heard of Bellhaven in all my months of book learnin'."

Thunder rumbled outside, distant and then close.

*Too fast for thunder.*

The boy's momma stepped away from the crates. "Horse hooves."

The ground vibrated. The music quieted upstairs and the folks stopped dancing.

The boy climbed down from the crates and approached the lone window half-sunk in the ground. The glass was mud smeared and concealed by azalea bushes fixing to bloom. He pulled an old stool under the window and balanced himself on top, his eyes just high enough to see horse hooves, white cloaks, and torches outside.

"They found us, Momma."

# CHAPTER 1

1920

BELLHAVEN, SOUTH CAROLINA

It was as good a day to die as any.

But first, Ellsworth Newberry would have his morning cup of joe.

He poured it from a dented pot, inhaled the earthy roast, and swirled in a finger's worth of medicinal whiskey. He'd begun stashing liquor the day the Eighteenth Amendment was ratified—a good year before Prohibition actually began—but as long as Dr. Philpot continued writing scrips for his bum leg, there was no reason to start using his stash of Old Sam. Whoever found his body could have what he'd hoarded.

He braced himself against the stove and took a step on his new wooden leg—a so-called Hanger limb, named after the man who'd designed it. *If ol' Hanger had any sense, he'd have made it so the knee would bend.* Leather attachments connected the leg to the stump above where his left knee used to be, and the leather pads on the heel and ball of the foot were prone to make him trip. "You'll need those pads for traction," the military doc had said.

1

*Soon won't be needing the leg for anything.*

Ellsworth used his cane into the living room, where his chair waited by the bay window. He dropped down on the wooden seat and unholstered the Smith & Wesson on the window ledge next to last night's dinner plate. Remnants of beef stew had hardened around the edges. He nudged the plate aside to make room for his coffee mug and then watched out the window.

Across the road, the façade of the town hall lay in rubble. Built by his late father, the building had once been the focal point of the town square, with sash windows and tall brick walls painted blue, eaves trimmed white to match the wraparound veranda that enclosed it all like a warm hug. Now the interior walls were visible, flame-scorched from the fire that had killed Bellhaven's soul and Ellsworth's wife.

The avenue of oaks was still there, though. Eliza once thought them magical—the way the Spanish moss draped their sprawling limbs, swaying in the coastal breeze and shimmering silver in sunlight. The live oaks overhung the road into town like a vault, evenly spaced on both sides for more than a hundred yards.

*"It's like a perfect tunnel,"* Eliza had said on their wedding day, nestling the top of her head into the pocket of Ellsworth's shoulder as he steered their new Model T over the bumpy gravel. *"Like driving under a dream."*

What was it he'd said in response? *"I reckon so . . ."*

She'd glanced at him before repositioning her head against his shoulder; a flicker of disappointment in those blue eyes. Breeze from the open windows moved strands of auburn hair against his cheek. Sometimes he could still feel the tickle.

Ellsworth moved hair that wasn't there, wishing now he'd said something different back then, something less dismissive than "I reckon so." But the truth was he'd been distracted by the rose-blossom scent of her hair, the puttering of the car engine, and the mockingbird trying to keep pace next to his window. That brief look she'd given him had been the first sign of her melancholy—what many in town referred to as her madness.

Instead of her smile he now saw chiggers and rat snakes. Boll weevils munching through cotton scabs. A long-abandoned town hall where 'coons lived in the attic, bats hung from rafters, and egret droppings covered the floorboards. Sea breezes passed through the broken windows like nothing of import had ever transpired in there—no festivals or potlucks, holiday gatherings or birthday parties, talent shows or theatrical plays. The music and singing had been something of wonder. Without it the town's heart thumped slowly and without much purpose.

Stacks of dirty plates rested beside his chair. No point cleaning them up now. No point grooming himself either. At twenty-two, his chestnut hair already had flecks of gray around the ears. The war had brought deep creases to an already rugged face, a bleakness to his blue eyes, and he swore now that Anna Belle Roper was trying to make him fat on top of it all.

Ellsworth's coffee was scalding, but he sipped it no matter. He didn't have time to let it cool. He had to get his business done before Anna Belle arrived with breakfast.

The coffee burned a trail down his throat. Steam opened his eyes and cleared his muddled head. He hadn't had a full night sleep since his return ten months ago, not with how the carnage flashed back every time he closed his eyes. *Better off not sleeping*, he'd tell himself nightly. *Better off not living at all.*

They'd been in such a hurry to fight the war President Wilson declared that they'd never stopped to think of why. Ellsworth thought maybe killing Krauts would help him grieve Eliza. Calvin and Alfred signed up because Ellsworth did. A mortar shell blew Ellsworth's left leg to bits during the battle of Château-Thierry.

Calvin never made it through the first American offensive. Alfred returned blind from mustard gas, and *his* insomnia had left him jingle-brained.

Alfred sat now on a bench in the shadows of the town hall, in full army gear minus the dented helmet, feeding bread chunks to squirrels he couldn't see. Probably already thinking of wandering over to share a cup. He visited daily, as did half the town, it seemed. Like it was their mission to get Ellsworth out of the house and back into Bellhaven's trickling bloodstream.

*Why can't they leave me be?*

Ellsworth finished his coffee, hurried through a cigarette, and squashed the butt into the window ledge next to his revolver. He braced his hands on the chair arms and stood, wincing at the sharp pain that resonated where nub touched prosthesis.

He grabbed his Smith & Wesson from the window ledge. It was fully loaded with .45-caliber bullets. He slid the barrel into his mouth, and it clicked against his teeth. He wondered if Alfred across the road would hear the gunshot and run blindly to help. Hopefully somebody would hear and come find him before Anna Belle came with breakfast. Maybe that crotchety Old Man Tanner across the road. He was just mean enough to deserve cleaning up the mess. And that way Anna Belle wouldn't have to do it.

Ellsworth pushed the barrel in too far and gagged, tasted metal against his tongue. He pinched his eyes closed, but thoughts of Eliza flashed. In the days before the fire, she'd seemed more at peace than he'd seen her in years, certainly since their first baby came out stillborn.

*"I talked with him, Ellsworth. Our son. Erik. I knelt upon the healing floor."*

Ellsworth had felt uncomfortable naming a baby that never once breathed on his own. But they'd done it anyway, for Eliza's sake.

*Till death do us part, Eliza. And brings us back together again.*

Ellsworth reapplied pressure on the trigger. Would one bullet even do the trick?

Something thumped against the window. He opened his eyes.

A cardinal bird fluttered outside the glass. An olive-gray female with a prominently raised red-tinged crest and a stark orange beak. It settled on the windowsill, stared at him.

He watched the cardinal right back, watched it until his finger eased and he'd moved the barrel out enough to take a deep swallow. No other sign could have coaxed that gun from his mouth. He lowered the revolver to his side, and his heart rate slowed.

Tears welled in his eyes.

The cardinal flew away.

Across the street, Anna Belle Roper's front door opened. She walked toward his house with a towel-covered plate of breakfast.

*Too late now. Shouldn't have hesitated.*

Ellsworth plopped back down on his chair and placed the gun on the window ledge, resigned to another day of living.

He sighed. "Hope she fried bacon."

# CHAPTER 2

Anna Belle was pretty as a sunrise and always dressed to the nines.

She'd been his first kiss at twelve, planting one on him while they waded in the Atlantic. *"Just so I could say one day we did, Ellsworth."* They'd all known she'd marry Calvin anyway. Now every morning Ellsworth battled the need to tell her about Cantigny, that small French village where Calvin was shot dead. About how he'd cradled her husband's head in his lap while he bled out from the throat wound. But every time he started, he'd choke up.

Today she wore a white sweater over a pink blouse, her strawberry-blond hair pinned up in a bundle atop her head. Her beige skirt hugged her hips and narrowed at the ankles, a soft silhouette of curves he tried not to notice when she placed the steaming plate of food on the window ledge. Bacon, fried potatoes, and two eggs over easy—just the way he liked them.

Anna Belle smiled, waited for a response.

He jerked her a nod. Lately he'd taken to staring at the floor-boards rather than meeting the walnut brown of her eyes. *I held him in my lap, Anna Belle. I couldn't stop the bleeding.* Any more than a nod would lead to conversation and, looks aside, Anna Belle talked too much. Never could leave quiet alone.

The rest of the town might visit, but they wouldn't stay. Ever since the night Eliza died in the fire—and with what Ellsworth had done to the Klansman after—they'd all acted a pinch leery of him, despite their innate fondness. But Anna Belle was the opposite. She brought Ellsworth breakfast and dinner every day, along with the newspaper from his porch.

He needed that daily paper even more than his morning coffee. He'd returned from war a month before Alfred and two months before his other pal, Omar, fearing more, daily, that both had died as Calvin had. He'd become obsessed with checking the news every day, even after both men had returned, each damaged in his own right.

But today Anna Belle backed away from his chair, the folded newspaper still in her grip. She didn't leave it next to his plate like usual.

"Why do you have the gun out, Ellsworth?"

"Might be Krauts in the woods, Anna Belle."

She grinned. Earlier, she'd knocked for two minutes before finally letting herself in his house. "A gentleman would get out of the chair and open the door for a woman."

"A wiser woman would catch a hint."

She huffed, looked at the gun. "So why didn't you shoot *me* for intruding?"

He slid a crisp bacon slice into his mouth. "This some kind of interview?"

She began stacking all the dirty plates he'd left around the chair.

"What are you doing?"

"Eat," she said. "I'll clean these, and then we can have more conversation."

"That what this is?" he mumbled, pulling the plate to his lap. The food was delicious. The potatoes were crisp. Eggs slid down like the grease they'd been fried in. He soaked the last piece of bacon in the remaining yolk and listened to Anna Belle clank dishes in the kitchen.

The sound of it brought back the urge to shoot himself. He and Eliza used to do the dishes together. She'd wash and he'd rinse. *"It begins with you in their arms and ends with your arms in the sink."* If she'd said it once, she'd said it a hundred times.

Anna Belle returned and sat in a chair opposite his. "So?"

"So what?"

"You've got to get out of this house at some point."

"Why?"

"To learn to walk again, for one."

"I walk fine."

"I haven't seen it."

"You don't see me using this chair as a privy, do you?"

She thought on it. "Then let's go for one."

"One what?"

"A walk, Ellsworth. It's a lovely day."

He grunted, kept his eyes on the street outside. She was relentless. She asked, "Do you have a nest egg I don't know about?"

"If I do it's none of your business."

"You'll need a job. There's still houses in need of painting about town, and your hands work fine."

He laughed, a quick burst, then poked the bottom of his clunky prosthesis into the floorboard three times. "I can't paint houses anymore."

"How about doghouses then? You wouldn't need to stand on a ladder to paint those. Or you could help Ned Gleeson paint those birdhouses he makes."

She glanced at his wooden leg, then looked away.

"I was a pitcher, Anna Belle."

For that she had no response. He *had* been a pitcher, one of the best South Carolina had ever seen. Before the war, the big leagues had been a certainty.

The summer after he and Eliza were married, Babe Ruth had come through Charleston between travel games to dine on fresh seafood. Ellsworth had caught wind of it and made the trip to Charleston. He'd approached the baseball star with a satchel of balls and a wooden bat and challenged him to three pitches, daring him to hit one into the harbor. Ruth took the challenge across the street at the nearby park—rolled up his sleeves and missed on three consecutive pitches. Ellsworth would later admit that Ruth had just finished his fourth pint of suds when he accepted the challenge, but he'd struck the man out no matter. When word reached the Dodgers, he felt sure his place in the minors would be assured.

Ellsworth knew that town folk whispered about the fact that now he'd never play in the big leagues like he'd dreamed. But this was the first time the tragedy had been spoken in his presence, and it felt like the air had been sucked from the room.

Anna Belle stood from the chair, opened the window. In came street noise, a subtle breeze, and the smell of blooming azaleas. "Have you noticed the hydrangeas are out? Along with the camellias?"

He'd seen it yesterday, but hadn't wanted to admit it to himself. Typically camellias flowered in winter, hydrangeas in the summer. But this spring both bloomed alongside the azaleas and the daffodils, and the magnolia trees were blooming early too. The town square was dotted with color—stunning shades of yellow and red, white and pink, blue and violet. *The oddities of the Bellhaven woods; rumors sometimes breed truths of their own.* But all Ellsworth said was, "What of it?"

"Just mighty peculiar is all." She watched out the window. "Pinch me, but everything is blooming at once." She breathed in the fragrant air. "Another good reason to take a walk."

Ellsworth watched Alfred feed squirrels in the distance. "Why do you care what I do?"

"Because that's what Eliza would have wanted. For you not to become a turtle."

"I can look after myself, Anna Belle."

"Like all men can?" She started away, stopped, turned back. "You know, that's what Calvin told me before he ran off and followed *you* to war. Alfred too. They'd follow you to hell if—"

"Don't do that, Anna Belle."

She looked down, fiddled with a button on her sweater. "I'm sorry. I'm sorry. But Calvin did say that. Told me not to worry, that he'd take care of himself. Well, he didn't. And here I am a widow raising a boy that I've come to love even though he won't talk." She pointed at Ellsworth. "And you don't even have the courage to mention his name. 'The boy. That boy.' His name is Raphael, Ellsworth, not 'that boy.' So don't be cold to me. I'm doing the honorable thing for *your* late wife. She's the one asked me to watch over him should anything happen to her."

Anna Belle folded her arms. "Are you going to say anything?"

He grunted. "Thanks for breakfast."

She shook her head. "Sometimes I wonder if Calvin wasn't the lucky one for dying." They shared a glance. "Have you noticed the cardinals?" she asked. "They're everywhere. Saw at least a dozen on the town hall roof this morning, and the woods are singing. There was one perched on your window on my way over. Don't tell me you didn't notice it."

"I saw her."

"Her?"

"The cardinal. It was a female." She was luring him to the past with talk of the redbirds, but he wouldn't take the bait.

"Ellsworth?"

"Yes?"

"Stop blaming him. Raphael. He's not the reason Eliza died." She turned toward the door. "I'll let myself out."

"Anna Belle, wait."

"Yes?" Her eyes lifted with hope.

"The paper?"

Her face sagged. She stepped toward him, but then stopped and grinned. Instead of handing him the newspaper, she walked back outside with it, slamming the door.

Halfway down the walkway to the street, she stopped to look at his window to make sure he was watching.

She dropped the newspaper in the middle of the sidewalk and walked off toward home.

# CHAPTER 3

Ellsworth made it out of his chair twice and even got as far as opening the door the second time before deciding to leave the newspaper on the sidewalk.

If she wanted to play games, then fine. He'd once stared down Babe Ruth with a baseball bat. He could outlast Anna Belle Roper. The current events could wait until tomorrow. *But what if she doesn't bring me my paper tomorrow either? Current events will soon become history.* And the smell of ink had now become as much of a daily necessity as the alcohol. Never should have fretted over his pals' return in the first place. Even the survivors died over there.

He hoisted himself up from his chair for the third time to retrieve that paper.

Alfred appeared out the window, crossing the road with his right hand gripping his cane and something boxlike and clunky in the crook of his left elbow. A blind man had no business crossing the road with both hands occupied. *How does Linda May let him out of the house like that?*

Alfred navigated the crossing easily enough. Not too many in Bellhaven had cars yet, and it wasn't a busy thoroughfare. And the townspeople knew to look out for Alfred, who roamed the streets like a stray mutt.

Alfred had the trip to Ellsworth's memorized down to the number of steps it took to get up the veranda and open the screen door. It was an unspoken rule that Alfred let himself in. But since Alfred had his arms full and Ellsworth was heading to the door anyway, Ellsworth helped him inside. Alfred handed Ellsworth the contraption he'd been holding—a series of copper coils and wires, a tin can, and an antenna, all mounted to two planks of wood fastened together at a right angle. He had been a machinist before the war and still tinkered.

"What in Sam Hill is this?"

Alfred felt for the wall and then counted his steps to the cushioned chair facing Ellsworth's wooden one. "Wireless telegraphy."

"Come again?"

"Made my own crystal radio, Ellsworth."

"But . . . how?"

"With my hands. Sometimes I think I can see better now than I could with eyes."

Ellsworth didn't think that made any sense. "Does it work?"

"'Course it works. Think I would've lugged it over here if it didn't?"

"Where's Linda May?"

"Charleston for some fresh air. She thinks I'm napping." He motioned for Ellsworth to put the contraption back on his lap. Alfred patted it like a loving pet that had been returned. "Linda May doesn't agree with it anyhow. She's a little leery about anything modern and has gone all high-hat about stuff like radio. Thinks it'll kill the, what did she call it?—oh, the cultural *sophistication* of the listeners. Thinks people will listen too much to the box and stop conversing."

Ellsworth plopped down in his own chair. "Maybe Anna Belle needs one then."

"Ha. Good one, Ellsworth." He scratched his nose, which he had a habit of doing since he'd come home from France addicted to morphine—the Soldier's Disease. Stuck a needle in between his toes every night after Linda May went to bed. Alfred patted the radio again and imitated his wife's voice. "How is this radio thing gonna influence today's youth, Alfred? That's what Linda May said this morning, Ellsworth. Kids growing up with a radio as a given right? Like I give two trouser coughs about that. I said, I don't know, Linda May. We don't have any kids. And I doubt we will since you don't lay with me anymore."

"You said that?"

"I did. And then she stormed out for fresh air and I went to feed the squirrels." He ran unsteady fingers through wispy brown hair that thinned daily. He'd pulled a good chunk of it out when the gas hit him in France, and it had never grown back. "I wish I wouldn't've said it to her, Ellsworth, but I did. And it's true—she won't touch me anymore. Linda May's a peach, and I love her, but it's one ing-bing after another with her, and she's convinced I'm jingle-brained enough to go see a lunatic doctor."

"Well?"

"Well what?"

"Don't you think you might be?"

Alfred paused and then leaned over the radio. "Let's have a listen. Where are you? Here, bring your chair over. We'll have to share the ear things."

Ellsworth scooted his chair closer and held one of the earphones to his right ear while Alfred used the left. Alfred stared at the ceiling as he adjusted knobs and dials and wires on his homemade radio. "These devices are becoming commercial, Ellsworth.

Pretty soon every household will have one. Not just the army and the government." Alfred had become one of those anarchists the country was so scared of, a US-born communist and angry veteran. Thought the government he'd given his sight and part of his mind to was oppressive.

Static burst through the earphones, and both men flinched. "Ah, there it is." After a few more adjustments a faint voice sounded through the crackle, talking about the Ford Plant in Detroit, ". . . that sprawling, modern industrial complex."

"Who is that?"

". . . America's Mecca . . . a breathtaking monument . . ."

"Hush now, Ellsworth. I don't know. Some man talking about factories."

"I can hear that much."

"Well I can't hear nothin' 'cause you won't stop bumping your gums." The radio voice was lost in static. Alfred adjusted another dial, maneuvered a copper coil. More static—louder, softer, louder again. "I'm going to get me one of them Model Ts. I'll go real slow, and you'll have to help me steer." He tinkered with his radio box. "Everyone's gonna have a car, Ellsworth. Heard it right on the radio here. Accidents might be on the rise. The roads are potted, cities clogged. And parking's gonna be a national crisis. But the automobiles are boosting this economy and getting us from here to—"

Alfred stopped muttering and held a finger up. Another male voice had burst through the static, clear as a bell. Both men leaned in, pressed the earphones tight. The new voice, surreal and seemingly sounding from nowhere, spoke about the Palmer Raids back in January, when the US attorney general had arrested and deported radical leftists. The announcer said the authorities were expecting more anarchist activity in the wake of last year's Galleanist bombings and were taking steps to prevent it.

Alfred's face reddened. He mumbled something about the state being unnecessary and harmful. The radio voice then told the story of how a maid had opened one of the Galleanist mail bombs back in May and had her hands blown off.

"Ah," Alfred grunted, waving it away as if he didn't believe it.

The radio jumped to static again. Alfred slapped the side of it, and the static got worse. "What'd we fight for, Ellsworth? Huh?" He adjusted the antenna and maneuvered some wires. "So we could come back to a country where our jobs were given to women and colored folk? Where they think it proper to chisel a man's corn liquor and throw folks in the hoosegow for partaking in rum punch? Don't get me started on the drys."

Out the window, Ellsworth saw Anna Belle's drapes move. "She's spying on me."

Alfred, quick as a snakebite, pushed the radio off his lap. It clunked on the floor. A dial popped off and rolled across the hardwood. He jumped from the chair with his revolver out. "Who's spying, Ellsworth? Who's out there?"

"Put your gun down, Alfred. It's just Anna Belle. She's spying on me from her window."

Alfred stood with his back to the wall, the gun poised next to his chest. He turned his head toward the window and then back against the wall. "Why's she spying?"

"She's watching to see if I've gone out to get my newspaper yet."

"What newspaper?"

"The one she left on the middle of my sidewalk."

"I didn't see any newspaper."

"You can't . . . Just holster your gun and sit back down."

Alfred didn't holster, and he didn't return to the chair. He slid his back down the wall and sat cross-legged on the floor. Tears welled in his eyes.

Ellsworth knew not to touch him when he got like this. Last time he'd put a hand on his shoulder, Alfred had fired and nearly taken Ellsworth's ear off. The bullet was still lodged in the wall above the couch where Ellsworth slept every night. So Ellsworth let him cry. He'd help him fix the busted radio later.

Ellsworth waited for Anna Belle's drapes to move again, but they didn't. His stomach growled, and he suddenly feared she'd hold out on dinner unless he went out to retrieve his newspaper. He'd never been a big eater before the war, but since his return he'd done nothing but, and his increasingly chubby body now expected food. A healthy portion of it.

This was a battle he was going to lose, so he got up out of his chair for the fourth time and hobbled to the front door. "If you hear me cussing, it means I fell down the steps."

Alfred didn't even give a hint he'd heard him.

The sun would drop behind the woods in a few hours. Anna Belle usually brought dinner well before sunset. Ellsworth opened the door and started down the single step to the veranda with his prosthetic leg first, but then stopped, realizing he hadn't navigated a step since he'd lost his leg. The house had a second floor with three bedrooms, including his and Eliza's, but he'd yet to go up since her funeral.

He put his good leg first and used it to guide the other one down. He inched his way out onto the porch, where the air was cooler than it looked from inside. His heart beat rapidly. His forehead broke out into a cold sweat. With every slow step across the veranda, he felt more exposed, more ashamed of how far he'd fallen. He should have pulled the trigger. Should have ignored the arrival of that redbird. Should have ignored what Eliza would have said the bird signified. Then he wouldn't have to deal with Alfred's daily breakdown in his living room. Wouldn't have to deal with any of it.

He gripped the wooden handrail. One at a time, slowly, good leg and then prosthesis. He made it to the sidewalk and stood beside the newspaper. He'd yet to think of a fluid way to pick up things—it wasn't easy to bend or squat with one leg straight.

He knew better, but he still couldn't shake the feeling that the Krauts were out there watching him. Just like in his nightmares, with spikes on their helmets and shadows for eyes. He surveyed the cluster of buildings inside the town square, then the houses on either side of the road leading to and from it. He *was* being watched—not by a Kraut, but by Sheriff Lecroy, who hiked his belt into his overhung belly and waved from the jailhouse parking lot. Bellhaven, despite the small size, was a county seat. The multipurpose town hall, before the fire, had also acted as the courthouse, but now those matters had been pushed into the squatty jailhouse.

Ellsworth tipped an imaginary hat. The sheriff, albeit a smidge lazy, was a good enough guy, but lately he'd gone overboard with Prohibition and begun to confiscate alcohol. Thought himself mighty when he poured it out right in front of the sinners.

*Step foot in my shed, I'll put a bullet in that fat belly.*

The sheriff smiled, probably happy Ellsworth had finally emerged from his house. Beverly Adams stopped sweeping her porch steps to stare at Ellsworth. Dooby Klinsmatter nodded as he steered his horse wagon around the square, and Ellsworth jerked a nod back. Ten houses down the road, Ellsworth's childhood friend Gabriel Fanderbink, the local blacksmith, stood in her front yard. She put her hands on her head and then waved like she was swatting a swarm of bees.

Ellsworth waved back, although without her enthusiasm.

The town still looked to him for stability. Didn't matter to them what he'd done in the tense moments after Eliza's death. If anything, his actions had solidified the notion that he, not Mayor Bellhaven or Sheriff Lecroy, was the bedrock of the town.

Word would soon spread now that he'd finally ventured out of his house.

Out here, the town hall didn't look quite as dilapidated. Might even be salvageable had he been motivated toward the betterment of things. *How many gatherings did we have inside those walls?* Back when the candles burned long and entry cost only a smile and a hug. The town had ignored the times and welcomed all skin colors and means of worship, all unified against whatever lurked in the Bellhaven woods—all those warnings and horrifying half-truths their parents had told them as children to keep them from wandering too far.

Anna Belle was convinced Ellsworth could give Bellhaven life again, a sense of normalcy lacking since the tragedy. Since the night the music died.

Ellsworth didn't know about that.

*There he is.* That black boy, Raphael, stood at Anna Belle's window, waving.

Ellsworth pretended not to see him. Instead he used his cane to maneuver the rolled newspaper upright. When he raised the cane, the newspaper flew into the grass.

Two houses down from Anna Belle's, Old Man Tanner laughed from his front yard. Instead of coming over to help, Old Man Tanner pointed at Ellsworth's folly and laughed himself into a coughing fit, his face red as a tomato. *Breeze off, old man.* The sentiments of most the town. Two weeks ago, Mr. Kilkelly's prize hound had barked all night until suddenly he'd stopped. The next morning the dog was found in a burlap sack with his mouth tied shut, the sack hanging from the gnarled limb of a live oak. The dog was so terrified he didn't bark for weeks. Everyone knew it was Old Man Tanner who'd done it.

The old man stared at Ellsworth's house like it was plagued. Probably blamed Eliza for bringing death to Bellhaven. For bringing that strange boy in and hiding him. He pointed an arthritic finger at Ellsworth and mumbled something.

"Go dangle," Ellsworth said to himself. He'd never seen a man age like Tanner. Looked to be eighty at least, like he'd aged twenty years in the past two. Nobody in town could agree on how long the old man had been living in Bellhaven, but the most common answer was "sometime around the big earthquake."

Tanner went into the woods every day around the same time—after lunch—with a shovel and saw or limb cutters, and he returned a couple of hours later. A man that old had no business venturing into the woods alone, and certainly not past the yellow-painted trees. For years, Tanner had kept the outskirts of the woods behind his property cleared of deadfall, brush, and weedy saplings. Maybe he'd decided to tempt fate and clean out some of the woods beyond the yellow trees. Ellsworth thought it likely that the rumors they'd heard as children were just not true, so there wasn't much fate to be tempted. But then again, they'd all seen just enough to be leery.

Old Man Tanner pulled what looked to be an ice pick from his trouser pocket. He pointed it at Ellsworth, made a stab motion, and then headed inside.

Ellsworth shook off a shiver.

He used the cane on the newspaper again, and this time it stayed on until he raised it to his free hand. He tucked it under his armpit and turned back toward the porch.

*Anna Belle can breeze off too.*

\\|///

20

High on the hillside overlooking the town stood the old Bellhaven plantation house.

In the 1800s the small plantation had thrived, its cotton fields worked by slaves who occupied wooden quarters on the edge of the woods. Many of them had fled after emancipation, some saying they feared the woods more than they feared their former owners. The rest had stayed on as hired hands and eventually raised families in town.

Once a sprawling, bustling organism, the property had long stood out on the hill as a blighted eyesore. The yellow paint on the three-story brick colonial was flaking badly. On the north side of the house, edging the avenue of oaks, the cotton field lay scorched from too many summer suns—scab blackened and overgrown with weeds. It had been decades since cotton had grown full on the plantation, five years since any cotton had grown there at all. The boll weevils had killed what was left in the summer of '15.

The mayor, Loomy Bellhaven, was the only Bellhaven left in town, a distant relative whose name held enough sway to win him an uncoveted office but not enough to inherit the house on the hill. He'd twice battled for it in court but lost. Instead it had gone to a great-great-great-grandson of the plantation's founder, Limus Bellhaven. This heir, a distant relative to the mayor, had allowed the house to fall into disrepair while he wasted away from cancer in a third-floor bedroom overlooking the woods. Two consecutive owners had stayed a short time, then hurried off in the night.

Every time the house went up for sale, Mayor Bellhaven had made offers the banks had no trouble refusing. Being Mayor of Bellhaven didn't pay much, and Loomy didn't have old money. What little money he did have, he usually lost betting on bangtails at the racetrack.

The plantation house had again been on the market for months.

But now the For Sale sign was gone and some migrant workers were clearing out weeds from the suddenly vibrant flower beds. Loomy sat in the shadows of the town hall, on the portion of the wraparound veranda still accessible behind the rubble. From his window, Ellsworth could see him sipping from a flask and wallowing as he watched the migrants clean up the property he'd dreamed would be his.

Ellsworth would respect the mayor more had he not dodged the war with a hinky excuse like color blindness. He didn't dislike Mayor Bellhaven; he just thought the town could do better. The man always seemed to walk around on a pedestal made of cracked glass, giving that forced impression that he was on top of the world when deep down he knew he was sinking beneath the cruel weight of it.

Ellsworth settled back into his chair, still leg-weary from the short jaunt to the sidewalk a couple hours ago. He hadn't walked that far since the army doc fitted him for the prosthesis and forced him to use it. *"Lucky you didn't have both legs blown off,"* the doc had said. *"Miracle you're alive at all, considering what happened to the rest of the men with you."*

Alfred was still on the floor with his back to the wall, no longer crying but on the verge. At least he'd holstered his gun. He was prone to sit there all day and looked like he was planning to do just that.

*What this town needs is a gathering like the old days.* Cram inside the town hall, share stories, and talk the day away. Sip sour mash on the veranda while the evening breeze from the salt marshes spins the tree moss. *If Loomy Bellhaven wants to be the high pillow he portrays, he'll get the town hall fixed. Plain and simple.*

Ellsworth snapped open the newspaper and read. Klan continued to grow. No surprise there. But race issues weren't a Southern thing anymore. Lots of blacks were migrating up north, looking for opportunity, and sometimes they found it. Up in Harlem, a new movement was starting to spawn some interesting art and ideas. But gangs of whites who blamed the blacks for taking their jobs and housing had attacked them in the streets. Sometimes they fought back. Race riots were breaking out all over the country.

Ellsworth turned the page.

More tension between labor and bosses—another article about the fallout from the United Mine Workers coal strike that had finally ended in December. And Prohibition agents had busted whiskey barrels in the streets; the drys were claiming victory.

Maybe Alfred was on to something. *The government can just go dangle.* They were to blame for much of the unrest. Prohibition was leading to more crime, the organized sort where gangsters murdered to prove points.

Ellsworth took two heavy pulls from his medicinal whiskey and read about a religious stage play in New York City called *The Wayfarer* that was attracting full audiences, with themes of despair and hope and redemption. Looked like something Eliza would have drug him to.

He thought about killing himself again.

*After* dinner.

Anna Belle finally exited her house and crossed the street with a basket of food covered with a white cloth to keep the steam in. Ellsworth folded the newspaper and placed it on the window ledge. "Here she comes," he told Alfred, who was snoring now.

Anna Belle carried the basket with two hands, proud of her achievement. Ellsworth just hoped she'd made corn bread. Or some of her hoppin' John with ham hunks and onions. And then she stopped suddenly before the porch. She spotted him in the window, grinned, and turned away from the house, the food still in her hands.

"Where you going?" Ellsworth leaned forward in his chair, knocked on the window.

Anna Belle walked past where she'd dumped the morning newspaper and acted as if she was heading back home with the food. But then she stopped at the road, contemplating.

But what was there to contemplate? The food was all but in his mouth.

Anna Belle opened Ellsworth's mailbox and slid the basket of food inside it. She smiled at him, closed the small mailbox door, and returned to her house.

At least now he didn't have to hear her gloat.

*But I'm starving like I don't know what.*

He leaned back in his chair, slapped the window ledge with an open palm.

Alfred's eyes popped open. He pulled his gun and fired.

Ellsworth lunged, fell out of his chair. He crawled across the floor, lowered Alfred's arm, and secured the gun.

"Did I get him, Ellsworth? Huh? Did I?"

Breathing heavily, Ellsworth eyed the fresh bullet hole in the wall, which was less than a foot from the hole Alfred had put in the wall two weeks ago.

He patted Alfred's arm.

"Yeah, pal. Don't worry. You got'm."

# CHAPTER 4

No one heard the gunshot.

Not even Bellhaven's postman, Berny Martino, who'd been sliding mail into Beverly Adams's box when the bullet hit Ellsworth's living room wall. Berny didn't react much to anything anymore. After delivering eleven death telegrams during the war and comforting each new widow at their doorstep, his will to smile had been siphoned.

By the time Ellsworth pulled himself up and helped Alfred back into a chair, Berny was opening Ellsworth's mailbox and finding it full of food. Ellsworth knocked on the window to get Berny's attention, but Berny never looked up. He did stick his nose in there for a whiff of what Anna Belle had fixed. But instead of bringing the food to Ellsworth's door, he crammed Ellsworth's mail inside, closed it up, and went on down the road.

Ellsworth stood flabbergasted. Berny knew he was crippled. He could have at least knocked on his door to make sure everything was okay.

*What's Anna Belle trying to prove anyway?*

Alfred got to his feet, made sure his revolver was secured in his belt, and felt for his cane.

"Where you going?"

"Home." Alfred was sullen, gloomy, his energy sucked into a deep void Ellsworth knew too much about, the same void that would later churn out horror disguised as nightmares and leave both of them sleepless and suicidal.

"Can you make it back okay?"

Alfred nodded.

A real friend would have walked him home. Would have taken him by the elbow and escorted him across the road and up to his porch. Maybe flicked on a few lights for him, because the sun was going down and it didn't look like Linda May was back from Charleston yet.

Ellsworth chuckled at this, a blind man needing his lights turned on.

"What's funny?"

Ellsworth said, "Nothing." Which was true. Nothing was funny anymore. He didn't like it when the sun went down. Didn't like it much anymore when the sun came back up either, but at least the morning was the beginning of something. "What about your radio?"

"It's not my radio," said Alfred. "Made it for you. Thought maybe it could help."

Ellsworth didn't ask what it would help. Too much to pick from, but he assumed Alfred meant *help you get out of the house.* He thanked his pal on their way to the front door, and Alfred said, "Same time tomorrow." Not a question but a statement. Ellsworth watched him shuffle across the road and disappear into the shadows on the far side of the jailhouse.

Tree moss swayed, silver tendrils turned pink by the setting sun. The woods were quiet except for the birds, the square spotted with so many colorful flower blooms it looked like one of those Impressionist paintings. Cantigny had looked like that just before the Kraut counterattack when Calvin was killed.

Peaceful before the sting.

Ellsworth closed the door and returned to his chair with a headache. Too much whiskey without food to soak it up, his dinner growing colder in the mailbox. But he just couldn't convince himself to go out there again.

He closed his eyes and nodded off. But every time he got close to deep sleep, he'd hear bullets, screams, fearful breathing. His eyes would snap open. He'd drink more bourbon whiskey until weariness dragged him down and then doze off again. But then came the crunch of shovels in soil, the artillery whizzing over the trenches, the rivers of blood churning on like a talkie movie stuck on repeat.

His leg was on fire, his foot lost somewhere in the blast that should have killed him like it did the others. He opened his eyes and took a drink. The whiskey no longer burned. Went down like water. That was a problem, but not one to be dealt with pronto. So he took another swig and wondered if there were any crackers in the kitchen, maybe some leftover corn bread muffins.

He found three oat cookies wrapped in brown paper next to the kitchen sink. Anna Belle must have left them the day before. They weren't fresh, but a cookie was a cookie.

He took them back to the living room and sat on Eliza's piano bench, facing the music stand where he kept the only picture he had of his late wife. Eliza leaned against a sprawling live oak with the Charleston harbor in the background, her curly auburn hair wind-tousled. The picture was sepia-toned, but he remembered her dress was red that day, her eyes blue like his own. Lucky the picture took as she'd laughed—her smile frozen for eternity.

Cookie crumbs gathered on the black and white keys. He blew at them and one got stuck in between. Didn't matter. Nobody to play it anymore. He scooted to his side of the bench and imagined the curve of her hip kissing his own as her foot pressed the levers, her wrists at hard angles to the keyboard. She'd been an animated pianist. In the short time they'd been married, she'd made the walls of the town hall sing more times than he could count. She was always happiest when playing.

He pressed a few keys and stared at her picture. Wished she'd never gone back into that town hall after they cleared it. After he *thought* they'd cleared it. The Klan had come that night for a reason, and no one knew that reason was still hiding in the basement— the little boy and his mother. Eliza had sneaked them into town the night before for reasons that still eluded them. That was why, during the party, Eliza had insisted they play and sing louder so her stowaways could feel included too. That was just how her heart beat—for others, sometimes, more than her own.

Ellsworth wiped his wet eyes and finished off the second cookie. He would have gladly run into the burning town hall in her stead. It wasn't something the town discussed aloud, but he'd already made a reputation for surviving things he had no business surviving—from the polio and cancer as a child to the train derailment that took his mother's life but not his own as a young man. He never would have let Eliza go back in there, but he'd been too busy ushering the others out to see that she'd already run back into a building engulfed in flame, even as the town's fire truck blared its siren and the firemen sprayed heavy water from the hose.

Eliza had forced that boy through the tiny basement window and into the grass. But she and the boy's mother had been too big for the opening, and they'd perished hugging each other.

He'd heard them screaming for help and set to work clearing collapsed bricks and boards from the basement stairwell. Flames had caught his left pant leg, and two firemen had dragged him out. He'd pleaded that she was just on the other side of that rubble.

Couldn't they hear her? Couldn't they see her two ashy fingers protruding through the smoke?

Truth was, she'd stopped screaming several minutes before he began tossing aside the debris, and the two fingers he'd seen weren't moving. There was nothing he could have done short of marrying a woman who didn't have such a kind heart.

Ellsworth tried a few more keys, but they came off as clunkers. Nothing melodious like he'd imagined in his head. He'd had nightmares of her screaming. Those nightmares had pushed him toward the war, where he exchanged them for new ones.

*She died from the smoke. Not the flames. I heard her coughing.*

Telling himself that was the only way he'd found solace in the days after.

He needed a drink to wash down the cookies. He'd eaten all of them, although he didn't remember the third. What he remembered clearly was the fireman's voice. *"You're gonna get yourself killed, Ellsworth. She's gone. Come on now, before the whole building collapses."*

He should have stayed in there to see if it was even possible to get himself killed.

Maybe he'd eat a bullet tonight and see.

But his dinner was still out in the mailbox getting cold.

He plopped down in his chair and swallowed a gulp of Old Sam, and then something caught his eye out the window.

Anna Belle hurried down her front porch, her voice filled with panic as she called that boy's name over and over. "Raphael! Raphael!"

Linda May Dennison showed up a minute later. The two women headed to the backyard together, still calling Raphael's name. Next they searched the road, peering into the shadows between the trees, and then stepped inside the town hall, only to come out a minute later disappointed. Anna Belle had her hands on her head, looking up into the sky, distraught.

More neighbors arrived in front of the town hall, even Alfred.

"Raphael!" they all yelled into the night, some in unison, some in alternating pitches, most of them facing the woods and probably praying the boy hadn't gone in there alone.

Ten minutes later, six dozen men and women, including Mayor Bellhaven, had gathered with lanterns and torches. Berny Martino was out there with his mail pouch over his shoulder, wandering from person to person as if he had his own mission and agenda and it didn't include finding the boy. Instead of letters and packages, he passed out what looked to be flyers. Mayor Bellhaven took one from Berny, quickly read it, and then crumbled it up as if he disapproved.

Maybe Berny the postman had turned communist like Alfred.

Ellsworth took a step, and the room spun. How much bourbon had he consumed? He used the wall as a crutch and eventually made it to the front door, where he could watch the goings-on more easily. Father Timothy was out there with Reverend Cane, and behind them stood Rabbi Blumenthal.

Charleston was known for its numerous churches—steeples soared above darn near every street corner. But it was odd for a small town like Bellhaven to have so many checkered along the main road—Catholics and Baptists, Methodists and Jews, and the black church with all that singing. There were even groups you hardly ever found in little Southern towns. A group of Moslems, most descended from a handful of Bellhaven slaves brought over from Africa, met in a small frame building a stone's throw from the Jewish synagogue. A year before the town-hall tragedy, a group of Latter-day Saints had rolled into town on two mule wagons. And a month after that ten young men and women, members of some

Watchtower Society, had shown up and taken root on the outskirts of Wally Luchin's pumpkin farm.

Some said those Watchtower folks came from up north and were part of the Bible Student movement. But Ellsworth had complained to Eliza he didn't much care where they'd come from. He just didn't like the way they knocked on his door and told him he needed to be saved. Saved from what?

He'd told them he knew two people who were in desperate need of saving. *"Calvin Roper, right there across the street, the blue house with the white porch. Oh, and Alfred Dennison, back there on the other side of the town square, the porch with the wind chimes. He needs to be saved more than anyone I know."*

Ellsworth smiled at the memory of his two pals chastising him the next day. *"How come you sent them new religious folk to our doors, Ellsworth?"*

Brother Fox Bannerman walked among the crowd outside. He had a copperhead coiled around his right arm, and most everyone steered clear of him. Recently a cluster of Pentecostals had moved into Jimmy Claret's old home—a mere sign hammered in the front yard had converted it from residence to church overnight—and Brother Bannerman, all six-feet-nine inches of him, was the leader of their lot.

Because of all the different places of worship, Linda May Dennison had jokingly renamed the avenue of oaks the Highway to Heaven. And despite their religious differences, they had always somehow pulled together. That was always Bellhaven custom. And whenever the town folk got together at the town hall, you could find members of every church in attendance. But now Bellhaven was more of a mixed bag of nuts than a melting pot. The peaceful town had grown silent since the tragedy—sleepy and indifferent.

Ellsworth pinched his eyes closed, and along with the darkness came a memory. Black tar and goose feathers. The bald eagle tattoo on the side of a Klansman's neck. That acrid smell of smoke, like something overcooked on a spit. He swallowed two gulps of Old Sam to forget. *Focus on the now. The people crowding the street and searching. Do they even realize this is the largest gathering since . . . ?*

Ellsworth hobbled out the front door for the second time of the day. Anna Belle was mouthy, but she was a friend. He probably should be out there with them. Probably.

He watched the crowd split into six groups and scatter with tentative steps and lanterns into the Bellhaven woods. Another memory. The night of the tragedy they'd gathered to celebrate because a boy who'd ventured into the woods had been found. Timmy Tankersly, twelve years old then, had gone in on a dare, and he'd disappeared for two days. He'd turned up with rashes across his back and arms and scratches on his cheeks and a baseball-sized patch of white in his hair above the neckline, but no recollection of what he'd done or where he'd gone, other than into the woods. He just kept muttering something about the air being bad medicine.

Reverend Cane said the boy had been so badly scared he'd lost pigment in his hair. Ellsworth didn't know about that, but he had noticed that Timmy's right eye was stalled. The boy's father, Tommy Tankersly, had been too overwhelmed with joy at first to notice the thing with his son's eye. He'd simply corralled him in his arms and hugged him tight and insisted they celebrate his return with music and food in the town hall.

Not everyone had ventured into the woods. Half a dozen had stayed behind at the town hall, most likely to keep an eye out in case the boy returned on his own.

How old was the boy anyway? Ten? Eleven? He'd looked to be about eight on the night Eliza died saving him.

Ellsworth made it down the porch steps with no plan other

than stopping at the road for a closer look. The cluster of people waiting in front of the town hall waved. Probably wondered why he wasn't out there helping.

Ellsworth had been the one to find Timmy Tankersly that day, sleeping a few paces from the boundary of trees their ancestors had marked with yellow paint. No one was to go past the yellow trees. Timmy, now a teenager, was out there now with the rest of them. Not hunting—he was too jingle-brained and skittish to focus on any task more mundane than putting one foot in front of the other—but standing by himself and staring up at the moon, tapping the meat of his right palm against his right temple.

*Poor kid never recovered.*

Ellsworth shuffled onto the sidewalk, tripped because of the leather traction on the ball of his prosthesis, but managed to catch himself. He took another drink and slid the bottle back into his pocket. He blinked for too long and nearly fell over when he opened his eyes again. He righted himself and stayed put for a minute in the middle of the sidewalk while his brain leveled. That's when he saw Old Man Tanner emerge from the shadows of his backyard, walking backward around his house.

The old coot showed no sign he knew what was going on or had any idea that the boy was missing. He was too busy walking backward, carefully, as if backtracking in the snow and trying to find his old footprints. As he walked, he tapped his fists against his temples in a gesture not unlike Timmy Tankersly's. *What is he doing?* Old Man Tanner continued toward the front of his house and disappeared around the other side.

And then Anna Belle screamed from the woods.

Ellsworth knew her well enough to know it was a relief scream and not one of panic or fear. He took four careful steps toward the road but stopped when he saw Gabriel Fanderbink hurrying from the woods with Raphael cradled in her powerful arms. The boy appeared lifeless at first, but then shifted in the crook of her arm.

Ellsworth had always thought Gabriel was a funny name for a girl. Truth was, she didn't even look like one, not from afar at least. She was tall—well over six feet—barrel chested and thick limbed, and he'd never seen her in anything but overalls. During a baseball game four years prior—she was the only woman who played—Ellsworth had accidently plunked Gabriel on the shoulder with a fastball, and she'd acted as if it was a mere bee sting. Hardly even flinched before readying herself for the next pitch, that easy-to-please grin etched across her boxy jaw. Gabriel was girth and muscle, and some wrongly said her brain was no larger than a dung beetle's. But all agreed her heart was too big to measure.

Gabriel spotted Ellsworth at the street—he'd unknowingly made it that far—and jerked him a nod. Ellsworth nodded back. Then he spotted Anna Belle hurrying behind Gabriel. Her eyes shot daggers at him as she stormed inside.

He knew why she was angry. Except for Old Man Tanner, who was on another backward lap around his house, Ellsworth was the only one who'd acted as if he hadn't given a hoot that Raphael had gone missing. But truthfully—and maybe this was a repercussion of the war—he *hadn't* given much of a hoot. He'd never met the boy. It had been a minor level emergency, if it had been an emergency at all. The boy had simply wandered off. It wasn't as if a mortar shell had blown a soldier's head into the coiled barbed-wire. Not like Private Latchett taking one in the gut and running across no-man's-land cradling intestines like a football.

Maybe Anna Belle was right.

The war had taken more than just Ellsworth's leg. What rattled inside his head now was like a coin clinking in an empty tip jar.

Too much dead space. Too much had grown numb.

Gabriel carried Raphael into Anna Belle's house, and the door closed.

One of the flyers Berny the postman had been handing out skittered breeze-blown down the street and clung to Ellsworth's prosthesis. He stared, then bent over to snatch it.

Too drunk to read every word, Ellsworth crumpled it into a ball and shoved it in his trouser pocket, having ingested the gist. Berny had left First Methodist to join the newly arrived Pentecostals, and he'd bought into their ramblings.

Apparently the end of days was here.

*Oh well.*

Ellsworth opened his mailbox, retrieved his dinner, and hobbled inside to eat it.

Good thing fried chicken still tasted good cold.

# CHAPTER 5

The Cantigny forest was small but dense, and the charred-limb canopy did little to keep out the stench of dead Huns.

Ellsworth trudged on, leg-weary, following the piano music as trench mortars exploded all around him. A flamethrower whooshed, igniting nearby trees. Fog drifted. He reached out to grab a swirl, but it slithered through his fingers like he imagined a cloud would.

The music grew louder. He blocked out the whistle of bullets, the shaking of the ground, and focused on the familiar notes of Mozart's Piano Sonata no. 8 in A Minor. According to Eliza, it was one of the composer's darkest, written when his mother died and his father blamed him for her death. She had played it often.

His gear weighed heavy. He dropped his shovel and, three paces later, his flare. He moved low boughs aside and entered a clearing. A leafy floor and more fog swirls. He followed the haunting music—right, then left. Louder. He dropped his two canteens on the ground—one empty, the other full. Five paces later he unloaded his four sandbags and the rest of his ammunition rounds. He dropped his belt—only one of his grenades remained.

Through the brush he saw the corner of an upright piano that had no business in the middle of a battlefield. His pace quickened. He sidestepped more limbs. The piano rested in the center of another clearing, where five Kraut soldiers lay dead on the ground, the surrounding leaves and grass darkened blood-black.

It wasn't Eliza playing the piano, but a man. A slump-shouldered soldier, helmetless, with a gaping red wound at the neckline.

"Calvin."

Calvin turned on the bench, looked over his shoulder, but continued playing. "Been thinking, Ellsworth. About what you told me on the boat. I think I know what it means. Some got that special spark and aren't meant to go." His fingers danced across the keys as if he'd been playing for years, when in fact it had been his wife, Anna Belle, who'd taken lessons from Eliza.

Calvin said, "It'll all make sense soon enough."

"Calvin."

"Look into his eyes."

"Whose eyes?"

Calvin finished the sonata abruptly, then slumped unmoving over the keys.

The piano music drifted to silence. And then the static-crackle began, intermixed with unseen voices, but familiar.

He smelled vanilla and buttery Cavendish.

Felt himself falling . . .

\|||///

Ellsworth startled himself off the couch and hit the floor with a thud. His revolver spun across the hardwood and stopped against one of the piano bench legs. He'd only intended to nap last night, but he must have dozed off longer because the sun was up and the birds were singing.

"You okay der, Ellsworth?"

Ellsworth looked up toward the muffled voice across the room and choked on a scream. He knew the face well—Omar Blackman visited as regularly as Anna Belle, Alfred, and Gabriel—but it wasn't the most pleasant face to see first thing in the morning. Omar had been a Buffalo Soldier during the war, a member of the all-black Ninety-second Infantry. He'd fought bravely in the Meuse-Argonne offensive before shrapnel took off the upper portion of his face. He wore a plaster-molded mask that stretched from his hairline to the dip of his chin below the lower lip. There were nostril holes at the bottom of the fake nose so he could breathe. The slit-opening for the mouth was so that he could talk. When he ate he removed the mask, which meant he never ate in front of anyone. The sculptor had fastened glasses to the mask, all part of the leather contraption that held the clunky ensemble on his head.

Ellsworth would never get used to the contrast in color. Omar's mask was porcelain white while his skin was dark as coffee grounds.

Omar and Alfred sat in the two living room chairs by the window, tinkering with the knobs on Alfred's radio. Omar wore a brown suit with white pinstripes, white shoes with brown spats, and a matching white fedora. He liked to dress to the nines to make up for his face. He smoked a curved pipe, the stem of which fit perfectly into the mask slit. He puffed. Smoke escaped the mask holes, filling the room with the smell of vanilla and butter.

"You want dat der leg o'er yonder, Ellsworth?"

"No." Ellsworth pushed himself up to the couch, noticed his leg leaning against the piano, not far from where his revolver had just ended up. "Thanks. I'll get it in a minute."

"Okay den."

Omar had a funny way of talking, his English infused with hints of Jamaican gobbledegook and capped off with a bad French accent he'd adopted from the war. The American soldiers hadn't wanted the blacks of the Ninety-second and Ninety-third fighting with them, so they'd cast many aside to fight with the French. The white French civilians had treated them well, and Omar had befriended several. His newly acquired accent was a tribute.

Ellsworth rubbed his face and yawned. "How long you two been in here?"

"Since sunup," said Alfred.

"Time is it now?"

"Noon thirty," said Alfred, craning an ear toward the radio. "Caught a clear station for thirty minutes." He fought the static, twisted knobs and straightened wires. "It's gone now."

"Static der in den pop dat voice come."

Ellsworth rubbed his face. "I should really lock my door at night."

"What's that?" asked Alfred, eyes to the ceiling.

"Nothing."

"He said him der should lock dat door at night." Omar exhaled pipe smoke and laughed. "No matta. We jus' dem break dat window, Ellsworth."

Ellsworth didn't doubt it. Omar and Alfred were here more than they were home with their wives. They'd all spent the entire time overseas wishing to be back home, but once they returned they hadn't known how to interact. Omar, the leader of Bellhaven's black Moslem community, was one of a handful who'd stayed behind when others went north for jobs or fled the night the Klan burned the town hall. Those who remained followed Omar's every word whether faceless or not. Before the war, he'd been a virtuoso on the double bass, with a singing voice so deep it produced cold chills. He could juggle anything, and when he danced the Juba inside the town hall and got to energetically stomping against the floorboards, everyone had stopped to watch.

A man's voice carried through the radio static, spouting news. Alfred's hand froze on the knob. The Klan had lynched another black man in Alabama. Busted up a new juke-joint speakeasy in Louisiana. Tarred and feathered a Catholic priest in Dallas, Texas.

Omar, easily excited, grabbed his rifle, cocked it, and stood from Ellsworth's chair.

"What's going on?" Alfred said.

Ellsworth held his hand out. "Whoa, Omar. Where you going?"

"Gon' get me some dat white-cloak Klan. Smoke'm outta dose hidey-holes and bump 'em off fo' dat big sleep."

"Well, would you hand me my leg first?" Omar wasn't going anywhere. Not a day went by that he didn't threaten to smoke somebody out of their hidey holes. He'd brought back rage from the trenches and didn't always know where to put it.

He'd been a handsome man once.

Omar adjusted his mask and walked toward the piano bench, puffing his pipe like a freshly stoked chimney. He handed Ellsworth his leg. "Why dem not put no knee in der?"

Ellsworth attached the leg to his left thigh and put his weight on it. He patted Omar on the shoulder. "Go sit, Omar. And put the rifle down."

Omar straightened his fedora and did as suggested. A minute later he and Alfred were playing with the radio again, searching the static.

Ellsworth tightened the leather straps on the prosthesis and bit his lip at the familiar pain. There was a mirror above the piano, above Eliza's picture. His jawline was prickly with dark stubble. He had to go relieve himself anyway, so he shaved while he was in the water closet. He'd had the same shirt on for days, so he changed and combed his hair. Eliza had always liked it parted to the side, so he did that, too, while his childhood pals entertained themselves in the other room.

Anna Belle laundered Ellsworth's clothes once a week. After the war, since Ellsworth refused to go up steps, she'd gone to his bedroom and retrieved a suitcase of clothes, which he now kept next to the bathroom door to live out of. It took him several minutes, but he managed to change his trousers and sock while leaning against the sink.

*"Some got that special spark."*

He tried to ignore Calvin's dream voice. Had Calvin lived, he'd more than likely be in the living room with the other two, tinkering and bumping gums, adding a layer of levity to the scene.

Fully dressed, Ellsworth stood in the kitchen and listened to his stomach rumble. He'd angered Anna Belle last night. He should have gone out into the woods to look for the boy like everyone else. Maybe then he'd have some breakfast in his belly. Guilt was probably why he'd had that dream of Calvin bleeding at the piano. He could drink Old Sam to help quell the hunger, but that wasn't a viable long-term solution.

*"It'll all make sense soon enough."*

Usually the nightmares of Calvin quickly drifted, but this one hadn't, and he knew what he had to do.

In the other room, Alfred and Omar were going through their daily bellyaching and government bashing. Most blacks like Omar had viewed the war as an opportunity to show their patriotism, their chance to become equal citizens united to fight a common foe, one nation undivided. And early on they'd felt like they belonged. But things had soon changed, as early as their camp training, with immediate pushback from white soldiers and politicians across the South. There had been lynchings, unlawful court-martials, dead soldiers put in unmarked graves—and this was all before they'd left the States. And now that Omar had returned, having given his face for his country, the nation was as divided as ever. Ellsworth didn't blame him for being touchy about it.

He reached into his cabinet for a bottle of Old Sam he'd stashed and downed a quick swallow on his way into the living room. He placed the bottle on the window ledge between his two pals. "Drink up."

"Whey you come up wit' dat stash Old Sam, Ellsworth?"

"None of your business," Ellsworth said. "Just stay here. I'll be back in a little bit."

Omar puffed his pipe. "Whey you off to anyway?"

"To see if I can't get me some breakfast."

Alfred said, "Linda May said Anna Belle's furious at you."

"I reckon she is." Ellsworth opened the front door.

Alfred said, "Have a look at the trees, Ellsworth."

"What of'm?" Ellsworth peered out the door, saw mostly glare from the sun, but reckoned they were referring to the blooms he and Anna Belle had noticed yesterday.

"Dem trees all bloom same time," said Omar.

"Very strange," Alfred said, more focused on the radio than the conversation.

Ellsworth said, "Just don't shoot each other while I'm gone."

Omar held the bottle of Old Sam by the throat and raised it as if toasting Ellsworth's departure.

Ellsworth nodded and then closed the door. Just before it clicked shut, he saw Omar reach for his mask. Omar hadn't been toasting anything. He'd been waiting for Ellsworth to leave so that he could remove his mask and partake in the bourbon without showing his disfigured face except to Alfred.

He knew his face wouldn't bother Alfred Dennison one bit.

\\\////

Sunlight blinded Ellsworth on the veranda.

It had been a while since he'd felt that southern warmth on his skin, and it brought back memories of cicadas and palmetto trees, of sticky summer nights on the rocking chairs with Eliza, sipping tea or pulpy lemonade as the sun sank behind the woods.

Ellsworth stopped at the road. Sweat erupted across his brow. He suddenly felt fidgety, paranoid, like he was in the middle of no-man's-land and surrounded by hidden machine-gun nests. He looked around suspiciously, but all he saw was wind tugging the tree moss.

*"There's whispers in the wind."* Gabriel had once said that to him when they were twelve and sitting together on a log, pitching rocks toward the tree line. Some in town, she being one of them, claimed the different wind pitches were voices coming from the woods—ghosts even. Ellsworth had never believed in such things, but he didn't belittle those who did. He figured most of the rumors about the woods were overblown, but he knew there was something strange out there. Something had turned Timmy Tankersly's hair white.

Gabriel hadn't really been that worried about the whispers back then anyway. She brought them up to change the subject, having just asked him what it had felt like when Anna Belle planted that kiss on him in the ocean. Gabriel had inched closer to him, he'd noticed, probably with secret girl motives of her own. But when he'd said the kiss didn't feel like much of anything—implying he wasn't hunting for another and would rather be pitching a baseball—she'd scooted back away from him with an embarrassed face. She'd probably been fixing to plant one on him like Anna Belle had done, and his indifferent tone had deterred her. She'd always been so boyish and Anna Belle so beautiful. She'd probably figured what was the point.

And now Gabriel had been the one to find that Raphael boy

in the woods. Never once in her life had she shown a smidgen of jealousy toward Anna Belle, even when she married Calvin and Ellsworth married Eliza and every childhood friend in town except her seemed to be marrying someone. Maybe he'd invite Gabriel over for some Old Sam and they could sit on a log facing the woods like they used to. Maybe they'd even talk about what had happened in that slave house when they were nine.

*Enough stalling.*

Ellsworth homed in on Anna Belle's house and willed himself across the road. But even as he stepped forward, out of habit, he found himself scanning the trees and neighboring buildings for Krauts. The absurdity of it all stopped him in his tracks again. He was more likely to see a giraffe in the woods than German soldiers. Had he finally come to that realization now that he'd begun to get out and about? He'd seen enough paranoia from Alfred and Omar. Enough was enough. Getting run over by a car was a more likely threat, so he broke from his reverie and urged himself onward.

At one point the road had been gravel, but now it was hard-packed and rutted by car tires, dusty gray, and in bad need of a good rain soak to keep it down. He found the flat parts with his cane and labored across. Even with his eyes glued to the road, he couldn't help but notice the array of color all around him.

Eliza had once asked him to imagine what it would look like if all the trees and flowers of Bellhaven bloomed at once. Ellsworth had said it wasn't possible, so what was the point? Eliza, undeterred by his lack of imagination, had said it would be magical, *"as if a paint palette overturned and scattered across the land."*

That's what it looked like now.

Ellsworth blinked, but it didn't change things. He reached the other side of the road and stopped to look around again. The colors gave him cold chills.

The American beautyberries in front of Beverly Adams's house typically showed berries in the fall and early winter. But now Beverly was out on her sidewalk looking at them in full color—tiny morsels of white and bright magenta. All across Bellhaven, the dogwoods had flowered overnight with petals of pink, yellow, and cottony-white. The crabapple trees behind the jailhouse bloomed pink, and beneath them grew the perennial purple cornflowers. Every cherry tree was in full bloom, as were the magnolia trees, with white blooms the size of dinner plates. Dozens of town folk stood outside staring. The redbud trees bloomed a brilliant purple. Crape myrtles frothed violet, red, pink, and even yellow. In gardens up and down the street, on bushes and shrubs outlining porches, there was color everywhere—camellias, roses, and azaleas; hibiscus, lilies, and daffodils; climbing coral honeysuckle and Carolina jessamine.

He wasn't the only one to notice. One man stood in the middle of the road sketching. The Pentecostals prayed in a cluster in Bannerman's front yard. Gus Cheevers had paused in painting his fence to stare.

Ellsworth looked to the sky. Cardinal birds circled atop the colorful trees and live oaks, whistling—even more birds than the day before. Old Man Tanner's house looked quiet. Ellsworth wished he could unsee what he'd witnessed last night, the old man walking backward around his house, but the trampled footprints were still in the grass as a reminder.

*How many laps did the old man take?*

Ellsworth stepped up to Anna Belle's covered porch and knocked. Three quick raps. A minute later the door opened. There she stood in the threshold, her face made up pretty, her hair gathered up in a mass of curls he wanted to run his hands through.

He should pinch himself for even giving the thought life.

"What do you want?" she asked.

What he wanted was his breakfast, but instead he said, "Reckon it's a fine day for a walk, Anna Belle."

She folded both arms. "What are you on about, Ellsworth? I'm no easy mark."

He held up his hands. "Honestly, Anna Belle. Just thought it was a nice day for that walk you wanted yesterday."

"That was yesterday, Ellsworth, when I still thought you might have a heart inside that chest." She took in the sunlight and did her best to hide a smile. "But I reckon it wouldn't be a bad day for a stroll. Come in first. I've got a plate of food for you."

Ellsworth smiled. He didn't think there was ever a woman who could read his mind like Eliza, but sometimes with Anna Belle he wondered. "Have you seen the trees?"

"'Course I have. Blooming even more than yesterday. Raphael and I have been on the back porch all morning."

"What do you think's causing it?"

"Does it matter?"

"I'd like to think it does, but I reckon not."

"The moment you pause to think of the why, it'll be gone and you missed it."

He didn't think that made much sense, but he followed her into the house. The front room smelled like flowers. Air moved through open windows, carrying thick foody smells from the kitchen. Only now did he realize how musty and sterile his own house had grown. Dust covered and stale from being occupied daily by three war vets.

Anna Belle was too stubborn to allow all that gloom into her life. Her house was brightly lit, full of vibrant colors. Not that she didn't grieve Calvin as much as he did.

She just did it differently somehow.

"How's the boy?" he asked. She looked over her shoulder at him, glared. "I mean, Raphael. Isn't that his name?"

"It is." She folded her arms. "We found him lost in the woods, no thanks to you."

He didn't have an answer to that—not one she'd want to hear, anyway. He didn't tell the boy to run off. "But I didn't know he was able to get about. Thought he was bedridden."

"He's always been able to get about, Ellsworth. You've seen him and me on our walks. He's just been afraid to talk after what he saw. The town's taken to him like fish to water, which is why *most* everyone gathered to find him."

Ellsworth followed her toward the kitchen, smelled something delicious. "Well, what happened then? Last night?"

"He got about. Sneaked out of the house and wandered into the woods. Gabriel found him a quarter mile deep, well past the yellow trees, sitting against a tree trunk shaped like a violin."

"Didn't you warn the boy about the woods?"

"Of course, Ellsworth. You think me irresponsible?" She sighed, fixed a loose strand of hair behind her ear. "Odd thing was, we found him smiling."

"Smiling?"

"Oh, I forgot. You don't know what that is anymore."

Ellsworth forced one, but it only left his face tired.

"Nice try." She entered the kitchen. Ellsworth followed like a lost mutt. "I don't know why he was smiling. All I know is that he looked at peace. Finally."

Ellsworth sat at Anna Belle's kitchen table. Biscuit and gravy day. After a minute of fiddling at the stove, she placed a steaming plate in front of him and ten seconds later a cold glass of milk. He watched the curve of her hips when she turned. He told himself to stop, but he liked her blue dress. Her Tuesday dress.

She turned suddenly and caught him staring. "Eat up before it gets cold."

He ate the first few forkfuls like he hadn't eaten in days. "Does he talk yet?"

"No, not yet. But I believe he will."

Ellsworth ate more, then gulped some milk. "Did you see Old Man Tanner last night, walking around his house?"

"I did."

"And?"

"I think the poor man is off the tracks."

"Should we do anything about it?"

"I didn't think you did anything about anything anymore, Ellsworth."

"Made it across the road, didn't I?"

"Even Alfred was out looking last night, and he's blind as a bat."

Ellsworth returned to his food. No use beating a dead horse. "You knew the boy—"

"Raphael."

"Raphael. Right. You knew he was there that night, didn't you? Hiding in the town hall basement with his mother?"

Anna Belle nodded. "Eliza took me down there the night before. Introduced me in the dark. I could barely see more than the whites of his eyes, but he smiled then like he's smiling now. Sensed something in him right away. Something special."

"Special like what?"

She shrugged. "I don't know. Just brought about a warmth. Made me smile."

"And his mother?"

"Looked frightened. They nodded their hellos. Eliza hurried me back upstairs."

"Why did Eliza bring them here anyway? She never told me."

"Didn't tell me either. She only asked me if I'd look after him if something were to happen."

Ellsworth finished off another biscuit. "So he looked at peace?"

"Yes, he did." She studied him. "And he still does. What is it?"

"Nothing."

"Nothing doesn't make your eyes twitch." She sat down across the table from him. "You're not so dead to the world that you can disguise your emotion. Especially where Eliza's concerned."

He put his fork down. "In the weeks before that night, Eliza was just much calmer. At peace, like you said. That's what I'd think in my head—that she was at peace." He looked Anna Belle in the eyes for the first time since entering her house. "Did you notice that with her?"

"I did."

"Did you notice anything else, Anna Belle?"

"Like what?"

"Don't be coy. You know what I'm getting at. Her appearance?"

Anna Belle's eyes grew wet. She bit her lip, nodded. "She looked older, Ellsworth. For the life of me, I remember it. She looked noticeably older—every day, it seemed."

Ellsworth sighed, nodded. He wasn't the only person to notice it then. He dug back into his biscuits and gravy, fighting back tears. "Did she . . . did she mention anything about our son?"

Anna Belle wiped her eyes. "Said she talked to him."

Ellsworth tightened his jaw. He didn't mind that he wasn't the only person Eliza had confided in. Anna Belle had been her closest friend, after all. But talk of their dead son—that was personal. And that talk could have led to gossip that his wife was hearing voices and losing her mind. Ellsworth finished his milk and wiped his mouth. "You didn't tell anyone, did you?"

"Anyone what?"

"That Eliza thought she'd talked to our son?"

"No, of course not, Ellsworth." She reached across and touched his hand. He let it linger there for a beat and then slid his out from under it.

"Where's the boy?" he asked.

She shook her head in defeat. "In his room." And then looked up with a jolt. "Do you want to see him?"

"No."

It was quiet for a moment. Then Anna Belle said, "Maybe we can take Mr. Tanner somewhere. To a hospital or something."

"An asylum?"

"Something of the sort, yes."

Footsteps sounded in the hallway. Probably just the boy. The boy with the stupid name. Hopefully he wouldn't come into the kitchen.

Ellsworth finished his food and wiped his mouth with the cloth napkin. The footsteps were in the living room now. Ellsworth figured he'd sneak out the kitchen door so he wouldn't have to meet the boy. If he played it right, he'd get himself out of that walk too. Maybe Anna Belle would forget he'd even suggested it. Now that he was full, he wasn't in the mood. He wanted to get back out to those blooming trees and see if he could make sense of things.

Then take a good nap in his chair.

He started for the back door but stopped with his hand on the knob. Piano music sounded from the living room. Anna Belle's piano, the one Calvin had purchased for her lessons with Eliza. The playing wasn't tentative or rote, as he'd expect from a young boy, but confident. Ellsworth heard hints of greatness, even as Raphael flowed through warm-up drills.

Anna Belle caught Ellsworth's confusion and smiled. "I didn't know he could play until last night." She lowered her voice. "He's extraordinary, Ellsworth. He doesn't even need the music in front of him. He just plays."

Her voice was background static. As much as his mind wanted to be out of the house, his body moved across the kitchen floor and stopped in the threshold separating the rooms. There he was on the bench, sitting upright in a pair of brown trousers and a white button-down too big for his skinny frame. His bare feet barely touched the floor. His skin was the color of coffee after a tablespoon of milk was stirred in. His hair was dark, cut close to his scalp, notable for the coin-sized patch of white an inch above his right ear.

*They found him sitting against a tree. He stayed still too long.*

The boy stopped playing and turned toward the two adults. "Michael Ellsworth Newberry, how do you do?"

Hearing the boy speak for the first time, Anna Belle choked back a sob.

Ellsworth didn't answer. He was too taken in by the boy's emerald eyes, as bold and green as any he'd ever seen. He leaned against the doorframe, heard Calvin's voice from the most recent nightmare. *"Look into his eyes . . ."*

Ellsworth did.

Raphael's smile lit the room. "I can see your color, Mr. Newberry."

Ellsworth's good leg buckled. Anna Belle caught him by the elbow.

Raphael's thin fingers settled gracefully on the keys. He played like a virtuoso, but it was *what* he played that brought about the lump in Ellsworth's throat.

*Mozart's Piano Sonata no. 8 in A Minor.*

# CHAPTER 6

Anna Belle followed Ellsworth toward the road.

"Ellsworth, stop! You're going to fall flat on your face."

He knew he was walking too fast—the cadence between his prosthesis and the cane was uneven—but he had to get away from that house and that boy with the eyes green as summer leaf. How had he known to play that sonata?

"I don't want to talk about it, Anna Belle."

His hips were out of rhythm with his feet. The cane slid against gravel and spun from his grip. He went down in the middle of the road and tasted dust.

"Ellsworth!" Anna Belle came running and offered help.

He brushed her hand away. "Off me, Anna Belle. I can manage." He sat for a moment in the middle of the road to gather his bearings.

"What was that in there?" asked Anna Belle.

"You heard the same as I did."

She nodded, knowing darn well it was Eliza's favorite Mozart piece, but also looking as perplexed as he was. He squinted through the sunlight at her. She shook her head. "Don't look at me like that, Ellsworth. I did not tell Raphael to play that. He . . . he must have just . . . I don't know. He's an intuitive boy. But get on up out of the road. There's a car coming." A bright-red car with a fancy grill and headlights on tunneled under the trees on the avenue of oaks, spitting dust and gravel in a cloud behind it. "And he seems to be in a hurry."

It took him a minute to figure how to get up from the gravel, and ultimately he allowed Anna Belle to grab his elbow. The car was approaching fast.

"Where's my hat?"

"You didn't have a hat. Come back inside. Talk to Raphael."

"I should have worn a hat."

She brushed gravel dust from his shirt. "Those were the first words I've heard him speak."

Ellsworth straightened his collar, looked toward Anna Belle's house. "What is he?"

"You mean *who* is he?"

"I mean what I said. Something's not right inside him. You've seen his eyes."

"I've been seeing his eyes for more than two years now." She jabbed an index finger into his chest. "Since before all you men went off to war and came back jingled. Those beautiful eyes kept me out of the lunatic asylum. Do you know how hard it was to wait, not knowing if the men of Bellhaven were ever going to return?"

The approaching car passed the plantation house on the hill and slowed fifty yards from their position on the road. Anna Belle said, "You say there's something not right about him? I say there's nothing *but* right."

"Then tell me what you know about him."

"He keeps me company. He sits with me. I can sleep at night because I know I'm not alone. Sometimes I cry, Ellsworth. I miss the way things were. And you know what he does when I cry? He doesn't look down at the floorboards. He pats my hand. That's what I know."

Ellsworth turned toward his house. "I'm tired."

"I'm not finished."

"You never are."

"What about these blooming trees and flowers? And all the redbirds returning like they did the night the town hall burned?"

"Coincidence."

"I don't believe in coincidence. How do you explain the birds, Ellsworth?"

"I don't explain'm."

"Or should I call you Michael?"

"I go by Ellsworth, Anna Belle. Haven't gone by Michael since I was a kid."

"And what was that about him seeing your color? What color?"

"I've no idea."

"I think you do. You turned pale as a wind-dried sheet. I feel something in these woods, Ellsworth. And I think you can feel it too."

"I can feel my nub rubbing against this peg—that's what I feel. And I need to sit down."

"You're a stubborn troll, Ellsworth Newberry."

"You bump your gums too much, Anna Belle."

The car skidded to a stop on the gravel. Ellsworth shielded his eyes against the windshield glare and instinctively put an arm around Anna Belle to protect her from the impact. She didn't push him away. He pulled his Smith & Wesson from his holster and pointed it at the man getting out of the open-air car.

"Whoa. Hold on there, pal." The man closed the door to his fancy car. "You shoot all of Bellhaven's newcomers?"

"My lands, Ellsworth, put the gun away." Anna Belle stepped away from Ellsworth and closer to the other man. "Are you the new neighbor?"

The man nodded. He wore a three-piece pinstriped suit with a matching bowler hat. But no tie—his starched white collar was open at the neck. "Indeed. I'm moving into the old Bellhaven house." His eyes wandered toward the blooming trees, shrubs, and flowers. "Is this normal around these parts?"

"No," said Ellsworth.

"In fact, it's never happened before," said Anna Belle. "Very strange, indeed."

The man smiled at Anna Belle. "But how can something so bright and beautiful be strange?"

Ellsworth holstered his gun. "What do you see in it—that old broken-down plantation house?"

Anna Belle smacked his arm. "Ellsworth, be polite."

The man smirked. "Do you folks always converse in the middle of the road?"

Ellsworth didn't laugh—he was too busy staring at that fancy car—but Anna Belle did, and then she reached up to straighten her hair. "No, we don't. Sorry we didn't move."

"Not a bother." The man's voice was deep, yet soft. He was easily over six feet tall. His eyes were big and brown, as was his mustache. Skin tanned by the sun. His jawline was sharp, highlighting an angled face that revealed all kinds of handsome. He offered his hand to Ellsworth. "I'm Lou Eddington."

Ellsworth shook it reluctantly. He didn't like the way the man had glanced at his prosthesis, as if it conveyed inferior status. "Ellsworth Newberry."

"At one time, apparently, he went by Michael."

Ellsworth clenched his jaw, mumbled. "Close your head, Anna Belle."

Eddington faced Anna Belle. "And you must be Mrs. Newberry?"

"Not a chance," said Ellsworth. "Mrs. Newberry's dead. She didn't talk as much as this one."

Anna Belle offered her hand. "I'm Anna Belle Roper. A recent war widow."

"My condolences, ma'am." His face sagged, but then the broad smile returned. "I'm a recent widower as well. Seems like we already all have something in common." Instead of shaking Anna Belle's hand, Eddington gripped it lightly and raised it to his lips. He kissed her knuckles and let her hand drop.

"Don't do that," said Ellsworth—a thought he'd meant to keep to himself. Anna Belle noticed, but Eddington was looking over his shoulder at the yellow house on the hill.

"You asked what I see in that house, Mr. Newberry." He smiled—straight teeth, white as an ivory tusk. "I see potential. I see promise. I see those cotton fields one day thriving again."

Ellsworth's eyes strayed to the car again—the gleaming grille and spotless paint, the luxurious leather seats for four or five. He had never seen anything like it except in pictures. "What is this?"

Eddington proudly patted the hood. "It's a 1918 Rolls-Royce. Silver Ghost."

"It's not silver, it's red."

"I had it custom painted before they shipped it." He opened the driver's side door, which looked queer on the right side of the car and supported a large spare tire. "The body work is armored. No wind will blow this babe off the road."

"Where'd it ship from?" asked Ellsworth.

"England. But they'll soon begin making the Silver Ghost in Massachusetts. Springfield, to be exact." He'd left the car running—more of a purr than a rumble. "Made to last—quality like a Swiss watch. Nineteen miles per gallon. Got it up to fifty miles per hour along the coast. Care to take it for a drive?"

"No," said Ellsworth, although he badly wanted to. But his prosthesis wouldn't be able to manage all the foot mechanisms, and

Eddington probably knew that. Probably was trying to embarrass him in some way.

"Perhaps another time then."

"Doubt it."

"Well, I'd best get going. It was nice to meet you both." The man tipped his hat and started for his car.

"What do you do, Mr. Eddington?"

"Ellsworth!"

"Well, he comes into town like a big cheese, driving a car never seen in these parts. Just curious is all."

"Forgive him," Anna Belle said. "He's been through the war."

"As have I, Mrs. Roper. Veteran of the war with Spain."

Ellsworth scoffed. Anna Belle slapped his arm.

Eddington smiled. "It's no bother. I'm an artist of sorts, Mr. Newberry. I suppose you could say I paint and sculpt. To be exact, I make chess sets."

"Chess sets?"

He pulled a card from his pocket and handed it to Ellsworth. His fingernails were too neat, like a woman's. "I've opened a new store in downtown Charleston. On Bull Street. You should come and see the inventory." Ellsworth couldn't pronounce the name on the business card. Eddington said, "Eschec Mat—that's the name of my store. Old French, mid-fourteenth century, from the Arabic *shah mat*, which basically means 'the king died.'"

"The king died?"

"Have you ever played chess, Mr. Newberry?"

"Couple of times."

"The king is left helpless. The king is stumped. In other words, checkmate."

"We're in America," said Ellsworth. "Why not just call your store Checkmate?"

"Because I have too much love for the past. For history. And Checkmate sounds too boring. Too on the nose." He'd pointed to his nose when he'd said it, like Ellsworth was an idiot instead of just a cripple and needed things explained to him with gestures. "Stop by sometime. Look around the store. I'll give you a good deal, I assure you."

"We most certainly will, Mr. Eddington," said Anna Belle.

"Please, call me Lou. We're now neighbors, after all." He tipped his hat, returned to his car, but stopped before getting inside. He looked at the trees instead of them. "Is it true what they say about these woods?"

"What do they say?" Ellsworth asked.

"That they're magical?"

The lump in Ellsworth's throat rendered him temporarily mute. Anna Belle gave Ellsworth a guarded glance—she was clearly uncertain how to answer the man's question. But she tried. "Some believe them to be magical, yes. Been a lot of odd occurrences in the woods over the years."

"Perhaps sometime you can tell me about them over coffee?"

Anna Belle blushed.

Eddington, having gone out of his way to meet his first Bellhaven neighbors, stared at the woods for a moment before settling into his car. He backed into the town hall parking lot and purred off toward the yellow house on the hill.

"You could have been a pinch more cordial, Ellsworth."

"I don't trust him."

"Why?" she asked playfully. "Because he kissed my hand?"

"No. It makes me no never mind what he kisses of yours, Anna Belle." She spun away and started toward her house. He called after her. "Butter-and-egg man comes into town without warning, flashing some fancy car that's probably not even his."

She went inside and slammed her door.

Ellsworth watched the bright red Rolls-Royce putter up the hill in the distance to what had once been the thriving Bellhaven plantation. A main building and sunporch with two flanking wings, one holding a library and the other a music room. Although dilapidated, it was the original structure, having survived the earthquake in '86 and, before that, Sherman's march in '65. The Union troops had burned the nearby Magnolia and Middleton plantations but then halted at Bellhaven. Their horses had suddenly become skittish, neighing and bucking riders. General Sherman, after studying the woods, had ordered his men onward, sparing Bellhaven.

Eddington's car stopped in front of the three-story mansion, and the well-dressed man got out, standing tall and facing the woods behind the house.

Ellsworth wished he wouldn't have put away his revolver so fast when the man got out of the car earlier. Shouldn't have been so quick to listen to Anna Belle and act polite. Their new neighbor had been heeled. He'd seen the bulge under the man's coat—a gat big enough to do damage if he'd had the inclination.

*Have I ever played chess before?* Ellsworth shook his head, limped inside. *Enough to know I need to protect my pieces.*

# CHAPTER 7

It was cold out on the veranda, so cold they could see their breath. But Ellsworth and Eliza sat out there anyway in the matching rockers Calvin had made for their first wedding anniversary.

They'd been sitting out there almost every day since, watching the seasons unfold. Bellhaven had never been stingy with flowers. Daffodils and forsythia and hyacinths in early February. Dogwoods and redbuds through April. Lilies, honeysuckle, magnolias into the summer. Crape myrtle all summer, and roses well into the fall. Eliza jotted the blooming patterns in the brown leather diary she kept on the bedside table.

Eliza always preferred the outdoors, no matter the temperature. On chilly winter days like this one she'd simply drape herself with a blanket and keep on rocking. Ellsworth didn't like the cold, but he sat with her anyway, wanting to soak up her good moments any time he could.

Good moments had turned scarce since their newborn came out stillborn in the fall. Most days Eliza would just wander about the house, stoic on a good day, melancholy on a bad one, mostly silent. Not to mention the times she'd disappear for days on end. Traveling the trains, she called it, even when there were no actual trains involved.

Those solitary trips weren't a new thing, though. Apparently she'd been doing it for years, even before she met Ellsworth. In fact, she'd been on one of them the day they met—that time in a literal rail car.

Almost everyone in that car, including his mother, had died that day. Only he and Eliza had survived. They'd both called it fate, and he'd fallen in love with her in a blink.

A month into their courting, she'd told him she needed to go somewhere.

"Where?" he'd asked.

"I don't always know," she'd said. "But I'll know when I board the train, and I'll be back soon with a clear head."

It was just something he'd have to get accustomed to, she'd said— her leaving periodically. She'd promised she wasn't doing anything mischievous—said sometimes a woman just needed time alone. And she was never gone for more than a day or two, always returning noticeably refreshed. So he grew to accept her absences. Oh, he'd prod her a little about where she'd been, but not so much as to tinker with her improved mood. Besides, he trusted her, trusted her like the changing of the seasons and the rhythms of the ocean waves. Watching her smile was always better than any sunrise.

Now he couldn't remember when he'd last seen her smile. Nothing he did or said seemed adequate. Even their town hall gatherings she loved failed to rekindle her glow.

The rockers' legs creaked on the veranda. Despite the chill, some of the camellias bloomed. She pointed to the bush next to their front walk. "They survive the frost if their buds stay closed."

Ellsworth nodded. They hadn't even spoken much since they buried their boy in the Bellhaven cemetery. He'd buried his own sorrow in hours of countless pitches, urging that fastball closer to his dream of the big leagues. He was more determined than ever since his mother and the baby had died. But Eliza—Eliza had simply gone silent.

Recently though, at night and without a word shed, she'd cuddle close and make her womanly presence known. What followed was an odd combination of passion and sorrow that sometimes left her silently crying, her dead weight resting upon him like a warm blanket, her wild heart fluttering against his chest.

They'd never discussed it specifically, but it was obvious she wanted another child.

He wanted whatever would make her smile again.

They sipped dark coffee on that chilly winter day when the camellias were blooming. Fresh on Ellsworth's mind was what they'd done last night and the way she'd wrapped her arms around his neck and whispered in his ear so matter-of-factly, "It worked this time."

"I reckon so," he'd told her, although how did she really know?

Ellsworth sipped his coffee and stole glances at her through the steam. And that's when the cardinal bird arrived on the porch rail, a male by the look of the black mask and brilliant plumage. Its tiny talons clicked against the wood. The bird watched them both, and then took off into the woods.

Eliza's smile finally returned in full.

\\\\\//

Ellsworth recalled that winter day with the cardinal bird, and what Eliza said after it'd flown away. Cardinals represent loved ones who've passed. They visit you when you need them the most—in times of celebration or despair.

Eliza was a strong believer in signs. She was sure the bird represented their dead son, Erik.

Ellsworth leaned back in his chair and watched out the window. Watched all that color, the blooms tousled by the breeze. *What would our boy have been like had he lived? Would he have looked like me or Eliza? Would he have been a baseball player—a pitcher even?*

Ellsworth's eyes pooled with moisture. He'd thought that his emotions dried up long ago. That he'd left those tears over in Europe, when he'd close wet eyelids in the trenches and dream Eliza and his boy were still alive back home. A make-believe reason to keep fighting that nightmare war.

The nightmare still wasn't over.

Three cardinal birds landed on the steep pitch of the town hall's roof. Ellsworth stole a gulp of Old Sam and watched them until they flew away a couple minutes later.

By the time Erik was born dead, some in town had already begun to whisper about Eliza's sanity, and Ellsworth hadn't known how to take that. But now he did.

He'd told Anna Belle the arrival of the redbirds was a coincidence, but that was a lie. He felt it too—that something was happening. And he was sure that the redbird who'd visited him the day before and stopped him from pulling the trigger had been a representation of someone. But who? Eliza? His mother coming to tell him he was forgiven? Or maybe his father coming to say he was sorry for dying on the church steps when Ellsworth was a kid—sorry they'd never be able to dust the gloves off for one last Sunday game of catch.

*But you'd never look me in the eyes, would you, Papa?*

Ellsworth cracked the living room window open an inch to allow fresh air into his stagnant home. He breathed in the distant sea, the brackish marshes. Smelled shrimp, crab, and oysters, cord grass and salty mud. The breeze was familiar, but somehow different, as if the pressure in the low-country air was a smidge off-kilter in a way he couldn't yet determine, good or bad. The moss in the live oaks swayed and pulled and tugged almost cyclical, ushering in something unseen from the coastal salt marshes and tidal swamps where croaker, menhaden, and flounder swam through the muck.

The thought of fish made him hungry. The clock on the wall showed ten minutes after five. Almost time to eat again. But would Anna Belle still be cooking for him now that he'd told her she bumped her gums too much?

He reckoned so. The woman liked to cook, and somebody had to eat it. The boy Raphael was thin as a rail and didn't look like he ate much.

Ellsworth leaned forward in his chair to get a good view of the plantation house up on the hill. That man Lou Eddington had wasted no time. Three hours ago, about the same time Omar and Alfred finally went home to their wives, a half dozen wagons had arrived on the hillside, and two dozen workers had been hammering and sawing ever since. The roof was already off the house, and they'd begun to put on a new one. They'd replaced boards on the picket fence and were repainting it white. Three men on ladders scraped at the paint near the roofline. Several men trimmed the hedges, and even more collected deadfall, debris, and weeds from the vast lawn and cotton field beside it.

Ellsworth would have put down tarps to catch the flakes of yellow paint those scrapers were no doubt producing. He would have replaced some of the wood around those windows too. He would have done a more thorough job than these palookas.

Anna Belle's front door opened. She and the boy stepped out onto the porch and crossed the road together, empty handed. *Where's the food?* They approached the porch, and Anna Belle didn't bother knocking. She just walked in as if the house was her own.

Raphael stood sheepishly beside her.

"What do you want?" asked Ellsworth.

"Figured you were hungry," said Anna Belle.

"Figured right." Ellsworth leaned forward, squinted. "The food invisible?"

Anna Belle looked away. "It was his idea to come over. I was against it."

Raphael stepped forward, smiled, his teeth as white as his eyes were green. "Mr. Newberry. I thought mayhap you'd like to join us for dinner tonight."

"Where?"

"Our house. Across the road."

"I know where it is." He settled back in his chair. "What'd you cook?"

"Fried chicken," said Raphael.

"He helped me," said Anna Belle.

Ellsworth grunted. "What's your last name?"

Raphael shrugged. "Dunno, sir."

"You don't know your last name?"

"No, sir."

"How about a middle name?"

Anna Belle said, "Hard to have a middle without a last, Ellsworth."

He grunted again. "So it's just Raphael?"

The boy smiled again. "Yes, sir. That's what I'm called."

Ellsworth was dubious. "Where'd you learn to play the piano?"

"From some man named Jive."

"Jive? What kind of a name is that?"

Raphael shrugged. "Name he was given. As Jive says it, I learned to play the minute I was born. But Jive taught me how to read the notes."

"Is that so?"

"I reckon it is."

The retort took Ellsworth aback. "I reckon" was his line. "Where'd you come from?"

Anna Belle said, "This isn't an interrogation, Ellsworth. We can conversate over dinner. You coming or not?"

Ellsworth grunted. "Reach me my hat."

\\\///

Ellsworth sometimes wished second thoughts came first.

If they had, he wouldn't have come. At Anna Belle's kitchen table, he sat opposite Raphael and steamed. Piano virtuoso or not, green-eyed monster or not, the boy was the reason Eliza had run back into the burning town hall. And when Ellsworth asked him again where he came from, the boy's only answer was "Somewhere down south."

"How'd you get here?"

"I don't remember." Raphael bit into a crisp chicken leg. "It was nighttime, though."

"You remember it was dark, but not how you got here?"

Raphael nodded, took another bite of chicken.

"Was it a train? A wagon? A car?"

Anna Belle sipped her sweet tea. "Ellsworth, we're taking it slow. There's a lot he doesn't remember."

"It's okay, Mrs. Roper." He looked at Ellsworth. "Your ex-wife was nice."

"She's not my ex-wife. She's my late wife. There's a big difference. And what do you know about her?"

The boy shrugged so deep his neck might have disappeared between his shoulders. "She saved my life. And my momma's. And she's the one told me your birth name was Michael."

Ellsworth felt better. The boy hadn't inferred it after all. "Your momma died in the fire."

Raphael nodded.

"How did Eliza know about you?"

"I don't remember."

Ellsworth leaned back in his chair and tossed his napkin beside his plate. "I think I need to leave. That story's got more holes than Swiss cheese."

"Wagon," said Raphael.

Ellsworth said, "What'd he call me?"

"What about a wagon, dear?" asked Anna Belle.

"We come up from somewhere south in a wagon. Hid under a wool blanket that smelled like burnt leaves."

"Who?"

"Me, my momma, and your ex-wife."

The boy said ex-wife with a smirk, like he was trying to get under Ellsworth's skin.

Ellsworth ground his teeth, thought about Eliza traveling the trains. "What was my *late* wife doing somewhere down south?"

"Saving us."

"From what? From who?" Ellsworth leaned forward. "Did it have something to do with the Klan showing up here that night?"

"What Klan?"

"What Klan? How can you not—"

"Ellsworth," cautioned Anna Belle. "He's been through something terrible. I think his mind forgets out of necessity. I'm sure you know about that."

"Would you like to play a game of catch sometime, Mr. Newberry?"

"Is that supposed to be some kind of joke?"

"No," he said. "Mrs. Roper said you used to play baseball."

"Well . . . not anymore."

"How come?"

"One of my legs is made of wood, smarty-pants."

"But she said you have two gloves, and you still have both your arms, don't you?"

"I don't have to listen to this." Ellsworth made as if to get up.

Raphael said, "I know how to make you not remember the bad stuff, Mr. Newberry."

"What are you talking about?" The boy had stolen Anna Belle's attention too.

Raphael finished his tea. "That's why I went into the woods last night. I prayed that I'd forget all the bad stuff. And I did."

"Prayed to who?" asked Ellsworth.

"I don't know exactly. I can show you. It's in the woods."

"What's in the woods?"

"The healing floor."

Blood rushed from Ellsworth's face.

Anna Belle touched his arm, asked if he was well. He didn't answer. He was remembering what Eliza had said after she insinuated she'd talked to their son, Erik—the one born dead, not the one they'd created in passionate winter silence, only to miscarry four months later.

*"He's with the angels. I knelt upon the healing floor."*

Anna Belle reached across the table and held the boy's hands. "Raphael, what are you talking about? What healing floor?"

"In the chapel."

"What chapel?"

"The one in the woods. It's not hidden anymore. I think that's why everything's blooming."

# CHAPTER 8

They'd agreed to meet behind the town hall.

Ellsworth showed up with a flare and two canteens of water attached to his belt, his revolver in his holster, and a rifle in his hands.

"Is all that necessary?" asked Anna Belle.

"Everything's necessary." Ellsworth straightened his brimmed hat and stared into the woods.

Anna Belle seemed distracted by the goings-on at Eddington's house—the hammering and painting hadn't slowed a bit. Ellsworth touched her arm. "We best get along. I don't want to be caught out there after sundown." He nodded toward Raphael. "Lead the way."

Raphael went right in. There wasn't a definitive path to follow, but the woods weren't very dense. Between the trees were open spaces accentuated by red azaleas, purple redbuds, and delicate drifts of dogwood. Unlike the evenly spaced trees of the avenue of oaks, the live oaks here were more scattered. The canopy of limbs and moss allowed in cross-hatchings of sunlight, casting shadows across the leaf-and acorn-covered ground.

Ellsworth walked carefully, on the lookout for mud because his prosthesis was prone to stick. Every time Anna Belle and Raphael turned to wait for him he urged them onward, pointing with his rifle.

"Keep that thing pointed low." Anna Belle walked with her skirt hiked up to her shins.

"Krauts hide behind trees, Anna Belle."

She rolled her eyes. But the deeper into the woods they walked, the more he *could* have been back in Cantigny. He flinched when a squirrel skittered past. Raphael said, "Just a squirrel, Mr. Newberry." He pulled his revolver on a copperhead snake hanging from a limb. "He's more scared of you than you are of him, Mr. Newberry." Two minutes later Ellsworth pointed his rifle at a deer.

"Don't shoot, Mr. Newberry."

Ellsworth had already lowered his gun. *I'll shoot when I want to shoot.*

It had been years since he'd gone this deep into the woods to find that Tankersly boy. Now they were a good two hundred yards past the trees marked with yellow paint. So far, nothing had seized control of Ellsworth's mind like Alfred's mother had once told them would happen if they entered the woods—that the air would kill brain cells just like cocaine would, and soon they'd be unable to remember the simplest of things. His hair hadn't turned white like Timmy Tankersly's had.

Anna Belle walked hand-in-hand with Raphael now, but her free hand covered her mouth and nose while her skirt hem brushed the deadfall. Her mother had told her the woods would cause cancer if too much of the air was taken in. *Old habits die hard.*

Seemed like the breeze would lessen there among the trees, but it only grew stronger the deeper they walked. Red, white, and purple blooms reflected majestically in a nearby stream crossed by a small white bridge. *Who built it?* The bridge was dilapidated, with a few missing floorboards, but it still gave the scene the charm of a beautiful painting.

But his mother had once told him that the beauty of the Bellhaven woods was like a desert mirage—an optical phenomenon inviting trouble, an illusion of light rays that disguised the truth. She'd warned him not to be fooled.

After all, people disappeared in these woods. The legends went back centuries to the town's founding in 1682. Winds with voices. Fog taking on human silhouettes.

*Nonsense,* Ellsworth told himself, but he still watched the gnarled, oddly shaped trees as if they were about to *do* something.

"Are you sure there's a chapel out here?" he asked Raphael.

The boy nodded. "We're halfway there."

*Halfway there? We're liable to end up at the coast. Or in the Ashley River, depending on which way we're headed.* He'd long passed knowing where they were. Still, the boy showed no sign of fear.

They pressed on. Honeysuckle with red flowers and yellow centers coiled around the trunk of a slanted live oak. Raphael stuck his nose right in among them, and Ellsworth told him to be careful. Three hummingbirds hovered near a patch of bright red cardinal flowers. To the right was ground cover of deep blue and green foliage that Ellsworth couldn't place.

He was getting short of breath and anxious, and his brain began to feel muddled. He decided to take a break and told the others to go on. They waited. He shared his water canteens and took in the surroundings. Moss sparkling silver in the threads of waning sunlight. Tree bark so dark it was nearly black. Leaves green, stiff, and leathery.

The limbs of the live oaks had always reminded him of arms, the way they often grew sideways and went in any direction they wanted, large and spreading. He spotted one tree whose limb dipped inches from the ground for five yards, only to take a sharp upturn toward the light again. Ellsworth sat on that horizontal limb. It moved beneath his weight but then settled.

He wished Eliza was with him. They'd often walked the outskirts of the woods and occasionally ventured just past the yellow trees. But they'd never gone this far together, although now he knew Eliza had traveled here on her own at least once.

It *was* magical. But it was a magic that made his heart beat slower rather than faster.

Anna Belle turned in a circle, surveying the trees. "Maybe we should go back, try again in the morning when the sun is fresh."

"We're close now." Raphael squeezed her hand, the child protecting the adult.

Raphael hadn't grown up in Bellhaven. He hadn't heard the tales as they had. Amelia Jeffers had seen werewolves. Connie Vargas had seen spirits. Trudy Valient had told her son that there was a man in there dressed as a hooded monk who took children every full moon, *so never go past the yellow trees.*

Raphael watched them both. "Old Man Tanner warned me not to go into the woods."

"When?"

"Right before I went in," said Raphael. "Told me little boys who enter the woods never come back out."

Part of the woods' aura came from all the stories people told to keep kids out of them—unworldly stories, all of them, but fun to repeat. Which was no doubt why they grew more fantastical with every generation.

Raphael climbed atop the limb and sat so close to Ellsworth their legs touched.

Ellsworth scooted an inch away from the boy.

Anna Belle laughed. "Room on there for me?"

"There's room, but . . ." said Ellsworth.

"But what?"

"Not sure if it'll hold."

Anna Belle sat on it anyway, with Raphael in between them. She bounced to prove she wouldn't break the limb, which amused Raphael. Ellsworth slurped water from his canteen and wiped his mouth. He'd propped his rifle next to his leg. Part of him wished for a Kraut to jump out so he could shoot something. Some deeply strewn seed longed to see blood splatter against a tree.

Two cardinals flew beneath the canopy, chasing a sparrow. A cloud-white egret slow-walked behind distant trees. The sun ducked behind a cloud, and the woods darkened.

Sundown wasn't far off.

Ellsworth sucked in a deep breath but couldn't fill his lungs. His chest tightened, and his heartbeat slowed even more. Sweat dotted his brow. Anna Belle looked to be struggling for breath too.

*Stay still too long and your heart will stop.* That's what Berny Martino's father had told him when he was seven.

Ellsworth hopped down from the tree limb and grabbed his rifle. "Break's over."

"You're the one who wanted to stop," said Anna Belle.

"Well, now I'm the one moving on." He motioned with his rifle for them to move along. "Don't think it's a good idea to stop moving for too long." He nodded toward Raphael. "I think that's how come that white spot showed in his hair."

Raphael scratched the white spot as if it suddenly itched, then smiled. "I like it, Mr. Newberry."

"You would."

Anna Belle stared at the white patch in the boy's hair. She held worry in her cheeks the way a squirrel would hold a nut, but for

Raphael's sake she held her hands in the air, pretending to be a prisoner. Ellsworth was glad they were in front of him so they couldn't see his smile.

Eventually she put her arms down, and for a good ten paces he watched her hips sway. Two minutes later, Ellsworth found it easier to breathe again. Anna Belle's breathing appeared less labored too.

*Best to keep moving.*

Five minutes later they came upon a narrow stream lined with red and mauve asters. Anna Belle helped Ellsworth across. He liked the feeling of her hand around his arm, but as soon as they got to the other side, he pulled his arm free.

"We're getting closer," Raphael said in an awed voice. "I remember these funny-looking trees." He nodded to several live oaks growing in hard, gnarled tangents that looked like arthritic fingers.

"The Indians bent them to serve as trail markers," Ellsworth said, "and they grew that way." He pushed aside a branch. "From what I was told, the deep roots spread out into a system under ground," he said. "So these trees are connected. Makes them resistant to floods and such, and to the strong winds from the ocean storms."

Raphael nodded, interested. For a moment Ellsworth feared the boy was growing on him. So he shut up, and for the next few minutes they moved in silence. Even this deep in the woods, redbuds bloomed in purple profusion. A speckled thrush hopped in and out among the blooms. A threesome of white-tailed deer watched from a nearby stream.

"Almost there." Raphael's pace quickened as a blue butterfly landed on his shoulder.

Ellsworth checked his timepiece. They'd been walking for nearly thirty minutes, and his nub throbbed. Up ahead he heard birdsong—loud like an exhibit he'd once seen at the menagerie, out of place even in these woods. His chest tightened again, so he moved on.

Raphael pushed a tangle of limbs aside to reveal a small clearing lit by the setting sun. Ellsworth lowered his rifle and stepped through.

His heart swelled.

Curtain-like tree moss surrounded the clearing. Hundreds of birds flew about—blood-red cardinals, sleek mockingbirds, royal eastern bluebirds, purple martins, and egg-yolk yellow warblers—all of them singing. Long-necked, stark-white egrets moved about on the edge of the clearing, far from their swampland home. Dogwood trees bloomed pink and white. A wide-growing butterfly bush showed flashes of purple beneath a cloud of colorful butterflies.

Anna Belle stood with hands over her mouth, tears in her eyes. "What is this place?"

The chapel rested near the back of the small, rounded clearing, in front of a trickling stream with a giant live oak slanting over the water. One of the limbs dipped down like a black elbow into the stream, disappearing for a yard under the water before swooping upward again toward the far side. Two silver-barked river birches leaned like fingers touching from either side of the stream.

The tiny chapel looked to be about eight feet wide and ten feet tall, stone-walled with a pitched roof and small steeple at the front. The long walls bumped out on one end so that the building would resemble a cross if viewed from above. Centered in the façade was a rounded wooden door that leaned slightly from a broken top hinge. A buttery yellow warbler emerged from the gap atop the door, sang for a few seconds, and then joined the rest of the flying birds. The leaf-bed clearing was spotted with bird droppings, as was the poorly shingled roof—there was a hole on the right side where rain could get in.

Anna Belle turned slowly in a circle, said again, "What is this place?"

Ellsworth stood speechless. Seeing it all made him want to paint. To sing. To do something. He looked up, turned as Anna Belle was turning. "Must be three hundred birds here, Anna Belle. You ever seen so much color?"

"More color than the Magnolia Gardens up the river."

Ten redbirds sat in a line atop the roof's pitch.

"This is where I came," said Raphael. "To forget all the bad stuff."

Ellsworth recalled seeing Old Man Tanner enter the woods every day after lunch with a shovel and limb cutters. *Could he have found this place?* The grounds resembled the woods behind Tanner's house, plucked free of weeds and cleared of vines, the woody tangles and brambles trimmed back and cleared. The exterior chapel walls were stained green and brown, as if they'd recently been covered by vines and deadfall.

Hidden.

Raphael reached for the door.

"Don't," said Ellsworth.

"Why not?"

"I don't know," Ellsworth said. "Beautiful don't always mean safe, is all." *Mother told me not to be fooled.*

Ellsworth placed his hands on the boy's shoulders. "I once went into a Kraut trench with some fellow soldiers. The Boches had fled. The dirt walls were full of lithographs. Peaceful landscapes. Hunters in the Alps. Winter cottages, windows aglow with warm light. Made us think for a bit that they were human. But next to those lithographs were some sketches so degrading and vile—"

"Ellsworth." Anna Belle warned.

"Caricatures in positions of all kinds of coupling," Ellsworth went on. "Demonic and evil. Images only a diseased mind could think of."

"Ellsworth."

"We come upon a young Kraut dead in the trench. Couldn't have been more than twenty. In his hand was a picture of his wife and little son. One of our men, Private Barnich, felt bad about that. He knelt down next to that dead Kraut and reached out to take that picture. I screamed for him not to, but he did anyway. The Boches had placed a bomb under the body, put the picture there to lure us close. As soon as Private Barnich grabbed that picture, he was blown to bits."

"Ellsworth, stop."

"God rest Barnich's soul." Ellsworth stared at the chapel door. "'Cause we never found his head."

Anna Belle said quietly to Ellsworth, "Was that necessary?"

"Everything's necessary, Anna Belle." He approached the chapel with his rifle. He curled his fingers into the door gap and ducked as two goldfinches and a painted bunting flew out.

Raphael said, "If you open your mind to it, Mr. Newberry, you can hear'm talkin'."

"Hear who?"

"Those that already passed on. Like they trapped inside some-how." Raphael looked up at Ellsworth. "She told me about this place 'fore she died."

"Who told you?"

"Eliza."

Ellsworth gulped, turned from the boy, and faced the chapel. Anna Belle's hand touched Ellsworth's shoulder, and they stepped inside.

A cardinal and two white sanderlings fluttered across the arched, rib-vaulted ceiling. *Too ornate and overconstructed for such a small place.* Sunlight beamed down at an angle through the hole in the roof. Dust motes floated in the light. Ellsworth reached his hand out as if to grab them. The air was warm, hugging him like a blanket.

*How old is this place?* The chapel seemed much larger than it had appeared on the outside. Set into the far wall was a circular stained-glass window that cast a colorful prism of light on the floor. Matching stained-glass windows lined the side walls. They made him think of the Charleston cathedral. Ellsworth looked down. The floor from wall to wall was tile, thousands of tiny pieces inlaid to form the picture of an angel with wings flying away from a family gathered around an arched doorway.

"A mosaic." Ellsworth studied the family portrayed in the tiles. *Were they praying? In fear? Thankful?* He knelt awkwardly and brushed his hand across the floor. It was scattered with bird droppings, dusty and cold, yet when he pulled away his fingers tingled with warmth.

*I knelt upon the healing floor.*

Ellsworth stood.

Raphael had followed them into the chapel. At the right wall outcropping, the boy was on his knees with his hands folded, bowed in front of a five-foot-tall statue of a winged man holding a staff and standing on a fish. In the niche opposite stood another statue, Mary holding the newborn Christ. The plaster walls were painted white, peeling in places. Near the ceiling, a foot-tall bas-relief carving stretched around the entire chapel, a continuous scene of winged angels and serpentine devils in confrontation. Below the bas-relief ran a fresco of the same height and with similar themes portrayed in vibrant colors—brilliant white clouds and royal blue skies, blackened rocks licked by orange-red flames, life-like figures.

Anna Belle ran her hand across the fresco and then the sculpted panel, walking alongside them until she'd paced the small chapel in full. More birds had entered—two more cardinals and a bluebird. A woodpecker stared down from the hole in the ceiling. A purple finch sat on one of the ribs above, whistling as three purple butterflies spun past.

A memory flashed like a lightning bolt, exiting just as soon as it entered. *"Your father was sterile, Ellsworth."* The voice of his mother was in his head.

Ellsworth blinked it away, just as he'd tried to do the first time his mother said it.

Too real. Too close.

His father's voice this time: *"Doctor said we wouldn't be able."* Ellsworth didn't remember the exact timbre of his father's voice. He'd died before some memories started to stick. So why could he hear it now?

"Ellsworth?" It was Anna Belle now, in the present.

*That's why he could never look me in the eyes.*

"Ellsworth, what's happening?"

He gripped his rifle in both hands, turned in a circle. Dust motes spun in rays of dizzying light. Suddenly the air seemed suffocating. His heart slow-thudded and his palms went clammy.

The chapel grew brighter. Colors faded and then swarmed back full and deep like fresh oil paint. He felt the flutter of bird wings, but he couldn't hear the birds. He heard a heartbeat though, loud like a drum, echoing off walls that were now alive and moving, the bas-relief and fresco angels and devils clashing with swords and shields.

And then he heard another woman's voice.

*"Ellsworth."*

This one wasn't a memory forced back to the now, but Eliza's

79

voice strong and true, as if she stood right beside him. *Voices of those who'd passed on.* He closed his eyes, dreamed up her face, then shook it away. Refused it. He kicked open the door and stumbled outside, fell to the ground and sucked in the Bellhaven air. It was fresh but somehow not as pure as that inside those walls.

*Pure but deadly. Not of this world.* "Don't be fooled." He panted, wiped his dry mouth.

He could hear the birds now. They circled above, singing. They perched on colorful branches, on the roof. He made it to his feet, brushed off his hands, tried to deny the clarity he now felt inside his head. The peace and tranquility.

*It's just a chapel. Just a small chapel in the woods.*

Raphael stood beside him. "Did you forget the bad stuff, Mr. Newberry?"

Ellsworth shook his head. *No, I didn't.* All he'd heard was a voice that had no business being boxed inside those walls, walls that had somehow churned up stored memories he'd thought long forgotten.

The chapel door trembled in the breeze. Anna Belle was in there. The bottom of her feet were visible, the pale flesh of her calves as she knelt on that floor. He should get her. He should run in there and pull her out before she took in too much of it.

Just as he started forward, the chapel door opened and Anna Belle emerged. She wiped her eyes, eyes so clear she appeared a different person. She smiled and then placed her hands on Ellsworth's arms.

"I talked to him, Ellsworth."

"Talked to who?"

"To Calvin."

Ellsworth shook his head, spun away from her hold. *Don't be a pushover, Anna Belle. Don't be such an easy mark.* He clumped out of the clearing and reentered the Bellhaven woods, where dusk seemed to overtake him. He could hear Anna Belle and Raphael behind him.

He was tired, his leg throbbed, and he needed to get back home to his chair and bottle of Old Sam. But he couldn't seem to distance himself from those voices. He refused to believe, but still they haunted him.

Voices of the past.

Voices of the dead.

"Ellsworth, I heard him." Anna Belle hurried into the woods after him. "He spoke of you. Calvin did."

Ellsworth froze. "What'd he say?"

She looked at him cockeyed. "He said the war was to blame. And that you're forgiven."

# CHAPTER 9

Sunlight cast rainbows across the nave of the Cathedral of Saint John the Baptist.

Colorful stained glass sent directly from God—or so his mother had said about Broad Street's soaring new cathedral.

Michael rested his head against the pew. The creamy columns stretched to an arched ceiling that looked like an overturned boat. The pews were hard and uncomfortable. His mother said they were meant to be that way, that church was not a place to lounge about. His father said they were Flemish pews. The cathedral was built of chiseled brownstone from Connecticut. The three altars were made of white marble from Vermont.

"So the pews came from Flem?" asked Michael.

His father smiled but didn't look at him. He never really looked him in the eyes. "Yes," he told Michael, "that's exactly where they came from. Pews from the land of Flem."

Michael's mother gave them a stern look.

Father and son straightened against the hard-backed pews from Flem, and Michael tried not to laugh. Why did they have to get to the cathedral twenty minutes before mass anyway? The first few times, Mother had just wanted to take in every nook and cranny of the newly completed church. Last week they'd ventured down to the crypt and found a chapel there as well. But what was there left to see?

Dust motes floated through colorful light. The Opus 139 pipe organ warmed up in the rear gallery. The colored windows across the nave represented the life of Christ from nativity to ascension. Above the high altar was a series of windows duplicating Leonardo da Vinci's painting, *The Last Supper*, and higher up Saint John himself baptized Jesus while angels played musical instruments. Rose windows, the Gallery of Saints—his father had explained them all over the past weeks. He seemed to know a lot about religious art, but not so much about religion. When Michael asked him why they genuflected before entering the pew, his father had looked confused and said, "That's a question for your mother."

Michael's father had big-knuckled hands, broad shoulders, and thinning hair he typically kept combed beneath a brown bowler. He was a builder and made little pretense of being smart on topics such as religion or politics. He and some friends had built the town hall where they lived in Bellhaven, and he'd helped rebuild many of the houses in Charleston after the earthquake in 1886 leveled it.

Michael's mother touched her stomach and leaned toward her husband. "I'm feeling a little unsettled. I'll be back promptly."

"Where's Mother going?"

"To the bathroom," said his father, his eyes focused a familiar spot just above Michael's right shoulder. And then he smiled and waved to another suited man across the aisle.

His father had a lot of friends who attended mass at the new cathedral.

Michael ran a finger along his neckline. His tie was too tight. This morning while his father tied it, he'd asked why they even went to church.

Papa had smirked. "Because your mother makes us."

But it was more than that. Other than the building of it, his father didn't have many answers on what went on inside the new cathedral every Sunday. He didn't understand Latin and hadn't even tried to learn as Michael was doing now at school. Sometimes his father dozed off during mass. Mother would nudge him awake and he'd snort in the pews from Flem, mumble something about praying with his eyes closed.

They had a small Catholic church in their hometown of Bellhaven, which was only about ten miles outside of Charleston, tucked and forgotten in the woods surrounding Middleton and Magnolia and the Ashley River. But even his father insisted they take the carriage ride into Charleston to the cathedral every Sunday.

Truth was, Michael had never seen his father smile more than he always did after church was over. He'd mingle on the sun-drenched steps on his way out to Broad Street, shaking hands and patting backs and giving hugs, chinning with one and all as his chest swelled with joy and their bones hummed from the choral music escorting them out the doors.

Michael looked up at his father. "Why are you sweating?"

His father wiped his brow. He looked pale and clammy.

"I'm not sweating."

"You are." Michael looked straight ahead as more people arrived. "You going to be able to play a game of catch when we get home?"

His father nodded.

It was something new they'd begun—playing catch every Sunday after church. Michael could already feel the hard baseball in his grip, the stitched thread beneath his fingers. His father was throwing harder now because Michael had proved he could catch it. Michael's pitches were gaining steam as well. His father's glove popped every time he caught one flush. He'd pretend the impact broke bones in his hand, and Michael would flush with pride.

What was taking mother so long? Mass would be starting soon.

His father leaned closer. "Watch this." His hands were out in front with the fingers interlocked. The two index fingers were extended upward and touching at the tips like a steep house gable, while the thumbs ran upright and parallel to each other.

"Here's the church," said his father. "And here's the steeple." The upright index fingers. "Open up the doors." He moved the thumbs apart and wiggled the rest of the fingers hanging downward from his coupled hands. "And here's all the people."

He leaned back against the pew and grinned, then wiped more sweat from his brow. He wouldn't have done that trick had mother been in the pew with them.

What was that about anyway? Church and steeple and door thumbs and finger people?

Michael's father spoke from the side of his mouth as the nave began to fill. "You asked earlier, why we go to church? For me, it's the people. I don't pay much attention to what they're doing up there in the front. But I've never been to mass where I didn't feel better afterwards. You know, from having gone."

Michael nodded like he understood, but he didn't. Maybe one day he would.

His father wiped his brow again. "My friends are here, Michael. Church is people. People are the church." He motioned toward the stained-glass windows. "Church is art too." And then toward the choral singers warming up. "And church is music."

He imagined his father smiling and shaking hands on the front steps after mass and realized that he too always felt better from having gone.

Michael's mother returned to the pew. A minute later organ music soared, filling the cathedral's belly with beautiful sound. The procession started down the aisle and mass began.

Michael's father sweated all through church, until eventually mother made him take off his suit jacket. His shirt was stained wet, with deep pits under the arms and across his back.

He made it through mass, smiling on the way out despite the lack of color in his cheeks, and even got to shake the hands of a half dozen friends before he collapsed on the cathedral steps. The doctor would later call it a heart attack. But Michael's mother would eventually explain, guiltily—when Michael was more of an age to understand the dimensions of the adult heart and mind—that it wasn't so much an attack of the heart that had killed his father as it was a heart mistakenly broken.

Michael was first to his father's side after he'd collapsed outside the cathedral. He guided his father's sweat-drenched head to rest on the first step so it faced the clear sky. His eyes settled directly on Michael's, and a look of peace swept across his father's pale face.

He said, "Blue."

Michael shook his head. "What's blue?" He knew his eyes were blue—some said the bluest eyes they'd ever seen. But his father didn't elaborate.

Instead he smiled at his son, and just before he took his last breath he said, "There is no land of Flem, Michael. They're from Flanders. The pews. They're Dutch."

\\//

For the first time since the war, Ellsworth slept free of nightmares.

He awoke the next morning rejuvenated, fresh and alert, knowing the chapel visit had something to do with it. *But is it possible?* He tossed the blanket aside and sat up on the couch. *Just a coincidence? Like the boy playing that Mozart sonata?*

But he'd heard the voices. His parents'. And then Eliza's. She'd said his name, and in that instant her voice had been as real as drizzle on a tin roof. If he'd stayed inside the chapel longer, she would have said more.

Anna Belle had been the brave one.

*"He said you're forgiven."* If only she knew what he'd done.

Ellsworth drank his morning coffee, and on his way into the kitchen he stopped before the stairwell and eyed the second-floor landing. Today was the day he'd go up.

He rested his coffee mug on the first stair and used the wall railing for support. He placed his right foot on the first step, followed by the prosthesis. It worked well enough, so he used that cadence all the way up, and he was sweating by the time he reached the landing. His bedroom was down the hallway to the right. A crack of sunlight shone under the door.

The last time he walked this hallway, he'd had two legs. A dream to one day pitch in the big leagues. A wife to cling to at night.

He turned the knob. The door clicked, swung open to sunlight, dust motes, and warm, musty low-country air. In the summer they used to move their bed to the middle of the room for better breeze. Eliza would stand at the window and watch the woods when she couldn't sleep. Ellsworth would roll over in bed, pretend his wife wasn't losing her mind.

Dust covered the floor and baseboards. The bedcovers were pulled back and tangled. They'd never gotten around to making the bed the morning of the fire. Eliza used to wait until night to do it, tucking and smoothing until all the creases were just right, only to pull back the covers minutes later. She couldn't slide into an unmade bed. She had those adorable quirks.

*"Ellsworth, there's a black woman walking backwards in the woods."*

*"Come back to bed, Eliza. You'll feel better in the morning."*

On the far side of the bed was the easel Eliza had gotten him the week before her death—the easel he'd said he would probably never use, the type of painting he'd thought pointless. A blank canvas rested upon it, the red bow still secured to the top. A clean wooden palette, new paintbrushes, and several tubes of paint rested on the floor below it.

He ran a finger across the canvas, blew dust off, and then turned toward the bed. The mattress was lumpy and cold. Dust puffed out when he patted it. He blew into the cloud and particles scattered. He pulled his legs up and lay back on Eliza's pillow. It still held her scent—the vanilla extract she liked to dab behind her ears, plus the jasmine powder from her nightly bath. Her dressing table was centered on the near wall next to the window. A tin of facial cream had been left open, now dried out. Next to it sat a small container of rouge, a stack of blotting papers, and the lipstick tube she'd been so pleased to purchase, that clever push-up stick. Ellsworth had said it looked like a bullet cartridge, to which she'd pointed a finger gun at him and fired a pretend shot across the bedroom. He'd acted like he'd been hit. She was upon him in a flash, her breath on his neck, her hair against his cheek as she leaned close to kiss his lips.

"I know you're not dead," she'd said, giggling.

He'd opened his eyes. "How could you tell?"

"I can still see your color."

\|||//

Ellsworth woke up starving.

The wall clock read five. He'd slept through breakfast and lunch.

Pots and pans clanked downstairs, accompanied by a familiar man's voice.

Ellsworth sat up in bed and rubbed his face. His cheeks were like sandpaper. He stood and stretched. Dust no longer covered every surface of the bedroom. The hardwood shone and smelled of cedar oil. Two flies tapped against the inside of the window, and a third circled. He'd have to find the swatter. His father used to roll up newspaper and bop them.

*"Your father was sterile, Ellsworth."*

He pushed it away, focused on the clean room. Anna Belle, no doubt, had cleaned while he slept. Food aromas wafted from the first floor.

Descending the stairs was more awkward than climbing them.

Raphael appeared at the bottom when Ellsworth was halfway down. He directed him toward the kitchen, where the table was full of steaming bowls, plates waiting to be filled, and glasses of sweet tea. Anna Belle wiped her hand on a dish towel and smiled as she took a seat at the table.

The man's voice he'd recognized earlier was Alfred's. He was at the end of the kitchen table next to his wife, Linda May, who sat with a giddy smile, her dark hair cut into a neatly parted bob. She didn't look to Ellsworth like a woman Alfred had described to him, one who'd fallen into despair because of a blind, brain-damaged husband.

"Ellsworth." Alfred held his hand out in the general vicinity for a shake. Instead of his war uniform, Alfred wore a suit. He didn't look like the same troubled man who spent his days feeding the squirrels and filling Ellsworth's living room with communist rhetoric.

Ellsworth shook Alfred's outstretched hand and sat down in a chair next to Anna Belle's, looking over the contents on the table. Mashed potatoes. Green beans. Hoppin' John with chopped onion and ham hunks. Southern spoon bread. Baked ham with brown sugar and peppercorns. He piled food on his plate during Anna Belle's prayer, oblivious to the moment, aware only when he finally looked up and caught her glance of annoyance. Besides the clanking silverware, they remained quiet as they ate. After a few minutes, Alfred broke the silence with a quivering jaw.

"Ellsworth, I talked to Sergeant Bathoon this morning."

They stopped eating, all eyes on Ellsworth, who shoveled a forkful of green beans into his mouth. Alfred was clearly still jingle-brained. "Bathoon's dead. Got cut in half by a big gun in Château-Thierry." He motioned to Linda May with his fingers. "His legs ran for another five feet even as the rest of'm blew back against a tree trunk."

"Ellsworth." Anna Belle covered Raphael's ears.

"I don't mind," said Raphael.

"I talked to him all the same." Alfred lifted spoon bread toward his mouth. "Inside that chapel. I knelt down on that floor."

Ellsworth looked at Anna Belle. "You took them into the woods?"

"I did."

"We don't know if it's safe in there."

"Power in numbers."

He shoveled mashed potatoes and hoped to let it go, but he couldn't. "How could you?"

"Do you own the woods, Ellsworth? Is it *your* chapel?" He clenched his jaw, then stuffed his mouth with ham. Seeing that Eliza had apparently found the chapel years back, he did feel it was more his than theirs. She had no right to show anyone else.

Anna Belle said, "Look what it did for you, Ellsworth."

"What did it do for me, Anna Belle?"

She scoffed.

Raphael said, "You slept in your room for the first time since your ex-wife passed."

"Late wife."

"What?"

"Late, not ex."

Raphael didn't follow. "Did you have nightmares last night? About the war?"

"Close your head, boy." He knew his refusal to answer the question was answer enough. He'd slept like a baby all night and then again during most of the day. "How'd you know about my nightmares?"

"Mrs. Roper told me."

"Well Mrs. Roper needs to zip her gums."

Alfred pointed with his fork. "There's a slice of heaven inside that place, Ellsworth."

"You've been dipping the bill in too much giggle juice, Alfred. It's just a chapel."

"I'm not out on the roof today. I promise. That ship done sailed."

Linda May said, "He hasn't had a drink since yesterday."

*What about the morphine he injects between his toes while you're asleep?*

Alfred said, "At first the place gave me the willies, but then . . ." He teared up. Linda May gripped his hand and he pulled it together. "I'm just sayin', for the first time since I come back, I feel proper in the head."

Anna Belle said, "We can't pretend it's not there, Ellsworth."

"You plan to go back?"

"Of course I do. I've never felt so . . ." she put a fist to her mouth to steady herself. Raphael patted her shoulder and she smiled lovingly at him.

Ellsworth asked, "Never felt so what?"

"Safe, Ellsworth. Never felt so safe. And peaceful. Is that so bad a thing?"

Ellsworth rubbed his face. "Did you go in there again?"

"Yes. Don't look at me like that."

"Like what?"

Anna Belle stabbed her fork into the table, the tines a quarter-inch deep in the wood. "Like I'm some easy mark. Like we're a bunch of saps. I know what I saw, Ellsworth. I know what I heard. Calvin didn't speak to me this morning, but I felt him in there. The air was like a hug, and he was so close I could smell his cologne."

Ellsworth pulled the fork out of the table, staring at the tiny holes it'd produced.

"I'm sorry," said Anna Belle. "I shouldn't have done that."

Ellsworth wiped the fork off on his napkin and rested it on her plate. She picked it up again and this time used it to scoop mashed potatoes.

Ellsworth said, "We don't know anything about that place. We don't know who built it. We don't know *why* they built it. Or how long it's been there, or who all has been inside it."

"Does it matter?" Linda May asked, rubbing her husband's back. "Today's the first day in forever I feel I have my husband back."

"And it could be sap poison. There's two sides to every coin, Linda May."

It grew silent. They all resumed eating, chewing, drinking. Silverware clanked again. Wooden chairs shifted beneath their weight. No one looked up from their plate. After a few uncomfortable minutes of it, Ellsworth turned to Alfred. "What did he say?"

"Who?"

"Sergeant Bathoon. You said you talked to him. What did he say?"

"Told me it was kill or be killed, Ellsworth. And I'd done right by my country. And . . ."

"And?"

"And that I was forgiven too."

# CHAPTER 10

Eliza was lifeless when he pulled her from the rubble.

Ellsworth's tears dripped grooves through the gunk on her cheeks. He carried her outside to place her on the lawn. Kneeling beside her, he stared vaguely at the chaos surrounding him.

Trees burned nearby, sparked by the burning building. Sheriff Pomeroy, Bellhaven's first Negro sheriff, hung from a live oak next to the jailhouse, crooked-necked and limp, stripped of his uniform and covered with tar and goose feathers as white-cloaked figures circled on horseback. Half-drunk from the town hall party, they'd been over-whelmed, unarmed against Klansmen with shotguns, clubs, and steel pipes. Hundreds of cardinal birds circled the trees, spiraling in and out of the smoke.

Calvin lay in the grass, moaning. Alfred took a punch to the jaw and spun against the grill of the tractor Berny Martino had driven to the party. Omar lay in the middle of the road unconscious. Even Gabriel, with all her size and strength, was losing her fight against four men swinging clubs and lit torches at her. She'd consumed an entire bottle of Old Sam by herself during the party and been nearly passed out with her head on the table when the Klan arrived.

A car revved, squealed, and swerved as if driven by a blind man—Reggie Vargus fleeing in a panic, clutching the wheel of his brand-new

Model T. Kenneth Rapido, screaming about the smoke in his eyes, stepped in the car's path, and his body folded under the vehicle's front left wheel. Kenneth writhed on the ground, legs pinned, while Reggie cried and screamed, still gripping the steering wheel, "I didn't see him. I swear I didn't."

Ellsworth jumped to his feet and ran over. He squatted down for leverage and gripped the front fender of the Model T, yelling as he raised the car front inch by inch off Kenneth Rapido's body. His feat of strength put a pause to the goings-on all around him, but it was clear he still needed help. Gabriel freed herself from her attackers, and together she and Ellsworth walked the front of the car five feet to the right, away from Kenneth's legs.

Except for the fire hose spraying water on the town hall flames, everything else went quiet. Even the Klansmen held still, their eyes focused on Ellsworth. He'd later claim it was adrenaline, but the town folk weren't so sure. In their minds it had given credence to thoughts they'd had all along. About him being different from everyone else. A special kind of different that had always made him the leader while they all followed.

Just as Reggie's car tires settled in the dust, a hooded Klansman came at Ellsworth with a steel pipe and cracked him hard across the back of the head. Ellsworth staggered but didn't fall, which stunned the Klansman into a stutter.

"W-where you got'm—where's that black boy?"

Ellsworth plucked the pipe from the Klansman's hand. He spotted Eliza in the grass, and his heart splintered. The chirping and twittering from the cardinals went mute, and all he heard was his heart thumping. He swung the pipe in a violent arc toward the Klansman's right shoulder, dropping him to the middle of the gravel road. He hit him again and again and again, screaming with every swing even as the white-cloaked Klansman begged for mercy.

No one moved, not even the man's robed cohorts, who still stood stunned from when Ellsworth had lifted the car. After what must have been twenty blows with the pipe, it was Anna Belle who talked him down. By that point she'd already hidden Raphael in Calvin's closet.

The bloodied Klansman moaned in the middle of the road. His brethren, careful to avoid Ellsworth, pulled him away and draped him over the haunches of a tall mare. The hood on one of them slipped, and Ellsworth glimpsed a bald eagle tattooed on a sunburned neck. The Klansman frantically tugged the hood back into place.

And then the earth shook.

It was just a quick one, a three-second tremor that left everyone steadying for balance. The area wasn't unaccustomed to a quick rumble every now and then. But there was still no getting around the suddenness of it.

In the lull, the cardinal birds attacked, swooping toward the white-cloaked men, flapping and pecking and clawing until the Klansmen thundered away on their horses without the boy they'd evidently come for.

The town folk stood still, watching each other, watching the ground, watching the birds they'd seen gather for days.

After a while, Ellsworth went to cut Sheriff Pomeroy from the tree.

His lifeless body dropped heavy into Gabriel's arms.

\||//

Ellsworth stared at the blank canvas.

Painting a picture had been a bad idea.

He was a baseball player, a soldier, a house painter, not an artist. But Anna Belle and the boy had been persistent, and he'd caved just so they'd close their heads about it. So here he stood for his third attempt in as many days, without the first notion of what to paint.

Today he'd set up the easel on the veranda. That was the boy's idea—said the sunlight and trees might inspire him. But so far Ellsworth just felt frustrated.

"What about that dogwood?" Raphael pointed at the tree blooming pink in the middle of his yard. Ellsworth shrugged and stared at the canvas while the boy chattered on.

"The woods—they're alive, you know. But they smell funny, like burnt leaves and chimney smoke."

Ellsworth sniffed but didn't smell anything. "Of course they're alive," he said. "They grow leaves and branches and such. And trees like that dogwood bloom every year."

"But this bright? And everything at the same time?"

The boy had a point. The trees did look more vibrant than normal. But when Raphael pressed about painting the blooming dogwood, Ellsworth said no out of spite.

"Those trees are called live oaks for a reason, Mr. Newberry."

"That's 'cause they hold on to their leaves nearly all year like an evergreen."

To that the boy shrugged, then asked Ellsworth if he wanted to play a game of catch. Ellsworth said no, and told the boy to quit bothering him. Raphael walked off with his hands in his trouser pockets. A minute later he was in Anna Belle's house playing the piano. Eliza's Mozart sonata again, sounding clearly through the open window.

*So the boy's a wise-guy as well as a pest.*

The music stopped after a while, but Ellsworth still had a hard time concentrating. It wasn't just the woods that had come to life; it was the town. Just as he'd feared, Anna Belle had begun telling others about the chapel. Alfred and Linda May Dennison too. Alfred claimed that chapel contained a smidge of heaven and kept encouraging everyone to go see it, especially the war veterans. Now town folk had been walking into the woods all day.

So far no one had gone missing or come back with a patch of white hair. Maybe they were in and out of the woods too fast to feel the effects. "Best not to stand still for too long," he'd heard Anna Belle warn some of them. Many, though, had returned crying, claiming they'd been in the presence of loved ones who'd died. Said they'd never felt so calm and peaceful as they'd felt inside those walls.

Ellsworth begged to differ. What he felt hadn't left him peaceful. Not for long, anyway.

The way he saw it, Anna Belle and Linda May and Alfred had jumped the gun, telling everyone about the chapel before they knew if it was a good thing or not. And now the main road teemed with people who'd previously spent their days in their homes, looking out windows, paranoid since the night the town hall burned and death knocked on Bellhaven's door.

"Ants on an anthill," mumbled Ellsworth, trying to focus on his canvas again.

After two dreamless nights, his nightmares had returned. His brain had reached down deeper than the war to recycle Eliza's death and its aftermath again.

The outcome never changed.

He hadn't told Anna Belle about the nightmares. If he did that, he knew she'd insist he make another trip into the woods to visit that chapel. But something in the way she'd looked at him in the morning made him think she already knew. She and the others had tried to get him to go into the woods with them earlier in the day, but he'd told them no. Insisted he didn't need to, was getting by fine without it. He had Eliza's picture to look at, and that was all he needed.

But the truth was he felt the pull like a drug. He'd been given a dose the other day, and now he was jittery from the lack of it. His grip shook. The paintbrush wavered. He couldn't quite think straight.

Up the hill, Lou Eddington's house was half painted, a bright new yellow reminiscent of the warblers at the chapel. The cotton field had been cleared and plowed. Eddington stood atop the hill, hands on his hips and smoking a pipe, wearing glad rags no one else in town could afford. According to Anna Belle, he'd ventured into the woods a dozen times over the past three days.

Yesterday Anna Belle had taken their new neighbor a basket of blueberry muffins. He'd let her inside, and she'd later told Ellsworth that the ceilings were high and the doorways wide. The wood was nicely polished, and fancy furniture had been moved in.

"What about a family?" Ellsworth had asked. "Does he have kids?"

"They passed two years ago during the flu epidemic. His wife and two sons."

"Where'd he come from?"

"I didn't ask."

"Why didn't Raphael go with you? To give that man those muffins?"

Anna Belle had paused before answering. "He didn't feel well, but he's better now."

Anna Belle had been hiding something. The boy looked well enough. Raphael watched that big yellow house and the new neighbor just as Ellsworth did—like he didn't trust the man. It may have only been a thread, but an unsaid bond had begun to form between Ellsworth and the boy because of that shared distrust. *How can the man get so rich from selling chess sets?*

According to Anna Belle, Eddington's hands and shirt had

been covered with dust when she dropped off the muffins. He'd been sculpting—"furiously sculpting," he'd told her—ever since he'd entered that chapel. He'd never worked so fast, so focused. Never had his creative vision been so clear. He'd worked through two straight nights without sleep and still felt the energy to do more. He'd embraced her, kissing both cheeks before she retreated, giddy herself, down the hill to Ellsworth's house.

"You should have seen him, Ellsworth."

"I'd rather not."

"He said he heard the voice of his wife in that chapel. And his little children. He said it's true what they say, that the woods are magical."

To that, Ellsworth had grunted and closed the door.

Eddington now puffed on his pipe and blew out smoke like a steamer, watching the crowd filter in and out of the woods. He spotted Ellsworth watching from afar and waved.

Ellsworth didn't wave back. Instead he uncapped a tube of fresh red paint and spilled a dollop on his thumb. He smudged a line across the center of the canvas and thought of blood.

\\\\///

Ellsworth stepped back to view in full what he'd done on the easel.

*It's a little violent.* But at least his hands no longer shook.

Once he started painting, the canvas had entranced him. He'd been at it for close to two hours now, and his hand was cramping. *But what a mess!* He'd never painted a picture before, and it showed. He'd set out to paint a war scene—a French village at sunset, with scorched trees and land pocked with bomb craters and a soldier with an arm blown off pulling another soldier across no-man's-land. But what showed on the canvas looked more like a multicolored paint spill. *Stick men would've looked better than this. Why did Eliza ever think I'd be good at such a thing?* Even so, he felt better having painted it, as if some poisonous toxin had been purged from his system.

Town folk were still roaming the street with tears and smiles and laughter, and their voices carried—even seemed to be magnified somehow.

Dr. Philpot was sitting on the brick rubble in front of the town hall, and Ellsworth could hear him telling Carly Jennings that he'd been to the chapel and spoken with his little brother, who'd died from polio in 1908. And Carly, with tears in her eyes, confided to the doctor that she'd heard her father's voice there. They'd had a falling out, and she'd told her father she hated him—an hour before he collapsed from a heart attack. She'd never had a chance to tell him she hadn't meant it. But now she related in wonder that "he said he knew I loved him and I was forgiven."

Ellsworth stepped closer to the veranda railing. Some of the town folk eyed him just as they had the night he took a steel pipe to the noggin and barely wobbled—with curiosity and a bit of awe. Jonah Livingston walked down the sidewalk with his wife, Mildred. They held hands and smiled. He'd never seen them show any affection before on their walks. Typically Jonah walked a step or two behind his wife. Their only son had drowned in the lake five years prior, and they'd stopped talking to one another after his burial. Now, as they passed, Jonah said something to Mildred and she laughed, squeezed his hand, and blushed.

Behind the town hall and near the edge of the woods, Ellsworth saw Gabriel hugging Donald Trapper, the town barber, pressing his face into the bosom of her overalls and patting his back. She dwarfed the little man, who sometimes had to stand on a stool to clip hair. They both looked like they were weeping, and Ellsworth wondered what the story was there.

Father Timothy exited the woods, his face pale. He kissed the cross around his neck and then motioned the sign of the cross over his forehead, neck, and shoulders. He passed Gabriel and Donald Trapper, staring at the tall woman as if in some strange new light.

Twenty yards away, Rabbi Blumenthal stood at the edge of the trees as if afraid to enter. Reverend Beaver from the First Methodist Church took the rabbi by the elbow, and the two men entered the woods together just as Reverend Cane from First Baptist walked out crying and eyeing all the birds.

Down the road, in the front yard of the recently claimed worship house for the Pentecostals, Brother Bannerman knelt in the grass and stretched his arms to the air, preaching about heaven and hellfire to a small crowd gathered around him on the sidewalk.

And up there on the hill, Lou Eddington still stood outside his house, viewing the town from above as Ellsworth did from below.

Ellsworth couldn't shake the picture in his mind that the whole foundation of the town was shifting, loosening—like a porch board that was sturdy now but could give way underfoot at any moment. And it was all because of that chapel. Most who visited it went just the one time, but Ellsworth noticed others had begun to enter the woods daily, sometimes multiple times a day. Anna Belle had told him just a few hours ago, after she and Linda May came back from the chapel after lunch, that she'd probably not go for a couple days—give her mind a break and let the rest of the town have their turn. But there she was again, entering the woods for the second time of the day, and Ellsworth felt the need to stop her.

*The town's been plugged into an electrical socket.*

And now he, too, felt the pull again.

The solace he'd found after painting the picture had faded. He craved the woods like the rest of them. Craved Eliza's voice. Craved the air that had felt like a warm embrace.

He turned away from the railing and then stopped abruptly. Old Man Tanner stood two feet away from him on the veranda, chewing the inside of his mouth. Ellsworth had never seen the old man up close, and now he saw that Tanner's eyes weren't old at all, though the skin around them was pinched and wrinkled. His back was hunched and his head bobbed as if palsied, but somehow he'd walked right up onto the veranda without Ellsworth hearing him.

"My place," said Tanner. "Not the towns'."

By the time Ellsworth realized what the old man was talking about, Tanner had raised the knife high and brought it down in a quick arc toward Ellsworth's chest. The blade punched through his shirt, and he felt warm blood around his heart.

The handle protruded from Ellsworth's chest. His vision swirled too much to pull it back out. His heart twitched. He spat blood and stumbled back into the easel, spinning his painted canvas to the floorboards where it probably belonged. He heard Gabriel's voice screaming his name as he hit the floor, landing on his back.

At the corner of the veranda a small yellow birdhouse with a red roof and blue arched door spun, breeze-blown, from a ceiling hook.

Every house in town had one. *For all the birds.*

His vision darkened, and Old Man Tanner's voice echoed across the void.

"Sorry, Ellsworth. The devil made me do it."

# CHAPTER 11

Ellsworth floated through the woods on his back, shivering.

He was being carried on a stretcher like after his leg was blown. Anna Belle gripped his right hand. Dr. Philpot applied constant pressure to the wound, his thoughts readable across glazed eyes: *This man shouldn't be alive.*

Father Timothy and Reverend Cane gripped the handles at the foot of the stretcher while Gabriel walked backward, carrying the head by herself. Her overalls were stained from the smithy, her blond hair uncombed to the tops of her bulky shoulders. Her blue eyes were pretty—didn't match the rest of her. A copper-colored light surrounded her face like a halo.

Was this it? Was he finally dying?

Anna Belle squeezed his hand, pleaded for him to fight. Part of him now wanted to. *Where are they taking me?* Birds circled above, red and blue birds. Yellow warblers and rainbow butterflies. Ellsworth squinted against the sunlight. Flower blooms flew wind-blown across the sky.

*No, don't take me in there.*

The door creaked open. Raphael held it.

Gabriel ducked under the threshold, looking less confident than the others. *She doesn't like this either.* Ellsworth lifted his head to see that half the town had followed them into the woods—concerned for him. Lou Eddington was among them, watching from afar, fidgety.

*He wants to come in too. But he can't. It's too full.*

Something shrieked in Ellsworth's brain. Tiny bee stings. He tried to scratch at his face, but his arms were restrained by someone's hands.

"Keep your head down," said Dr. Philpot.

"Relax," said Gabriel, backing into the chapel.

The chapel air's warm embrace soothed his shivering. They placed the stretcher on the mosaic floor, and he did relax. Light beamed down from the hole in the roof. Dust motes. Stained glass casting rainbows. Angels and demons in combat along the walls, swords clanking on shields across fields of fire and snow, sunlight and dark.

"Now what?" someone asked.

Ellsworth didn't hear an answer. He'd closed his eyes. His heart barely thumped.

*Where am I?*

"Ellsworth . . ."

*Who am I?*

"Michael Ellsworth Newberry."

*Mother . . .*

\|\|//

He'd insisted on sitting alone in the train car.

Told his mother he needed space, some time to think on the ride back to Charleston. And she'd obliged, although not without that hurt look when she turned away.

The Brooklyn Dodgers were officially interested in signing him.

He'd just pitched for their scouts in Florida, and they'd shaken his hand and talked to him like he was a man. Not a boy, he thought, glaring ahead at his mother, who'd taken a seat four rows up. By the tilt of her shoulders, she might have been crying.

Maybe he shouldn't have told her to butt out of his life, especially now that he was so close to achieving his dream of pitching in the big leagues, but the way she'd asked all of those questions of the scouts had embarrassed him.

*"Michael here is prone to accidents, so when the time comes I'll have to know he'll be watched over."* How many times did he have to tell her not to call him Michael anymore?

*"And we have to make sure he eats proper and stays away from the giggle juice. And the broads."* Broads? Where had that come from? But she just wouldn't stop.

*"I know how those ballplayers are, and I know how the women who follow them can get—on the road and whatnot. Michael here has been at death's door more times than you know . . ."*

The two scouts had thanked him and moved on, promising to be in touch when he got another year or so of pitching under his belt.

She shouldn't have come anyway. He was seventeen, after all— old enough to catch a train by himself. Calvin and Alfred and Omar had wanted to make the trip with him, but she'd said boys their age didn't need to be gallivanting across state lines without chaperones.

She just didn't want him leaving Bellhaven, clear and simple. Didn't want him leaving her. Father would have been more supportive had he been alive. He'd been the one to plant that pitching seed in the first place, and those Sunday games of catch had fertilized it to grow.

Up ahead, mother rested her head against the window and watched trees zip by.

Ellsworth felt the urge to hug her. Ten more minutes, and maybe he'd join her up there, tell her sorry for what he'd said. He smelled the baseball glove on his lap, inhaled the scent of leather, and imagined pitching in front of big crowds while they ate hot dogs and sipped suds.

And then his mother suddenly stiffened in her seat, as if she'd seen something out the window to startle her. The train shrieked and squealed. She held her ears and looked over her shoulder with fear in her eyes. He stood as if to run to her, but then the windows shattered and the train car folded in on itself.

Everyone was screaming. Everything spinning. Ellsworth shouted for his mother but couldn't see her.

Arms enveloped him. A soft voice told him to get down. A woman's voice, but not his mother's. He turned to look. She had pretty blue eyes, a curtain of auburn hair, and a face meant for a painting.

She told him he'd be safe.

And he believed her.

\\\\///

"His pulse is stronger," said Dr. Philpot.

"Mother . . . I'm sorry . . . Mother . . ."

They told him not to talk. Anna Belle told him to close his eyes and rest. So he did, but he held on to her hand for dear life.

\\\\///

His mother lay red-faced and straining on the operating table, her knees propped up beneath a white sheet stained with blood.

*The day I was born? But how?*

Was the chapel somehow filling him with memories that couldn't have been his own?

A gray-haired doctor pulled a baby from the tented folds, and his eyes narrowed in concern.

The baby boy didn't cry. He lay blue-faced and limp, the umbilical cord wrapped tightly around the neck. The doctor worked quickly, cut the cord, waited.

Mother assumed her miracle baby was dead. She wailed.

But then the baby's fingers twitched. The right hand then the left.

The doctor felt for a pulse. Color returned to the baby's face. A minute later he cried.

*Almost died the day I was born.*

*That's when it started.*

\\|//

"How long do we leave him here?" someone asked.

"Until his color returns," said Raphael.

Gabriel hovered above him, her presence giving him strength.

A yellow warbler landed on her shoulder, and she didn't move it.

\\|//

Eliza lay beside him on the stretcher, nestled in the crook of his arm.

Her lips against his ear, breathing life, just like on the train.

"Not yet," she whispered.

\\|//

He was on a picnic blanket now with Eliza, looking up at the clear blue sky, finding pictures in the clouds.

Eliza pointed. "There's a buffalo." The swells of her chest rose and fell beneath a yellow dress with red flowers. She slapped his arm. "Pay attention, Ellsworth."

He didn't see the buffalo cloud but claimed he did. Eliza's hair fanned out on the blanket. His left hand held her right, fingers inter-twined. Now that she'd agreed to marry him, he didn't see what could stop them from holding hands all day if they wanted.

"Are you sure you want to live here?"

She pointed to the sky. "That one looks like one of those incandescent lightbulbs."

"Eliza?"

"I'm sure, Ellsworth." She inhaled the summer air, and her chest rose and fell. "Every soul has its match, and I found mine. I felt the pull toward Bellhaven, just as I felt the pull toward you on that train."

*The train. The derailment. The only two in the car to survive.*

"Can you not feel the pull, Ellsworth?"

"I reckon so." He looked back to the sky and pointed. "Hey, look, there's an alligator."

\\||//

Ellsworth opened his eyes.

The air was colder, drafty. A real blanket now hugged him.

Eliza was memory—scent on a pillow.

Anna Belle sat by his bed. Her smile must have been conta-gious, because Dr. Philpot smiled next, and then Gabriel at the foot of the bed, who squeezed Ellsworth's left foot and then patted it.

Anna Belle ran the top of her hand across his clammy brow. "His fever broke."

Dr. Philpot placed a cold stethoscope to his bare flesh, near where the bandages wrapped his chest. "Welcome back to the land of the living, Ellsworth."

It was dark outside. A fly buzzed at the window sill.

Music sounded from the first floor—Raphael on Eliza's piano. That was okay. Something about it felt right.

"What day is it?"

"Thursday," said Gabriel.

Ellsworth tried to remember when he'd been stabbed.

"It's been two days," Anna Belle said.

"You're very fortunate to be alive," said Dr. Philpot. "The blade went into your heart. To be perfectly honest, I see no rational reason why it's still beating."

Anna Belle patted his hand. "Most stubborn man I've ever met."

She looked antsy and a little pale herself, as if she hadn't slept in days. She hadn't made her face up or fixed her hair.

*It was the chapel.*

"I best get going," said Dr. Philpot. "Let me know immediately if anything changes."

Anna Belle said she would. Gabriel squeezed Ellsworth's foot again and then followed the doctor out of the room. Ellsworth asked for water, and Anna Belle helped him with a sip. She wiped his damp hairline. "Do you remember talking just before you opened your eyes?"

He remembered watching the clouds and holding Eliza's hand, not Anna Belle's. "What did I say?"

"Something about following the fault line," she said. "Finding the crack where the plates don't line up and . . ."

"And what?"

"And that's where the bad medicine gets through?"

He shook his head. "America Ma. While I was out. She told me those things."

"Ellsworth, who is America Ma?"

He shrugged because he didn't know, but something in the way Anna Belle had asked made Ellsworth wonder if she already knew about America Ma and was looking for some answers herself. "The pressure forces it up like a geyser. Like steam hissing from the ground, except invisible. That's why the chapel was built there, Anna Belle. In the woods. That's where they come up."

"That's where who comes up, Ellsworth?"

He didn't understand his own thoughts. "I don't know what you're talking about."

"Don't worry yourself with it." She squeezed his hand.

"Where is he?"

"Where is who?"

"Old Man Tanner?"

"He's locked up. Sheriff Lecroy put him in a cell."

"He talking?"

She shook her head. "In tongues. He's gone completely off the tracks. Thrashes against the bars. Curses and spits. Leroy said that at night he paces inside that small cell—not forward, but backwards. Round and round he goes. Leroy said he can't take it much more."

"He's suffering from withdrawal."

"Sheriff Lecroy?"

"No, Old Man Tanner. He's used to going into the woods every day. And now he can't."

\\||///

"Your father loved you, Michael."

"But not completely, Mother. He would never look me in the eyes. It's like he was ashamed of me."

"Oh, Michael . . ."

"I go by Ellsworth now, mother. You know that. All my friends call me Ellsworth. They've done it for years now. I know you don't like it, but I'm not Michael anymore."

"Don't say that."

"Why did Papa never look at me? It was like he wanted to love me but couldn't."

She stared down at the table, sighed, finally spoke.

"Your father was sterile, Ellsworth. Do you know what that means? To be sterile?"

"I know about the birds and the bees, if that's what you're asking."

She drank tea and watched out the kitchen window toward the woods. "We tried to have children for years but were unable to. We saw several doctors."

"And?"

"And it was determined by all of them that your father could not reproduce."

"Yet here I am." Ellsworth leaned back in his chair, folded his arms defiantly. "I see."

"No, you don't see." She slammed her cup down, spilling tea on the table. "It's the same way the rest of the town looked at me. Like I was some harlot. Do you know what that is too?"

"I read the Bible."

She picked up her tea again. "Your father had made our issues known to the public. He was a drinker. He talked a lot when he was boozing and drank even more after he found out his ailment. The entire town knew why we couldn't have children."

They sat silent for a moment. Ellsworth remembered the pop the baseball made in his mitt after one of his father's throws. He'd relished the sting it made on his palm. "Was he?"

"Was he what, dear?"

"Was he even my father?"

She cried silently and nodded. "I loved your father. I'd never stray. I prayed every night for us to conceive. Despite what the doctors told us, we never stopped trying."

"But then it worked. You were with child. With me?"

"Yes, dear. It worked."

"Because you prayed?"

"That's what I believe, yes."

"And Papa?"

"Your father was not a very religious man. You know that."

"He liked going to church."

"He liked seeing his friends. He liked the artwork in the cathedral. He liked the music."

"He told me that once. Told me he felt better for going because of those things."

She smiled. "He dozed off during mass more times than not."

"Still . . ."

She watched him. "Do you see, though, why he could never look at you?"

"Not really."

"There was always that doubt that you were his child. He didn't really believe God had answered my prayers. As much as I denied it, the suspicion that I'd been with another man was always in the back of his head. And the more the town whispered about it, the more he believed it—all the way up until he died on the church steps."

\\\////

The room was dark except for the triangle of moon glow against the wall.

The boy with the green eyes hovered bedside on a stepstool. His hands pressed against Ellsworth's chest, warming the wound beneath the bandages. The boy told him to close his eyes, so he did. *He's healing me from within.* But that made no sense. *It's only a dream.*

"Sleep now, Mr. Newberry. And don't speak nothin' of this."

Ellsworth nodded, half in and half out of delirium. He lay silent for a while, reveling in the warmth where the boy's hands had been. He dared not open his eyes. The boy was no longer touching him, but he was still in the bedroom. The stepstool scooted across the hardwood, and the boy's weight settled into the wooden chair beside the bed.

"You know the night she brought us here," said the boy, "and hid us down in the basement . . ." Ellsworth was aware enough to know that the moment called for a monologue. The boy assumed he was asleep and was unburdening himself. "I saw something in the woods that night, and I've yet to tell anyone. There was a man in the woods. Not a man really, but a bunch of birds . . . in the shape of a man. Cardinal birds, like the ones coming here now. All beaks and red feathers." Ellsworth waited for more details, but none came.

And then he dozed off.

\||//

Night passed and the sun rose.

The fly on the windowsill had died, but four more had replaced it. Ellsworth recalled Raphael's hands on him overnight, pressed against the wrapped hole in his chest, the wound Dr. Philpot said was healing faster than it should. And there was something about a man made of birds—cardinal birds. When Ellsworth turned his head he spotted Raphael in the bedside chair.

"Hi."

Ellsworth said, "Where's Anna Belle?"

"Went into the woods with Linda May."

Ellsworth looked at Raphael's hands, then fell back to sleep.

\||//

"I just don't understand it," said Eliza.

"What do you mean?" asked Ellsworth. Nearly a foot taller, he still had to take long strides to keep up with Eliza's pace. She walked quickly, constantly in a hurry. "It's America's pastime, Eliza. It's baseball. And I'm probably going to be in the minor leagues next season."

"It's nonsensical. You hit a ball with a wooden club and run in circles."

"It's actually a diamond. But even so, it's a dream of mine. One day soon I'll play in the big leagues. For the Dodgers." Ellsworth laughed. "Eliza, slow down."

Eliza suddenly slowed her pace, then tightened her grip in his hand and swayed their arms as they strolled along the seawall promenade of the Battery. The row of colorful antebellum homes always lifted her spirits. She hardly watched where she was going, and everything caught her attention. Occasionally he'd have to steer her away from a passing couple so as not to collide. She'd flinch whenever a bike zipped by, startle every time a car honked. Wind whipped upward from the converging Ashley and Cooper Rivers, tossing her auburn hair into a frenzy. She made no effort to corral the loose strands, while other women nearby worked desperately to keep their fancy hats on.

"It's too hard anyway," Eliza said.

"What's too hard?"

"That baseball." She'd suddenly grown melancholy. "It's too hard. And that bump on the field is too close. I worry you'll take one in the face. And I like your face."

"I have a glove. And I'm quick. And it's called a pitcher's mound," he said playfully. "Not a bump."

"I like your face, Ellsworth."

He said no more on the matter. He'd never told her he'd already taken one off the face when he was sixteen. Broke bones around his right eye, and his brain swelled. Dr. Philpot had told his mother he might not live. A month later he'd been back on the mound.

Eliza smiled—deep dimples and red-painted lips a stark contrast to porcelain skin. Sailboats, barges, and passenger ships sent waves throughout the Charleston harbor.

It had been Ellsworth's idea to take a day trip to the city. He'd witnessed her bouts of melancholy numerous times—they'd been married for nearly three months now, and the moments rarely lasted long. But last night, for the first time, she'd unnerved him. Out of the blue, during dinner, staring out the window with her mashed-potato-filled fork paused inches from her open mouth, she'd said, "I saw her last night."

"Saw who?"

"The black woman."

"What woman?"

"America Ma. I saw her in the woods."

Ellsworth had put his fork down. He'd heard of people around the world who saw visions of the Virgin Mary or made pilgrimages to Lourdes to seek cures for the sick or disabled. But this made no sense. "You saw this woman in a dream?"

"No," she'd said, her fork still suspended in front of her mouth. "No, I was awake. I was outside fetching clothes from the line. I saw her on the edge of the woods. She smiled at me." Eliza slid the mashed potatoes into her mouth. "I think she smiled at me."

Ellsworth had watched her chew and swallow and then asked her to pass the salt. They'd spoken no more about the woman. But the next morning he'd suggested they take a trip into the city.

Eliza had a thing about not stepping on pavement cracks. She'd skip to avoid them. Sometimes she'd hum. Sometimes she'd talk nonstop. And sometimes she'd grow so painfully silent that Ellsworth wanted to pick her up like a fragile bird and hug thoughts from her head. Feel her shoulder blades against his palms and her chest against his and squeeze her tight until her breath released against his neck. She was older than him by five years but often acted like the younger one.

A steamer blinked over the horizon. Eliza pointed across the shimmering water and spun into a dancer's twirl right there on the Battery wall. In doing so, she accidentally bumped into a couple passing in the other direction, the wife in particular, who was desperately trying to hold onto her feathery, wide-brimmed hat. Ellsworth saw it coming but couldn't stop it in time. The woman was not amused by the brushing of shoulders. She'd been caught off guard and would have tripped had her mustachioed husband not caught her arm.

The man straightened his hat and looked down upon Eliza, who apologized profusely. He muttered something about "lunatic" and "asylum" and ushered his wife along.

Ellsworth clenched his right hand into a fist.

Eliza caught his arm. "It's nothing, Ellsworth. Only words."

But words once said couldn't be unsaid. Words did damage like an ice pick, chipping away. Some words stung more than bullets. Ellsworth wrestled free and was upon the mustachioed man in seconds. He pasted the man on the right side of his jaw, spinning him like a top. The man's bowler hat popped from his pomade-slicked hair, and the wind took it out into the harbor.

"Oh, my lands," the wife shrieked, her gloved hand to her mouth.

The man righted himself and removed his jacket. He rolled up his sleeves as if ready to brawl right there on the Battery, even as his wife begged him to ignore the insult.

Ellsworth hunkered down into a fighter's stance, fists poised, and the mustachioed man did likewise. But then something splashed in the water behind them.

Ellsworth looked over his shoulder. Eliza swam through the dirty water toward the man's bowler hat, which was floating next to a log.

Her arms chopped the water. Her beige dress billowed out around her like a sun-dappled lily pad. The water had to be freezing.

Eliza snatched the hat and turned back toward the seawall. She navigated the rocks below and reached up toward Ellsworth on the wall. He pulled her dripping body to the pavement. He could see straight through to her undergarments and wanted to cover her immediately. He tried to with his own coat, but Eliza sidestepped him with the same twirl that had gotten them into the situation in the first place. She poured river water from the hat, tiptoed over, and plopped it right back atop the mustachioed man's head.

"There you go." She patted the man's shoulder. "All better now."

Water dripped down the man's brow. He watched her with wide eyes, grabbed his coat from the ground, and hurried down the Battery with his distraught wife.

Ellsworth gripped Eliza's shoulders. "Are you all right?"

"A tad cold." Her teeth chattered.

His knuckles were sore from the punch. He covered her with his jacket and walked with his arm around her shoulders, rubbing to keep her warm.

"The hat was more than a hat," she said after they'd walked several blocks into the city. "It was important to him. That is why I retrieved it."

"How do you know it was important?"

"I saw fear in his eyes."

"Because I was about to paste him again."

"No," she said matter-of-factly. "It was the hat. He was terrified of losing it."

They walked arm in arm for another block, the focus of everyone's gaze—she was soaked to the bone. "She tells me to look out for such things. To help those in need."

He stopped walking. "Who, Eliza? Who tells you this?"

She began walking again. "Just a voice."

A lump formed in his throat. He rubbed her shoulder as they walked. "You said 'tells,' not 'told.' Eliza, how long have you been hearing this voice?"

"Since I was five."

\\\//

Ellsworth awoke with an appetite.

Anna Belle was with him again. She had chicken noodle soup. She helped him sit up in bed, but he insisted on spooning it in himself.

She was distracted, fidgety, in a hurry to be somewhere else.

\\\//

That night Ellsworth opened his eyes to slits.

Raphael had his hands on the bandages again, pressing against the chest wound.

Ellsworth closed his eyes and acted like he hadn't seen a thing.

\\\//

The next morning he found Raphael on the bedside chair again. They watched each other for a minute. Ellsworth sat up against the headboard on his own. The bandages had been changed.

Raphael said, "Dr. Philpot doesn't have words."

"About what?"

"About how quickly your wound is healing."

There was a sandwich on the bedside table. Ham and cheese between two thick pieces of wheat bread. Ellsworth ate it, ravenous.

He grunted against the headboard. Raphael handed him an apple, and Ellsworth took a healthy bite.

"Anna Belle in the woods?"

The boy nodded.

"Why don't you go with her?"

Raphael shrugged.

Ellsworth took another bite of the apple. "That place isn't all good, is it?"

"I don't know, Mr. Newberry. But I do know that some answers aren't found between walls."

"You didn't visit Mr. Eddington the other day with Anna Belle. Why not?"

Raphael paused. "I don't trust him."

Ellsworth waited for him to elaborate, but he didn't. He took another bite of apple and asked the boy to retrieve his bourbon from downstairs. Raphael was back in a minute. *Your father was a drinker.* Ellsworth shook his mother's voice away and took two gulps that left his throat burning and his chest on fire. "How'd you know to play my wife's sonata? The Mozart."

"Her songbook was on Mrs. Roper's piano. First page looked crinkled, like it'd been used a lot. So that's what I played."

*That page was stained with Eliza's tears.*

"How'd you know my first name was Michael?"

"Your . . . *late* wife told me that one, Mr. Newberry."

Ellsworth smiled, took another gulp of Old Sam. Maybe the boy wasn't as strange as he'd first thought. "Call me Ellsworth. You've fondled my chest the past two nights. Might as well be on a first-name basis." Raphael's caramel skin blushed, but he didn't deny touching him. "Conversation for another day?" Raphael nodded. Ellsworth didn't push him on it, but he wondered if his rapid healing didn't have more to do with the boy than the chapel.

He offered Raphael the bottle. "Take a nibble."

Raphael hesitated, but then took a drink. He choked into his fist and patted his skinny chest. "Burns." They shared a laugh. "Don't tell Mrs. Roper."

"I won't if you won't."

Ellsworth pushed the bedcovers aside and slowly swung his legs to the side of the bed.

"What are you doing?"

"What's it look like I'm doing? Where's my leg?"

Raphael retrieved it from across the room, leaning next to the window.

Ellsworth latched it on, wincing. "The other day . . . you said you saw my color?"

"It's blue. Like your eyes." Raphael helped him off the bed. They went silent; it was hard to discuss what made little sense.

Eliza had talked about such things and he'd just gone along with it, accepted that if she believed or saw them they must be true. But until he'd met Raphael, had he ever seen it for himself—that faint thread of color shimmering like horizon glow around another person's contour? It dawned on him now that possibly he had, on another person in town, another who'd been inside this very room with him here during his recovery.

Ellsworth stepped away from the bed. "Yours is green, by the way. Your color. Don't know what it means, Raphael, but it's green as lima beans."

# CHAPTER 12

Four days after he was stabbed, Ellsworth stepped out on his veranda and filled his chest with flowery air.

Everything still bloomed with brilliance. People moved along the street, in and out of the woods in greater numbers. Some he'd never seen before.

"Recent arrivals," Anna Belle told him. She looked tired, like an overworked mother of a wild brood, when in reality she only had under her charge one boy more self-sufficient than half the adults he knew. She was starting to get that aged look he'd seen on Eliza in her last days.

"You need rest, Anna Belle."

"You're the one who needs rest, Ellsworth."

"Nonsense." He paced himself down the steps and down the walk, stopped at the mailbox.

Dozens walked the road, glancing at him in disbelief. He'd seen the look before; they were all surprised he'd lived through the stabbing.

Lou Eddington's house on the hill was nearly finished, bright yellow now except for a lone patch on the upper south side under the roofline, where two men leaned with brushes from a scaffolding.

"He's gone into the city," said Anna Belle, following Ellsworth's gaze.

"How do you know?"

"This morning he invited me to come see his store. You can come too."

"I can't drive with this leg."

"I'll drive."

He laughed. "You don't know how."

"I do now."

Ellsworth started across the road toward the destroyed town hall and the squatty brick building beside it that now served as both courthouse and county jail. The back of the building sported three barred cells, one of which currently held Old Man Tanner. "Since when do you know how to drive, Anna Belle?"

Anna Belle followed. "Since yesterday." He looked over his shoulder. Anna Belle grinned. "Lou Eddington taught me."

Ellsworth stopped in the middle of the road. "Did he now?"

"In that fancy red car." She pointed down the avenue of oaks. "Up and down the road."

Ellsworth chewed the inside of his mouth and headed toward the sheriff's office.

"Well?"

"Well what?"

"About him teaching me to drive."

"You've got my blessing, Anna Belle. Marry him for all I care."

"Marry him? What? I hardly know the man. And don't think I need your blessing either. I can do anything I darn well please." She peeled off in the opposite direction.

"Anna Belle, where you going?"

She quick-walked behind the town hall and gathered momentum into the woods, where she passed Rabbi Blumenthal on his way out.

\\|//

Leroy Lecroy had taken over the job of town sheriff the night Isaac Pomeroy was killed by the Klan.

He'd been Pomeroy's underling, his do-this-do-that man, and Leroy had always been happy to oblige. He'd liked wearing the deputy badge, the silver star that twinkled in the sun but was never quite straight on the left shirt pocket of his beige cotton button-down. And when it came time to bury Pomeroy and pin the gold-star badge to his own shirt, he'd done it with pride, but also reluctance. He had never once coveted the job of sheriff—or so he'd told Anna Belle one night, half drunk two weeks after the town hall burned, confiding in her that he didn't think he had the sand to do it.

When Ellsworth entered the jailhouse, Sheriff Lecroy looked like he hadn't slept in days. His belly overhung his waistline, and his shirt was untucked in the back. In the far corner cell, Old Man Tanner stood naked, his face pressed between the bars.

"I keep tellin' him to put clothes back on, Ellsworth, but he won't listen to reason." Sheriff Lecroy nibbled on a fingernail he'd already taken down to the quick. "He's off his nut, Ellsworth, and I'm stuck with him day and night."

Old Man Tanner started peeing on the floor, and the splatter made Ellsworth chuckle.

"Ain't funny," Leroy said. "He's done that six times if he's done it a dozen. Should make him clean it up."

Old Man Tanner finished. He spat on the floor and shook the bars hard enough to loosen ceiling dust. And then he started walking backward, pacing around the cell the same way Ellsworth had seen him do around his house days ago. He watched Ellsworth like a predator would prey, a lion in a cage.

*"The devil made me do it."*

"How's he doing otherwise?" Ellsworth asked Leroy.

"What do you mean? He's a lunatic. Everyone knows that."

"I mean at night. Doing his business on the floor is rebellious behavior. But Anna Belle said he was thrashing the bars and speaking in tongues the first few nights. Is he still doing that?"

Leroy hefted his belt. "Suppose that's eased now that I think on it. Why?"

"You once told me your father died from the bottle."

"He did. Been ten years now."

"Did he ever try to stop drinking?"

"About every Sunday." Leroy smiled but then grew serious. "Twice that I recall. Once for about a month and another time for two."

"Remember those first few days? The nights? Was he fidgety?" Leroy nodded. "Restless?" Another nod. "Easily agitated? Violent?"

Leroy chewed his fingernails again. "Only time he ever hit Ma was when he sobered up. Then he went out to the tavern for a growler."

"I think that's what we're dealing with here. With Tanner."

"He misses his alcohol?"

"No . . . well, yes, in a sense. Leroy, have you been inside that chapel? In the woods?"

Leroy paused. "I have."

"How many times?"

He counted on his fingers. "Five. Plan to go again when I leave here this evening."

"Why?"

"Well, you know why, Ellsworth."

"Then say it."

Leroy shook his head, smirked, but didn't answer.

"You can't say it aloud because it sounds so impossible. But it isn't, is it, Leroy? It makes you feel good, doesn't it, breathing in that air? Who do you talk to in there? Who do you think you see? Your father?"

Leroy bit his lip, looked away. "I don't want to be the sheriff anymore."

"But you are."

"I am."

"And you're coming down so stringent with Prohibition because of your father's problem with the suds."

Leroy didn't deny it. That was another story for another time.

Ellsworth grabbed Leroy's shoulders and looked into his eyes. "Ever since I returned from the war, I've seen Old Man Tanner going into the woods every day after lunch and returning a few hours later. My guess is he's been visiting that chapel, and who knows for how long. We don't know how long it's been there or who built it. But there's something about that place that makes people need to go back. Old Man Tanner's suffering from withdrawal, just like your father would from the lack of drink. You get it?"

Leroy watched Old Man Tanner pace backward. "You think the chapel did this?"

"I have my suspicions."

"But I've been inside, Ellsworth. It ain't bad in there. It's a slice of heaven, just like Alfred says."

"You ever been to heaven, Leroy?"

"No."

"Then we don't know, do we?"

Leroy clenched his jaw, then pointed a fat finger at Ellsworth. "Don't you dare make that place bad for me or any of the others. Rumor is Eliza went in there before she died. And that's how come she acted so peaceful before . . . you know, like . . ."

"Like what?"

"You know, Ellsworth."

"No I don't."

Leroy wiped his brow. "You know what the town thought of her."

"That she was a lunatic?"

Leroy gulped, stepped away. "I'm sorry. I shouldn't have brung it up."

Ellsworth clenched his hand into a fist. "But you did."

"Do it," Tanner yelled across the room. "Do it. Plunge your knuckles into his fat neck."

Ellsworth said, "Close your head, Tanner." Tanner hushed. Ellsworth eased his fingers and stared at Leroy. "Tuck your shirt in. Walk with your shoulders up. Act the part, Sheriff Lecroy. Maybe then your prisoner will respect you. Now, you mind if I have a word?"

"Go on," Lecroy said, tucking in his shirt. "Suit yourself."

Old Man Tanner stopped pacing. "You gonna shoot me, Mr. Newberry?"

Ellsworth gripped the handle of his Smith & Wesson but left it in the holster. "Probably should. Put your clothes on."

Tanner retrieved his underwear across the cell. His skin was wrinkled and liver-spotted and his hair was white, yet he moved nimbly and his eyes seemed sharp.

"How old are you, Tanner?"

"Old enough." He slipped his shirt on and buckled his pants.

"You still want to kill me?"

Tanner shook his head. "No."

"You did three days ago."

Tanner slid down the wall and sat against it. "But I don't anymore."

Ellsworth sat, too, awkwardly on the opposite side of the bars with his prosthesis jutting out. "Why not?"

Tanner shrugged, crossed his arms.

"How long you been going into the woods?"

The old man rolled the back of his head against the cinder-block wall. "Oh, Ellsworth."

"What?"

"You really want to know?"

"Wouldn't have asked otherwise. Ain't got time for game playing."

"Okay, then. Longer than you been alive—that's how long I've been going into those woods." He closed his eyes and smiled. "Longer than you been alive."

# CHAPTER 13

Ellsworth felt stomach sick by the time Anna Belle navigated his black Model T into the city.

The car had lurched and puttered the whole way, threatening to run out of gas before they reached Charlie Thurston's fuel station outside of Bellhaven. The car had been used when he and Eliza bought it in 1914, and Anna Belle drove it like a battering ram. She'd clipped Moses Yarney's mailbox backing out of the driveway. And before they'd made it through the avenue of oaks, Ellsworth had volunteered to walk to Charleston, questioning whether she'd paid enough attention during her so-called driving lesson.

"Close your head, Ellsworth," she'd barked.

Instead he'd closed his eyes, preferring surprise to actually *seeing* his front fender fold around a tree.

At first her feet had moved so frantically atop the floor pedals that she appeared to be dancing, all while fumbling with the throttle lever on the steering wheel, still stressed over how she'd struggled to hand crank the engine. The second try, after he'd pumped the gas, had gone a little smoother, and eventually, until they'd entered the busier thoroughfare in Charleston, they'd enjoyed a few minutes of easy coasting, with the windows down and the low-country sunlight on their arms.

But now Anna Belle gripped the wheel with both hands, eyes pinpointed on the road. "And that's all he said? That he'd been going into the woods since before you were born."

"Turn here."

"I know where I'm going, Ellsworth. What did he say?"

"That he's known about that chapel for decades. Until recently it was concealed by foliage and weeds and brambles and whatnot. Even the door. But he cleared that all out."

"Why did he do that? Why now?"

"Said he felt his time coming near, and when he passed he was going to leave a note with directions. But until that time came, he considered the place his."

"And then what? What'd he say after that?"

Anna Belle's long fingers wrapped the steering wheel. The knuckles weren't bone white anymore, and he favored the red color she'd painted her nails.

"Ellsworth?"

"Oh, sorry. Nothing. After that he started beating the back of his head against the wall, crying like I'd never seen a grown man cry before. Mumbling about his late wife—her name was Susannah— and the old White Meeting House over in Summerville. And the earthquake that leveled Charleston."

"The '86 quake?"

"The same."

"Supposedly Susannah and Tanner were in the area because of that earthquake. I have no idea how that could be—how they knew it was coming." Anna Belle turned carefully onto Bull Street, the tip of her tongue protruding from the corner of her mouth in concentration. "But the meeting house was left in ruins, with Susannah still in it." She straightened the car and leaned forward. So many cars were parked in diagonal tangents from the curb that it made for a narrow passage. "That's why he went into the woods every day."

"Also why he started losing his mind." He watched her for a reaction, but none came. He recalled Sheriff Lecroy's words as Ellsworth had left the jail. *"Don't make this bad for me. Don't ruin this for the town."*

"While you were convalescing, Maisie Cannon took her daughter Marlene in there. The daughter with the tuberculosis she keeps quarantined. She knelt upon the healing floor."

"Anna Belle . . ."

"The girl still coughs, Ellsworth, but at least she smiles now." He thought about how rapidly he'd healed from the knife wound but was hesitant to tell her about Raphael's possible role in it. Or had it been because they'd carried him into that chapel on a stretcher? She continued, "Not everyone goes into the woods to . . ."

She trailed away, but he knew what she'd wanted to say. *Not everyone goes into the woods to communicate with their deceased loved ones.* But he also knew that he'd recently been stabbed in the heart by the man who'd been visiting that chapel for at least two decades, and that man claimed the devil had made him do it.

Ellsworth spotted Eddington's store up ahead on their right, a narrow brick building pressed between a clothing store and a butchery. "There it is. Eschec Mat."

"I see it." She slowed the car. It choked and lurched.

Ellsworth braced his hands on the dashboard. "There's a spot. Park there." She eyed the open spot. Her tongue moved to the corner of her mouth again, and Ellsworth suddenly imagined kissing her. "Right there, Anna Belle. Turn."

"I'm turning." She spun the wheel like a fisherman hurriedly righting a shrimp boat.

"Slow down. Slow down!" He braced his good foot into the floor-board. The Model T rammed against the curb, and they bounced forward. He wasted no time opening the car door and balancing himself against a palmetto tree. "My lands, Anna Belle. It's not a tractor."

"We made it here, didn't we?"

"Next time I'll hire Alfred to drive."

She slammed the driver's side door. "Lou was much more patient than you."

"So he's just Lou now?"

"I assume he's been Lou since he was born, Ellsworth."

Ellsworth started toward the shop. "Has nothing to do with being patient, Anna Belle." He leaned forward, whispered in her ear. "He just wants to run his hands across those getaway sticks of yours."

He didn't see the punch coming.

But in hindsight maybe he did, which is why he said it.

\\\\////

The sign on the door said the shop was closed on Sunday, but the doorknob turned when they tried it. "He said he'd be here," Anna Belle said as they stepped over the threshold. Eschec Mat was win-dowless and dark except for the hazy glow from lamps in each of the room's four corners.

Wooden countertops stretched along every wall, holding what looked like a hundred intricately carved chess sets, the pieces two-to-three inches tall. More countertops and chessboards filled the middle of the room.

"Not one board is the same as another," Ellsworth said, in awe of the talent. It was quiet inside the store. No one emerged from the back room to greet them, even though the bell had tinkled as they'd entered the front.

Anna Belle leaned over one of the sets and lifted a painted frontline soldier, a warrior knight dressed in armor and chain mail, holding sword and shield.

"Don't touch, please." Lou Eddington appeared from the shadows in a black suit and shiny shoes. A folded red kerchief jutted up from the pocket below the right lapel, matching his bow tie. He looked taller and thinner in the meager light, but his toothy smile stretched the room.

*Has he been there all along?*

Anna Belle was quick to obey and placed the pawn back on the board, crooked.

Eddington straightened it. "So glad you could both come. I'm sorry I wasn't in here to greet you properly. My wife used to run the store while I carved in the back. Now I try to do both. Though of course I am closed on Sundays."

"And you actually make a living from selling chessboards?" asked Ellsworth.

Anna Belle slapped his arm in the same place she'd pasted him earlier. "Ellsworth's as subtle as a mule tiptoeing through a tulip garden."

Eddington's laugh was a little fidgety, but his manners remained smooth, almost courtly. "I am blessed to have some family money—not a fortune, but enough to keep me comfortable." He patted down his pomade-slick hair, which was parted so carefully up the middle his scalp was visible. He wasn't as put together as he'd been days ago. He'd missed a button on his shirt, and the collar was wrinkled—slept on. His skin was ruddy.

"We used to have a little store in Savannah," he said, eyes darting, preoccupied. "Along the river. But when my family died I found the memories of our home too difficult a burden to bear, so I decided to move. I looked many places, but fell in love instantly with Bellhaven. In a sense I felt pulled there." He'd begun to sweat. His neck flushed and suddenly looked too thick for the collar, like a sausage about to burst its casing. He wiped his brow, slid a finger under his neckline.

Anna Belle put her hand on his arm. "Lou, are you all right?"

He nodded, forced a smile.

"You talk to your family in that chapel?" Ellsworth asked.

"Ellsworth, that's none of your business." Anna Belle looked at Lou. "Maybe you should sit down."

Lou stepped away from her touch and straightened his coat. "I'm fine. I've been suffering from bouts of dizziness lately. But they pass as quickly as they come."

"Have you been sleeping?"

"I've been working too rapidly to sleep," he said tersely. He sucked in a deep breath as if to compose himself and then offered an olive branch handshake. His hand was a vice grip, thick and muscled from carving, and beneath his cuffs the forearms were roped with sinewy muscle, the dark hairs faintly touched with what looked like rock dust, as if he'd quickly changed upon their arrival. "Where are my manners?" He patted Ellsworth's back hard enough to nearly unhinge the prosthesis. "Welcome back, Ellsworth."

Ellsworth looked confused. "I've never been here before."

"I mean from your deathbed. Your recovery was nothing short of . . . a miracle. I hope that man Tanner will be prosecuted to the full extent of the law."

"I had the charges dropped."

Lou let go of his hand. "But the man tried to murder you."

"He failed." Ellsworth surveyed the store.

After a beat, Lou clapped his hands and smiled pearly white.

"Nevertheless, you're here, and I should show the two of you around. I've just finished painting my newest set." He slid his arm inside Anna Belle's and guided her toward the front of the store, gesturing with his free hand, acting now more like the confident man they'd met in the road. "Eschec Mat. The king is dead. The king is lying down. Chess is a game of strategy, a battle to kill another's king. Us against them. Good against evil. Chess is history. And as you can see, that is my passion. History. Battles. Uprisings." He glanced at Ellsworth. "War."

"Do you play?" asked Ellsworth.

Eddington thought on it. "I'll partake in a game from time to time." He motioned them to the countertop. "This one I created twelve years ago. It portrays the Ottoman-Hapsburg Wars. With no support from the pope in Rome, the Austrian Hapsburgs were left alone to stop the Ottoman Empire's northern advance. With the help of a few northern allies, the Danube, and a timely winter, they did. Held the Ottoman Turks with their janissaries off at Vienna—fought back the Turks and the spread of Mohammadism."

Ellsworth leaned in. He couldn't believe the detail on the figures, from the tiny eyeballs to the fingernails of every pawn, which were all slightly different, yet real enough to walk right off that checkered board and start fighting. He pointed to the next chessboard. "And this one?"

"Ah, one of my favorites, the Peloponnesian War. Athens and Sparta. Took me months to finish it. I research tediously."

"Months? I would think it would take longer for such detailed work."

"Once I set to carving I barely sleep or eat. And since I moved into Bellhaven, it . . . um, the work has taken me over."

Eddington walked Anna Belle along the wall, describing each board. The British and the French at Waterloo, with Napoleon as the king. The Battle of Antietam during the War Between the States. The American Revolution. The Battle of Hastings in 1066. He described not only the battles, but the major players and why the wars had been fought. The Boxer Rebellion. The Crimean War. Rome versus Carthage in the battle of Metaurus in 207 BC. The Crusades—one board for each. Caesar's Gallic Wars. The Beaver Wars and the French and Indian. The War of the Roses. And dozens more.

By the time they'd walked the entire room, Ellsworth stood speechless.

"Well?"

Anna Belle said, "I've never seen anything so splendidly done."

"About that we are in agreement," admitted Ellsworth.

"You're an . . . artist yourself," said Eddington. "Your painting— the one you created the day you were attacked. Amidst all the commotion, I came down the hill and saw it on the veranda. I placed it back on the easel. It was of a town and a traveling circus— was that it?"

"Ever heard of the town called None of Your Business?"

"Ellsworth!"

Eddington grinned. "It's no problem, Anna Belle. Really." He looked to Ellsworth again, his lips hooked in a grin. "How long have you been painting?"

"Couple hours, give or take."

Eddington chuckled. "Well, it shows."

That response drew a queer look from Anna Belle.

Ellsworth grunted, then acted as if he hadn't heard the retort or was ignoring it.

Eddington stared briefly at Ellsworth's fake leg, clapped, and changed course. "I've noticed a black boy in your house, Anna Belle. Is he a servant?"

She threw him another strange look. "Of course not!"

JAMES MARKERT

Eddington slid his arm from hers and stepped away. "Yet he lives with you?"

"It's an involved story."

"One you should tell me about some day? I can see that you care for him dearly."

She paused. "He's a good boy."

Eddington was prodding. But why? Did he hold the same reservations about Raphael that Raphael had against him?

"Why did he not come with you today?"

"He was feeling ill," said Anna Belle. Ellsworth knew the boy was perfectly fine. *He didn't want to come.* Anna Belle was quick to add, "He's staying with the Dennisons for the afternoon."

"The blind man and his wife. How unfortunate to be unable to see. He seems in fine spirits for being wounded so."

"It's only of late that he's become that way," said Anna Belle.

Ellsworth said, "Ever since he visited that chapel, he's been better. I think."

"Yet he's still blind." They watched each other for a moment before Eddington's eyes lit up. "Wait here. I've got a gift." He returned a moment later with a carefully crafted wooden box. The top was a checkered board, and on the front was a polished knob for a drawer. He handed the heavy box to Ellsworth. "For you. The Battle of Cantigny."

Anna Belle went pale.

Ellsworth wanted to grab her elbow but his hands were full, so it fell to Eddington to hold her steady. Ellsworth did take a deep breath to right himself. "We better go, Anna Belle."

She regained her composure and backed away from Eddington.

Ellsworth saw the sudden gleam in Eddington's eyes. But before he could steer Anna Belle away, Eddington grabbed her hand and kissed the top of it.

Ellsworth nearly dropped the chess set.

Eddington's eyes settled directly on Anna Belle's. "Do you like to dance?"

She looked up at Eddington with sadness in her eyes. And a look that implied that this man, though she hardly knew him, was the only one now capable of taking that sadness away.

\|||//

Ellsworth sat with Anna Belle at her kitchen table, both of them staring at the wooden box containing the Cantigny chess pieces they'd yet to pull out. He pulled a flask from his jacket pocket and took two gulps of Old Sam.

"You drink too much, Ellsworth."

"I don't drink enough, Anna Belle." He slid the flask across the table. Anna Belle stared at it for a few seconds before taking a sip. She wiped her mouth and slid it back. Raphael was in the other room playing the piano.

"Would you go?"

She stared blankly out the window toward the orange-blue sunset. "Go where?"

"On his invite. To his house for dinner and dancing."

She shrugged, chewed her fingernails, eyed the wall clock across the kitchen. She hadn't been watching the sunset. It was the woods she coveted.

He pulled the drawer from the chess box; each piece nestled on a bed of red velvet. "Care for a game?"

"I don't know how to play."

"I'll teach you. I taught Eliza."

"Eliza was smarter than me."

"You're plenty smart, Anna Belle."

She exhaled two cheeks of air and kept her attention out the window.

Ellsworth began removing the Kraut soldiers of various rank and order, all unique down to their hair and noses, the height being the only similarity. The pawns were the same height, as were the men acting as bishops and rooks and knights. Ellsworth placed each pointy-helmeted soldier on the front line and explained their movements to Anna Belle, but she didn't seem to be paying attention.

"I told him I was in the war. Do you remember?" She did. "But I never mentioned Cantigny." She didn't respond. He continued removing the pieces from the drawer beneath the checkered board. "How did he know? Or was it coincidence?"

She stood from the table. "I'll be back."

"Where are you going? Anna Belle, it's too late to be going into those woods. The sun is going—" She'd already closed the door. "Down."

Through the window he watched her enter the woods. She'd be safe, he guessed. She wasn't the only one in there. Mayor Bellhaven was on his way, too, moving as if possessed. Or maneuvered.

*Like chess pieces on a board.*

He removed the first American soldier from the drawer and placed it on the board facing the line of Krauts. A general posing as king. Colonels and sergeants with faces that all looked familiar to him. Too familiar. *"I research tediously."* Ellsworth aligned the back row and began to assemble the privates acting as pawns.

Raphael had stopped playing the piano. He entered the kitchen and sat in the chair Anna Belle had just vacated.

Ellsworth asked, "Do you play?"

Raphael shook his head no but looked eager to learn.

Ellsworth continued placing the pieces.

"It's you."

Ellsworth looked at the boy. "What's me?"

Raphael had a pawn in his hand—a private with a rifle and bayonet. "This one. It's you."

Ellsworth took the piece from Raphael and studied it until his hands shook. *Holy Moses.* It *was* him, but in small scale. "*I research tediously.*" When he tried to place it on the board, his fingers were so unsteady the piece fell over.

"You all right, Mr. Newberry?"

Blood rushed from Ellsworth's face. He rubbed his stubbly cheeks and forced himself to look back in the drawer, where four pawns remained.

The next one looked just like Calvin.

# CHAPTER 14

Ellsworth tossed and turned in bed until he'd entangled himself in the sheets.

It was the middle of the night, and he was wide awake.

This used to happen to Eliza. She'd go to the window and watch the woods. He'd ask her to come back to bed, but she never would right away. Too often she'd see things out there—people, she'd claim.

*"Sometimes they come through."*

*"Through where, Eliza?"*

*"The doorways."*

Ellsworth sat up in bed, kicked the twisted sheets to the floor. The night she'd mentioned the doorways, he'd asked what doorway? She'd never answered.

*The chapel—was it a doorway? Some conduit?*

He hugged Eliza's pillow. Closed his eyes and breathed in what remained of her scent.

He'd left Anna Belle's in a hurry earlier that evening, right after Raphael placed the chess piece that could have been Calvin right next to the chess piece that could have been him. He'd hurried across the street and downed the rest of his Old Sam while sitting on Eliza's half of the bed. He'd gotten drowsy wondering what their kids would have looked like had the first not been stillborn and the next two miscarriages. What kind of father would he have made? And then he'd passed out trying to remember exactly what Eliza's face looked like.

Even now, as he sat up in bed, her features were still a blur. He should have had more photographs taken of her. Of them together. But he'd always thought they'd have more time, and he didn't like his picture taken anyway. Didn't like how Eliza always pointed out his color when he claimed never to see it himself. But that had only been denial. He'd seen the color even in those black-and-whites, just as he'd seen Raphael's color the first time he met him in Anna Belle's living room. And what about the faint color he sometimes saw around Gabriel, that coppery light he'd always pretended not to see as far back as when they were children, daring each other to run to the yellow trees and back.

He got out of bed in a hurry, needing to see Eliza's face like flower blooms need sunshine, to hold the picture he kept atop the piano of her standing next to the oak in White Point Garden, with the Battery in the background and her hair tousled by the harbor breeze. He hobbled down the stairs, skipped to the piano, but the picture wasn't there. He scoured the living room to no avail. It wasn't in the kitchen or bathroom or dining room, either.

He hustled back upstairs in a panic, looking through the nightstand drawers, her vanity, her dresser. Her face was slipping in his mind. The more it faded, the more frantic his search became. He pulled out every drawer, scattered contents to the floor. He tore through the closet, ripping shirts and dresses from hangers. *Where did it go? Someone took it.* But who would take the only picture he had of his dead wife?

He searched the other two bedrooms, then he headed downstairs again—but too fast. He stumbled the last five steps, rolling into the wall. The impact knocked a framed oil landscape painting down on him. He shoved it aside, winced as he made it back to his feet.

*Her voice.* Now he couldn't imagine the sound of her voice. He punched the wall, denting it and bloodying his knuckles. The headaches she'd begun having upon moving to Bellhaven had often pained her to tears. Those he could see clearly now, the way she'd curl into the fetal position and try to squeeze them away with clenched fists.

*"Don't show me the bad stuff."* The bad medicine, Eliza called it. *"Show me her face."*

He stood for a minute, heart thumping, looking out the living-room window as Bellhaven slept content until morning, when they'd venture into the woods again without thought of the consequences, falling into the same pattern Tanner Whitworth had succumbed to decades ago. *Look at the old man now.* The bad medicine, whatever it was, had dug into the folds of his brain and begun eating away, eating and eating and eating.

But perhaps that was an isolated incident. Perhaps it wouldn't happen to the rest of them.

Wouldn't happen to *him.*

Ellsworth had denied himself the simple pleasure for too many days now, chastising everyone else for going while doing his best to bury his own urge to hear his wife's voice one more time, to feel her embrace.

*One more visit won't hurt.*

He grabbed the oil lamp from the kitchen, lit it, and headed out into the Bellhaven woods.

\||///

The next morning Ellsworth woke to birdsong.

He sat up in bed with a clear head, an easy smile, and a detailed image of Eliza in his mind. He found Alfred, Omar, and Gabriel in his living room, all hunkered over that radio.

"You wait right der, Ellsworth," Omar told him, returning a minute later with a dining room chair. The four of them leaned over the radio like it was a bonfire and the air was cold. They found stations and listened hard, all three men less somber, even smiling. But after fifteen minutes of news and static, they lost focus.

Ellsworth found himself glancing at Gabriel, sometimes watching her for seconds at a time. Twice she caught him and he looked away.

Alfred said, "Gonna have to find the perfect spot so this will work regular."

"Maybe it was a flaw in the building of it," said Ellsworth.

"Looks better than that painting you attempted over there." Alfred pointed in the wrong direction. "Van Gogh, Monet . . . should we now add Newberry to that list?"

Ellsworth said, "Go dangle."

Omar chuckled, then stood and left the house without warning. Just stood from his chair, grabbed his hat, and walked out the door. Through the window they watched him enter the woods. Alfred left a minute later, as if he'd become suddenly nervous about something. He put on his hat and felt his way to the door. Before going out he said, "Linda May lays with me now." He tipped his hat and walked outside. He, too, entered the woods. Max Lehane, the town's volunteer fire chief, escorted him.

*Linda May lays with me now.* Ellsworth fought back envy, not because he carried a torch for Linda May—although, like Anna Belle, she *was* a striking woman—but because it made him realize how long it had been since his lips touched anything so soft as a woman's.

He and Gabriel sat with each other for a minute. What had never been uncomfortable before was suddenly awkward now, and they both looked to the floorboards. Seemed like ever since the woods took on all that color, *their* colors had turned brighter as well. Colors he might have noticed faintly before but now were unavoidable to his eye. Maybe she noticed it, too, but like him was afraid to bring up something so strange.

"Where'd you go last night, Ellsworth?"

"Nowhere. Why? You spying on me?"

"No." She stood, straightened her overalls. "Just be careful is all."

Then she left.

Ellsworth ate a butter sandwich for lunch. Anna Belle had become so preoccupied with the woods that she'd stopped cooking for him.

As the afternoon wore on, Eliza's image began to fade from his mind again, and he missed his pals. He promised himself he wouldn't go into the woods again. But he did.

And he went the next day too.

\\\////

Ellsworth hurried through his coffee, but it did little to settle the nerves he'd begun to develop, the shaking that would start the moment he'd swing his legs from the bedsheets and promise himself that last night would be just that—the last.

But each time he stepped inside the chapel at night, her voice would become closer, the caress of air more penetrating and real, to the point where he wouldn't want to leave. And what made it harder was her begging him to stay. And he would, getting up only after the line of people outside the chapel grew, their chatter audible. *"How can a person be so selfish? Sheriff Lecroy should put a time limit inside those walls."* Everyone seemed to think that those inside were taking too long.

Raphael's voice, of course, would accompany him back home, real enough to make him look around to make sure the boy wasn't shadowing him.

*"It's bad medicine, Ellsworth."*

Ellsworth finished his coffee and placed the mug on the kitchen table. *It's too good to be bad. My wife's in there. Till death do us part.*

He hurled the coffee mug into the wall and felt better after watching the pieces dance like dice across the hardwood. His tension oozed much like the coffee remnants down his wall, and his hands stopped shaking. Smashing that mug had flashed through his head and he'd done it without thought of having to clean up a mess. He flexed his fingers and wondered if Anna Belle was home. Wondered if she'd ever gone dancing with that boob Eddington. Wondered why she'd stopped coming by every day to check on him.

He had a sudden urge to see that chess set, the one with him and Calvin as pawns. He holstered his gun and walked across the street.

Behind the town hall, Alfred and Linda May walked hand in hand toward the trees. The woods were busy, crowded with people walking to and from. None of them talking or looking at one another in passing. All of them too on edge for conversation.

Up the hill, Lou Eddington's house stood sunflower yellow against the blue-sky backdrop. In front of the house, a swath of yellow goldenrods bloomed beside cherry red bougainvillea and a row of violet oleander. The oleander and goldenrods had never bloomed so early—a garden never grown so quickly. Bellhaven dripped with color that conjured visions of Van Gogh, Renoir, or Monet.

In contrast, massive black birds clustered on the trees around Eddington's yellow house.

*Vultures*, Ellsworth realized. *Two dozen, at least.* As if they'd flown in to combat the arrival of all the cardinals and the dozens of other colorful birds flying around that chapel.

Ellsworth crossed the street and stopped on Anna Belle's front lawn, looking around. Outside the jailhouse, in the shadows facing Maddie Horn's garden, he spotted Sheriff Lecroy. The sheriff—of all things to do on a bright spring day—stood urinating on Maddie's cucumber patch, humming while he watched the golden stream arc over her picket fence.

He spotted Ellsworth, turned away, and finished peeing in the gravel next to the jailhouse. He zipped up quickly, then ducked inside where Tanner was still locked in the cell.

What in the world was the sheriff doing?

And then a past conversation flashed into Ellsworth's head from back when Lecroy was still a deputy. Miss Horn's cucumbers were the largest in town, and she'd defeated Lecroy's mother's cucumbers in a local competition. Mrs. Lecroy had cried on her son's shoulder, claiming she'd never won anything in her life. The next day, Deputy Lecroy had jokingly told Ellsworth that he was going to urinate all over Miss Horn's cucumbers and see how they grew then. "What if it makes them grow bigger?" Ellsworth had asked. "I don't think it would," Deputy Lecroy had said after some thought. But his foolish words had never amounted to any action.

Until now.

Sheriff Lecroy had gone and peed all over Miss Horn's cucumber patch. Had he felt the same lack of control Ellsworth had experienced before hurling his coffee mug into the wall? Ellsworth laughed, even though the widow Horn was a nice lady and didn't deserve to have her cucumbers vandalized.

Ellsworth didn't deserve to have his leg blown off either.

*Sometimes life ain't a bed of roses. Sometimes life ain't duck soup.*

He grinned all the way up to Anna Belle's front porch and didn't bother knocking. The door was unlocked. Raphael stood against the living room wall, two paces from the piano bench he'd just vacated.

The boy glanced toward the kitchen, where pieces of something crashed to the floor. "You don't look good, Mr. Newberry. You've got to stop going to the woods. Please. Both of you." He tried to block entry to the kitchen. "Don't go in there. You shouldn't see her like this."

Ellsworth gently nudged the boy aside and entered the kitchen anyway. Anna Belle wore an untied nightgown that showed glimpse of a naked chest and a bare leg as she twirled away from the counter. His heart rate sped up. He should have looked the other way, but he didn't. Couldn't. Wouldn't. He'd always wondered what her getaway sticks looked like unhampered by those long dresses. Calvin had been a lucky man.

Anna Belle tried to hide what she'd been doing before his sudden arrival. Her hair was disheveled, and she looked older. Her face was unmade, her lips a pale natural color he found alluring. There was something about the plainness; he'd never seen her look prettier.

Or maybe he was just tired.

Maybe they both were.

She held a roll of tape in her right hand. She trembled like Ellsworth had done before he'd smashed that mug into the wall.

To ease the pressure.

Ellsworth stepped toward her. His forehead was clammy, and he wanted nothing more than to hug her tight and smell her hair and then possibly ask for her hand in marriage. But that was crazy talk. They'd fight from sunup to sundown.

*But that smile, and those legs . . .*

She hid the tape behind her back.

"What are you doing, Anna Belle?"

"Go away." She bit her plump bottom lip. Chess pieces were scattered across the kitchen table as well as the floor beneath it. Two pieces remained on the board—Ellsworth and Calvin face-to-face in the middle. She pointed. "You going to explain that?"

"Explain what?"

"You've got secrets about Calvin. About how he died."

"Who told you that?"

"Alfred told me this morning. Told me I should talk to you about how Calvin died."

Ellsworth clenched his jaw. Alfred had promised he'd never tell. And Alfred didn't even know the full truth.

"What happened, Ellsworth?" She approached slowly, her nightgown flowing back against her hips. She pushed him against the wall. Stood inches from his face, her chest heaving. She kissed him on the lips and then stepped back, as confused as he was. Her eyes were watery, tired, and reddened from lack of all kinds of necessary things.

She pounded her fist into his chest. "Why did Lou give us that chess set?"

As quickly as the thought entered Ellsworth's mind, he acted on it. He grabbed the tape from Anna Belle's hand, ripped off a six-inch piece, and stuck it across her mouth, pressed it nice and tight too. She backed away and tore at it, but before she could he'd taped another piece across her lips, sealing the first one down good and hard.

"Been wanting to do that for years now, Anna Belle."

She screamed something that was muffled by the tape and then ripped it off her mouth, crumbled it, and threw it at him. "Eliza was mad," she screamed. "A lunatic. She heard voices and saw things. Yet you loved her still. And so did he."

"So did who?"

"Calvin. And all the men here in Bellhaven. I think they all secretly carried a torch for her."

Ellsworth shook his head, started to tell her she was wrong, but then spotted what Anna Belle had been doing at the counter with the tape when he'd walked in. Eliza's picture had been ripped into a dozen pieces and she'd been trying to tape it back together.

"You took that picture off the piano? My only picture."

She was crying, mouthing the words "I don't know" as a stream of saliva and tears stretched from top lip to bottom.

She knew why she'd done it. Her so-called best friend. The thought had popped into her head, and she'd acted on it without thought of right and wrong. But that was no excuse. She had no right . . .

He approached her, clenching his fist like a man never should toward a woman.

"Don't do it, Mr. Newberry." Raphael stood in the doorway, tears dripping from his emerald eyes. "It's that place. It's bad medicine."

He stopped. Bad medicine—why did people keep saying that?

"You the devil?" Ellsworth asked, wishing he hadn't.

Raphael teared up, shook his head no.

Anna Belle cowered at his feet. "I'm sorry. I'm sorry, Ellsworth."

He looked down at her, unclenched his fist. They watched one another. He helped her up from the floor. She tied the folds of her nightgown together, suddenly modest, and hurried from the kitchen.

Ellsworth reached down and began picking up the scattered chess pieces, but then remembered the picture of Eliza that Anna Belle had been taping back together. He found it on the counter, mostly put back together, yet still ruined.

Raphael was on the floor gathering the chess pieces. Ellsworth helped him. Neither spoke until every piece was back on the board, and then Raphael said, "She visits him at night."

"Who?"

"Mr. Eddington. The house with the vultures. She goes there every night now."

\\\//

Ambulances sounded in the distance. Smoke belched from pockets of fire. Wreckage smoldered over sun-caked mud and twisted rails.

Their train car was smashed like an accordion. No one moaned or cried.

"Mother?" Ellsworth blinked, tried to get up but couldn't move. Sunlight blinded him. "Mother?"

"She's gone."

There she was again, a beautiful face in shimmering halo. She'd saved him. Protected him. Embraced him right before the car derailed. Bright embers floated over her shoulder. Her cheeks were blackened by smoke.

"Are you hurt?" Her voice was angelic and her eyes a brilliant blue, a cloudless azure eerily similar to his own.

"A little sore." He wiggled his fingers, moved his arm, then his legs. *I'm alive. I can move. But can I still pitch?*

"Is your name Michael?"

*How does she know? Who are you?* "My name is Ellsworth now."

She rubbed her hand over his brow. "I can still see your color."

"Are you real?"

She'd looked down at her dress, felt her hips, patted her arms and chest, and gave him the kindest smile he'd ever known. "I reckon so."

He smiled.

Knew right then he loved her.

# CHAPTER 15

Ellsworth woke with half his face numb, his cheek pressed against a cold mosaic floor.

Birds twittered; flapping wings echoed. Sunlight beamed through the hole in the roof. He got up weak kneed and fell into the frescoed wall. The door creaked on its broken hinge, and he stumbled out into the clearing, into swirls of color and blooms and butterfly wings. A yellow warbler landed atop the swaying chapel door. He dropped to the ground, closed his eyes, and recalled what Raphael had told him yesterday.

"Wagons arrived the other night, Mr. Newberry. At Eddington's house."

"What wagons?"

"Wagons filled with heavy crates. Covered with tarp. Men in dark suits unloaded them into his house."

Yesterday, while Raphael was telling Ellsworth about Anna Belle's visits to Eddington's house, they'd heard her leave through the front door, and moments later they saw her enter the woods. Raphael had pleaded for Ellsworth not to go back to the chapel. Made him promise. Ellsworth had looked the boy in the eyes and said he'd not go in, but after he'd awoken from the dream about his mother's death and meeting Eliza, he'd had to. Not only had he gone into the woods, in fact, but evidently he'd spent the night.

Even now as he lay in the clearing, barely able to move, he already craved a return back inside. He made it up to his elbow, then knee, and then started crawling toward the chapel as a trio of redbirds swooped inches from the ground, stirring up a patch of leaves.

Had he told his mother he was sorry for what he said on the train? He couldn't remember. Forgiveness was only feet away.

He wobbled toward the chapel door, and then a large hand clutched his forearm.

Gabriel blotted out the sun. She hoisted his weight over her shoulder, and he was too drained to fight her. His prosthesis had fallen off. She bent down under his weight and grabbed it too. "Let's get you home. Town can't see you like this."

"Leave me, please."

"Close your head, Ellsworth." She stepped out of the clearing and entered the woods. Four deer watched. Voices sounded in the distance. Early visitors. Gabriel moved away from them on a quick tangent in the opposite direction so they wouldn't be seen.

*Put me down. I have to tell my mother I'm sorry.*

He couldn't muster the strength to form words.

Deep breaths expanded Gabriel's chest and the muscles of her back as she walked. Her boots crunched against deadfall, the cadence soporific, soothing. She was so strong. Always had been. *Strength of God. Remember Blue Fire? I used it to help free the slaves. Me and you.*

She looked back at him and smiled as if she'd just read his mind.

He closed his eyes and allowed himself to fall limp.

\\\///

Ellsworth awoke in his bed, warmed by daylight.

Across the bedroom, Gabriel and Raphael sat in wooden chairs brought up from the kitchen. They stood when his eyes opened. Gabriel's head reached nearly to the ceiling, while Raphael was just tall enough to prop his elbows on the footboard.

"What are you two doing in here?"

"Doin' what needed to be done," said Gabriel.

He grunted, got out of bed. They followed him from the bedroom and down the stairs, giving him space but not so much that he could slip out the backdoor.

"Might as well throw me in the cell with Tanner," he said at the kitchen table, eating rice and beans that Gabriel had made. She was no cook.

"No jail cells left."

"What do you mean there's no cells left?"

Raphael ate like he hadn't eaten in days, so Gabriel did the talking. "Tanner is still in the one. Last night Sheriff Lecroy filled the other two with John Stone and Beverly Adams."

"What did they do?"

"John Stone blew Ned Gleeson's shed up."

"Tried to burn it down," Raphael said, chewing.

"Don't speak with a full mouth," Gabriel told the boy. She'd apparently taken over the motherly role for Raphael. She looked back to Ellsworth. "You know how Ned doesn't sleep but a few hours at night. Then he goes out to his shed and makes those birdhouses?"

"I've got three of them," said Ellsworth. There wasn't a house in Bellhaven that didn't have one of Ned's colorful birdhouses on their porch. "Eliza liked them. The whole town likes them."

"Well, as Ned's neighbor, John Stone wasn't so fond of all that hammering and sawing in the night, right outside John's window. And you know he gets up before the roosters. Must have had enough.

So he set the shed on fire and watched it burn. All those birdhouses gone, along with Ned's tools. "

Ellsworth shook his head. "Had John been visiting that chapel?"

"Like everyone else," said Gabriel.

"Except the two of you."

Gabriel and Raphael shared a glance, and she said, "And now you. You're not going back there."

"Why do you not feel the pull?"

Raphael said, "Because once was enough. What seems good can also be bad."

"The town is falling apart, Ellsworth. We need you before it crumbles."

"Why me?"

"It was always meant to be you." Gabriel blushed. "I've known since we were kids. Saw that color."

Ellsworth shook his head, didn't want to hear it.

"Clear as a daylight sky," said Gabriel.

Ellsworth dropped his fork and pounded the table with his fist. "The town was fine . . ."

"Town's never been fine, Ellsworth. It was built on hate. Founded by evil. Those original Bellhavens were terrible people. They built this town on the sweat, blood, and oppression of slavery. It's no coincidence that it was *your* father's idea to build that town hall out there. It's why you're here just as we are."

"Who is we?"

"Me and the boy."

"Why? Why are we here, Gabriel?"

Tears welled in her eyes. Her jaw quivered. "For my entire life I've been looking for answers to why I am like I am. A man in a girl's body. A girl in a man's body. Only now are some of the pieces coming together."

"What pieces?"

"Me, him, you. The earthquake. That house on the hill coming back to life. Something's happening. And somebody's got to do something."

"You think Eddington is here for a reason?"

"I think he's just a man who felt the pull of forgiveness from those woods. It's the house that worries me more. I think he's just an unfortunate pawn."

Ellsworth paused. "I don't understand."

"Neither do I, but at least I'm trying. And it starts by keeping you sane."

"How long has that chapel been in the woods?"

"That I don't know."

"And what about the earthquake? Old Man Tanner was mumbling about the earthquake. The one in 1886 that leveled Charleston?"

"A lot of people back then believed the center of it was around the Middleton plantation, not the immediate city of Charleston. And Tanner believes it was here in Bellhaven. He was in these woods when the earth started moving."

"Why these woods?"

"Tanner's a scientist," she said. "Or he used to be—studied earthquakes. In '86, when the foreshocks hit Summerville, he and his wife headed east from Tennessee. Says he felt the instability in the air and followed it first by train and then by wagon, and by the time he reached Bellhaven he was on foot in the woods. The instability was stronger the deeper he went. And then the earth started moving."

"Does the earthquake have something to do with that chapel?"

Gabriel dug back into her rice and beans. "My gut says it does." She eyed him. "Eighty-six wasn't the only time the ground here has rumbled."

She was right. The last time he remembered was the night Eliza died, that three-second burst of shaking that had put a halt to the violence. But according to the stories passed down, the ground in these parts had been rumbling periodically for generations, long before the '86 quake ripped Charleston apart, and he remembered several in his lifetime. Did all those little bursts mean the pressure was building up? Was another big one coming?

The three of them ate in silence for a minute, and then Ellsworth said, "Beverly Adams. You said she was jailed last night as well. What did she do?"

"She made Reverend Cane a pie," said Raphael.

"And?"

Gabriel put her fork down and sighed. "Instead of apples, she put in dead crickets."

\|//

By dinner, which was warmed up rice and beans from lunch, Ellsworth was pacing the house from living room to kitchen and back again, biting his fingernails to combat the trembling in his hands. *Beverly Adams fixing Reverend Cane a dead-cricket pie? John Stone blowing up Ned Gleeson's work shed? All those lovely birdhouses destroyed!* He stopped pacing to look out the window. Would Anna Belle go up the hill tonight?

He'd follow her if he could, but he was a moth trapped in a lampshade. His skin was covered with goose bumps. He'd already downed his seventh coffee of the day, and Gabriel wouldn't let him have any more. Said it made him jittery. He could make a run for the woods, but they'd catch him. His days of running were over, just like his days of pitching.

"You should paint a picture," said Raphael. "To take your mind off things."

"Last time I painted I got stabbed."

"This time you'll do better." Raphael grinned. "Mayhap we'll be able to tell what it is, and the town won't be as hard on you."

"You should be on a stage with that sense of humor." Ellsworth turned from the window toward Raphael. "What should I paint?"

He shrugged. "Paint out the bad stuff like last time." Then he turned to exit the room.

"Hey."

Raphael stopped.

Ellsworth looked at the piano with a nod. "Maybe you should play, you know, while I paint."

# CHAPTER 16

While Ellsworth painted deep into the night, most of Bellhaven slept.

But not all.

\\\\///

Ned Gleeson stood on his back porch watching drizzle fall from a purple sky. The moon looked like a cat's eye, and as a cloud drifted by, he convinced himself the moon had winked at him.

He took it as a sign.

He'd always been taught to forgive and forget, to turn the other cheek, but somehow those notions didn't feel right anymore. Not when the rain still sizzled off the ashy rubble that used to be his work shed. How many birdhouses had he built inside it? Leanne had kept a logbook, and the number she'd last tallied was in the four hundreds, but she was three years dead now, and he'd long stopped keeping track. Every house in town had at least one of them. Some had as many as a dozen, with all the colors of the rainbow.

There *were* a lot of birds in Bellhaven. Always had been. Which is why, twelve years ago, Leanne had given him the birdhouse idea in the first place. *"If it doesn't make you wealthy, at least it'll keep you busy, Ned."* And this afternoon in that chapel, when she'd spoken to him through all that wonderful air and told him to start anew, he'd promised her that he would.

But first he'd have to build a new work shed.

Before he left the chapel, Leanne had told him one other thing—about John Stone, the man who'd burned his life work to the ground. At least he'd thought it was her voice. By the time he stepped out of the chapel's clearing, he'd carried with him an inkling of doubt. But the words had been clear: *"John Stone says the rosary every night, Ned. He collects them. Those silly papist rosaries."*

Ned had thought on what Leanne had said and come to a decision. It was the right thing to do, all things considered.

He went inside to get a hammer and a towel—the latter so that he could muffle the sound of breaking glass. He breathed deep, expanded his chest with fresh Bellhaven air, and then stepped out into the drizzle toward John Stone's backdoor.

\|||///

Tanner Whitworth leaned over his bathroom sink and stared into the mirror.

He'd never liked that the town called him Old Man Tanner. But truthfully, now that he'd finally taken a long gander at how white his hair was—*like dove wings*—and how wrinkled his face was—*like a doggone prune*—he reckoned he did look like an old man.

*Oh, well. Some boozehounds drink to get drunk. Some drink because they can't not drink.* He supposed his situation was a combination of both. It wasn't like he didn't know what he was doing; he'd noticed the repercussions years ago, and now the crow's feet around his eyes had grown feet of their own.

He wondered what his brain must look like after so many years of entering the woods. Mushy applesauce came to mind. He liked applesauce, just as he had come to like walking backward—it made him feel relaxed, made him feel like he could rewind time and start working against those crow's feet. And also, he'd seen a black woman in the woods doing it. Years ago, on a night when the moon was completely round and looked full of blood.

An escaped slave was what she'd looked like, with that coarse white dress in need of washing and the brightly colored textile she'd wrapped around her head. Just her by her lonesome, walking barefoot and backward through wisps of fog. He'd tried blinking her away, but every time he opened his eyes she'd been there. She'd put a finger to her lips as if to shush him. Whispered something that sounded like "Good crows don't tell . . ."

*America Ma.*

Somehow Tanner had known her name. Like she'd magically passed it from her mind to his because they'd both been inside that chapel.

He'd never told a soul about that place and didn't plan to. *Good crows don't tell.* But he wasn't even a crow. He was as white-skinned as they come. He freckled in the sun. *And now everyone knows about it.*

He missed America Ma and often wondered where she'd gone to. Wondered why she'd been walking backward through the woods all those years ago when the moon was bloody.

*Oh well. She might not have even been real.* His mind had already half turned to applesauce by then.

For now he was just glad Sheriff Lecroy had let him out of jail. The pudgy sheriff had looked flustered unlocking his cell, made him promise he wouldn't stab Ellsworth Newberry again. But apparently Ellsworth was in the process of dropping the charges, and with what had happened with John Stone and Beverly Adams, the sheriff had hinted that he might need more future jail space.

*Just don't go fleeing town.*

Oh, Sheriff Lecroy didn't need to worry himself with that. Tanner wasn't going anywhere but his bed. That jail cot had wrecked his back. He entered his bedroom and smiled. He'd told Ellsworth he was sorry for what he'd done and promised to never go into that chapel again. And he'd meant it—for now, at least. They needed to know what he knew about the earthquake and the chapel, and for that he'd need to stay somewhat clearheaded.

Somewhat.

At the foot of his bed was a wooden chest. He unlocked it, and his heartbeat accelerated. He counted twenty jars inside, all tightly sealed. He grabbed one, started to open the lid, and then decided that tonight called for two. After securing both jars in the crook of his elbow, he locked the chest and shuffled to his bed.

The covers had already been turned down, and the pillow looked primed to swallow the side of his face. He sat on the side of the bed and watched out the window. Wondered why Ned Gleeson was walking across his backyard in the drizzle. *Is that a hammer he's carrying? Oh well.* Tanner had more important things to tend to.

He placed one jar in between his legs and opened the other— slowly, so as to not let anything slip out unused. Both jars looked empty, but they were far from it. He put his nose up close to the lid and inhaled so deeply his lungs ached. *You never know how badly you miss something until it's gone.* And then he completely removed the lid and stuck his entire nose in the jar, breathing in the air he'd trapped inside. *Months ago? Years?* What did it matter? He felt alive again. Youthful for the first time in days.

He dropped the jar to the floor and relaxed against his head-board, both feet now strewn across the bed as he untwisted the lid on the second jar. He closed his eyes and inhaled—once, twice, three times until he felt he'd gotten every last bit of it.

By then the bliss had taken over and his eyes grew heavy. He remembered America Ma whispering to him one night—that's right, he'd seen her more than once—that there was slave blood on those walls.

He'd never understood how one man could own another. His father had been an ardent abolitionist. Sounded like nasty business.

Dirty old nasty business.

*I picks all the cotton, massa.*

Tanner grinned, on the edge of slumber. "Mayhap now we have some dat corn bread."

\\\\////

Reverend Ephraim Cane didn't like crickets.

His wife was scared of them, just like she was of mice and spiders and flying beetles and June bugs. She'd climb up on a chair and scream like the dickens until Cane squashed the culprit under his shoe.

So ever since she'd cut into Beverly Adams's new pie and heard the crunch of dead crickets instead of the soft cinnamon apples she expected, she'd closed herself off in the bedroom. Hadn't even come out for breakfast, lunch, or dinner. Every time Reverend Cane knocked on the door she told him to go away, as if it was somehow *his* fault.

He'd couldn't think of a reason why their neighbor of twenty years, who had baked them many an apple pie, had suddenly baked them a dead-cricket one. He supposed it was better than a live-cricket pie. That would have been a sight.

He smiled when he shouldn't have been, thinking of all those crickets exploding through the cut and him giving chase with one of his shoes. He liked Miss Adams, and he'd already forgiven her. But that didn't mean he'd turn the other cheek. He'd prayed on it, and for the first time in his life he'd come to the conclusion that retaliation could be fun—and just. But what could he do?

Moments ago when he'd asked his wife if she needed anything, she'd shouted that she needed to be fully immersed into the baptismal waters again. To pronounce her faith in Jesus in front of one and all, as if the first time hadn't fully taken root.

"At least neither of us took a bite," he'd said. To that comment she'd thrown something at the bedroom door—probably her hairbrush—and he'd scurried away to sit at the kitchen table with his Bible and his thoughts.

He'd been having those more often of late—random thoughts that didn't make much collective sense. *Did I ever kill a cricket in front of Beverly Adams? Was she a lover of crickets and took offense to it? But if she was a lover of crickets, it wouldn't make much sense to fill a pie with dead ones—unless, over the years, she'd collected all the ones he'd scraped off the bottom of his shoe. Maybe the wind blew them from my yard into hers.*

He opened his Bible and flipped through the Old Testament, but couldn't find anything calling to him. He scanned a few psalms and part of John's gospel, but his mind was too muddled to concentrate. Maybe he'd take a trip into the woods. No, it was a bad idea to go into the woods at night. His mother had always told him so. The tree limbs turned to arms, and they'd snatch you. Kids disappeared in those woods at night.

He'd wait until morning. First thing. Maybe he could get Mrs. Cane to go with him. Entice her out of the bedroom with a bit of that fresh chapel air.

He closed the Bible much too hard and wondered if that was a sin. And then it dawned on him, clear as day. Beverly Adams was a strict Catholic, and a few days ago he'd let one slip in front of her, one of the condescending comments he and Mrs. Cane liked to make in secret about the pope. "Pope Benedict, the one who sits on his throne in Rome like some king."

He remembered how Beverly had folded her arms and smiled. But it had been the kind of smile that wasn't really a smile, the kind that hid the opposite of a smile. The kind that said watch your back because you've got something coming to you—like a dead-cricket pie on a Sunday afternoon. Come to think of it, she'd slammed the door on her way out. Mrs. Crane's framed painting of Jesus being baptized in the water had tilted askew on the wall.

Reverend Cane stood abruptly from the kitchen table. He knew what he was going to do.

Beverly Adams volunteered to clean Saint John's Church once a week. That's where he could gut-punch her. He'd give her something to clean up all right. And Father Timothy? Well, he and the good priest had always been cordial with one another. They'd swapped stories and shared enough meals at the town-hall gatherings over the years to be considered friends. Good ones, even. But the way those Catholics baptized infants before they could even walk or talk just made no sense. It had always gotten under Reverend Cane's skin. And all those crazy rituals—and the doctrine of transubstantiation! Truly believing they were eating the body of Christ like a bunch of cannibals?

*Yeah, they've had this coming for years.* Longer than that, even. Since way back when the Catholic Church was selling indulgences for remission of sin and Luther decided enough was enough and hammered his ninety-five theses to some door. It was about time to do something about all that. But first he'd need to coax Mrs. Cane out of the bedroom. He needed her to sew something for him right quick—she could sew a small doll faster than he could wash a sink full of dishes.

And oh, he almost forgot.

He'd need his sledgehammer from the barn.

\\|////

Father Timothy couldn't sleep.

Despite the drizzle, the moon glowed, and the thin window covering did little to keep out the light. But that wasn't the only reason he was awake in bed, getting sore. He couldn't wrap his mind around the thoughts he'd been having.

A priest shouldn't have those kind of thoughts. But with how Anna Belle Roper had bounced down the street the other day in her pretty dress stretched full from her figure and wiggled her fingers his way, in what he took as a flirtatious wave, he couldn't much help himself, now could he? Every time he closed his eyes now he imagined what she looked like without that dress on.

As a boy, he hadn't been completely immune to the seductive nuances cast by the opposite sex, but whatever urges he may have had were strongly overshadowed by those he felt from the church. The Lord had called him, and he'd obliged, willingly and without a second thought. He'd taken the vow of chastity, and for years now he'd had no issue keeping to it. It was like he'd successfully flipped a switch when the time came, casting that room into perpetual darkness.

Well dad-blame if Anna Belle Roper hadn't somehow flipped that switch to a bright light again. Even the thought of her sent his heart fluttering.

He got out of bed and prayed on his knees for strength. Anna Belle was a widow now, and he'd heard of priests leaving the church before. Or maybe he hadn't. Maybe that was just wishful thinking. Jingle-brained thinking. He wasn't all that handsome of a man. Anna Belle was probably just being nice with that wave she'd done.

He removed his belt from the hook on the bedroom door and flung the metal part over his bare back to chastise himself for having impure thoughts. He flinched and cried out. It hurt like hell, so he didn't do it again. He needed to restore himself to a religiously pure state with something maybe not so painful. Maybe he'd fast tomorrow. No, he liked food too much. And Anna Belle was a great cook. *Too bad she spends all of her energy fixing food for that crippled Ellsworth Newberry down the street.*

He placed his palms to his head and cursed himself. What was he saying? Ellsworth was his pal. Ellsworth was the unspoken leader of this town. Always had been—before the war, anyway. Sheriff Lecroy was a wrong number, and Mayor Bellhaven was basically useless. The town had been started by Bellhavens, and they'd dwindled for a reason. Rumor was they'd been cruel to their slaves, so cruel the slaves sometimes tried to escape to the neighboring plantations at Magnolia and Middleton, where they'd be treated better. And cruelty had a way of finding future generations. Mayor Bellhaven wasn't cruel, as far as Father Timothy could tell—he was distant kin from the jingle-brained line of Bellhavens—but he was a boob who didn't know when to give up.

He stared at the belt in his hand. Maybe self-castigation was not the way to go. Maybe he should take his confusion out on someone else. Just paste someone and see if it made him feel better. Father Timothy had a notion to go right up to Mayor Bellhaven and dry-gulch him in the noodle.

He hung the belt on the door, walked down the hall to his living room, and sat on the sofa to ponder his options while staring at the cross on the wall. It only took him a minute to decide Mayor Bellhaven shouldn't be his target. He was too irrelevant.

He spotted a bucket of red paint and a wide-bristled brush next to the front door. He'd picked up both from the store. The storage shed behind church needed a good painting, and red was his favorite color. That was an idea. Instead of pasting someone, maybe he'd vandalize something instead. Besides, he'd never been in a fight in his life, and wasn't sure he could go through with it. But spreading paint on something that wasn't meant to be painted on? That he could do. That would probably shut the door for good on all these thoughts he'd been having about Anna Belle Roper. Then he could get back to the Lord.

Maybe he'd knock on the door of those Watchtower people and paint their faces before they could open their mouths to protest. That would teach them for trying to witness to the entire town. Or he could paint the front door of Reverend Cane's First Baptist Church. Or was it Pastor Cane? The Baptists seemed to call him both. He and Ephraim were friends, but it needled him how the man thought he was right about everything—like it was the Baptist way or no way. And the way he was always thumbing his nose at the Holy Father. Besides, it looked downright silly to completely immerse a grown adult in the water.

*What if they can't swim?* Father Timothy laughed to himself. *Salvation through faith alone, Scripture alone? Please. They need a good dose of all the sacraments is what they need.*

Then again, the person in town who needled him the most was Reverend Solomon Beaver over at Bellhaven First Methodist. He and his flock were always thumping their Bibles and quoting Scripture and claiming to be servants of the Lord when they didn't even allow blacks in their church. At least Ephraim Cane at First Baptist allowed them up in the balcony.

Rumor had it that Reverend Beaver was Klan, and he was in thick with that Methodist minister in Georgia, William Simmons, who'd organized the resurgence of the Ku Klux Klan on Stone Mountain. He'd gotten inspired by that moving picture, *The Birth of a Nation*, and now the Klan numbered in the millions across the South.

*Talk about a hypocrite. I should paint First Methodist red, from the flower beds to the roof shingles.*

But then again, Emma Briscoe was a Methodist, one of Beaver's original flock, and she was as sweet as Anna Belle's tea. *There I go again.* He forced himself up from the couch and headed for the front door.

There was always Rabbi Blumenthal over at the Bellhaven Temple. He could paint something all over that little stone hut. The Jews didn't even think Jesus amounted to much. Said he was just a regular man and nothing special. Well, Father Timothy didn't think Bellhaven Temple amounted to much, and *it* wasn't that special, either, not with the funny way they had of talking over there. Bellhaven Temple sounded boring anyway. With all the other Firsts in town, why didn't Rabbi Blumenthal name it *First* Bellhaven Temple?

Ah, but the rabbi wouldn't hurt a fly, and they bowled together on Saturdays. He'd have to pick another target.

Father Timothy felt more confused than ever, so he opened the door, grabbed the bucket of paint and the brush, and walked down the dark street in the drizzle.

Like the messages in his sermons, he figured the right path would come to him.

He'd know it when he knew it.

\|////

Reverend Beaver usually counted sheep when he couldn't sleep.

Tonight, though, he imagined shooting them one by one with his rifle and watching them pile up like an Egyptian pyramid. He gave up on slumber and swung his legs from the bed. Normally the drizzle on the roof would prove soporific, but tonight it was a nuisance, although not as much as his wife snoring like a bear.

He looked down at her before leaving the bedroom and thought about what he would do if she were dead. Maybe then he wouldn't have to keep his secret anymore. That he didn't love her. Never really did. She was nice and all, but he'd never felt that spark. And now that he'd been doing some serious soul searching in that chapel, he'd come to realize that maybe it was women in general he didn't like, and maybe that was the root of all his anger and hate and pulpit chastising.

Lately, and maybe it had been festering for a while, he'd found himself looking at the men in his church in ways a man shouldn't.

*Lord, please tell me I'm not bent. Strike me down now if it's true.*

He waited. Nothing happened.

He'd kicked a man from his church just two years prior for admitting to being one of those homosexuals. He'd preached from his pulpit about the evil of all the sodomites. What was that man's name, the one he'd verbally terrorized in front of his flock? Middle-aged man with thin red hair combed and parted on the left side. Green eyes and freckles on his cheeks, looked kind of like a squashed tomato.

*Holy Moses, Solomon Beaver, get hold of yourself. You know his name was Frank Jessups. And you called him out in front of everyone. Sent him on the path to fire and damnation, and all because you felt guilty about your own thoughts.*

He filled a glass of water and chugged it in the kitchen. *I'm not that way. It's just funny thoughts coming into my head of late.*

Then why did he find himself always looking down the street toward where Frank Jessups lived in that small blue house with the wraparound porch? Why did his heart jump like an excited puppy in a cage when he thought of knocking on that man's door to apologize?

He finished his water and slammed the glass down so hard on the counter it shattered.

His hand was bleeding, right on the index finger knuckle where one of the shards must have nicked him. He wrapped it in a dish towel until it stopped, and thought that at one point in his life he'd carried a torch for Anna Belle Roper. All those curves on the back end.

*What is wrong with me?*

*Nothing's wrong with you.*

*Things is what they is, massa. Yes'm, things is what they is.*

*Who is that? Who's there?*

*Just a voice in my head. Same voice I heard inside that chapel. America Ma, I think she called herself.*

Reverend Beaver took a deep breath to compose himself and opened his eyes with cold fury in his heart. Amazing how focusing on what he hated calmed the confusion.

He hated how the people of Bellhaven had always been so willing to mix races inside that town hall, singing and dancing in the same space as the blacks. That's where the town had made a wrong turn, establishing that strange reputation of being so tolerant. It wasn't natural, not the way things were meant to be. And what about those Jim Crow laws that had been instituted? Those brilliant Jim Crow laws that would keep things the way they were supposed to be—separate. In Bellhaven at least, those laws had basically been ignored.

He dropped the bloody towel on the counter. His finger had

stopped bleeding. He was glad the Klan had come that night and burned the town hall. He'd been sad to see Sheriff Pomeroy tarred and feathered, and he never expected the man to be *killed*. But some kind of message needed to be sent. Never should have been a black sheriff in a mostly white Southern town anyhow. And now that weird green-eyed black boy was out walking the streets like he belonged—living with a white woman, no less. The very idea made him grind his teeth. It was just . . . wrong. Wrong like the notions the town had about his part in the tragedy that night. He had some sympathy for the Klan, thought some of what they were doing was needful, but he wasn't one of them. And he sure hadn't called them.

Solomon taxed his brain for something to do, something to relieve the pressure.

First person to pop into his head was Moses Yarney, the pastor of the black Methodist church down the road. But not really Methodist. It was one of those AME churches that had been sprouting up like weeds. African Methodist Episcopal? How dare those blacks call themselves Methodist anyway, when they'd gone and made up their own church?

And now Reverend Moses Yarney was getting all uppity and preaching about ministering to *all* people. What was their motto? "God our Father, Christ our Redeemer, Man our Brother?" *No one of them will ever be my brother.* Open to people of all ethnicities, nationalities, and color? What could be more dangerous?

More *unnatural.*

He slipped on his field boots and grabbed his fedora from the coatrack. He had something in the shed that good ol' Reverend Yarney needed to see. Something all those folks at Bellhaven First African Methodist Episcopal Church needed to see. That was a mouthful. No church should take that long to say. It was as bad as that Jew synagogue in Charleston. What was that place? Kahal

Kadosh Beth Elohim Synagogue. *Christ the Lord Almighty. We speak American in America.*

He opened the door, stepped out into the drizzle, and slammed it shut, part of him hoping he'd waken up Alethea and the kids. Given them a little startle.

He had a plan for Bellhaven African Methodist Episcopal. A partial plan, at least, and it had to do with his cherished collection of slave memorabilia he kept in the tool shed, the stuff he'd found ten years ago in a moth-eaten satchel in slave house number five.

\|||//

Moses Yarney sat in the dark and prayed for forgiveness.

Not so much for something he'd done, but for what he was about to do, although the "about to do" had no definite shape yet. He only knew that his thoughts were dark like storm clouds, the kind of thoughts in need of future forgiveness. So he sat alone in his church, Bellhaven African Methodist Episcopal. The church he'd founded and built with his own hands three decades prior, back when his posture wasn't stooped and his hair was black instead of white.

He knelt in the pew and closed his eyes, squinting until he'd felt the connection, the one he'd sometimes get when Jesus felt close enough for a handshake. Usually they were in total agreement, but this time they weren't. Moses had a swelling ball of fury in his gut, and he couldn't sleep. The solace he'd hoped to find inside his church had only made matters worse. He'd need to act on it or burst.

His folded hands shook atop the pew. He prayed for good thoughts, but his mind kept coming back to the one that made him smile—the one in which his big knuckled hands clenched Reverend Beaver's throat and squeezed until his eyes popped.

What would it feel like to kill a white man? To kill any man, for that matter. It was something he'd never imagined doing until now. But if any white man had it coming, it was Solomon Beaver, the man he and others around Bellhaven knew was secret Klan.

That fury ball in Moses' gut burned hotter. Moses was descended from the Bellhaven slaves, and his parents, like Omar Blackman's, had been just stubborn enough to stay as hired hands after emancipation. This was his town as much as any white man's, if not more so. It was the blood of his ancestors that had kept this town running when the cotton fields were pregnant and full.

Slavery had finally been made illegal after the war, and then here came Jim Crow and all that forced segregation. Different bathrooms, back of the bus, Jim Crow cars on trains when you hit that Mason-Dixon Line. Moses was tired of it all. Yes, ma'am. No, sir. Smiling when you wanted to slap someone. Mayhap you no longer called them master, but they still acted as if they soared higher. Take off a hat when addressing a white man. Callin' us boys when they know darn well we're grown men.

Moses stood from the pew, already feeling his thumbs press into Reverend Beaver's neck and crushing that crooked Adam's apple. But then he winced at the pain in his lower back and hunched over as he walked down the aisle. Some of that arthritis Dr. Philpot spoke of.

Now there was a nice white man, that Dr. Philpot. That Ellsworth Newberry too. Come to think of it, most of the white folks in Bellhaven were polite and tolerant. Their parties in that town hall had been like no others across the South. That's why he'd liked it here. That's why he'd stayed. That sense of camaraderie— the why of it that he'd never been able to put his finger on.

Besides, as much as he wanted Reverend Beaver under the ground, he'd always preached to his flock that they were better than the hatred of their enemies. Hatred was a sign of weakness in the Lord's eyes, and they would continue to rise above it all.

Maybe he wouldn't kill Reverend Beaver after all. The man was younger, anyhow, and more agile. Probably had a mean streak and would fight an old man back. Moses shook his head and prayed for answers as he walked down the center aisle toward his pulpit. Moonlight illuminated the colored-glass windows, and Moses looked to it for guidance.

Maybe he'd go into the woods and visit that chapel. He seemed to think more clearly in there. America Ma always had good advice. He didn't know exactly who she was, but he knew she was former slave kin, and her voice was downright soothing, like warm maple syrup.

And then Moses stopped cold, facing the front of church where his choir normally stood.

Best choir in town, they were, and everybody knew it. Boy, how they'd sing it up inside that town hall. And even now, every Sunday they filled his church with song so angelic that some of his flock wept. He felt the Lord himself through the rhythm and rhyme, the words like omens of good times ahead, full of hope and happiness. If any church in town had a stronghold on music it was this one, the passion for song deeply rooted in those ten slave houses on the back of the hill. For that was one thing those slaves were allowed to do every Sunday—sing and pray to their heart's content. And sing they would, according to his ancestors.

Sing loud enough so that the missus and massa could hear.

An idea then came to Moses Yarney, a plan to extinguish that fireball in his gut. That other something that really stuck in his craw was Bellhaven Lutheran Church across the street, run by that German pastor Josef Hofhamm. It hadn't really dawned on Moses until now, but the way they carried on with *their* music really bothered him. Not the way Reverend Beaver bothered him, of course, but the annoyance had been building for far too long.

At all the town hall gatherings, the Germans always seemed to try to outsing the rest of them or outplay whoever else was holding their instruments. And now every Sunday they had that fancy new pipe organ blaring loud enough to crack windows, like *they* were the ones with the best music in Bellhaven.

"Well they ain't," whispered Reverend Moses Yarney. "Not by a long shot."

That stuffy German music might have a certain *presence,* but it wasn't close to the emotion rooted from what the slaves had sung. And if he heard those Lutherans play "A Mighty Fortress Is Our God" one more time he'd burst. And lately, now that the war was over and the German internment camps had been shut down, Reverend Hofhamm had gone high-hat and begun preaching in German again. The sand of that man. "Ein Feste Burg Ist Unser Gott"—they'd sung it that way so often now that Moses had memorized the German.

*Well, no more.* He didn't even know why they were even allowed in the US border. They'd lost the war. They should go home to what was left of their country and take that guttural language with them.

Moses might not be able to send them all back across the ocean, but he would do his part, and that pipe organ was calling to him. Pipe organs didn't fight back like Reverend Beaver would have. Moses had a ball-peen hammer in the back that would do the trick. Come to think of it, he had a nice handsaw too.

He had two hands, so he grabbed them both, then headed out into the moonlit drizzle with a smile.

He could already feel that fury ball in his gut waning.

He crossed the street, whistling "A Mighty Fortress Is Our God."

Seconds after he entered an unlocked door in the rear of the

Lutheran church, Reverend Beaver entered the back of Bellhaven African Methodist Episcopal with a dusty satchel over his shoulder and a plan of his own.

\\\///

Fox Bannerman looked forward to future days.

His flock of Pentecostals, for now, was content with having their revival meetings in Bannerman's house, but he already had the plans for a brick-and-mortar place of worship etched in his mind. The Lord had sent the plans to him one night in a dream, just as he'd sent the power to heal and speak in tongues. He'd build it on that sliver of land between that building where the Moslems met and Rabbi Blumenthal's synagogue. Heathens all of them.

This new place of worship would protect his flock when the end of days came. Or when Jesus came back to town in the promised Second Coming. Either way, his flock would be ready.

Never had he felt so united with the Holy Spirit than he did now in Bellhaven, and especially after visiting that chapel in the woods.

Brother Bannerman stretched out on his bed. Moonlight shone through his bedroom window, highlighting his long, lithe body. His two copperheads slithered around his legs—one at the ankles and the other around his left thigh—burrowing in and out of the twisted sheets. He imagined having a harem of fawning women with him, that Anna Belle Roper one of them. He'd love to put his healing hands on her head. That Linda May Dennison too. She was too pretty to be with a man who could no longer see her beauty.

His stomach growled, and his thoughts went elsewhere.

He still had leftover pork in the icebox.

He swung his feet from the bed and left his room, closing the door on his snakes as they tried to follow. If there was one thing he liked more than the formation of the Bellhaven Church of God, it was pork. He sat at his kitchen table and ate what was left of the last roasting, knowing he still had three full pigs smoked and salt-cured in the basement. He'd promised his flock a pig roast, and he was determined to give them a feast of all feasts. He hoped the smell would lure the lost town folk so he could evangelize them. Help them get born again and heal their pain. Watching the new ones speak in tongues excited him almost as much as a good pork feast. He'd even take his chances with those Latter-day Saints or that new group of Bible kids going door to door and witnessing to people. He was so good at what he did, he knew he could make them see the light. The one true light.

His mouth watered at the thought of the skin charring on the spit, the grease-and-bubble dripping to the grass below. He'd already decided he'd have the pig roast on his new lot. It was only grass now, with a sign that read The Future Home of Bellhaven Church of God. But soon its steeple would soar taller than the synagogue and mosque on either side of it.

He'd met both of those men, the rabbi and that black Moslem leader without a face. That mask was enough to scare anyone on the right path, if not for his preaching being on the completely *wrong* path. Mohammadism had no place here in Bellhaven or even in the States, for that matter. All that praying like they did to some God named Allah, bowing and babbling about that Moslem bible of theirs. What did they call it—the Koran? It was enough to make his blood boil.

And Judaism, with all that weird talking and those strange rituals. The fact that they believed Jesus was just some Jew and nothing more. It was blatant blasphemy. Jesus was Christ, plain and simple, and one day he'd come knocking on their door again. Except not on any Jewish or Moslem door, that was for sure. But what needled Bannerman even more than all of that was the fact that neither one of them ate pork. And here he was planning a grand pig feast right smack dab in the middle of both of them.

He laughed so hard his side ached when the idea hit him.

Wasn't it custom to give new neighbors a welcome gift? Or maybe it was the other way around and they were supposed to gift him? Either way, he knew what needed to be done. All those rules about cloven hooves and kosher meat and dirty animals chewing their cud or not, wallowing in mud and their own feces or not—it all was nonsense to him.

Pork tasted good, and he thought it silly not to eat it.

One pig was enough for his roast; he'd hold back the biggest one. The other two pigs in his basement, for an idea as good as this, could be given away—presents for his new neighbors. He'd give them a couple of knives and forks too.

The pigs were heavy, so he'd have to make two trips, but that was okay. It was drizzling outside, and the wetness just might feel good on his face.

It was the perfect plan.

But first he needed to feed his snakes and put some rain gear on.

\\\\////

Gabriel sat at the kitchen table, her chair situated so she could watch Ellsworth paint in the other room. It wasn't so much that she liked to watch him paint—his painting was a new thing she wasn't so sure about. It was more that she'd always liked to watch Ellsworth do anything. It wasn't really a matter of talent, though Ellsworth certainly had some. She'd never seen anyone throw a baseball like he could. But it was the other things about him that made him special in her eyes, things not grounded in ability but instead heightened by the unexplained.

Raphael had stopped playing the piano ten minutes ago and was snoring on the couch. She could hear brush strokes against canvas and wondered what Ellsworth was painting this time. Probably another horrific image from the war, although she liked to imagine he was painting her in a pretty dress.

She liked to imagine she was pretty in the first place.

In the front pocket of her overalls was a bundle of old newspaper clippings Ellsworth had thrown in the trash after his mother died. His mother had saved them since Ellsworth was a little boy, back when he was called Michael, and Ellsworth had thrown them away. But Gabriel had rescued them from the trash without him knowing and had kept them now for years.

She patted them in her pocket, imagining them warm against her chest. She didn't need to take them out. She'd long ago memorized them, and she didn't want to risk him suddenly coming in for a nip of Old Sam and seeing them spread out on the table like she sometimes did in the solitude of her own home, trying to make sense of it all. Trying to make sense of the *other* things.

The headlines ran through her head. *"Bellhaven boy survives polio." "Bellhaven boy miraculously defeats cancer." "Bellhaven man strikes out Babe Ruth." "Bellhaven boy survives . . ."*

Gabriel stiffened in her chair, thinking Ellsworth was on his way in, but he'd only cleared his throat. Bristles still brushed canvas in the other room. Not that it would have mattered; the newspaper clippings were still in her pocket. The only sin had been committed in her mind.

She imagined being married to Ellsworth with an entire brood of kids. She'd been picturing it since she was seven, back when all of them would dare each other to go into the woods and Michael would be the only one to do it. In her head he was still Michael. Michael with the sword she'd carved from a tree branch, the sword he'd called Blue Fire. He'd wield it and pretend to be a knight.

He'd held Blue Fire on the day they dared each other to go into the old slave houses.

They'd all been around the age of nine—her, Michael, Calvin, Alfred, and Omar. Linda May and Anna Belle had watched from atop the hill. Their parents had told them to steer clear of the old slave houses, and they'd obeyed. Many in town thought those houses should've been leveled decades ago, but they'd left them up to remember the injustice of slavery, a reminder that nothing of the like could ever happen again.

Michael had led the way that day with Blue Fire. The carved stick was no more than three feet long, more of a dagger than a sword, but it made Gabriel proud the way Michael cherished it.

The plan was an imaginary one, of course; the slaves were decades gone. But the mission was to rescue every last slave from the evil Bellhaven masters.

As they approached the first wooden slave house with its lone window and crooked concrete stoop covered in weeds, the others grew fidgety and began mumbling that maybe this wasn't a good idea after all. That they weren't supposed to be playing around the slave houses anyway.

Calvin peeled off first, saying he was hungry for lunch, and Omar followed, dropping the stick he'd been pretending was a pistol. Alfred lasted another ten steps before claiming he was hungry, too, and thought he'd heard his mother calling him anyway. He ran up the hill and escorted Anna Belle and Linda May back home.

Only Gabriel and Michael remained, and she wanted to turn around as well because the air felt queer. She thought she heard whispers coming from those shadowy, open-air houses. Folks said they always stayed cold and dark in there, no matter what the weather outside. But she stayed put with Michael. Didn't want him to think her chicken.

Michael held up a hand, and she halted with relief. He whispered a strategy: he'd go in first, alone, and if things were clear he'd call for her. *But be ready to attack. I'll need you by my side.*

Even now those words brought a smile.

After a minute she called his name, but he didn't answer. After two minutes she inched closer to the stoop and called his name again. Nothing. Not even footsteps or shuffling or the sound of his breathing.

She gulped back her fear, climbed the stoop, and peered into the shadows to find . . . nothing.

Michael was gone, vanished from that slave house altogether. The window was too high for him to have climbed through. And there was no other door.

She fell back off the stoop and rolled in the grass, nearly hyperventilating as she stared down the row of ten slave houses, one just as old and abandoned as the next.

She heard his voice call her. "Gabriel?" It was distant, but somehow close enough to resonate.

She waited, her heart pounding her ribcage. *Where'd he go?* "Michael!"

And then Michael emerged, not from the first slave house, but from the third one down the row. His eyes were glazed. She ran to him, hugged him, asked if he was all right.

He asked, "Where am I?"

"In Bellhaven," she answered.

"They took my sword. I fought them back, but they took my sword."

With tears in her eyes she promised to carve him another. She took his arm and walked him home with full intentions of prying after dinner. She'd ask him exactly what had happened in that slave house. But she didn't ask, and the next day he never mentioned it. He set out instead to scrounge up everybody for a game of baseball, like yesterday never happened. Like he hadn't vanished and ended up two houses down from where he entered.

It was the woods' doing, she decided. She knew the Bellhaven woods could do strange things like that.

But she also knew that Michael was Michael.

As the days passed she promised herself that she'd ask him, but she never did, and he never offered. He never even brought it up. She wondered if there wasn't a part of him that enjoyed her uncertainty about that day. Maybe that was his way of flirting with her.

After time, she'd realized she enjoyed the mystery of it all more than the knowing.

Gabriel sucked in a deep breath and exhaled until her cheeks puffed out. She knocked her knuckles against the kitchen table, realizing exactly what she had to do, what she should have been forging in her smithy long before now.

His brushstrokes whisked canvas in the other room. Concrete proof that the Michael she knew was still alive after all of it.

*Michael . . .*

She'd get to work on it first thing tomorrow.

\||//

At one time in his life, back when his wife and kids were alive, Lou Eddington had believed in God. But he wasn't so sure anymore, and he wondered if that now made him an agnostic. Or was it an atheist?

One thing he knew for sure was that he no longer needed sleep.

What had it been now? Days? Weeks? And he didn't feel the least bit tired. He looked a little different in the mirror—with the heavy bags under his eyes, the red splotches across his flesh, and the fact that his skin felt tighter than an overstuffed pillow and all-around bloated, especially around the neckline of his collared shirts. But then again that all could have been because the lighting was poor in the bathroom.

Otherwise he felt swell, what Anna Belle Roper downstairs sometimes called peachy.

Lou sat alone in his bedroom with the door locked. He'd invited several of the town folk over to dance with him in recent days, and now they'd begun to stay, to sleep over right there in his living room. He'd danced with them all, but so far none of them could hold a candle to Deborah, deceased now for what—going on three years? She'd been such a good dancer, so fluid you would think her feet never hit the floor. It was folly for him to think he could find another, and right now he just wanted to be left alone. They could sleep on his couches downstairs; he wouldn't stop them. But tonight he wouldn't bless them with his presence either. He didn't like the way they'd started to fawn over him every time he entered the room, like he was some kind of something when he knew deep down, behind all this newly found energy and flare, that he was some kind of nothing.

It was the house's doing. Or, to be more precise, the woods'. Because whatever had come into the attic that day had come from the live oak trees. Or maybe from those old slave huts that needed to be leveled.

Anyway, he was too busy playing chess to go downstairs with what Anna Belle Roper had begun calling his "flock." So in his room he remained, orchestrating both sides of the chessboard and finding more pleasure with every move.

He'd fallen in love with this house on the hill, only doubting the purchase of it once, when he'd ventured up into the attic on that first visit and felt whatever he'd felt and seen whatever it was he'd seen—or thought he'd seen. He only knew that ever since that visit to the attic, the house had called to him, seeped into him like water into dry-parched ground, and he had the feeling now that he couldn't leave even if he wanted to. And he'd never gotten so much work done so fast. In the past it would take him months to complete a chess set, but now he was down to a week, two at the most. Take sleep out of the equation, and there was no limit to what he could get done.

He only wished Deborah and the kids were around to see his newest pieces of work. They'd always been so fond of his craft— even his two little boys, who'd only just begun to learn how to play when they fell sick, all three of them at the same time. It haunted him still, seeing them overcome with weakness and nausea. And the pain—that had been worst of all. Lou couldn't stand to see them in pain, and that was how he'd rationalized what he did in the end.

What Deborah had begged him to do.

He'd moved to Bellhaven seeking forgiveness, and that's exactly what he'd gotten inside that chapel, that little sliver of bliss that had no rhyme or reason for being there. That memory lane where voices weren't so dead anymore.

They'd forgiven him. America Ma had told him so, and then she'd allowed him to speak with them. It was like she was some kind of gatekeeper, although she sounded more like some long-ago slave.

Lou swallowed the lump in his throat and moved another newly carved piece on the board. Somewhere, buried deep, a tiny voice wanted out. It kept asking if what he'd done was the right thing or not. Whether coming to Bellhaven had been right or not.

"How could it not?" he answered it aloud. "Look at me now." He moved another piece, solemnly this time. *My new fancy car, my freshly painted house on the hill. More people coming to dance with me daily.*

What did it all mean?

He would have felt empty had his body not been so filled to near-bursting by whatever had entered him in that attic months ago, those seconds when he felt all tingly and dizzy.

Across the room, flies—a good dozen of them—buzzed against the glass. He'd thought about shooting them with his rifle downstairs, but that might alter the delicate balance of things. Or imbalance of things.

He moved another chess piece, a pawn, to the middle of the board. "Brother Bannerman likes his pork. He likes to eat with a knife and a fork."

He moved another piece, this one a rook. "Moses Yarney, old as sand, once had thoughts of killing a man."

Lou grinned, licked salt from his lips from where unknowing tears had settled in his mustache, and then touched another chess piece, this one a king.

"Ellsworth Newberry got stabbed in the chest. Some still think him better than the rest."

# CHAPTER 17

In the morning sunlight, Raphael viewed the painting Ellsworth had done last night. The canvas depicted bloody body parts strewn across charred trees, coiled barbed wire festooned with dead soldiers, crows circling—or so Ellsworth said.

Raphael looked suspicious. "If that's what it really is, it's disgusting."

"So is war," said Ellsworth, full of energy and ready to face the day. "It ain't neat." He looked over at Gabriel, standing next to the front door. He was still a prisoner in his own house. And what was that gleam in her eyes?

"Am I free to go yet?"

"It's your house. You can come and go as you please."

"Somehow I doubt that."

"Where is it you want to go?"

"Check on Anna Belle, then maybe Alfred and Omar. They haven't been around for a few days."

Gabriel opened the door for him. "Go on."

"And what if I run for the woods?"

"You won't. Because you know now that it's fool's gold."

Ellsworth stepped out onto the porch, no longer craving the bliss the chapel offered, at least not at the moment, and somehow

Gabriel knew that. She'd told him earlier in the morning that she liked the look in his eyes. The sturdy prewar look.

Raphael followed Ellsworth across the street. "We should play catch today, Mr. Newberry."

Ellsworth grunted away that notion, then took in his surroundings. It felt good to be outside again. Every flower in Bellhaven stood perky from last night's rainfall—so many bright, vibrant colors. The rain had knocked petals off like oil-paint droppings in the grass. Pink crape myrtles, blue hyacinths, and violet rhododendrons reflected majestically across a large puddle.

"Danger can disguise itself in the most beautiful of things," Gabriel had said of those voices in the chapel.

Static crackled to his right. High in a sprawling live oak, Alfred sat on a thick limb with his radio, fooling with the knobs and wires.

Raphael said, "What's Mr. Dennison doing up there?"

Ellsworth shook his head. "Alfred, what *are* you doing up there?"

"Radio comes in clear as a bell up here, Ellsworth."

"Doesn't sound like it."

"Just in the process of locating a station."

A stepladder leaned against the tree trunk. "You get up there all on your own?"

"No. Omar helped."

"And he just left you?"

Alfred nodded toward the street. "Had something urgent he needed to tend to."

"Well don't try getting down on your own. We're gonna run in and check on Anna Belle and then be back out."

Ellsworth knocked on Anna Belle's door and got no answer. It was unlocked, so he let himself inside, calling her name as he passed through every room, his apology for taping her mouth shut on the tip of his tongue for the instant he saw her. Of course, she probably owed him one, too, for cutting up the only picture he had of Eliza.

He recalled that sudden kiss Anna Belle had planted on his lips, reminiscent of the one she'd put on him in the ocean when they were kids, except this one had jostled him. He missed her voice, her constant blabbering. It shook him to realize he'd been so close to pasting her right there on the kitchen floor. *It was the chapel's doing. And now it was still doing it to her, turning the screws against the grooves.*

Raphael lifted a piece of paper from the kitchen counter. "Looks like she left me a note."

She'd gone to visit Eddington last night. Ellsworth crumbled the note and left the house.

They hadn't been in Anna Belle's house long, no more than five minutes, but in that short time the town had come unglued. A crowd of about two dozen had gathered in the town hall parking lot. Sheriff Lecroy stormed from the jailhouse, parting the onlookers like a man on the run. The crowd shouted at one another and jeered at Sheriff Lecroy. Gabriel was in the middle of it all, keeping the enraged people at bay with her long arms.

Ellsworth caught the sheriff before he jumped into his old blue Model T, where he'd hand-painted the word *Sheriff* on the back. "What's going on?"

"I quit, is what's going on." The man's face was pale, his eyes strained red. "I left a note on my desk, right next to the badge I won't be wearing any longer."

"You can't just walk off the job. What happened?"

"Where do I start? The town went to hell in a handcart overnight. You heard about John Stone and Beverly Adams, right?" Ellsworth nodded. "Well, last night Reverend Cane thought it a good idea to break into Father Timothy's church and hang a homemade Pope Benedict doll from the giant Jesus cross above the altar. Then he knocked the Mary statue on the floor, and her head snapped clean off at the neck."

"Reverend Cane?" Ellsworth asked, half-chuckling in disbelief.

"You see me laughing, Ellsworth?" Sheriff Lecroy pulled a bottle of Old Sam from the deep well of his pants pocket and downed a gulp. "Well, Father Timothy retaliated."

"Wait. Where'd you get that?"

"Get what?" Sheriff Lecroy looked to the bottle. "Oh, from your shed out back."

"You knew but didn't confiscate?"

The sheriff nodded, wiped his mouth, shrugged. "Well, you're different."

"How so?"

"You know, you're . . . you."

Ellsworth massaged his brow, annoyed at Lecroy and even more so at the growing crowd behind them. "Go on. Father Timothy retaliated?"

"As if he had a bucket of paint at the ready." Sheriff Lecroy unabashedly took another swig of Old Sam. "He kicked in the backdoor of Bellhaven First Baptist, walked in with a brush and a bucket of red. Painted each of the seven sacraments on the walls. And get this—he spells the words 'child baptism' and 'original sin' in letters as big as a man up the center aisle."

"You don't say."

"Just said, Ellsworth. Ain't you listening? And then that new Pentecostal preacher, the one with the copperhead snakes that's a little goofy in the noodle."

"Bannerman?"

"The same. Well, you know how he's purchased that narrow corncob patch of land between the Moslem meeting house and the Jewish synagogue? Well he decided to welcome his new neighbors with a little gift. Puts a dead pig inside each of their doors and sticks a knife and fork in it. You get the angle here? The Jews and the Moslems don't eat pork 'cause the pig has cloven hooves or some nonsense. Or chews its cud. Or doesn't chew its cud. I don't completely get it myself. But anyway . . ."

Sheriff Lecroy paused, his attention stolen by the sight of Rabbi Blumenthal entering Brother Bannerman's side yard, where a clothesline stretched between two trees. One by one the rabbi plucked articles from the line—Bannerman's undershorts, trousers, shirts, and socks. Methodically he placed them all into a laundry basket he carried.

"What is this?" mumbled the sheriff.

Ellsworth watched the rabbi with curiosity. "The old gooseberry lay."

"*That's* how he's gonna retaliate for the pig?" The sheriff said it as if the rabbi had disappointed him. "By stealing Brother Bannerman's skivvies?"

But then the rabbi poured gasoline into the basket and lit it on fire. The whooshing flame stole the attention of the arguing crowd.

"See," said Sheriff Lecroy. "Hell in a handcart." He opened his car door and paused before getting in. "Who knows what your masked friend's gonna do when he sees the pig inside his mosque."

"Where is he?"

"I don't know, and I don't much care at this point. I'm done."

Ellsworth caught the door before it closed and nodded toward the rabbi, who stood watching the basket of burning clothes. "Shouldn't you go handcuff him or something?"

In Fox Bannerman's yard, Rabbi Blumenthal was shouting something in Yiddish.

"If I had enough nippers I would," said Sheriff Lecroy. "Reverend Beaver broke into Moses Yarney's African church and hung old slave shackles and iron masks from the pulpit. But Moses was too busy taking a ball-peen hammer to the new pipe organ at Reverend Hofhamm's First Lutheran to stop him." Sheriff Lecroy took another swig of Old Sam and didn't wipe the dribble on his chin as he nodded toward the jailhouse. "They're all in there, Ellsworth, hopefully not killing each other. Or maybe that'd be a good thing. I ain't even told you the half of it."

"You're really leaving?"

Sheriff Lecroy got into his car, cranked it up, and drove about ten feet before stopping abruptly, tires skidding on gravel dust. He got out and left his car door open.

Ellsworth said, "Second thoughts?"

Sheriff Lecroy walked toward the woods with his bottle. "No. Just need to visit that chapel one last time before I go."

\\\\////

The jailhouse sounded like a chicken coop and was about as crowded.

Sheriff Lecroy hadn't told him about every arrest. Ellsworth counted eleven people inside the three cells. Leroy had managed to separate the ones who'd committed hate crimes against each other. But almost every one of the offenses had been church on church, religion on religion.

Reverend Cane gripped the bars and shouted two cells down at his former friend, Father Timothy. He called the Catholic Church the whore of Babylon, then went into a tirade about the new Catholic parochial schools popping up across the country, to which Father Timothy responded that something needed to be done to protect the Catholic youth from Protestant teachers—especially Baptist ones.

Gabriel had followed Ellsworth inside and was now attempting to quiet the jailhouse—not only the prisoners, but also the dozen or so visitors outside the cells, who weren't so much visiting as adding fuel to the fire. Ellsworth pushed his way through the crowd and found Sheriff Lecroy's keys on the desk. He'd left them right next to his badge and resignation note.

When he returned to the cells, Reverend Cane spat in between the bars, hitting Ellsworth in the chest. "Communist! Catholic harlot!"

Ellsworth hadn't been to mass in two years and wondered if his Catholicism still counted. He reached his arm through the bars quick as a snakebite and grabbed Reverend Cane's shirt, but he let go when he noticed the dazed, lost look in Cane's eyes.

In the middle cell, Reverend Hofhamm pointed at Moses Yarney through the bars and said to Ellsworth, "He ruin my new pipe organ."

Moses Yarney yelled, "Spaetzle spattzle. He won't stop talking that German, Ellsworth. I say we send him to Camp Oglethorpe with the rest of them Kraut aliens."

"War's over, Moses," Ellsworth said.

"Who says the war's over? Huh? I say the war's just startin'. Them Lutherans try to drown out our singin' with their singin' every chance they get. That pipe organ had it comin'." Moses sat back down and hooted, "Never asked what he done back to me, Ellsworth." Louder. "Never asked what he done back to me."

"I did nothing," claimed Josef Hofhamm with his heavy German accent.

"Came over on the wrong boat," shouted Reverend Beaver. "That's what he done."

Moses turned on Reverend Beaver in the next cell. "Well if I'd gone with my first notion, I would've strangled your Klan neck, Beaver-Dam."

Reverend Beaver grunted like a monkey, and Moses nearly came through the bars.

Outside the cell, Gabriel pinned an enraged Dooby Klinsmatter to the far wall with a forearm. The short, fat man had been trying to get at Father Timothy through the bars. Dooby was in charge of keeping the Baptist church clean. He had gout in his right foot, and now would have to repaint all the walls and scrape letters from the tiled floor.

Father Timothy knelt in his cell and cried into his hands, mumbling what sounded like his own confession to himself, playing the role of both sinner and saint simultaneously.

Reverend Hofhamm repeated himself loudly. "He ruin my pipe organ, Ellsworth. Ruin it good. So you know what I do? I had five pounds of sauerbraten marinating. So I open lid on piano they have in that African church and dump it all in. Now it sounds like duck soup when you play. Ain't that a hoot?" Hofhamm then went into some tirade in German, and his face turned red.

Brother Fox Bannerman was in the middle cell pleading for the company of his two copperhead snakes, which he'd evidently named Adam and Eve. He spoke in tongues, put his hands atop Beverly Adams's hair as if to suddenly heal her, and she pasted him in the stomach.

Reverend Cane yelled something about how dead cricket pie didn't taste so good, and Beverly Adams started crying.

John Stone was still in there from blowing up Ned Gleeson's birdhouse work shed. And there, two cells down, was Ned Gleeson, who must have retaliated overnight.

John Stone called out, "Ned ruined my rosary collection,

Ellsworth. Sheriff Lecroy got him for breaking and entering, but when he come in here, he had all my rosaries in his pockets. He started ripping off the beads one by one, and I couldn't do nothin' to stop it. Then, once he had my attention he started stripping them off by the dozen, like he was plucking dry corn from a cob." Hundreds, if not thousands, of rosary beads had been strewn across the jailhouse floor. John Stone said, "I begged for him to stop, Ellsworth. Told him I was sorry for blowing up his birdhouses. But he had a look in his eyes, and I got those rosaries from my grammy."

Reverend Beaver mockingly shouted, "John Stone got rosary beads from his grammy."

John Stone ran at the neighboring cell and stuck his arm between the bars, reaching for the Methodist minister. Reverend Beaver bit the outstretched fingers, and John Stone screamed.

Ellsworth had to get outside and find some fresh air before *he* steamed over. His gun was holstered but loaded, and he was afraid he'd be too willing to use it.

Before he reached the jailhouse door, Raphael entered.

"What is it?"

The boy gulped, pointed outside. "There's a man here to see you."

"Who is he?"

"Don't know. Just come here from down the road, asking for Ellsworth Newberry."

Ellsworth pushed the door open and limped into the sunlight. The crowd outside had grown. Alfred was still up in the tree with his radio, but crying now. "Alfred, what is it?"

Alfred fumbled with the knobs. "Linda May's up there with him, Ellsworth. She got invited to dance, and she never came home last night."

"What are you talking about, Alfred? Up where?"

"Eddington's place."

Ellsworth looked up the hill. Vultures circled the trees around the yellow house. Lou Eddington stood outside it, gazing down the hill.

"Ellsworth Newberry."

Ellsworth looked toward the new voice, the newly arrived man with the worn brown suit and bowler hat. "I've seen you before."

The man stepped forward. "I've been here before, Mr. Newberry."

"Don't come any closer." Ellsworth pulled his pistol.

"I come in peace this time." The man dropped to both knees. "I come for forgiveness. I've got death on my conscience. I was lost, but I've been found. I know my place now."

"Start making sense before my finger gets heavy, 'cause this trigger sure don't care."

The man looked around at the treetops where dozens of redbirds circled. "I felt the pull to come here even back then, but I was confused as to why."

And then Ellsworth saw it—the bald eagle tattoo on the left side of the young man's neck. He'd glimpsed something like that on the neck of a man the night Eliza died in the town hall fire, except then the tattoo had been half-concealed by a white Klan hood. Ellsworth staggered toward the man, knocked him to the ground, and planted the gun barrel against his temple.

The man folded his hands as if praying, tears streaming from his eyes.

Ellsworth cocked the hammer.

"No." Raphael put his hands on Ellsworth's arm. "Don't. Please. Don't let the bad stuff back in, Mr. Newberry. He knows things we don't."

Just then Omar shouted in the distance. "Fox Bannerman, you

come out, take yer med'cine." He must have found the pig in his mosque. He walked down the middle of the road with his rifle against his shoulder, a lit pipe smoking from the mask slit. "Fox Bannerman, you come on out of dat der hidey-hole."

Rabbi Blumenthal looked up and stepped away from his smoldering clothes basket.

Omar had Bannerman's copperhead snakes draped over his shoulders like two leather belts. Adam and Eve were dead.

Ellsworth looked back to the man he'd pinned to the ground.

Raphael said, "Mr. Newberry, let him live."

After a beat, Ellsworth removed the gun from the man's head and stood. He yanked the man from the ground and escorted him toward the jailhouse.

"I'm here for forgiveness, Mr.—"

"Close your head or I'll put a bullet in it."

The man quieted, followed obediently.

Gabriel stood at the door, held it open. She and the new arrival locked eyes. Ellsworth noticed the exchange of familiarity and yanked the man toward the door.

Ellsworth nodded toward Omar, steadily approaching with Bannerman's dead snakes. "Go handle him," he told Gabriel.

Gabriel went right away.

Inside the jailhouse the crowd parted and went quiet as Ellsworth unlocked the first cell, where Father Timothy had just finished his confession and was now reciting the rosary, plucking a loose bead from the ground as he recited each Hail Mary. He stopped when the new man entered and then motioned the sign of the cross.

Ellsworth slammed the cell closed and locked it. The crowd resumed talking, shouting, pushing, and shoving. The noise escalated. Ellsworth sidestepped and brushed people aside until he made it to the desk in the corner. He took Leroy's old gold-star badge, pinned it to his shirt, and battled back through the throng. He removed his revolver and fired it up into the ceiling. Plaster dust rained down, and the jailhouse went silent once more.

Ellsworth said, "Go back to your homes, or I'll pack these cells tighter than a log jam in a crooked river. There's a new sheriff in town."

One by one the citizens of Bellhaven began to disperse, but Ellsworth didn't lower his gun until the last one exited the jailhouse. He followed them out the door and fired another shot to move the crowd in the parking lot. The shot echoed. Birds scattered from trees, even some of the vultures at the Eddington place.

Eddington was still watching from atop the hillside. He tipped his hat, but Ellsworth didn't return the gesture. Anna Belle and Linda May were both still inside that yellow house.

*Dancing.*

Gabriel had subdued Omar, although he still wore the dead snakes like suspenders over his shoulder. He'd always preached about the peaceful nature of his Moslem religion and was doing so now, explaining to Gabriel that his urge to retaliate was over now that he'd lopped the heads off of both Adam and Eve. Now he seemed more concerned about his good friend Alfred crying up in the tree.

Ellsworth found Old Man Tanner next and told him not to go far, or he'd track him down and throw him back in a cell with the Pentecostal.

Gabriel approached Ellsworth. He surprised her by pinning a silver-star badge to the right pocket of her overalls.

"What's this?"

"Every sheriff needs a good deputy."

She grinned, eyes misty.

As Omar secured the ladder on the tree for Alfred to get down, a voice burst through the radio static, the voice of a woman from the past rather than some broadcasted studio in the present day.

*"This here's good ol' America Ma comin' to the town of Bellhaven from the land of no-way-no-how. A town founded on that foundation of evil. Tha's right, massa Bellhaven. No mo' pickin' that cotton. Now we gettin' down to cleanin' some slave blood off them walls. Slave blood from yo' hands, massa. You don' never know what you walked in and saw. You don' never know and never will now. It was us try and stop'm. Us tryin' to protect these here woods. But now they be gettin' through 'cause of you, massa. Now they gettin' through . . ."*

The radio fell from Alfred's grasp and crashed on the ground. Dials spun loose and wires popped free. Alfred cried silent tears, and Omar escorted him down the ladder.

Those that remained outside stood speechless, staring at the busted radio. From their expressions and the whispers that followed, it soon became apparent that many in the crowd had recognized the voice of America Ma.

Ellsworth sidled next to his new deputy. "I saw the look you shared with that new man earlier. You know him?"

Gabriel's silver star glistened in the sunlight. "I don't."

"Then why were your lookers peeled?"

"You saw it the same as I did, Ellsworth."

"Saw what?"

"His color."

Ellsworth chewed the inside of his jaw. He'd seen it, all right. That thin glow shimmering redder than any cardinal bird he'd ever seen.

# CHAPTER 18

Alfred may have been blind, but he had enough spatial sense to know where the window was.

He stood next to Ellsworth's chair, facing the street, as tears dripped down his cheeks.

Ellsworth gripped his elbow, and Alfred jumped.

"Sorry." He helped Alfred into the chair. "Here, have a seat."

Alfred gripped the chair arms and lowered his voice so those in the kitchen couldn't hear. "I'm sorry, Ellsworth. I told Anna Belle you had secrets about Calvin. It just came out. I think that's what's happening. People have thoughts, and usually our minds sort out the bad ones, the ones we shouldn't act on. But now we're all listening, doing what comes to mind. It's because of that place, isn't it?"

Ellsworth patted his shoulder in agreement. Alfred gnawed on his fingertip, spat a fleck of nail to the windowsill. "People won't stop going. You know that, don't you? Even now, knowing what I know, I'm itchin' to go back. And by nightfall it'll be a full-out craving and cold sweats."

"Close your eyes, Alfred. Take a nap. There's a bottle of Old Sam on the ledge."

Alfred patted his coat pocket. "Got my own from your shed."

He removed it, downed two gulps. "She didn't come back. Said she'd only be a few hours. To dance? What does that even mean? Why would she need to go dance with a man she hardly knows when I can still dance perfectly fine?"

"I'll think of something. Now rest up." Ellsworth turned toward the kitchen.

"Ellsworth."

"Yes, Alfred."

"I know we've been needling you about it, but you think maybe you could do a painting for me sometime?"

"What kind of painting?"

"One of them that you do." He made a few rapid brushstrokes through the air. "Raphael told me about it. Said it's a good way to get the bad stuff out. Like bloodletting—let out some of the humors. Thought maybe it would help keep me out of the woods."

"How 'bout I set you up with a canvas and a brush, let you paint something yourself."

"But . . ."

"You're still seeing it, Alfred. Makes no difference that you're blind. Yours might end up looking better than mine anyhow."

\||//

Old Man Tanner sat with his elbows on Ellsworth's kitchen table. He looked around at Ellsworth, Gabriel, and Raphael as steam floated up from his coffee mug.

"I've studied earthquakes all over the country. Got a knack for sensing them. A sulfur smell in the air. Shifts in the wind. Energy. The hair on my arms stands up." He sipped coffee with unsteady hands.

"Need some whiskey in that?" asked Raphael.

Tanner winked at the boy. "Wouldn't hurt." Ellsworth poured a finger's worth into the mug. Tanner swirled it, took a healthy gulp. "The first foreshock hit on August 27, 1886, in Summerville. Had an acquaintance there who took a train to Tennessee to tell me. Me and my wife, Susannah, packed right quick."

"She was a scientist too?"

"Not by training, but she'd worked with me for years. Like a ball team of two, we were. Any rate, we arrived in Summerville the next day, two hours before the second foreshock hit on August 28. Folks there thought that was it because there were no shocks the next day, but I sensed more."

"How so?" asked Ellsworth.

"The wind. It was taking me east toward the coast, and Susannah agreed I should go. Short trip by train and we ended up in Charleston. The energy there tugged at my arm hair. Susannah took notes, like always. Every night we'd return to Summerville to stay with my acquaintance. He put us up in the old White Meeting House. At sunup we'd return to Charleston. I'd follow the air. Record shifts in the wind. The water in the harbor was unusually still. So many birds circled above the Battery."

"What kinds of birds?" asked Ellsworth.

"All kinds. I just noticed there was more than what would be considered usual. Everyone walking the harbor had their eyes peeled to the sky.

"It was closing in on nightfall on the thirty-first of August, four days after the first foreshock. Susannah and I were about to board the train to Summerville when I got this numb feeling up my left arm, and then the hair on my head stood up. Susannah said it was just windblown, but I didn't think so. Didn't feel any gust. I told her to go on back to Summerville and that I'd catch up later. I insisted she go. It would be safer there at the meeting house. If something was going to happen, I was convinced Charleston would be the center.

Tanner stared into his cup as if searching for answers, then shook his head. "I told her I'd be safe, and smart. That I'd see her in a few hours. I kissed her and watched the train pull away. And then I followed the energy in the air. An hour later, after a short ride on a mule cart and walking the rest on foot, I'd followed it here to Bellhaven." He pointed out the kitchen window. "Town I'd never heard of. But I knew right away that I needed to go into the woods, just by the cyclic way the moss spun on the trees.

"The sun was setting, so I knocked on a door and asked to borrow a lantern. Man asked what for. So I could go into the woods, I said. At night? He looked at me like I'd gone off the tracks. I told him it was important, that I was a scientist. And you know what he told me? Said a priest would do me better than a lantern, but to give him a minute and he'd fetch me one."

"A priest?" asked Raphael.

"I didn't know," said Tanner. "I waited on the stoop, and he returned with a lantern and a gun. I said, what do I need a gun for? Just in case, he says, shoving it in my hand. Just in case what? He didn't answer. He said if I come back out to just leave the lantern and gun on the back porch. And then he closed the door."

"Remember his name?" asked Ellsworth.

"I don't." Tanner's hands had stopped shaking. He gripped the mug and gulped more coffee, his arthritic knuckles bone white. "He moved out of Bellhaven in the days after. I took the lantern and gun into the woods and followed my nose. That sulfur smell was strong."

Tanner stared at the whorls in the tabletop. Flicked a bread crumb into his hand, only to drop it right back to the table. "I held that gun out as I walked because I felt I needed to. Heard voices in the wind, noise swirls that didn't sound human. The energy pulled me deeper. Ten minutes in, I noticed the animals going out. Hundreds of them. Deer, squirrels, 'possums, woodchucks, 'coons—all heading in the opposite direction because they felt it too. Saw a deer ramming its head into a tree repeatedly. Another deer walking backwards."

Ellsworth shifted in his chair, caught Gabriel's eye. "Backwards?"

"Like backing away from something you don't understand. Like you gotta get away but at the same time you still gotta see.

"I dodged the fleeing animals, walked deeper, but I felt sick to my stomach. Two times the gun drifted to my right temple like I was some puppet on a string. Like I had no control. Once my finger flirted with pulling the trigger. I was being pulled to something like quicksilver spinning onto a funnel—lured to exactly where this thing was starting. I moved aside branches, stepped over deadfall, resisted the urge to use the gun on myself, and eventually I made it to the clearing we all now know about. By then, every hair on my arm was standing on end, as were all the hairs on my head—straight up and rigid—and my skin tingled. Hundreds of birds circled through the moonlight."

"Was the chapel there?" asked Ellsworth.

"It was there even then," said Tanner, wide-eyed. "The door was opening and closing fast, whapping against the stone wall like hammer blows. Then water in the creek behind the chapel suddenly rose, and fish were jumping in it. One of them landed on the ground and flopped around in the grass. I went to kick it back in, and that's when I saw a light flicker inside the chapel. A glow against the stained glass, and then it darkened.

"The earth started shaking seconds later—at nine fifty-one, to be exact. Lasted thirty-five, forty seconds. Knocked me off my feet. It sounded like a heavy bowling ball rolling along a wooden alley. Trees uprooted and split. Tiny fissures opened, and I swear the creek widened. More fish jumped, and the birds were singing so loudly it was like one continuous screech. The chapel door kept opening and closing, and light flickered even though there were no candles in there, no electric current. Swamp water belched high in the air, and sand blows popped up like small volcanoes all over the woods. It was the most violent shaking of the earth in my entire career, and here I was in the middle of the woods—in the dark. The lantern had gone out, and I couldn't find the gun. It's a wonder I wasn't killed by a falling limb."

"But you weren't hurt or anything," said Ellsworth.

"Nope. Just scared out of my wits. And then it all stopped, and everything got silent. Even the birds closed their beaks. The chapel door was open, and I heard a woman crying." Tanner pulled a kerchief from his pocket and wiped his eyes. "I knew right away it was Susannah. I went into the chapel, dropped to the floor, and felt the mosaic tiles. Moon glow entered through the hole in the roof, showed me the picture on the floor.

"I heard Susannah's voice clear as day." He bit his lower lip and then downed the rest of his coffee. "Told me she was okay. That she was in a good place."

"She died, didn't she?" asked Ellsworth.

Tanner nodded. "The White Meeting House where we were staying was leveled, reduced to ruins. Her body was crushed by bricks and ceiling beams, and she died instantly. Even though I'd told her she'd be safer there."

Gabriel said, "You couldn't have known."

"Maybe not. But I still should've kept her by my side." He sucked in a deep breath. "Don't know how I heard her voice inside that chapel or how it happened so fast after the meeting house went down. But I spent the next several minutes in there talking to her.

Taking in that burst of fresh air that was so right it couldn't have been wrong."

Tanner motioned for Ellsworth to slide the flask over. He downed two gulps, blew out air, and looked from chair to chair. "That was the largest earthquake ever recorded in this part of the US. Eight minutes later we were hit by another aftershock, and six more followed over the next twenty-four hours. The main quake was felt as far away as Boston and Chicago, Cuba and Bermuda. Wires snapped. Train rails were torn apart. Nearly every building in Charleston was damaged. It was so severe that some speculated the Florida peninsula had broken away from the continent."

Ellsworth said, "How long do you think that chapel has been there, Tanner?"

"I don't know. But the reason it was built there and the reason I was pulled to the center of that earthquake are one and the same."

"What do you mean?" Gabriel put an arm around Raphael's shoulders.

"I don't know exactly, but there's pressure needing to come up. And it isn't done."

"Eliza, my wife—she used to go there. At one time she said something about doorways."

"*Sometimes they come through.*"

Tanner put his hands to his temples and blinked hard, forming crow's feet upon crow's feet around his eyes. He opened them sharply. "There's a mystery to it all. To my knowledge—and other scientists agree with me—there are no fault lines here. Not for sixty miles in any direction. From what we know, earthquakes occur when the earth's tectonic plates—think of it like puzzle pieces fit together—get pushed together at the places where they join, the fault lines. The plates will slip and then jump past each other, and that's what causes the ground to move. That's what happened in San Francisco in '06."

"But how could it happen here?" Gabriel asked. "You said there are no fault lines."

Tanner shrugged. "It's befuddled me for years. I don't know how it could—unless somehow it happened *inside* the plate. Some believe that's what happened with the big New Madrid quake a hundred plus years ago—some kind of an intraplate movement. But I don't know." He folded his hands on the table. "I just wonder if that chapel, whenever it was built, was placed in that exact spot for a reason that goes beyond science."

It was silent for a moment as they chewed on their thoughts.

Ellsworth said, "You mentioned earlier that you don't think it's done shaking."

"No, I don't. I still think there's potential for another quake. And soon. I felt aftershocks for weeks. Two strong ones on October 22 and November 5 of that same year. On January 3, 1903, another quake shook houses along the South Carolina and Georgia border, near Savannah. In April of '07, another quake affected Charleston, Augusta, and Savannah, rattling dishes and knocking items from shelves. Another quake hit Summerville in June of 1912, felt as far as Wilmington, North Carolina, and Macon, Georgia. Union County had a small quake in 1913. And another one in Summerville in September of 1914 knocked pictures from walls. Folks said it sounded like a train coming into their homes. Hundreds of minor quakes have occurred that are barely noticeable. Then, of course, there was the one the night the town hall was set on fire."

"And you feel the energy again?" asked Raphael.

"I do. It was harder for me to pick it up on account of how far I'd fallen, but now that I've regained my wits, I feel it strong. It's always been hissing, but I think that quake in '86 busted something open."

Ellsworth said, "Why did you stay in Bellhaven? Was it the quakes or the chapel?"

"Both. Scientifically I was curious to learn why an earthquake of that magnitude happened here."

"And the other?"

"For the first time I believed in heaven. I talked to Susannah inside those walls the day after the big quake. And the day after that. I went nearly every day since. Couldn't stop going. But what I didn't realize—not at first—was that going there was changing me. It aged me like the dickens. And it made me selfish. Jealous. Like it was my own special place and no one else could ever have it. It was already mostly concealed beneath vines and branches, but I hid it even more with deadfall and brambles. I was determined that no one else would ever find it. Only recently had I begun to clear it out, so someone else could maybe find it after I died."

"Eliza found it," said Ellsworth. "She spoke to me of the healing floor, about talking to our son who died stillborn. In the weeks before she died, she looked calmer, more at peace. But the aging was starting to show with her too." He looked at Tanner, changed course. "When you stabbed me, you claimed the devil made you do it. Was it a voice you heard?"

"No, just a thought that popped up in my head. You went into the woods, and I didn't like it. So I needed to kill you." Tanner leaned back in his chair, ran fingers through his white hair. "I saw the age marks in the mirror. Felt the goodness drip out of me like candle wax until all that remained was the bad stuff. I knew it all, and still I went. That was the power of hearing Susannah's voice every day. I was willing to make a deal with the devil if I could be with her just a little more. And apparently I'm not alone."

"Just how old are you, Tanner?"

He scoffed. "How old do I look?"

"Honestly?"

"Wouldn't want it any other way."

"Eighty plus," said Ellsworth. "On a bad day, maybe pushing ninety."

Tanner looked around the table, grimaced. "Well you're about three decades off, you cake-eater. I'm fifty-five." He looked at his hands. "Place has shriveled me up like a prune." He winked at Ellsworth. "But at least I got both my legs."

Ellsworth chuckled at the bluntness.

"Ask a man his age, you can't always expect a nice answer."

Gabriel leaned with her elbows on the table. "Tanner, you spoke of believing in heaven earlier."

"Yes."

"But then you also spoke of the devil and his doings? Why?"

Tanner stood from the table. "Because now I also believe in hell."

# CHAPTER 19

While Alfred slept in Ellsworth's chair and Gabriel and Raphael went to check on the prisoners in the jailhouse, Ellsworth and Tanner headed up the hillside together to confront Eddington and bring home Linda May and Anna Belle.

It was slow going up the hillside, one man with a fake leg and the other stooped and depleted from having gone into the woods too many times.

"Sorry about that leg comment," said Tanner. "It was one of them thoughts that got through."

Ellsworth waved it away. "You simply stated a fact. You have two legs, and I don't."

Tanner stared off toward the woods behind the yellow house. "I still have the urge. It's strong." They walked for another ten yards. "You actually have one and a half legs. It's the foot you're missing. And the knee."

"Close your head for a bit. Can you do that?"

"I can."

"Next thing you know you'll be walking backwards again."

Two men in pinstriped suits stood stone still on either side of the steps leading to the white sunporch. The man on the right had a flat nose and full lips. He pulled a pistol from his coat. The other guard did the same.

Ellsworth had never seen either man before, so he held up his palms. "Just need to bump gums with your boss."

"G'v'm gun," mumbled the flat-nosed guard.

"What'd he say?" Ellsworth asked the other guard.

"Said give him your gun."

Ellsworth removed the Smith & Wesson from his holster. Flat Nose handed it to his partner and patted Ellsworth down, then nodded his boxy head for them to proceed up the porch steps.

"You heeled, old man?" asked the other guard.

Tanner paused, then slowly opened his coat and came out with his hand pointed like a gun, index finger as the barrel and the thumb as the hammer. "Bang." Flat Nose grunted, then decided to give the old man a quick pat down. Tanner said, "Careful, Frankenstein."

Flat Nose nudged him along toward the steps.

"You trying to get us killed?" said Ellsworth.

Tanner smirked. "Why does a maker of chess sets need armed guards?"

Ellsworth didn't know, but before he could knock on the front door it opened.

"Gentlemen, welcome." Lou Eddington stood tall in a white suit and shiny black shoes with spats. His neck was still bloated, and his cheeks were rosy. "Please come in."

Ellsworth said, "No need. We're just here to see Anna Belle and Linda May back home."

Eddington laughed—a broad smile, teeth too white. "They're welcome to leave whenever they want. I hold no hostages here."

"Then why the two boobs out front?"

"Can never be too careful. Not in these times. Were you not

just stabbed recently at your own home?" He gave Tanner the hinky eye. "By the very man now standing beside you?"

"We made amends," said Tanner. "Where are the ladies?"

Eddington stepped aside, opened the door wider. Linda May was asleep on a plush couch in the middle of the room, dressed in stockings and a garter and red undergarments, her head resting on the crook of her elbow.

Ellsworth hurried to the couch and shook her gently, then more violently when she didn't wake. "Linda May."

Her eyelids fluttered. "Ellsworth?"

"You're drugged, Linda May. What did he do to you? Where's Anna Belle?" He looked over his shoulder at Eddington. "What did you do to her?"

"We danced all night, Mr. Newberry. She's exhausted."

The room was dimly lit by wall sconces. Red drapes covered the windows. The floors and furniture were polished to a museum-like sheen. More couches were scattered about the room in no particular arrangement, each occupied by a man or woman who was fully clothed but either drugged or asleep. Ellsworth recognized most of them. Miss Ribidoe from the bowling alley. Nancy Tankersly from Father Timothy's choir. Berny the mail carrier. Brenda Baker from the food market stood with her back against the far wall, holding a rifle and smoking a butt. Janie Janks, Berny's assistant at the post office, leaned against the stone hearth with a bolt-action British machine gun. Four men in top hats and suits stood in the shadowed corners, all heeled with rifles. Another suited man faced the wall, marching in place, knees kicking high. Three half-clothed women lay pell-mell atop a square plush floor carpet, all passed out or asleep.

"Opium," said Tanner, sniffing.

Ellsworth stepped toward Eddington and gripped the lapels of his jacket. "Where is she?"

Eddington grinned.

"She done did the dance, Ellsworth," said Janie Janks from her place against the fireplace.

"Where is she?" Ellsworth screamed into Eddington's face.

Eddington brushed his mustache and motioned toward the middle of the room, where a small rounded table held a chess set. "Let's sit for a moment and work out our differences over a game of strategy." He put his arm around Ellsworth's shoulders, and for four steps Ellsworth went with him willingly—no, not willingly, but obediently. Eddington had that seductive charm, and Ellsworth quivered at how easily he'd done his bidding.

Ellsworth broke away from Eddington's embrace and eyed the chess set. The pieces were not historical. They weren't from any famous battle he'd ever seen. They were expertly carved, as usual, but they looked like regular people, the women in dresses and skirts and blouses, the men in suits and top hats, overalls, trousers, and button-downs.

Ellsworth bent down and overturned the board, scattering the pieces across the floor.

Lou remained calm. "You've no idea what you've just done."

Ellsworth turned, gripped the strange man's throat, and squeezed. "Tell me where she is. Or so help me, I'll put you down."

Every conscious man and woman in the room cocked their guns and aimed at Ellsworth. Even the man marching the wall turned around with his barrel poised.

Tanner hunkered down, covered his ears, awaited the flurry of bullets.

Eddington gave no hint of pain or discomfort from Ellsworth's grip. Eying the chess pieces on the floor, he raised his right hand high, a gesture that immediately eased the tension. The firearms lowered. Lou kept his eyes on the chess pieces but spoke evenly to Ellsworth. "Sometimes they slip through. Sometimes the flies tap so hard against the glass, it makes me want to jump with glee."

Ellsworth's grip tightened on the man's throat and then eased. "Slip through what?"

"The cracks, Ellsworth. Sometimes they slip through."

"Who? What are you talking about? Where is Anna Belle?"

"I'm right here."

Ellsworth let go of Eddington's neck and spun toward Anna Belle's voice. She stood three feet away, barefoot, in a wrinkled blue-and-white polka-dot dress he'd seen her in days ago. Her eyes were distant and glossy, her hair disheveled, her face pale. But most unnerving was the pistol she held in her right hand.

Ellsworth stepped forward, reached out for her, but she slapped his hand away.

"Don't touch me."

"Anna Belle?"

"I know what you did."

"What? Anna Belle, put the gun down."

"I want to hear it from you, Ellsworth."

"Hear what?"

"You know what." Eddington straightened his lapels. "The reason you put the gun in your mouth and nearly pulled the trigger."

"How do you know that?"

"America Ma sees all."

Anna Belle pounded Ellsworth's chest with a closed fist and screamed, "I want to hear it from you! Don't lie to me!"

Ellsworth clenched his jaw, blinked his lashes like bird wings, and then said what he had one day hoped to confess, but not like this. He grabbed Anna Belle's flailing hands and secured her wrists tight so she couldn't hit him anymore. Her pistol dropped to the floor, and he kicked it away. All the rifles and guns around the room were on him again.

He looked Anna Belle in the eyes. Somewhere behind those distorted pupils was the woman he knew and not the one she'd suddenly become.

Maybe the truth would bring her back.

"I shot Calvin, Anna Belle." He gulped, filled his chest with a deep breath, not surprised with how quickly the tears filled his eyes. "At Cantigny. There was fog. It was an accident, but I shot him. And he died in my arms."

# CHAPTER 20

Ellsworth limped down the hillside, his right cheek stinging from Anna Belle's open palm.

He'd seen the hint of forgiveness in her eyes and thought maybe she'd return with him now that the truth was out. But instead she'd slapped him twice in quick succession and insisted he leave. *That* sting had been worse than the slaps. On their way out, Ellsworth had called across the room toward Linda May, told her Alfred was worried about her and wanted her to come back home. *"Alfred?"* She'd acted like she didn't know who Alfred was.

"Slow down." Tanner struggled to keep up on the grassy decline. "You're gonna fall."

Ellsworth didn't slow. If anything he gained momentum down the hill, getting more used to the prosthesis and the odd, clunky cadence. *Anna Belle with a gun?* She was the last person he'd ever thought he'd see with a weapon—the last person next to Eliza.

*Eliza.* He could get to her now. Hear her voice. Feel her breath on his neck. All he needed to do was go into the woods, open that door, and kneel on the floor. If ever he had needed to hear her voice, it was now.

*"Fool's gold,"* Gabriel had warned him. She was right. The voices weren't what they seemed.

Even so, Ellsworth veered off toward the woods.

Tanner clutched his elbow and straightened his path back toward the avenue of oaks, where a line of six cars—five puttering Model Ts and a Morgan Runabout—spit dust on their way into town. The lead car stopped at the bottom of the hill, and the rest of the cars halted. Doors opened and closed. The new arrivals—men and women, husbands and wives, a few children—stood with suitcases, staring up toward the yellow house.

"They can't park there," said Tanner.

"That's what you're worried about?"

In the distance, more cars arrived in a cloud of dust down the avenue of oaks.

*Players on a chess set. Two sides facing off.*

"Ellsworth, did you hear what I just said? Did you see the wooden crates against the wall? Inside the house back there, next to the fireplace?"

"No, no . . ."

"They were filled with guns. All of them. Pistols, rifles, parts that could have been disassembled machine guns. Hundreds of guns."

Ellsworth's pace quickened. He hadn't noticed the crates or the guns. He'd been too preoccupied by the chess pieces he'd scattered across the floor. "I saw you in there, Tanner."

"What are you talking about?"

"On the floor. One of the chess pieces. It was you."

Tanner went silent until the bottom of the hill. "What do you think it means?"

"You were a pawn, Tanner. A piece moved across a checkered board."

Tanner chuckled.

"What could you possibly find amusing?"

"You called me a pawn, Ellsworth."

216

"So?"

"It's just that as a kid, I always dreamed of being a knight."

They turned toward the town hall and jailhouse. A family of four from Bellhaven First Baptist passed them, carrying suitcases and hurrying toward the hillside and Eddington's house. Suzie Cohen, a regular at Rabbi Blumenthal's synagogue, jogged toward the hillside, avoiding eye contact but rambling about the evil congregants at Bellhaven Lutheran.

"Miss Cohen?" Ellsworth called out.

She didn't look his way.

More people from Bellhaven followed with suitcases, bindles, blankets, and bedrolls. Among them, and pointing the way as a leader of sorts, was Mayor Bellhaven, who walked with the Bible held out before him like one would carry a cross into church. He glared at Ellsworth as he passed and then spat at his feet.

Ellsworth stepped away even though the wad fell yards short of the target.

They walked in silence for a minute as more people passed and then noticed smoke in the distance, coiling around the white steeple of Bellhaven Methodist. Ellsworth got as close as he could to running, ignoring the pain around his stump, the jolt in his hip every time the prosthesis touched the ground.

A man stood outside the Methodist church with a lit torch.

Tanner said, "It's one of those new Latter-day Saints."

A crowd had formed around the torchbearer, hands in the air, chanting. Another man shattered a window with a brick, and the woman beside him hurled a lit torch through the hole in the glass.

Ellsworth fired his gun in the air.

The Saint faced them, then dropped to his knees in prayer.

Ellsworth and Tanner turned toward the jailhouse and saw Rabbi Blumenthal hunkered in the shadows. At first he appeared to be tying his shoes, but there was something bulky at his feet. He lit something and hurried away from the jailhouse toward the woods. Ten seconds later a bomb exploded. Dust and bricks flew from the back of the jailhouse and bounced like dice across the parking lot.

The blast knocked Ellsworth and Tanner to the ground. They sat up to find there was a gaping hole in the back of the jailhouse. The prisoners, dust-covered but alive, hurried out into the brick-speckled sunlight. The rabbi had set them loose.

Reverend Cane shielded his eyes as he stumbled through the rubble, looking around in confusion. John Stone, who'd blown up his neighbor's shed and the hundreds of birdhouses inside it, walked out behind him, then headed straight toward the woods. Ned Gleeson limped across the town hall lot, dragging an injured right leg but still in a hurry to get to the yellow house on the hill. Reverend Hofhamm emerged, coughing, and then dropped to his knees.

Gabriel hurried from the main doors, carrying Raphael in her arms. She placed him on the ground, and the boy rolled onto his side, choking and spitting in the grass. Gabriel looked up, her face smeared by brick dust, then scrambled to help others from the building.

Omar stumbled out next from the back. He straightened his mask, the glasses still attached to it, and seemed to be looking around for something. "Omar," Ellsworth called from the ground, but his friend didn't hear.

Gabriel emerged again from the smoking building with Miss Dead Cricket Pie, Beverly Adams, and walked her toward the town hall to rest on the rubble. Reverend Beaver passed her as he stumbled away from the jailhouse next, squinting against the sunlight. Then he noticed his church burning and broke into a run. The Latter-day Saint stood from his kneeling position in front of the burning church and ran toward Beaver. The two men crashed and rolled in a flurry of punches and eye-gouging.

Ellsworth was on his feet now, turning in a slow circle of agitated gravel and brick dust and screams. He found his gaze drawn to the house on the hill, where Lou Eddington stood silently watching.

*Did I cause all this by overturning that chess set?*

Three houses down, Dooby Klinsmatter had a shovel in his hands. Cletus Merryweather held a rake. The two men battled in Dooby's front yard as if the garden tools were swords.

Father Timothy stepped from the jailhouse, hacking and coughing, so he didn't see Reverend Cane coming at him. Didn't see Cane's bent knee and loaded weight, and had no way to brace himself against the kick to the face that splattered blood from Father Timothy's nose.

Father Timothy rolled upright and kicked Reverend Cane in the groin, doubling him over.

Omar grabbed Father Timothy by the clerical collar. He nudged him aside and then kept Reverend Cane at an arm's distance so the preacher and priest wouldn't kill each other.

Raphael moved toward Reverend Hofhamm, who was coughing so hard his eyes bulged. He placed his hands on Hofhamm's chest, and the man calmed. Moses Yarney, who, seconds before had been threatening to strangle the German preacher, stood still as he watched the little boy's hands on Hofhamm's chest. He whispered something about a miracle, about Moses parting the Red Sea, and then he dropped to his knees and begged Hofhamm's forgiveness for destroying his pipe organ with the ball-peen hammer.

Down the street, Gabriel ripped both the shovel and rake from Klinsmatter's and Merryweather's hands. After defusing that scuffle, she headed next to where the Latter-day Saint leader was still engaged in fisticuffs with Reverend Beaver in the middle of the road. In the background, neighbors and members of First Methodist Church filled buckets from the nearby hydrant and futilely tossed them at the burning church, while some of the Saints and a handful of Moses Yarney's AME church did their best to stop them. Some of them kept chanting "Let it burn."

The lone Bellhaven fire truck approached from the opposite direction, siren churning. Someone had had the sense to signal the box. The truck stopped, and Max Lehane pulled a long hose from the back of it. He stood for a minute watching the blaze, before finally hooking the hose to the hydrant. But instead of aiming the water at the burning church, Max, a devout Baptist, sprayed the Saints and the Methodists and the African Episcopals, one after the next, until he'd knocked every last one of them to the ground. Only then did he aim the water toward the fire.

Old Man Tanner brushed dust from his shirt, stared toward the hole in the back of the jailhouse and counted. "Not everyone escaped."

"He's still in there," said Ellsworth. "The man with the neck tattoo."

Tanner looked up. The hair on his arm stood on end. "Brace yourself."

Ellsworth took a step toward the hole in the jailhouse wall, and the earth moved under his feet. A three-second bowling-ball rumble, and then the quake was over, but it was long enough to stun everyone back to rationality. The fighting stopped. All eyes were on the ground. Hundreds of birds circled above the woods, squawking.

"The first foreshock." Tanner nodded toward the jailhouse. "After you, sheriff."

Ellsworth navigated the brick rubble and ducked into the opening Rabbi Blumenthal had blown in the jailhouse. The floor was covered with plaster and brick dust. The second and third cells had clear openings from the blast, but the first cell did not. Even so, someone had found the keys on the desk and opened it, which was how Father Timothy had gotten out. But the man with the neck tattoo was still there.

He sat on a chair in the cell, looking at the floor as if contemplating something. He gave off the faintest glow, that thin sliver of red contouring his body.

"You see it?" Ellsworth asked Tanner.

"See what?"

"His color."

"I don't know what you're talking about, son."

*He can't see it. Only a few can.*

"It's red."

"What's red?"

The man with the neck tattoo finally looked up from his seat inside the cell, his face smeared by sweat and dust. Yesterday Ellsworth had nearly killed him, and part of him still wanted to. Wanted him dead for having anything to do with Eliza's death.

The man said, "I saw it that night. You're blue."

Ellsworth nodded. "So I've heard."

Tanner watched both men. "What's going on here?"

The tattooed man said to Ellsworth, "Michael."

Tanner stepped closer, right off Ellsworth's shoulder. "What's he talking about?"

"Michael is my first name." The front door of the jailhouse opened, and in with the sunlight walked Gabriel and Raphael, their colors as clear to Ellsworth now as the white plaster dust on the floor. "Green and Copper."

Ellsworth looked back toward the tattooed man. "So what's your real name, red?"

"Been called Tony-Too-Tall ever since I was six," said the tattooed man. "But my parents claimed to hear a voice when I was born. Said to name me Uriel. So they did."

# CHAPTER 21

The town grew quiet after nightfall.

The three-second quake had subdued the afternoon tensions, and most of the town returned home to clean up broken dishes shaken from cabinets.

Alfred, Tanner, Raphael, Gabriel, and the new arrival Uriel gathered in Ellsworth's kitchen. Not long afterward, Father Timothy arrived with Reverend Cane. The two men weren't cordial, but they had set their differences aside and come with their arms full—Father Timothy with a heavy, cloth-covered basket and Reverend Cane with a plate of pastries leftover from a weekday prayer service. Minutes later Rabbi Blumenthal knocked on the door with a basket of corn bread.

Ellsworth brought in extra chairs and they ate around the kitchen table. He missed Anna Belle, and he'd be willing to fight for her, but she was there of her own free will, after all. He'd need to come up with a better plan to lure her from Eddington's influence.

Not much was said as they ate, although they from time to time stared at each other surreptitiously, like they were all adding two and two together but were afraid to admit they'd all come up with five.

"What kind of a name is Tony-Too-Tall?" asked Ellsworth with a bit of venom. "You're not that tall."

"I was when I was a kid." Uriel spoke like he'd been itching to. Chewed with his mouth full and clinked the spoon against his teeth with every bite. "I was always the tallest in my class. Shot up young, then stopped around thirteen, when all the rest of the boys were getting going. But before that, they always used to say, Tony, you're too tall for this, too tall for that." He shrugged. "Tony-Too-Tall."

Ellsworth stared at him like he was a dumb bug who didn't know better than to walk across his kitchen floor in broad daylight. "I get that. I mean the Tony part. Where'd Tony come from?"

"My mother let me change it when I was six because who would ever name their kid Uriel? You know? So why'd you change *your* name?"

"I didn't."

Tony nodded, waited for an elaboration, but when none came he went back to eating. He clinked the spoon against his teeth again, and Ellsworth banged his fist on the table.

Everyone jumped. Tanner spilled a dollop of stew on his shirt. Ellsworth glared at Uriel and said, "Why were you with the Klan that night?" He glanced at Raphael. "What did you want with Raphael? How was my wife involved?" He leaned with his elbows on the table. "And why are you here again?"

Uriel took another bite before answering, careful not to click the spoon on his teeth this time. "I think why I'm here now is obvious."

"Is it?"

He surveyed the room, then settled on Ellsworth. "What has the boy told you?"

"He doesn't remember much. Just that he was secretly carted up here during the night."

Uriel pushed his bowl aside and folded his hands atop the table. "I was born in Bellhaven, back before the turn of the century."

"I don't remember you."

Gabriel said, "Let'm talk, Ellsworth."

"If you're going to understand what brought me here with the Klan that night and why I've returned, I'll need to start from the beginning."

"Then start."

"Okay then. I was born three months early. Doctor told my parents I wouldn't live to see past my first year. Mother prayed the rosary at my crib every night, while Father buried himself in a bottle. If I may?" Uriel unbuttoned his shirt low enough to reveal a birthmark on the left side of his abdomen. It was about two inches tall and fuzzy along the edges, but the shape was clear. "What does this look like?"

"It's a cross."

Uriel buttoned his shirt. "My mother was very religious, and she believed I was touched by God. The early delivery. The birthmark. The fact that I slept all night from day one, even as wind from the woods thrashed at the window above my crib. She was convinced it was spirits and demons trying to get at me. When I was four months old she walked past the yellow trees with a rosary, felt as long as she kept going she'd make it. But then she stopped. The longer she stood still, the slower her breathing became. She heard voices but somehow broke free from them. Then, as she hurried back through the woods, she felt pain in her hands. The rosary had burnt scars where it was wrapped around her fingers and across her palms. She had gray in her hair where before it was brown."

"So you moved from Bellhaven?"

"The next day," he said. "My parents argued, but Mother

insisted we go. She was convinced there was something in the woods trying to kill her child."

"Where did you go?" asked Gabriel, suddenly more curious than the rest of them. She sat on the edge of her chair, looking like she had something to tell and was learning from the new arrival just how to do it.

"San Francisco." Uriel looked around the table. "Mother wanted to get as far away as possible, so we didn't stop until we hit the West Coast." His eyes settled on Tanner. "I was seven going on eight when the great earthquake hit the Bay Area."

Tanner leaned forward, alert. "The one in 1906. Yes, I arrived in the aftermath, felt the aftershocks. It's the only time I ever left Bellhaven since the quake here in '86."

"How long did you stay?" asked Uriel.

"Not long," Tanner said with guilt. "Two days. I'd long past become addicted to the chapel by that point. I had to hear my wife's voice again."

Uriel went on. "There was a strong foreshock twenty seconds before the main quake. My father was a firefighter. He was on his way to check on me and Mother when the main quake hit. Rumbled like a train for forty-two seconds. I counted every one of them, hunkered in the doorway between our bedroom and the kitchen. Our chimney collapsed on my father, killed him. Mother was distraught. I took her hand and guided her from the house."

"At seven," said Gabriel. "The son protecting the mother."

Uriel nodded. "It leveled the city, but the worst was still to come."

"The fires," said Tanner, with eyes that relived it. "The entire city burned."

"Four days they burned," said Uriel. "Four hundred and ninety city blocks destroyed by flames. Gas pipes broken underground. Downed electric lines. One fire broke out on Hayes Street. A mother was cooking breakfast for her family and accidently burned the house down."

"The ham and eggs fire," said Tanner.

"That's what it became known as, yes," said Uriel. "Mother cried every night, prayed for her Uriel to give her strength. And I did. I wasn't scared. But the memories are etched in my mind. The fires and all the destruction—it changed people."

Tanner looked at Ellsworth. "They picked sides."

"How so?"

"Hundreds of thousands were left homeless," said Uriel, taking back over. "Refugees evacuated across the bay to Oakland and Berkeley. People camped at Golden Gate Park, the Presidio, and the Panhandle. All along the beaches too. Many were homeless for two years after. And people did help. Many people risked their lives to help others. There were superhuman acts of strength in rescuing others from debris."

He looked at Tanner. "But he's right. They did pick. There was humanity aplenty but also terrible riots and violence. I saw men and women beaten for no reason. A lot of looting, even by the soldiers brought in to protect us. People wandered with crazed eyes—good people gone off the tracks. There were fights in the streets over food and water and shelter. Some people shot looters on sight or set fires with intent to harm. I saw violence no seven-year-old should have to see. And once I did, for years I couldn't unsee it."

Uriel rubbed his face, exhaled. "Even at that age, I played my part in the cleanup efforts. I couldn't lift anything heavy, but I had ideas no child my age should have. Engineering ideas on how best to remove the debris, how to clean the streets, how to keep the crowded parks and beaches in order and handle garbage disposal. That sort of thing. I was ignored initially, of course, but then the men started to listen. Some of my ideas really helped."

Uriel took a drink, raked fingers through his hair. "One night I was tired and crying from having seen too much. I'd been having nightmares about it all. My mother rubbed my back and told me what she knew about Uriel the archangel—the angel of the earth. That he was one of the wisest archangels, an expert in problem solving and spiritual understanding, weather and changes in the earth."

Father Timothy said, "The archangel who helps with floods and fires, hurricanes and earthquakes and natural disasters."

"Yes, Father. But I told her to stop. I didn't want to hear any more, didn't want everyone in town looking at me like I was different. I wanted to be a regular boy with a regular name. My mother asked me what name I would like to be called, and I said Tony. My father's name was Anthony. At the fire station they'd called him Tony."

Ellsworth rubbed his face and blew wearily into his hands. He bit into a piece of corn bread and chewed. "It's good," he said to Rabbi Blumenthal. "The corn bread."

"My mother's recipe." The rabbi spoke solemnly, not like a man who had blown up the back of the jailhouse earlier that day. He nibbled on his fingernails, twirled the hairs of his beard, and repeatedly glanced out the kitchen window toward the woods. The chapel was calling him.

Reverend Cane was restless too. And Tanner looked uneasy, but he tended to get more fidgety at nighttime anyway. Alfred bobbed in his chair. He hadn't touched his food.

"I was born with a caul." Gabriel waited for their eyes to turn toward her. "It's rare. A membrane covers the baby's head and face, except mine covered my entire body like a cocoon. The midwife had a difficult time removing it, but from what I was told, I busted through. My mother said I was aware, even then. I had enough control of my arms to do it."

Tanner said, "I remember when you were born."

"Biggest baby the midwife had ever seen." Gabriel chuckled. "Nearly killed my poor mother. Word traveled fast about my size, but not about the caul. My mother had made the midwife promise not to tell about it. Some see the caul as good luck, a sign of future greatness, but not everybody. She named me Gabriel because of a voice she heard in a dream. 'God is my strength,' the voice said."

Father Timothy had gone pale. "Gabriel is the only archangel sometimes depicted as female in art and literature." He removed the white cloth from the basket he'd brought with him, revealing ten bottles of red wine. "We'll need an opener, Ellsworth. And glasses."

"Second drawer on the left. Glasses are in the cabinet. Where'd you get all that?"

"Prohibition loopholes." Father Timothy rooted through the drawer. "Sacramental wine. I suppose now is as good a time as ever to admit that I manipulate the numbers in our congregation in order to get more of it. I can't do without my wine, so I've been stockpiling. Consider this my donation to . . . whatever it is we're doing here tonight. Free of charge."

Reverend Cane said, "You imply that you typically sell it?"

"Of course I sell it," said Father Timothy. "What are they calling it? Bootlegging? The money all goes back to the church, I assure you." While he removed glasses from the cabinet, he looked over his shoulder at Reverend Cane. "Judge not, that ye be not judged." And "He who is without sin among you—"

"—let him first cast a stone," continued Reverend Cane. "I know how it goes."

"Then either cast more stones or help me with these glasses."

Reverend Cane pushed his chair from the table to lend a hand. "I don't drink."

"Well, tonight you do." Father Timothy popped the cork and

poured Reverend Cane the first glass of red wine. "It seems the end of days is right outside our door. No better time to start drinking than now." Father Timothy poured himself a full glass and downed a third of it in one tilt of his head. He refilled and then poured wine for the rest of them.

Reverend Cane sipped his.

"Good?" Father Timothy asked.

Cane took another drink, his teeth already stained red. "I've been to burlesque shows." Gabriel coughed on her wine. All eyes in the room focused on Reverend Cane, who continued with his loose tongue. "The kind where the ladies are scantily clad and they dance on the stage to music. I go into Charleston, to a little place called Delly's. In disguise, of course, so no one can place me."

Father Timothy smirked. "You don't say?"

"I do, and I pray for forgiveness daily."

"Are you coming to me for confession, Ephraim?"

Reverend Cane took a full gulp of wine.

Father Timothy said, "Well, in that case I absolve you from your sins. Don't go to Delly's anymore."

"I've been to Delly's," said Alfred, looking down at the table. "But don't tell Linda May. It was before we got married."

Ellsworth said, "Am I the only one who hasn't been to Delly's?"

Rabbi Blumenthal said, "I've never been to Delly's."

Father Timothy sat back down. "I absolve everyone who has entered Delly's. Now can we get back to Bellhaven? 'God is my strength,' the voice said. Gabriel, please continue."

Gabriel gulped wine like it was water and refilled it from the second bottle Ellsworth had just uncorked. "What my mother called a blessing, I viewed as a curse—my strength and courage and, well, my size. I was walking at five months, carrying pails of water from the well at two years. Even as a child, I had the strength of a man.

And I was larger than any of the other children—certainly the girls. That was enough to earn me ridicule in the schoolyard. I always felt confused. Uncomfortable in my skin." Her eyes teared. "The giant with the strength of an ox but with the brain of a mule."

Ellsworth reached across the table and squeezed Gabriel's hand, gave her a look that said, "You're one of the smartest people I know." He then turned his focus back to Uriel. "You never finished your story."

Uriel poured more wine. "Like her, I was uncomfortable with who I was, and what I saw after the earthquake was always on my mind. And to make things worse, my mother died of a weak heart when I was only nine. I lived in an orphanage until I was sixteen but never really belonged. I kept to myself, and the other kids teased me—and worse. They hit me, pinched my skin, put cigarettes out on my back. So I ran away. Stole every bit of money I could find inside the orphanage, hopped a train, and headed east."

"Why east?" Ellsworth asked.

Uriel shrugged. "Because west would have put me in the ocean. I wanted to get as far away as I could. Each state where the train stopped was going to be my home, but after only a few days I'd feel the pull to keep going. I hopped one train after another until ultimately I ended up in Savannah." Uriel glanced at Ellsworth. "What is it?"

"Nothing. Just something similar to what my wife would say. She felt a pull to come here. A pull towards . . . a pull towards me." Ellsworth poured more wine, thought of the train wreck. He filled Rabbi Blumenthal's glass again and told Uriel to go on.

Uriel said, "I got into more fights than I could count. Made a friend named Shakes, who gave me a book called *The Clansman.* Read *The Leopard's Spots,* too, and was taken in by it all. Then me and Shakes, we went to see that film, *Birth of a Nation,* about the original Ku Klux Klan. It was like a light went on in my brain. I'd finally found some channel for my hate. I was there on top of Stone Mountain in 1915 when William Joseph Simmons roused up the Klan again. Me and Shakes were recruited by a local Kleagle—that's what they called the Klan organizers."

"They?" asked Father Timothy. "You're no longer a member?"

"No, Father, of course not. I left them the night after what happened here in Bellhaven, I promise. I saw the sins of my ways, and I hope for forgiveness."

Father Timothy watched Uriel suspiciously. The new Klan was violently anti-Catholic.

"I was misguided," said Uriel. "But I thought I'd found a home. I was convinced the Klan was the reason I'd been pulled across the country—to help guard the nation against the sins that were causing it to crumble. The Jews, the Catholics, the foreigners coming across on boats by the thousands. Divorce and adultery. The blacks. We preached 100 percent Americanism. Nativism. I went and got this bald eagle tattoo on my neck to show how committed I was."

He eyed everyone. "I apologize to you all. My thoughts have changed since then. Anyway, I paid my initiation fees, and they handed me a white costume and Bible. I didn't have a religion so to speak, but I became a Methodist. And I have to admit, I never felt so comfortable as when I was able to hide my true self behind a hood. I wasn't different anymore, you see? With the white hood and cloak, I looked like all the other Klansmen. We all had the same thoughts and ideas."

Uriel laughed as he sipped more wine. "And now the Klan is violently enforcing Prohibition—busting up speaks and stills all across the South. Believe you me, I wouldn't be sitting here drinking with a Catholic priest, a black boy, and a rabbi if I was still in the Klan." He smiled, then his laughter died. He swirled red wine around his glass. "A couple years in, one of our Kleagles got word that a plantation owner near Macon had an incident with a black boy—a Catholic black boy to boot, which was about as rare a find as a four-leaf clover in a desert. Shakes said we couldn't get luckier than finding Catholic blacks." He looked at Raphael with apologetic eyes. "So thirty of us packed our belongings and headed to Macon, but by the time we arrived at the plantation, the boy here had already been sneaked out during the night."

Ellsworth said, "It's Raphael."

"What?"

"You called him the boy. His name is Raphael."

Ellsworth and Raphael shared a glance. "Is any of this coming back to you yet? Eliza sneaking you out here? How did she know?"

"I don't know," Raphael said. "We never seen her before."

"She just showed up?"

"And said she'd been watching over me."

Reverend Cane leaned in, his elbows on the table. "Why?"

Raphael didn't answer, so Ellsworth did. "After I was stabbed, you all rushed me into the woods. To the chapel. Perhaps that initially saved my life; perhaps it didn't. But it wasn't the reason for my rapid recovery. At night, at my bedside . . ."

Raphael shook his head. "No, Mr. Newberry. Don't."

"I need to tell it." Ellsworth nodded toward Raphael. "He put his hands on me, directly on my wound. Did it several nights in a row when he thought I was asleep. I know that's how come I healed so rapidly. Raphael, does this have something to do with the incident at that plantation?" Raphael nodded. "You remember everything don't you?" Raphael nodded again. Ellsworth said, "You claimed not to because it frightened you."

"Yes, Mr. Newberry. I'm sorry."

"It's okay, son. But now it's time to talk."

Raphael wiped his eyes, the green so brilliant it sparkled under the kitchen light. "When we were hiding in the town-hall basement, my mother told me a story. She lost a lot of blood when I was born. Her heart nearly stopped. Then the midwife placed me against her chest, folded her arms around my body. And her heart started beating again."

He looked around the table for reactions. "My father just thought his prayers had come through. They had me baptized a week later. When I was three, I found a bird on the ground with a wounded wing. I cupped it in my hands, and a minute later the bird took off flying. My uncle, my mother's brother, had fallen into using cocaine. My father tied him up in a barn so he couldn't partake. He screamed out like the devil had took him. My father told me to sit with him, and I did. I held his hand, and my uncle relaxed. I stayed with him until he stopped, and the demons soon left him."

Father Timothy leaned back in his chair, motioned the sign of the cross over his forehead, chest, and shoulders. "*Raphael*—the name refers to the healing power of God. God heals. In Christianity, Judaism, and Mohammadism, Raphael is the archangel who works to heal people's minds, spirits, and bodies."

He sighed into his hands, looked at Reverend Cane, then Rabbi Blumenthal. "I assume you have noticed the artwork in that chapel? The mosaic on the floor? It's a replica of the Rembrandt painting, *The Archangel Raphael Taking Leave of the Tobit Family*. The statue depicted there, the one holding a staff and standing on a fish? That's Raphael. One of the stained-glass windows shows Raphael healing a blind man. In the other he's driving a demon from a woman I assume to be Sarah—the demon Asmodeus. Part of the mural has Raphael stirring the water at the healing pool of Bethesda. That chapel is like a monument for Raphael."

*The healing floor.*

Rabbi Blumenthal said, "His presence is supposedly like a burst of fresh air."

"Which is exactly what you feel upon entering that place." Ellsworth stared at Father Timothy. "Is Raphael associated with a certain color?"

"Ever since I went into that chapel I've been studying the artwork in it. The frescoes and reliefs are apocalyptic, the walls bordered by depictions of all the archangels and devils. And yes, Raphael is associated with a certain color. All the archangels are. Raphael's is green. Look at this boy's eyes."

"Uriel?"

"Red."

"Gabriel?"

"White . . . coppery light."

"And Michael?"

"Bright blue." Father Timothy poured more wine, gulped it down, and then poured more. "I won't pretend to ignore why you're asking, either."

Ellsworth looked to Raphael, who sat stoically but on the verge of tears. "Please continue. You helped heal your uncle. But what about the incident on the plantation?"

"Mr. Redfield was the plantation owner, and my momma and papa worked for him. He was a decent man until he started drinking, but that was just about every night. Mr. Redfield had a daughter my age, Patrice, and we were secret friends." He looked up. "Secret because her parents wouldn't have approved, you understand.

"There was a creek next to the plantation where she was warned not to go because the water was sometimes swift. We liked to sneak off to that creek, sit on a large rock overlooking the water, and skip pebbles. But one day she lost her balance and went into the water. I climbed down after her and knew she broke a rib.

"We sneaked in through the old slave entrance to the kitchen. She changed out of her wet clothes and into a nightgown, and I helped her into bed. It was getting dark outside. I knew I should get out of the house and back to my parents, but I couldn't leave her like that. I told her I thought I could take away her pain. She said I was sweet, but that she would manage. I told her I was serious. Without asking me to explain, she'd agreed to let me do what I could. She said she trusted me."

Tears welled up in Raphael's green eyes as he remembered what came next. "So I climbed atop the bed with her, put my hands on the left side of her chest, and felt warmth. She started crying. I asked if she was okay, and she said she was. Said the pain was already going away and then asked how I'd done it. Told her I didn't know exactly. That made us both laugh. But then—"

Ellsworth saw it coming. "Then someone found you."

Gabriel nodded. "Her father. He was pretty drunk. But when he walked in and saw me on the bed with Patrice, he went crazy. When he pulled a pistol, I rolled off the bed and hit the floor. He fired but missed. I ran at him and knocked him aside. He stumbled against Patrice's vanity table, and I escaped down the hall.

"I found my parents and told them what happened, and we knew we had to get away. We didn't even pack up, just ran off through the woods with Mr. Redfield and his buddies after us." Raphael bit his lip, gathered courage. "They shot my father in the back as we ran—just shot him dead right there—but Momma and I got away. Question was, where could we run? We didn't know what to do, so we just kept going. But then we heard a voice calling to us from behind a tree, a lady's voice telling us she had a wagon. We could hide under the tarp and she'd take us away from there."

He looked at Ellsworth, his green eyes tender. "Guess you know who that lady was."

Ellsworth wiped his eyes. "Eliza was young when her mother died. There was a flood, and she went in after a little girl who'd somehow fallen into the river. Saved the child's life, but then she got swept away in the high waters. Eliza saw the whole thing."

"What a terrible experience for a young girl." Father Timothy's voice was kind. Ellsworth could only nod.

"Eliza spent her entire life helping others like that. She insisted that's what she was born for, and she often spoke of that day when she watched her mother go. One night we were rocking on the porch, Eliza said something peculiar. She said that right before her mother jumped in the river, she called out that little girl's name. *Like she knew her, Ellsworth.*' That's what she said to me. *'Like she'd been watching over her like . . .'* Then she'd trailed away, you see, just like that. And when I asked Eliza what she was about to say, she locked up and didn't speak the rest of the night."

He looked at Raphael. "I'm only now beginning to piece things together. But how did she know about you?"

"I don't know, Mr. Newberry. She just said she'd been watching over me for years."

Uriel said, "Mr. Redfield called his Klan friends and gathered up some men to hunt the boy and his mother down. Shakes and me went with them. But I knew as soon as I got to Bellhaven that something was wrong. I saw the cardinal birds and told Shakes and the Kleagle that we were making a mistake. That we should turn around and go.

"I tried to stop the violence that occurred, I promise you all, but then things got out of hand. That day has haunted me ever since. But I understand why I'm here now. Why I was drawn here in the first place."

"Why we all were," said Gabriel.

Rabbi Blumenthal stood and pointed toward the other room.

"It's the same reason why people flock up the hillside and tent in the cotton field. Same reason why the town is choosing sides."

He grabbed his wine from the table, finished it, and then pointed the glass at Uriel. "The Archangel Uriel warned Noah of the great flood. Now you warn us of a looming battle. We're going to war, and you're the brains here. Gabriel is the strength, Raphael the healing." He pointed to Ellsworth. "And now the limping leader. The Archangel Michael, the first angel created by God. The source of protection and truth, strength and courage."

He stood and leaned on the table. "I assume you've known from birth as well, Ellsworth. So tell us why. Why do you no longer go by Michael?"

They looked to Ellsworth.

But before he couldn't answer, the earth started shaking again.

# CHAPTER 22

The house shook for five seconds.

Wine spilled across the table. Two glasses walked off the cabinet shelf and crashed against the icebox.

Ellsworth braced himself against the counter, surveyed the room. "Everyone okay?"

Rabbi Blumenthal emerged from under the table. Father Timothy and Reverend Cane wiped ceiling dust from their hands. Gabriel hunkered protectively over Raphael.

Tanner stood from the floor. "Another foreshock."

"How do you know it wasn't the main quake?"

"Same way my wife could tell when the cake was done."

Alfred's head perked to the sound of static. He felt his way toward the sound in the other room. Ellsworth followed.

Alfred's painting had fallen from the easel. Plaster dust had settled like snow flurries atop the piano. The center light fixture swayed from the ceiling. And the busted radio on the windowsill hissed and calmed.

A woman's voice burst through the static. ". . . they come up from the magma . . ."

"America Ma," Tanner whispered, and the room nodded in agreement.

Then Eddington's voice burst through. ". . . and what do I do when I'm done dancing? . . ."

Static.

Eddington's voice was replaced by a young woman's voice. An English accent. ". . . there's people out there in the woods, Harvey. Can you . . ."

A man's voice, English as well. ". . . I just don't see 'em . . ."

". . . here. Look closer . . ."

Static. Children's laughter.

". . . Father . . . help us, Father . . ."

Alfred said, "Turn it off."

The children's laughter grew louder.

A woman's voice. ". . . Get off those walls . . ."

"I said turn it off."

More static.

Another man's voice, Italian accent. ". . . I cast you out . . . I cast you out in the name of the Father and of the . . ."

Static.

America Ma. ". . . please . . . don't . . . we wasn't tryin' to 'scape, massa . . . We was fixin' to . . ."

A woman's voice. ". . . Alfred . . ."

Alfred went rigid. "Linda May?"

Alfred held the radio to his ear, turned the knob, but could only find static, ebbing and flowing, bursts of loud and soft.

Then finally a voice. America Ma again. ". . . massa don' understand what he seein'. And now they's slave blood on those walls, all over that floor to mask up the Injun blood 'fo' it . . . all under them tiles . . . killin' floor . . ."

Alfred shook the radio. "Where'd she go?" Louder, more panicked. "Where'd she go? Linda May! Where'd she go, Ellsworth? Why doesn't she come home? *Where'd she go!?*"

Ellsworth touched his arm. "It's not real, Alfred. Linda May is up there on that hill, in Eddington's house. It's not—"

"... they been comin' up since the Good Lord cast 'em down ..."

And then a static that seemed finite. Alfred held the radio at arm's length. Reverend Cane and Father Timothy were now in the room, along with Gabriel and Raphael. Tears streamed down Alfred's face. He sat in Ellsworth's chair and cradled the radio as if it were a baby.

Ellsworth put his hand on Alfred's shoulder.

"Go away." He listened to the static. "Leave me be."

"Better check on what's going on outside," said Gabriel. "We've been in here awhile."

Ellsworth opened the front door to commotion up and down the street. Many town people had gathered in the twilight to discuss the second quake. Max Lehane's fire truck was parked in front of the jailhouse. The town ambulance had made it as far as the avenue of oaks, which was now gridlocked with cars as more people walked up the hillside toward the yellow house.

On the veranda, Ellsworth stepped into a cloud of vanilla-scented pipe smoke. Omar sat in one of the rockers with a shotgun across his lap, puffing through his mask slit. Six men from his Muslim congregation stood in the front yard with shotguns.

"We standin' guard, Sheriff."

"From what exactly?"

"Dem what's gathered." Omar's dark eyes flicked toward Eddington's house. Tents had been set up in the cotton field. Dozens of men walked the premises with torches, several wearing white cloaks and hoods.

"They're Klan."

Ellsworth turned to find Uriel behind him. "They back for Raphael?"

"I don't know."

"Keep an eye on him."

Uriel returned inside.

One of Omar's men had a book and pen out, writing.

"What's he doing?"

Omar exhaled thick smoke. "Ali recordin' all dis goin's-on."

A midnight-blue Model T puttered down the road, slowly navigating the thin opening under the avenue of oaks, and stopped in front of the town hall. The lot was full of haphazardly parked cars that must have arrived during their meeting in the kitchen.

A mustached man got out of the car with a hobo bindle over his shoulder.

Omar's men pointed their rifles.

The man stopped. "Don't shoot."

Omar stood from the rocker, gnawed on his pipe stem. "Why you here, palooka?"

"I don't know exactly."

"How dat yeller house make you feel drivin' pas'?"

"Made my skin crawl," said the man. "Can you aim that bean-shooter elsewhere?"

Omar lowered his rifle and nodded toward the town hall across the road, where candlelight flickered behind the broken windows. "Stay in der wit' da rest of dem. You on da right side."

"Thank you." The man hurried across the road and entered the town hall.

Shadows moved behind windows.

Ellsworth eyed the full parking lot. "Omar, how many people are inside that building?"

Omar removed the pipe and spat into the grass. "Two dozen, give or take. One dem come from far as Florida. Say he ready to fight."

Ellsworth removed his hat, wiped his brow. "Fight for what?"

Omar shrugged casually, then puffed on his pipe. "Dey be a hole in dem woods, Ellsworth. Dat quake in '86 make it worse. Dat where dem bad stuff, it come up t'rough. All da way up from da magma."

"How do you know this?" Tanner had been listening at the doorway.

Omar looked over his shoulder. "America Ma, she been tellin' me it."

"You know her?" asked Ellsworth.

"Great-great slave kin. Tol' me dem war was comin'. She tol' me in dat chapel."

"She say why it was built?"

He shrugged. "Dunno. She tell me she foun' it der, right der in dem woods. She an' dose fellow slaves try and fill up dem hole so no more bad stuff get t'rough. But massa found 'em, t'ink dey tryin' to 'scape. Den Massa Bellhaven turn it into da killin' floor."

"Omar?"

"Make it his own dem personal torture chamber. Fit with all dem kind of evil gadget what even da Missus Bellhaven know nothin' 'bout. Kep' torturin' slave kin for years."

"Omar, ask her more. Ask her when the chapel was built. How old is it?" Ellsworth stepped closer. "She mentioned Indian blood, Omar. Does it go back as far as the Indians?"

"Not goin' back in der to fin' out, Ellsworth. Dead not only dem what talk." He exhaled, sat in the smoke cloud. "Demons in dem woods—dat who we should be fighting. But no." He looked up the hill toward the Eddington house. "Everybody dem choose sides 'gainst other folk."

Father Timothy hurried out the door and down the porch steps.

"Father, where are you going?" asked Ellsworth.

"Where do you think I'm going?"

Father Timothy was drunk and heading into the woods for a quick fix. Reverend Cane and Rabbi Blumenthal emerged from the house next, following in Father Timothy's footsteps. The rabbi said, "You still owe us answers, Ellsworth. Just something we have to do first."

Gabriel stepped out beside Ellsworth. "Let'm go."

They weren't the only ones going into the woods for an evening visit. Dozens of people entered, including the new arrivals. They returned in awe, some crying, some talking about the peace they'd felt inside those walls, the dead loved ones to which they'd spoken.

"They're giving it strength," said Ellsworth. Gabriel looked at him. "The chapel. It's using us for fuel."

Gabriel agreed. "When I carried you out the other day, the clearing was larger. But not with beauty or color."

"Fool's gold," said Ellsworth. "I saw it too. On the fringes the trees were dying. Green leaves curling brown. Moss blackened like candlewicks."

"Like boll weevils munching through cotton."

"And we let it out."

"We didn't let it out," she said. "We've just been letting it in. Into us. And we—"

A scream sounded from the kitchen. They were through the door in a flash.

They ran past Alfred, who stood with the radio above his head as if fixing to smash it. "Static," he told them frantically as they rushed by. "Static and static!"

They stopped short in the kitchen. The backdoor gaped open. Anna Belle stood across the room with Raphael in her grasp and a sharp peeling knife at his throat. Her eyes were wild, red, with heavy bags underneath. She still wore the polka-dot dress she'd had on inside Eddington's house earlier in the day. Her hair was uncombed and jutting in bunches.

Uriel lay on the floor bleeding, a steak knife protruding from the middle of his back. Whatever Uriel was, he bled like the rest of them. His color was fading.

"It's a test." Anna Belle pressed the tip of the knife against Raphael's throat. "It's a test. He said it's a test. Bring the boy back, and I pass. It's a test. He said it's a test."

Ellsworth took a slow step into the kitchen, found Raphael's green eyes. *Relax now.* Raphael closed his eyes and did just that.

Anna Belle tightened her grip around Raphael's chest. Tears dripped from her eyes. "Why'd you do it, Ellsworth?"

"Let him go and we'll discuss."

"He told me to go down and bring back the boy. He said it's a test. A test. The men that came for him years ago are back. It's a test, Ellsworth. He put our pieces on the board."

"It's a test you're gonna fail, Anna Belle. Let's talk this through, me and you. Let's take that walk now."

"I think Calvin loved Eliza and you knew it. That's why you shot him. He loved your dead wife, and you shot him because of it. All the men in town looked at her special. He loved Eliza more than he loved me, Ellsworth."

"That's not true, Anna Belle."

"How do you know?"

"He told me. He loved you until that final breath. The chapel's putting thoughts in your head. The voices in there aren't real."

"You lie."

Uriel crawled like a wounded soldier toward Gabriel, who squatted to pull him closer.

"I can help him," said Raphael.

"Stop talking." Anna Belle squeezed Raphael. A spot of blood turned into a trickle on the boy's caramel-colored neck.

"You're cutting him, Anna Belle. Let him go, and we'll talk things through."

Tears came harder, and she choked on a sob. "The Klan's up there. Like that night." She shook her head. "I can't be there with them. I've had nightmares ever since they hung Sheriff Pomeroy from the tree. I still hear the screams, Ellsworth."

"Anna Belle, drop the knife. Come back home."

She tightened her hold on Raphael again. "I don't know who I am anymore. I cut Eliza's picture into pieces, but I tried to tape it back together. I tried. It's a test. It makes me feel good, Ellsworth. Makes me forget. I cook food to forget—not for you, but for me."

Gabriel took a step forward, so heavy the floorboards creaked.

"Tell that big ugly broad to stay back."

Ellsworth held out his hand, and Gabriel stopped against his forearm.

"Drop the knife, Anna Belle. I'll do anything. I'll go up there myself. Meet Mr. Eddington face-to-face again."

This gave her pause. "He'd like that." Her eyes flashed. "He used to go into the woods every night. For hours he'd stay in that chapel. But then he stopped. And do you know why?"

Ellsworth inched closer. *Keep her talking.* "Why, Anna Belle?"

"Because now the chapel comes to him." She grinned. "The chapel's inside of him. He felt it the first day he came to visit that house. Except he's the king on that chessboard."

Without Anna Belle noticing, Raphael had raised his free arm to her face and lovingly touched her cheek. She flinched, fought his hand, but then settled her cheek into his touch. Her jaw trembled, her lips wet with tears.

She locked eyes with Ellsworth. "I want to go to the chapel."

"You can go to the chapel. Just drop the knife."

She dropped the knife and embraced Raphael, pressing him against her chest, kissing his head, telling him over and over again that she was sorry. "It was a test, and I failed."

Raphael squirmed from her embrace to help Uriel on the floor. He removed the knife, knelt beside Uriel, and placed his hands on the wound.

Anna Belle shuffled across the kitchen. "I'm ready to go now. Go back into the woods."

Ellsworth whispered something to Gabriel. She nodded, then circled around the kitchen table so that she was behind Anna Belle.

"Sometimes he doesn't want the chapel in him."

Ellsworth offered Anna Belle his hand. "Who?"

"Lou. He hurts like the rest of us. Except Lou isn't his real name. It's Lucius. And I'm a bad soldier."

Just as Anna Belle was about to grab Ellsworth's hand, Gabriel clutched her from behind, securing her arms in a sturdy bear hug. Anna Belle screamed as Gabriel carried her from the kitchen. "Let me down. Where are you taking me?"

"The safest place for you, Anna Belle." Ellsworth glanced at Gabriel. "My deputy here is going to lock you up for the night. Just long enough to—"

Anna Belle sprayed spit in his face.

He followed them out to the veranda and then to the street, where some of the people returning from the woods stopped to watch the scene. Gabriel now had Anna Belle over her shoulder, oblivious to the fists pounding against her back.

The bomb Rabbi Blumenthal detonated outside the jailhouse had left one cell functional. It would hold Anna Belle just fine.

"Liar," Anna Belle hissed. "Let me down. One more time into the woods. Let me go."

Gabriel was unfazed by the hysterics. "You did say she could go," she said to Ellsworth.

"It's for her own good."

"Okay by me. She called me an ugly broad. But I'd rather be called ugly than a liar."

Ellsworth struck up his first cigarette in days. "Lying is the least of my sins."

# CHAPTER 23

Ellsworth left Anna Belle alone in the jailhouse cell and promised to return.

She was screaming at him when he left, thrashing her shoulder into the bars, begging for one last trip into the woods, one more time with Calvin. And with the back of the jailhouse now open to the elements, her voice carried. Shouts of "murderer" and "liar" followed Ellsworth across the street. Some of the new town-hall arrivals watched in the parking lot. He told them to go back inside, and they obeyed without question.

Back at Ellsworth's house, Omar and his men remained on guard. Raphael was waiting at the door. "Uriel, he'll live. He's sitting up in the kitchen. Gabriel is bandaging his back." The boy continued as he climbed down the veranda steps and started on toward the road.

"Where you going?" asked Ellsworth.

Raphael nodded toward the jailhouse. "To calm her down."

Anna Belle's voice had continued, though hoarse from screaming, but it silenced a minute after Raphael entered the jailhouse.

"Dem boy is good," Omar said, packing fresh tobacco into his pipe. At the end of the veranda, Omar's man was writing in his diary again, jotting notes in the moon glow. "Get dem sleep, Ellsworth. Big days comin'."

Ellsworth knew he needed sleep, but with all the goings-on he doubted it would readily come. Instead he told Omar he'd be back. He walked to the street, surveyed both ends, and then headed south toward the churches, turning right before he reached Brother Bannerman's house, where the clothes basket Rabbi Blumenthal burned was now a heap of ash. He ducked under the clothesline and cut through Ned Gleeson's backyard, where Ned's work shed lay in charred ruins. Something winked yellow in the moonlight—a partially charred birdhouse. Ellsworth pulled it from the heap, blew ash from the rooftop. It was mostly intact—red roof, yellow walls, blue door, and green-framed windows on three sides—the kind that was big enough to be a bird feeder as well. Even the rope Ned had fastened to the roof was still connected, and it was by this that Ellsworth held it as he continued on through Berny Martino's backyard toward the Bellhaven Cemetery.

Hundreds of gravestones packed the graveyard tightly, knee high at the most, and decorated with so many bird droppings one might think they'd been carved from marble. Ellsworth found Eliza's easily enough—on the north end of the lot, wedged between the wrought iron fence and little Erik's gravestone, which was no wider than a foot and shorter than the tall grass that surrounded it. Ellsworth bent over and pulled the weeds, wiped the stone clean.

"Eliza, I know it's been too long since I visited, but you've been on my mind daily, no matter." He sat on her headstone and breathed in the cool evening air as hundreds of birds cast shadows against the clouds. "Give me the strength to do what needs to be done in the coming days."

The last time he'd visited her grave was the day before he enlisted. But instead of a birdhouse he'd held a baseball and glove, and he'd made a promise to her then that he'd come home and make a name for himself on the ball field. He would play every game like his life depended on it. Make every pitch like it was his last. Leave every city with the fans begging him to stay.

"I wanted to make you proud, Eliza." He stood from the stone and hung the birdhouse on the iron fence. Arms folded, he watched it for a moment. He started to leave, but then a cardinal bird dropped from the flock circling above and landed atop the fence, the tiny talons doing a dance to stay balanced. It pecked through the birdhouse window at food that wasn't there and then looked at Ellsworth like he was at fault.

"I'll bring seed next time." He stared at the bird. The bird stared right back. Ellsworth wiped his eyes and chuckled, wondering if it was the same bird he'd seen at his window the day he nearly shot himself. He'd like to think it was. It was a female. The feathers looked the same. "Is that you?" he said aloud.

The bird didn't answer. Of course the bird didn't answer. It flew off into the trees and lost itself in the shadows. Ellsworth thought about taking the birdhouse with him but then decided he'd leave it there on the fence. Maybe tomorrow he'd come back with some seed. He wrote himself a mental note and then paused, realizing what Eliza would have been doing had that bird arrived so timely, so personally. Like Omar's man on the veranda, she would have recorded it in her diary.

Her diary.

Eliza's diary.

Ellsworth turned from the cemetery, picked up pace through Berny Martino's backyard, and then jog-hobbled the rest of the way home.

Omar still stood guard on the porch. "Ellsworth, dem slow down. What da—"

Ellsworth flung the front door open and hurried inside. Upstairs in his bedroom he found the little book where she'd always kept it, in the drawer of her nightstand. She'd sit on the veranda rocker and take notes on the colorful blooms, chart their yearly patterns and seasonal tendencies. And the birds—sometimes he'd steal a glance and find her sketching them. She'd take that diary when she traveled the trains—wherever she went.

Sometimes, curious, he'd been tempted to sneak it out of its drawer while she was out in the garden or napping. He'd even made it as far as smelling the leather cover and cracking the spine. But each time he'd put it back and close the drawer in a cold sweat. He'd respected her too much not to trust her.

Then she'd died, and he'd refused to go into their room. Later he'd been too hobbled from the war to climb stairs. And in all that had happened, he'd completely forgotten about her diary.

The musty smell brought about tears. A thin network of cracks etched the leather spine. The pages were stiff, crinkled. He blew away dust and started at the beginning. "October 14, 1906." *She started it when she was thirteen years old.* On that day Eliza had written briefly about the sunny weather and a clear blue Arkansas sky.

He turned the pages carefully. Most entries were brief, some only a few words—

**January 5, 1907:** Hello, it's me again.

But mostly she'd written about the weather, flowers, pictures in the clouds, descriptions of sunrises and sunsets, imaginary friends she'd invite over for tea. She'd go weeks, sometimes months, without entries, and then she'd be back again, scribbling that next entry as if in a hurry to capture her days. Her mood changes were evident even in her writing, sometimes shifting in the same entry from excitement to melancholy, bliss to depression.

Why do I feel alone even in a crowd?

She wrote often about her mother, recording memories. Being read to at night, falling asleep in her mother's arms, taking walks hand in hand, riding the train together. *Riding the trains.* Here Ellsworth paused, allowed those familiar three words to gather in his mind, before looking back down to her writings. Then finally came the memories of watching her mother being carried away in the swift river current—memories that had turned to nightmares, nightmares she'd documented dozens of times in her diary.

February 9, 1907: The girl mother saved—her name is Clare.

That was it. So short, to the point. So . . . random. Ellsworth turned more pages, skimmed, stopped on various dates.

March 10, 1907: Very strange, but I woke up this morning and shouted out a name. Benjamin! And I don't know why. I know no Benjamin. Yet I shouted it out like he was one of my own.
February 3, 1908: I awoke this morning to find dots of blood on my undergarments. I hope I'm not dying. I wish my mother were alive to explain such things.

The next month the blood came again. She wrote:

March 5, 1908: Something is killing me slowly from the inside out. Perhaps it has something to do with the changing of the moon? I must clean up before father gets home!

The story of her young life continued to unfold as he turned the pages. He had known her so well, and yet there was so much he had never known.

**July 6, 1908:** A young boy at the market smiled at me today. He was licking a lollipop. He understands me. Does he bleed down there? Is he slowly dying too?

**August 6, 1908:** I met a friend today. Her name is Patricia. She explained my monthly blood. So if I'm dying, then all women are dying. I suppose it also means I'm now a woman!

Years passed before the next entry, her entries nearly as random and sporadic as her thoughts had sometimes been when she was alive.

**September 11, 1911:** I heard a familiar woman's voice in my head this morning. Again. Was it my imagination? I don't think so. I've been hearing her for too long for it not to be real. I can tell no one, not even Patricia. But I believe I may know who it is. I can only hope.

**September 19, 1911:** Patricia and I watched the clouds today, and I saw a sewing machine.

**October 17, 1911:** Father is forcing us to move to Atlanta today. I hate him.

There was another big gap before the next diary entry, which was one of the longer ones.

**December 9, 1913:** I'm twenty today. Father forgot my birthday, and here I sit eating a muffin alone at the kitchen table while he drinks at the tavern. I have no friends here. I wonder what Patricia is doing back home, if she's found a man to marry. There's a mouse in this kitchen. I think he likes our crackers. I must apologize to myself for going so long without an entry. It shall not happen again. But the voice in my head grows stronger. Perhaps she is my only friend here, and it's time for me to start listening to her. I don't think she's in my imagination any more. She's real and has been since I was five years old. I believe now that she's the voice of my mother. And so I now call her Martha.

Ellsworth's tears began anew. He turned the page, jumping another year.

**January 11, 1914:** There's a peculiar story in the newspaper today about a boy from Arkansas named Benjamin Stithe, nearly seven years old, who is apparently able to do complex mathematics. I feel myself drawn to him. Benjamin. They call him a prodigy. Is this the Benjamin I called out to seven years ago on the day of his birth?

**April 29, 1914:** Mother Martha's voice is like a goodnight kiss. She told me of a little girl named Lilly, who lives down the road, and said that I should watch over her.

The next pages chronicled the story of Lilly, with months-long gaps between the entries.

**June 23, 1914:** Lilly still has no idea that I watch over her daily. Even at age seven she has the voice of an angel. Her father drinks, though, and can get rather disagreeable with both Lilly and her mother. Sometimes they fight. I believe he hits them.

**August 5, 1914:** I took Lilly to my house this evening. Her father became violent and stormed from the house, probably to the tavern where my father slowly kills himself. Lilly's mother chased him, and he swatted her to the road, where she cried and pleaded for him not to go. I think he should never return. I heard Lilly crying, so I tapped on her bedroom window, and she opened it with a smile. She asked if I was an angel and I said no, but she sings like one. She asked if she could come over. She said she's seen me before and has always wanted to talk to me. I held her that night, and we cried together. I hugged all the bad stuff out of her mind, and she sang us both to sleep. Her mother returned to the house but didn't give any indication that she'd found her daughter missing. I'll walk Lilly back home in the morning, although she begs me not to.

Ellsworth turned another page, found another time gap.

**December 26, 1914:** It's been three weeks, and Lilly's father has yet to return. This is probably for the best. Both mother and daughter are in much better spirits now. I hear them both singing at night.

The next dozen pages included entries about the weather, about Lilly's voice, and about how the child was growing like a weed and seemingly happy.

**January 1, 1915:** I wonder if I am ever to marry like all the other women my age. Men tell me my eyes are beautiful, azure like a clear summer sky. Yet none of them ask for my hand.

Ellsworth scanned more pages, turning faster. He'd skipped too much, so he turned back to find entries he'd missed.

**April 11, 1910:** I saw a vision last night—a black infant in a cradle. A boy, I believe, and he was surrounded by the most brilliant emerald glow. I'm unsure how I know it, but I must watch over this boy, although I have no inkling where he is.

The next day she wrote about sunflowers. That was what fascinated him—the mix of the ordinary and the mystical. Reading it brought her spirit back to him more vividly than he had felt it since she died.

**July 7, 1912:** Father stays all night at the tavern and comes home smelling of sin.
**August 10, 1912:** Mother used to call me her little angel. That much I remember. I miss my mother, but at least now I am beginning to understand my purpose. Sometimes, in my dreams, mother doesn't have a face.

Ellsworth swallowed hard but turned another page, hands trembling.

**July 4, 1913:** Father didn't come home last night. That's three nights in a row. Strange that I don't really miss him.
**November 17, 1913:** The black boy has a name. It's Raphael. Yesterday he healed a bird by holding it in his hands. I watched him from behind a tree. But he never knew I was there. He never knows. Neither did Lilly or any of the others. Lilly is growing into a beautiful young woman.

By now Ellsworth was flipping pages back and forth, comparing, analyzing, snapping them palpably inside the quiet bedroom.

**January 17, 1915:** The little girl my mother saved when I was young is now a grown woman. I remember her name—Clare. She still lives in Arkansas. There's a story about her in the newspaper. They call her a saint, even though she still lives. Her orphanage has saved more than a hundred children from life on the streets. She'd founded it when she was only fifteen.

**March 10, 1915:** My father struck me on the face. My right cheek stings from the blow. His knuckles are large. He read my diary and threatened to put me in an asylum. He told me there would be no more talking or writing of voices. He says my mother is dead and that I'm a fool just like her.

Ellsworth's jaw tightened, as did his grip on the diary. Her father had died two weeks later. They'd found him on the sidewalk outside his favorite tavern, stabbed to death and robbed of a wallet that contained only a collection of pictures of Eliza's mother.

**June 25, 1915:** I had a dream last night about a boy who plays baseball. He's what they call a pitcher. Martha tells me his name is Michael and that I'm to watch over him. In the dream he had wings and a blue glow. I liked his smile. He has kindness in him.

A tear dropped from Ellsworth's cheek and plopped on the page, smudging his name. He skimmed the next pages quickly. More entries about the weather, about Lilly, about a tornado in Kansas, a flood in Louisiana, and a young boy in Atlanta who at seven had just written his first novel. He slowed when he saw his name again. How strange to see the story of his life through her eyes.

**August 5, 1915:** Michael is in Florida today, pitching for an important man in a suit who claims to be from the Brooklyn Dodgers, whoever they are. His mother is with him, but I have a feeling he's upset with her. She buzzes around him like a bee. Apparently Michael pitched well. The man clapped him on the shoulder and told him they'd hear from him soon. Of all the people I have guarded, Michael is the only one who has ever sent my heart fluttering, and I'm unsure what to make of this.

**August 6, 1915:** What does it mean to be in love? I try not to smile but it can't be helped. He's but five years younger than me. Does age matter with love?

**August 7, 1915:** Today Michael is due to return via rail to Charleston and then onto his home in Bellhaven. Something tells me I should go with him. Something feels wrong about this train. I bought my ticket and now sit inconspicuously across the aisle and three rows back. I wonder why he doesn't sit with his mother. They seem to have gotten into an argument, and she now sits by herself.

**August 8, 1915:** Yesterday I survived a terrible train derailment ten miles south of Atlanta. Just before the wheels screeched I was out of my seat and by Michael's side. I had him in my arms and told him to curl in tight. I didn't tell him who I was, but I think he knew. Everyone in the two train cars perished except for the two of us.

**August 10, 1915:** I can't leave him. I will not leave him. The two of us are inseparable. His bruises continue to heal from the wreck, as do mine. Is it possible for two hearts to beat as one?

Ellsworth hurried through the next pages, which described her decision to follow him to Bellhaven. She'd written that she felt *pulled* to the town, just as he'd felt pulled to return. Then he read through brief but numerous entries about their months of courtship. Their trips into Charleston. The restaurants where they dined. Walking hand in hand along the Battery wall. Tears rolled down his cheeks and dripped to the pages as he relived those days. Then came an entry that made him refocus.

**December 3, 1915:** Sebastian Nowark killed himself in prison yesterday. He was the man arrested for causing the train derailment months ago. He'd been a loyal worker on the railway for a dozen years, with a wife and three kids and no apparent motive. In the courtroom he'd appeared dazed, confused as he'd admitted to removing the rail on the northbound bend the night before the accident. When the judge had asked why he'd done it, he'd said with a straight face that he didn't know. But in his suicide note he claimed the devil made him do it.

**April 20, 1916:** I've found a home in Bellhaven. The woods are magical. Mother's presence is even stronger here.

**May 9, 1916:** After some research, I've learned more about the man who derailed our train and later killed himself, Sebastian Nowark. Seems like he spent time in Bellhaven months before the wreck. His dear mother showed me his diary. He wrote about the woods and the yellow trees and an odd patch of white that had grown in his hair. He wrote that he needed to do something to release the pressure.

Ellsworth shook his head, heart thumping. Why had she never mentioned this to him, this proof that the derailment was deliberate? It took him a minute to begin reading again.

The next entries took him through months and years at a time. Their first several months in Bellhaven as husband and wife. The sorrow of little Erik's stillbirth and the two miscarriages that followed. The guilt Eliza had felt for never giving him a son. Her first encounter with the woman called America Ma in the woods. And interspersed with all these momentous events were simple entries about the blooming azaleas and dogwoods and the moss hanging from the avenue of oaks. And she continued to write about Raphael. He counted ten trips she'd taken to Macon to spy on the boy at the plantation before the final one, when she'd rescued him and his mother and brought them to Bellhaven.

Ellsworth flipped backward, finding more that he'd missed. He was surprised to find short passages about visiting a doctor in Charleston.

**June 10, 1917:** I visited Dr. Blackburn today. Diagnosis still the same. Oh how I dread telling Ellsworth.

*Dr. Blackburn?* Ellsworth turned the page, shaking. *Tell me what?*

**June 26, 1917:** Ellsworth continues to work on his pitching—every day, throw after throw. The ball sounds like an explosion when it hits the other mitt. He grows stronger daily with strenuous exercise. The scouts assure him that next season will be his first in the big leagues. I don't have the heart to tell him about my condition. I fear he'd set his dreams aside to stay with me.

Ellsworth choked back the lump in his throat, wiped his eyes.

She was right. He would have done that. *Whatever the condition was.*

**July 17, 1917:** Dr. Blackburn says my color is improving. My strength is better. I didn't tell him about the chapel I found in the woods. Didn't say I've found a way to not only listen to my mother, but speak back as well. Her voice is inside those walls.

**August 2, 1917:** I feel drained, but I must go back. The woman in the woods, the one who calls herself America Ma, she keeps saying the name Radkin. I must learn who this is.

Ellsworth's eyes flicked over the words, skipping the dates now in a hurry to understand.

. . . One more time and I won't return.

. . . Ellsworth says I look tired. I think that place is aging me. But I can't stop going.

. . . I'm having strange thoughts today. I had a notion to stab Anna Belle Roper at lunch with my fork, and I even got as far as clutching it before my better senses won over.

. . . Inside the chapel today, Mary Bellhaven spoke to me. She used to live in that yellow house on the hill. She told me to watch out for the flies. I know not what she meant.

. . . I traveled the trains today and learned news of another similar to myself. His name is Asher Keating, and he watches over many in a city called Louisville.

. . . I finally may have found the Radkin America Ma speaks of. There's a Father Radkin, a priest in Charleston, retired due to health concerns. I should set up an appointment to see him promptly.

. . . After meeting with Father Radkin today, I'm nearly lost for words. His refusal to visit the Bellhaven Woods unnerved me. I could tell from his eyes that he knew of that chapel. He warned me to stay out of the woods, but I'm not sure that I can. I asked him about Mary Bellhaven and the yellow house on the hill, and he asked me to leave—to please leave. He made the sign of the cross over me and practically begged me to speak of it no more.

. . . I visited Dr. Blackburn today. He was stunned silent. He asked me if I believed in miracles.

. . . The old Bellhaven plantation frightens me. Odd things happened there.

. . . I saw America Ma again last night. She was walking backwards through the woods.

. . . I look older. There are strands of gray in my hair, and I'm not yet thirty. So I punched the mirror, and glass shattered. The chapel no longer brings me peace after I leave it. I cut my wrist with one of the shards, but Ellsworth found me in time. And now I sit bandaged to the elbow, fresh from a bath. Ellsworth combs my hair and tells me not to worry. But I do. I don't think moving to Bellhaven was a good idea at all.

Ellsworth wiped his face, exhaled. *Dr. Blackburn. Father Radkin. Why was she visiting a doctor? A priest?*

The next two entries mentioned Raphael and his mother hiding in the town-hall basement and Eliza's fear of them being found. Then there was an entry expressing her excitement about the town-hall gathering. She looked forward to the music and the displays of talent. She'd make sure they played loud enough for Raphael and his mother to hear from their hiding spot.

Ellsworth had already glanced at the final entry but looked away. She must have written it in a hurry before they'd walked hand in hand to the town-hall festivities that night.

. . . I love you, Michael Ellsworth Newberry.

Like she'd known those words would be her last entry.

Ellsworth closed the book, kissed his fingertips, and then pressed them against the cold, dusty leather.

# CHAPTER 24

At two thirty that morning Ellsworth returned to the jailhouse to find Raphael asleep on the floor outside Anna Belle's cell, curled up like a puppy and snoring with his head on a bent elbow.

He found a blanket and pillow under Lecroy's desk—it was rumored Lecroy slept on the job—covered Raphael with the blanket, and slid the pillow under his head. Anna Belle sat next to the bars with her back to the wall, feet reeled in and hugging her knees. She rocked, bit her lip, said nothing as Ellsworth sat next to her on the opposite side of the bars. He didn't know where to start, so he closed his eyes and eventually Anna Belle broke the silence.

"I didn't do anything with him. With Lou, I mean."

Ellsworth's eyes popped open. That wasn't where he had thought she'd start, but truth was he'd thought about it. "That's good, Anna Belle."

She chewed on her fingernails and lightly tapped the back of her head against the wall.

"Anna Belle, stop. Please. Stop hitting your head against the wall. Anna Belle."

She stopped. "I just wanted one more visit with Calvin. You lied to me."

"You threatened to kill Raphael."

She spoke under her breath. "It was a test."

"Where's Linda May?"

"Still up there, being a good soldier." She knocked her head against the wall, harder now. Tears welled. "Good soldier." Ellsworth slid his arm through the bars and gripped her hand. She banged her head again, but more softly, and then she stopped. "He has a chess set of the town, Ellsworth."

"I saw it."

"You're the king on the opposite side of the board. He knows about you."

"Why did he come here?"

"To grieve. He lost his wife and children to the flu you soldiers brought back."

"Why Bellhaven?"

"Bellhaven chose him, I think." She looked at him. "Ellsworth, what is happening here?"

"I don't know everything, Anna Belle. But I know more than I did yesterday."

"Don't hold out on me."

"Tell me who my queen is first. On his board? Who is my queen?"

Anna Belle squeezed his hand. "Gabriel."

"So he knows."

"Knows what?"

"What side does he have you on?"

"I'm a pawn," she said. "Sometimes he moves the pawns from side to side, the good soldiers and the bad. Linda May is a good soldier. She passed her test."

"You're a good soldier, Anna Belle."

"When the Klan arrived. I couldn't stay." She shifted against the wall, chewed her bottom lip. "Lou is physically changing. His skin has lesions on it. There's one on his neck, another on his forehead. He covers them with powder. You said he knows? What does he know?"

He faced her. "Do you believe in angels?"

"I'd believe in just about anything right now."

He pulled the flask of Old Sam from his jacket and took a gulp. He slid it through the bars, and she partook. As they shared the bourbon he told her about Uriel's arrival, the San Francisco earthquake, and the behavioral parallels with the great Charleston earthquake. About Gabriel's story, Raphael escaping the Macon plantation. Last he told her about Eliza's diary, about how she and her mother had both died saving children, special children. By the time he finished it was four in the morning.

They stared across the room at the wreckage from Rabbi Blumenthal's explosion. Two cardinal birds flew in, talons clicking against the floor, leaving tiny prints in the plaster dust.

Ellsworth said, "He talked about you every night, Anna Belle, from the day we left Bellhaven. We sailed across the ocean, trained as doughboys at Saint-Nazaire, and you were always in the front of his mind. He'd talk about you until his eyes grew heavy, and he'd fall asleep with a smile on his face, thinking about you."

Ellsworth wiped his eyes, regripped her hand. "It was like quicksand over there. Solid ground was never solid. We captured Cantigny, our first offensive of the war. We were tired but confident, getting acclimated to sleeping in the trenches. For three days the Germans launched heavy counterattacks. Truth be told, Calvin was better at it than I was. Better at war. I was still angry from Eliza's death, and I'd hoped to channel the anger, but all it did was make me fear for my own life."

He wasn't completely sure she was listening. Her expression didn't change, and she stared straight ahead. He took another sip of Old Sam before pressing on. "On the third night a fog set in across the forest, and the Krauts caught part of our line off guard, forced us out of the trenches. In some places it was hand-to-hand combat—a first for many of us. I knew Calvin was close by. We'd promised we'd watch each other's backs. One time there was a break in the fog, and I spotted a Kraut about thirty feet away, standing in between two trees. I aimed at him but then froze. I'd never killed a man that close. And because I hesitated, that Kraut shot and killed another of our men. Private First Class Wells. I watched him drop, then ran toward him. He was dead because I had hesitated to protect my fellow soldiers.

"Something in me snapped then, and I started firing at every Kraut I saw. I heard a twig crunch, I turned and fired. Heard footsteps, turned and fired. I fired at dying Huns all over the ground so they'd stop whimpering."

Ellsworth's heart raced as he relived the memory. He pressed on, determined to finish. "We'd lost some men, but we were doing all right. We were holding them off. And then I heard footsteps behind me. Someone screamed in the distance. I panicked and fired, Anna Belle. Blindly, like a fool. It was Calvin, and I'd clipped him in the throat."

Anna Belle gave a little gasp, but she still didn't look at him. So he just kept talking. "I looked around through the fog. No one had seen me do it. I ran to Calvin on the ground and held him in my lap. I don't know if he knew it was me who'd shot him. I kept saying, 'I'm sorry, Calvin. I'm sorry.' And his light went out fast. But he smiled." Ellsworth clenched his jaw. "He said, 'Tell Anna Belle I love her.' Said it twice. 'Tell Anna Belle I love her.'"

Ellsworth chuckled softly. Anna Belle looked at him now.

"'And tell her she makes the best doggone hoppin' John I ever tasted.'"

Anna Belle choked on a sob, then squeezed his hand, and in that touch Ellsworth knew he'd been forgiven. She'd given him a burst of air no chapel in the forest ever could. A dose of good medicine—the real, human kind. She cried out loud, then continued to weep silently. He let go of her hand and used the bars to pull himself up. He unlocked the cell, stepped over Raphael, and locked himself inside with her. He sat with his arm around her shoulders and rubbed her back until the sobs eased and she rested her head against his chest.

They stayed that way, feeling each other's heartbeats, their intakes of air. He kissed the top of her head and realized how much he'd missed the sounds of her voice in the few days she'd been in that house. It had been so long since he'd held a woman, he never wanted to let go. His eyes grew heavy, and sleep seemed possible.

"Ellsworth."

"Yes."

"Why did you stop going by Michael?"

"Thought it was bad luck."

"It's more than that." She burrowed deeper into his chest.

He rested his chin atop her head. "Ellsworth was my father's first name, but he always went by his middle name, Robert. When I was born my mother insisted the name Ellsworth be part of mine. In hindsight, I guess it was just another way for her to prove to him that I was his. You know he had doubts about that, right?" She nodded. He went on. "One day when we were out playing catch, I asked him why he went by his middle name. He said, "'Cause Ellsworth's a name that gets poked at in the schoolyard. Robert isn't.' 'I don't get it,' I told him. 'As Ellsworth I was weak,' he said. 'As Robert I had more confidence.' After a few more pitches I said to him, 'Well, maybe Michael's a name that's destined to be sick all the time.'"

Anna Belle chuckled.

"What?"

"Nothing. Just that you never talked about your father much. Feels good to hear it, is all. What did he say next?"

"He laughed just like you did and said Michael was the name I was given. That it was a good, strong name and to leave it be. I threw another couple pitches. Told him that I liked the name Ellsworth on him and that a name was just a name." Ellsworth took a deep swallow. "Told him strength comes from elsewhere, from somewhere down deep. After that he told me I was too smart for my own good sometimes and to go wash up for dinner. Anyway, I changed my name to honor him after he died. To show him."

"Show him what?"

"That a name was just a name. That there wasn't anything weak about him." He repositioned himself against the wall. "You know, he glanced at me that day. Right when he told me to go wash up for dinner. He smirked. I think it was that day that he started to know."

"Know what?"

"That I really was his son."

Anna Belle nestled into his shoulder, and he welcomed her body warmth. "Your mother saved all the newspaper articles. All those headlines about you beating sickness and accidents and such."

"I threw the box in the trash after she died," he said. "What of'm?"

"Gabriel got them out of the trash. She looks at them still. She carries a torch for you, Ellsworth. I think we all have at some point." They let that sink in, and then Anna Belle went on: "Bellhaven boy survives polio. Bellhaven boy miraculously defeats cancer. Bellhaven boy nearly drowns in lake but survives. Bellhaven boy overcomes the flu with little treatment. Bellhaven pitcher catches a ball to the face and returns to the mound in weeks."

"Anna Belle, stop."

"Bellhaven man strikes out Babe Ruth on three consecutive pitches. Bellhaven boy survives typhus; doctors befuddled. Bellhaven resident one of only two survivors in Georgia train derailment."

"Anna Belle, I've seen all the headlines. Stop now."

"You took that blow to the head the night of the fire and barely wobbled. You went into the burning town hall and came out untouched." Her voice accelerated. "That bomb that took your leg killed the other five men around you. Tanner stabbed you in the heart, and you're right here holding me."

"Anna Belle . . ."

"I don't think you can be killed, Ellsworth." Her words were a slap to the face. He'd thought them before but had never heard them aloud. "Your father was your father. He was wrong not to believe your mother; other men thought sterile have fathered children. Anyway, you've ended up looking just like him. He may not have believed in miracles, but I do."

Raphael squirmed outside the bars, repositioned himself, and resumed sleeping.

"I was born with the umbilical cord wrapped around my neck," said Ellsworth.

"That I didn't know."

"They said my face was blue as a summer sky and I wasn't breathing."

She nodded; he was proving her point.

"The military doc told me I'd lose my leg from the knee down but feared I wouldn't live through the procedure. I laughed at him. He asked what was funny, and I said life was funny. He said I was delirious. I closed my eyes and told him to start sawing." He rubbed her arm and sank his chin back into her hair. "The other side has been trying to kill me since before I was born, Anna Belle. I'm not gonna dust out now."

"He's brought in guns, Ellsworth. Crates full of them."

"I'll protect this town."

"Ellsworth, do you really think . . . that Eliza was some kind of guardian angel? And that you're . . . ?"

He rubbed her arm. "I don't know exactly what I am, Anna Belle. I'm just a man holding a woman, and right now we need to get some sleep."

# CHAPTER 25

Ellsworth awoke to sunlight and the flutter of bird wings.

At first he thought he was inside the chapel again, but then his eyes took in iron bars and broken bricks, the morning sun streaming in through the damaged jailhouse. Two redbirds flew from wall to wall.

He jerked up to a sitting position. *Anna Belle?* The door to the cell was open, lodged against the set of bulky keys she'd dropped upon her escape. He stood too fast and stumbled against the cell wall, his prosthesis only half attached. He secured it and hurried from the jailhouse. She'd better not have gone back into the woods—or to the yellow house. How could he have fallen asleep with the keys latched to his belt? How could he have trusted her?

He squinted against the sunlight and limped across the gravel road. Men and women, some of them strangers and some town folk, sat outside the town hall sipping coffee. Watching him, their supposed leader, stumble by hatless and with hair askew, covered with dust.

Omar was still at Ellsworth's, leaning against a veranda post with his legs crossed at the ankles and holding a rifle as he stared up the hill toward Eddington's house. There was no pipe in the mouth slit this morning, only focused eyes shining like wet coal behind the white mask.

"Dem good mornin', Ellsworth." Omar tipped his topper, a white fedora with a red silk band around it. It matched his suit, which was white and striped with threads of red.

Ellsworth smelled food. Omar's men sat along the veranda with steaming plates on their laps, taking in the Bellhaven air as azaleas bloomed purple and pink in the flower bed beneath their feet. Their eyes moved back and forth from their food to the armed men atop the hill, dozens dressed in suits, button-downs, and suspenders. Mayor Bellhaven stood front and center with his eyes shaded by the brim of a bowler hat.

"Been standin' der all mornin' like dat, our mayor."

"Where's Anna Belle? Have you seen her?"

Omar smiled under the mask. "Relax, Ellsworth." He nodded toward the house. "Whey you t'ink dem food come from?"

*Of course.* He let out a deep breath, eyed the full plates. Bacon and eggs. Biscuits and buttermilk gravy. Skillet potatoes and buttered grits. Only Anna Belle could have conjured up such a spread on little notice. He opened the screen door and found Alfred in his chair by the window, listening to the static of a newly repaired radio and mumbling about Linda May.

In the kitchen Uriel sat at the table with his back and shoulder bandaged. Gabriel was next to Raphael, both eating. Anna Belle stood at the stove, dressed to the nines in a pretty yellow dress that brushed past her knees. Her hair was done up in curls, and her smile showed fight. How could he have doubted her? *But maybe she went into the woods and came back with the energy to feed a town.* But he didn't think so. Her eyes showed clarity, not guilt. She was cooking to stay occupied. Cooking so that she *wouldn't* go into the woods.

Ellsworth hugged her and she didn't give him brushback. "Welcome back, Anna Belle," he said.

She smiled, patted his hand. "You stink, Ellsworth."

\||//

Belly full and face fresh from the blade, Ellsworth checked himself in Eliza's vanity mirror and straightened the lapels on his coat. He slanted his fedora—the look of a leader.

He met Anna Belle at his car and tossed her the keys. Gabriel, along with Omar and his men, was in charge of the town while they sneaked into Charleston. Father Radkin had been a priest at the cathedral when Ellsworth's father died on the steps years before, and, according to Father Timothy, he was now in his eighties and in failing health. They'd told Father Timothy that Radkin possibly knew about the chapel, so he'd insisted on going with them.

Ellsworth checked his timepiece. Father Timothy was five minutes late, and he'd only give him five more. He didn't like the idea of leaving town in the first place and was in a hurry to get back. He pulled a cigarette from the case inside his coat and offered Anna Belle one. They smoked side by side, leaning against the hood of the Model T. Ellsworth watched her red lips pucker against the thin butt.

"Eliza was seeing a doctor in Charleston," he said. "She kept it secret from me, but I read it in her diary. A Dr. Blackburn? Do you know anything about it?"

Anna Belle flicked ash to the gravel. "Do you remember her headaches?"

"How can I not?"

"Do you know when they started?"

"The first one I knew of was a week after I met her, after the train wreck. It really scared me. She told me she'd been having them for years and not to fret about it. So no, I can't pinpoint it."

Anna Belle exhaled smoke. "After she moved here, they grew a lot worse, a lot more frequent."

"I tried to get her to go see a doctor about them, and apparently she did. But why'd she keep it a secret from me?"

Anna Belle dropped her cigarette to the gravel and ground it under the flat of her black shoe. "She had one of those tumors, Ellsworth. In the brain. Dr. Blackburn told her it would kill her. He gave her months, a year if she was lucky. But she didn't want to tell you because she was afraid that if you knew you would stop your baseball training. It put me behind the eight ball. I wanted to tell you, but I promised her I wouldn't."

"Do you think the tumor had something to do with the voice that she'd hear?"

"Dr. Blackburn believed so."

"But Eliza?"

Anna Belle touched the dewy violet bloom of a rhododendron next to the driveway and then wiped the moisture on her dress. "She believed the voice was genuine. And I do too."

Ellsworth finished his cigarette and dropped it to the gravel. "She wrote about a miracle. Something even this Dr. Blackburn didn't understand?"

"The tumor started to shrink, Ellsworth. I think it had something to do with going to the chapel. The tumor had all but vanished by the time we had our last town-hall party."

"I don't know, Anna Belle. I don't think the chapel can work that way."

"Then what?"

"Something tells me that tumor could have started shrinking

275

about the time she started watching over Raphael." He checked the time again. "If Father Timothy doesn't—"

"I'm here, alas!" The priest arrived with an envelope and something shiny and mechanical wrapped in a leather case.

Ellsworth asked, "What do you have there, Father?"

Father Timothy climbed in the back and closed the door. "One of those snapshot cameras. Thirty-five millimeter. Simplex. Much smaller than those clunky Kodak Brownies."

"I wouldn't know."

Anna Belle slid into the driver's seat while Ellsworth moved to the front to crank the engine. The old car sputtered and caught, then finally settled into an asthmatic rumble as Ellsworth opened the front passenger door and climbed in. He reached over the seat for Father Timothy's camera and pointed it at Anna Belle as she began to back out of the driveway. "Smile."

Anna Belle braked the car and smiled, toothy.

"Say prunes," said Father Timothy.

"Prunes," said Anna Belle, attempting to hold on to the smile.

By the time the picture took, the smile had left her face, which was why in most portraits the posers were asked not to smile in the first place. It was too hard to hold it for as long as the exposure took. Better to not smile at all than get caught in between.

Ellsworth handed the camera back to Father Timothy and pointed down the road in the opposite direction of the avenue of oaks, where the main entrance to the town was still clogged with vehicles. They'd take the back roads out of town. Anna Belle kept both hands on the wheel, more comfortable driving now. Ellsworth looked over the seat back. "What's in the envelope, Father?"

"Ah, yes. The reason I was running late." He opened the flap and removed a thin stack of photographs. I just got these developed.

It's like magic. Jeremy Post down the road can do it in his barn. He has a self-made darkroom behind the chicken coop."

Ellsworth leafed through the snapshots. "The chapel?"

"I'd like to show them to Father Radkin. I took them days ago but only just now had a chance to see them developed. Keep looking."

Anna Belle kept her eyes on the road but glanced at the pictures when she could. There were several snapshots of the woods leading to the clearing. Five pictures of the clearing itself from several different angles. Ten pictures of the chapel's exterior from every viewpoint, even from the opposite side of the creek behind it. The beauty of the place was still evident in black-and-white. The next snapshot was an up-close image of the arched wooden door. The one after that was of a bleak darkness, as if a cover had been left over the camera lens and the picture didn't take at all.

Father Timothy leaned forward, patted Ellsworth's shoulder. "Those I took from *inside* the chapel. The statues. The mosaic floor. The reliefs. The stained-glass windows. They didn't develop at all."

\||//

Ellsworth had walked ten paces down Broad Street before Father Timothy asked if he was heeled. He pulled his coat aside to reveal the revolver at his waistline. Out of respect for Charleston's mother church, Father Timothy recommended he not enter the Cathedral of Saint John the Baptist with his Smith & Wesson. Ellsworth returned the revolver to the Model T and stashed it under the passenger seat.

"Sorry, Father."

Father Timothy waved it away, then led them into the shadows of the Gothic brownstone cathedral on Broad Street. "I've met Father Radkin numerous times. He's a kind man. Ailing, but still mindful."

Ellsworth paused on the front steps, pinpointing the exact spot where his father had collapsed and died, thinking he had an unfaithful wife. The doors were heavy. The nave still took his breath away, with its soaring columns and bright colorful light. Stained-glass windows. The rose window coat of arms surrounding the main doors. The Gallery of Saints. The chancel window above the high altar. St. John the Baptist baptizing Jesus with the Holy Spirit above and angels playing musical instruments. The replica of da Vinci's *Last Supper*.

Ellsworth hadn't been inside the cathedral since his mother died. He'd missed the tall walls and vaulted ceiling. Their footsteps echoed.

Father Radkin sat slump-shouldered in the front pew facing the marble altar. His hair was white as cotton. Instead of the colorful vestments he wore ceremonially, he now wore a simple black shirt and clerical collar.

Father Timothy genuflected before sliding into the pew behind Father Radkin. Ellsworth and Anna Belle genuflected, too, even though Anna Belle wasn't Catholic. Father Timothy hurried through the formalities and introductions. Father Radkin already knew who Ellsworth was—the son of the man who'd died on the front steps during his first year at the cathedral.

Father Radkin looked over his shoulder with rheumy eyes and white hair. "What can I do for you, Michael?" His voice was brittle but still penetrated the empty cathedral.

"I actually go by Ellsworth now, sir."

The old priest faced forward again, his smile obvious enough. "Sir?"

"I mean Father."

"That will do, but I'd answer to Francis all the same."

Ellsworth scooted forward, handed him the pictures. "I don't have a lot of time. Strange things are happening in Bellhaven. The town folk have . . . well, they've gone off the tracks. There's a chapel in the woods. From the outside it looks plain, but inside—well, the artwork, it reminds me a little of this cathedral. My late wife, Eliza Newberry—I believe she visited you years back."

Father Radkin nodded but offered nothing. He handed back the pictures after barely glancing at them. Ellsworth looked at Father Timothy and Anna Belle on either side of him. "We were hoping you could tell us what you know about this chapel. Before the town rips itself apart."

Anna Belle said, "There's been vandalism. Crimes of vengeance and intolerance. And people are starting to arm themselves. We're worried there might be more violence."

Father Radkin bowed his head. "I shall pray today for the town of Bellhaven."

"Do you know about this chapel?" asked Ellsworth.

The priest's head bobbed as if palsied. "Stay out of the Bellhaven woods."

"So you fear those woods too?"

Without turning around, Father Radkin held up a dismissive hand. He slid to his knees and bowed his head.

Outside, a cloud must have revealed the sun. A beam of light shone through the stained-glass windows and cast a rainbow across the pews surrounding the central aisle. A shaft of clean blue light reflected up the steps to the altar.

By then the three of them had already slid from the pew, and Father Timothy was inches away from placing his hand on the old man's shoulder to thank him for his time.

"Wait," said Father Radkin, staring at the blue light on the altar. "Wait. Sit back down. Please." He turned slowly toward Ellsworth. *He took the blue light as a sign. He can see my color.*

"I will tell you what I know." The old man closed his eyes. When he opened them they were more alert, his voice stronger. "If what you say is true, it is my duty now as a servant of the Lord to help out however I may."

"Thank you, Father Radkin."

The grin again. "At this point, Michael, I believe I'd rather you call me Francis. That's what the demons inside that yellow house on the hill called me." Father Timothy put a fist to his mouth. Anna Belle's eyes grew large. "I was newly ordained at the time," said the priest, "and stationed at St. Patrick's. I sometimes spend time on Sullivan's Island, which is where Henry Bellhaven found me in the summer of 1870. He begged me to come to Bellhaven. Pleaded. His wife and children were sick." He pointed an arthritic finger to his temple. "Not sick with disease, but sick in the mind. Henry told me I had to see it in person.

"I followed the man to Bellhaven. He went silent as our carriage stopped at the top of the hill. Once inside that yellow house, it soon became evident that something was amiss. Something . . . demonic. A swarm of big black flies buzzed throughout the building. 'We kill them by the dozens,' Henry Bellhaven told me, 'but they still keep coming back.'"

"They were so loud I had to cover my ears. First he showed me his wife, Mary, upstairs in the bedroom. He opened the door and a suffocating heat come out. She looked up from the bed, eyes bulging. She hissed something at me in a demonic language and then . . ."

Ellsworth put his hand on Father Radkin's shoulder.

Father Radkin found strength. "God strike me down, but Mary Bellhaven levitated above the bed. Two, three feet, and then four, the bedcovers coming right up with her like the skirt around a stage. She laughed. But it wasn't her. It was dark and from the gutter. She—it—told me to get out. Once we were out in the hall, the bedroom door slammed shut. A candle sconce on the wall flickered out and then relit itself as I passed."

"'You see, Father, it's just as I told you.'"

"The next morning Mary Bellhaven didn't remember what had happened. She ate breakfast with little emotion. But then afterward she scooted her chair from the table until it toppled. She started walking backwards—around the table and out of the room, then up the stairs. She hissed something about the woods calling her back.

"The flies returned at dinnertime. The Bellhaven's youngest boy, James, walked into the parlor naked as the day he was born. His older brother John joined him, and the two boys started tearing into the wallpaper like a cat would do. It was all very . . . disturbing.

"That evening things calmed down. We were all gathered around the fireplace when we heard footsteps pounding up and down the main stairwell. Up and down. Up and down. And laughter, but there was no one there. No one. Then Mary Bellhaven started screaming. We couldn't get her to stop. She fought us with the strength of ten men. Eventually, however, she calmed. Walked out to the back veranda and faced the woods.

"I looked at Henry, who was distraught and defeated and asked him why he had not been stricken with the same affliction.

"'There's something in the woods,' he told me. 'There's a place where Mary took the kids. They went deep into the woods and found some chapel half buried in the growth.'"

Father Radkin lowered his head. "He took me there the next morning. This chapel. A meager-looking, very Spartan place. I stayed in there for no more than a minute, but long enough to . . . to hear the voice of my father. He'd passed three years prior."

"We've all experienced similar things," said Father Timothy.

Anna Belle fidgeted in the pew. Ellsworth gripped her hand.

Father Radkin said, "We hurried away. And I told him never to go in there again." He paused, a stricken look on his face. "He begged me to perform an exorcism on the house. On the woods, even. But I told him that was something to be approved from higher up, by the bishop, at very least. And then I left the place. I'd already interviewed the family, didn't know what else to do. Truth was, I never requested a church-sanctioned exorcism. I knew they rarely granted them, and if I ever hoped for advancement I didn't want that bruise on my skin."

"So what did you do?" asked Ellsworth.

"I returned and told them their request was denied. The two boys, James and John, beat their heads into the wall. Mary, her voice deepened by the devil, spoke of demons coming through the doorway." Father Radkin massaged his brow. "I couldn't just leave them like that. So I went back to the city and gathered what I'd need for a private exorcism. You don't need church approval for that."

"So did it work?"

Father Radkin shrugged. "I said prayers, made statements. Felt demons all around me—in the house, the woods. Flies swarmed in through windows that opened and closed. Candlelight flickered on and off. I made a small altar on the living room floor, on a little table brought in from the kitchen. I burned sage and sulfur throughout the house. Read psalms at the top of my voice. And suddenly the house went quiet. We believed it had worked. I was exhausted, but elated. But then a week later it all started again. Henry visited me at St. Patrick's. The family was showing signs of falling back again. He didn't expect me to help but just wanted me to know. He had his own plan, he told me.

"'It involves the chapel, Father. I know you told me to never go back inside that place, but I believe the cure resides in there. There's good medicine in there, Father. But it needs more.'

"He knew a man from the docks, a recently immigrated Italian artist who spoke of a mosaic floor he'd disassembled from a Florentine chapel and brought with him from Italy. It had originally been built in the seventeenth century by one of the Caravaggisti, the artists who mimicked the style of the great Baroque painter Caravaggio. And it had been blessed by the Holy Father himself. The mosaic depicted the angel of healing, the Archangel Raphael. The Italian artist called it the healing floor. He swore whoever knelt upon it was healed of their sickness.

"Henry was paying the artist to install this very floor in that chapel—and more artwork as well. Frescoes and reliefs. Sculpture and colored glass. He believed that beauty would strike the demons away.

"This Italian artist spent the next year inside that chapel, laying the floor, installing the glass, painting pictures on the walls. He slept in there, working day and night." He looked over his shoulder. "Have you experienced the . . . acceleration of aging that happens because of that chapel?"

"We have," said Ellsworth. "We've all witnessed it."

"Well, this artist, he was thirty-seven when he began. He looked eighty when he finished. He celebrated the completion by slitting his own wrists right there on the healing floor. Henry Bellhaven had his sharecroppers clean it up. Then he brought each family member inside and performed his own exorcism, one by one. He prayed to the Archangel Raphael to free them of the demons."

"Did it work?"

"He claimed it did. But they were never the same afterward. They couldn't hold conversation or sleep. Couldn't stop going into the woods. I told Henry to destroy that chapel and never return, but he couldn't bear to destroy the work he had commissioned. So the chapel remained. And the next two generations of Bellinghams were weaker and more degenerate than the one before it, until the family essentially died off." He grinned weakly. "Dropping like flies. The house fell into disrepair. The cotton fields got eaten up. Henry Bellhaven shot himself with a rifle on the outskirts of those woods."

Ellsworth waited through a moment of silence before standing. He fingered the brim of his hat. "One more thing, Father. Even before the artist finished the interior . . . you said this was 1870. Do you have any idea when the original structure was built? Or why?"

Father Radkin shook his head. "I don't know. But I remember my short time in there very vividly. My father's voice."

"What did he say to you?"

"He said, 'Francis, close your eyes. Don't look. There's more than just slave blood in these walls.'"

# CHAPTER 26

Father Timothy squirmed like a caged animal on the way back to Bellhaven.

He had the car door open before Anna Belle pulled to a stop behind Ellsworth's house, and was off running toward the woods before they could stop him.

Ellsworth said, "Let him go. He'll return."

Omar and his men still stood guard outside Ellsworth's house.

Up on the hill, half the town roamed Eddington's property. Men and women held guns, but no one as of yet had fired a shot. *Patrolling as empty threats.* A vulture circled like a giant condor, casting an ominous shadow across the hillside, where Lou Eddington paced. *What is he planning? Is he an evil man or a by-product of that house? A pawn himself?*

Eddington's followers entered and exited the woods. Mayor Bellhaven watched over them, holding a massive gun. Upon second glance, Ellsworth recognized it to be a flamethrower like the ones he'd seen in the war. The mayor pointed it toward the sky, whooshing the flame upward like dragon fire.

Over at the town hall, more people had gathered. They milled around, watching the yellow house on the hill. Two men smoked cigarettes on the roof. Others stood in the grass, the road, and the parking lot. Some hid behind parked cars, ready for a shoot-out Ellsworth hoped to avoid.

"Ellsworth." Gabriel's silver-star badge sparkled in the sunlight. "I've locked up Rabbi Blumenthal. As soon as you left, he entered Father Timothy's church with a sledgehammer. Took chunks from the altar. Then he went to work on the pews and the stained-glass windows. Looks like a bomb went off in there."

"Keep an eye out for Father Timothy. I think he went to the chapel." Ellsworth entered the jailhouse after Gabriel peeled off. Two squirrels skittered across the floor near the hole in the back of the building. A swarm of flies buzzed over what could have been a charred raccoon.

"The mayor did it." Rabbi Blumenthal pointed at the burnt carcass in the corner. "He came in with that flamethrower." He gripped the bars. "Please let me out. I'm sorry for what I did. It's just that Father Timothy walks around like he's right and I'm wrong. And he takes orders from that pointy-hatted man in Rome. They're a cult, Ellsworth."

"What if they're all cults?"

Rabbi Blumenthal backed away, gnawed his fingernails. "It's accelerating. The energy from that chapel. Every time someone enters, it grows stronger." He laughed, hard. "But that's the thing, Ellsworth. We can't stop going. We can't stop going, and the trees are dying!"

"Around the clearing?"

Rabbi Blumenthal nodded, animated. He gripped the bars again and shoved his face between two of them. "The tree moss falls like ash. The leaves shrivel and drop. Its twenty feet deep now around the clearing—and growing. Let me out of here. One last time."

Ellsworth turned away. "Sleep it off, Rabbi."

"I don't think the chapel likes fire, Ellsworth."

Ellsworth turned. "Don't know many buildings that do."

"No, listen. I struck a match outside the chapel, to light my cigarette. It immediately went out."

"Wind."

"There was no wind. You've been there, Ellsworth. It's too calm. There is no breeze around that chapel."

"Go on."

"I struck another. It flickered as if ready to go out, so I moved away from the chapel, toward the trees. And the further I walked, the stronger the flame became. So I approached the chapel again, and the match went out."

Ellsworth chewed on the information. They'd need more than a match to burn that place down. He turned and left the rabbi alone.

"That's where they used to take the slaves," screamed Rabbi Blumenthal. "The ones who disobeyed." Ellsworth stopped at the door. "My great-grandfather, he's in the chapel. He told me. Master Bellhaven, the first Bellhaven. They'd hang slaves from hooks in the ceiling and lash them until they could no longer walk. Let their blood drip to the floor and then make them clean it up. Later, five slaves found the chapel in the woods and tried to destroy it. Master Bellhaven thought they'd run away, and he killed all five that night. But the chapel was there even before the Bellhavens arrived. There's slave blood in those walls, but that isn't all. There's those that came before the slaves. Before Master Bellhaven."

"What are you saying?"

"Colony plantations. They got attacked regularly by the Spanish from St. Augustine. And all the Indian tribes—the Catawba, the Peedee, Cusabo, Cherokee. The redbones, Ellsworth, and the Spanish. They bled in that chapel by the hands of the white men. The early settlers."

"How do you know this?"

"America Ma. She told me so."

Ellsworth turned and approached the cell again. *How far back does this chapel date?* But he stopped cold when people started screaming outside. He hurried out the door. Mayor Bellhaven was down the road in front of the churches, firing bursts from his flamethrower, igniting trees and mailboxes and fence posts and screaming, "I'm the mayor of this town!"

Gabriel approached the mayor. He fired. She jumped back from the flame.

Atop the hillside, Lou Eddington sprayed machine gun fire into the air. Mayor Bellhaven froze, looked up the hill as if reprimanded. He fired one more flame whoosh at Gabriel, then ran behind the town square and up the hillside, where three vultures circled.

Movement in the woods drew Ellsworth's attention. Eddington's armed men and women spread out in a line, like a disciplined Roman legion, right at the tree line. More came from deeper in. Ellsworth spotted Reverend Beaver and Linda May Dennison in their midst.

Just then Father Timothy burst from the trees with a dozen other town people, hurrying away from Eddington's makeshift army. "They won't let us past the yellow trees," he announced, panting. "They're claiming the chapel for themselves."

Panicked voices spread through the square. "How can they do this?" "They have no right." "I must get to that chapel." They were ready to fight then and there.

Eddington's soldiers had halted at the tree line with their weapons leveled—pistols, machine guns, and rifles. Mayor Bellhaven, with his flamethrower, stood in the center of the line next to Eddington, who craned a rifle against his shoulder.

Father Timothy started walking toward their line, hand raised in benediction, then broke into a frantic sprint toward the woods. A bullet tore a clod of mud and grass a yard from his next step—the first official shot fired. Father Timothy stopped in his tracks, took a pronounced step backward, and then ran for cover behind the parked cars at the town hall.

The crowd around the town hall grew by the second as word spread that passage to the chapel had been blocked. Raphael, Gabriel, and Uriel joined Ellsworth in attempting to calm their side down, but no one wanted to hear them. They wanted their chapel. They wanted their loved ones, the voices in that magical air.

Ellsworth stepped in front of the town hall. "That chapel is killing us. It's the devil's trick. He's luring us in and—"

"I say we fight," yelled a man Ellsworth didn't recognize.

Omar and his men forced their way into the middle of the crowd. "Listen to dem leader. Sheriff speak dem truth."

Gabriel towered above them all. "Something is coming out of the ground. Out of the chapel. It's moving into the woods. Every time we go in there, we're feeding it. We have to stop."

Anna Belle was on the periphery, pacing, antsy, as if torn between what she knew and what she craved. Ellsworth didn't trust the look in her eyes. He took a step toward her just as she approached Donald Trapper, and pulled the rifle from his grip. She walked toward the gap between the jailhouse and town hall and fired toward the woods. Eddington's soldiers ducked. She fired again and hit a man in the leg.

The man screamed and bullets started flying.

Ellsworth shouted, "Take cover!" They ran toward homes, behind cars and hedgerows. "Spread out!" If a fight was going to happen, he couldn't let it turn into a bloodbath. He couldn't have his side clustered.

He made his way toward Anna Belle. She turned toward him with the rifle pointed directly at his chest, her eyes crazed.

"Give me the rifle, Anna Belle."

"They can't take the woods from us."

He stepped closer, hoping she wouldn't shoot. "Give me the rifle, Anna Belle."

She lowered the barrel with shaky arms and tears in her eyes but didn't give Ellsworth the rifle. Instead she hunkered behind a rusty black Model T and returned fire toward the woods.

Ellsworth ducked with every gun pop. Dust scattered. People screamed. A woman was hit in the leg and Raphael pulled her to cover behind a hedge of azaleas.

Old Man Tanner exited Ellsworth's house, walking with a purpose and gathering a crowd behind him as he stormed toward his own place.

"Tanner!"

The old man didn't stop. Ellsworth followed the group into Tanner's house and down a narrow stairwell that led to the cellar. Along the far wall, highlighted now by a lantern Tanner had just lit, stood three wooden crates full of weapons.

"What is this? Where did you get these?"

They paid Ellsworth no attention. Eyes glowed as if they'd just been shown pots of gold. They reached into the crates and left with armfuls of ammunition and weapons—rifles, pistols, two machine guns, knives and daggers, dynamite, and what looked like one of those duck-hunting punt guns that was nearly as long as a car and needed two people to carry.

Tanner gripped a rifle in each hand. He and Ellsworth were the last to leave the cellar. "I've been saving up. I always feared this day would come."

"Tanner, stop."

"I don't see any other way. That's *my* chapel. My wife's in there."
He headed for the stairs. "You may have temporarily cured me,
Ellsworth, but you forgot to pluck out the seed." He stopped on the
stairwell and handed Ellsworth one of the rifles. "Listen, I've got
something to tell you. I knew your father. And I knew your mother
saw your birth as a miracle. Perhaps it was."

"What are you saying?"

"All those years, I told no one about that chapel. I kept it hidden. But every time I went, I'd take an empty jar with me. I'd fill it
up with air from the chapel and bring it back to inhale at night. I
kept a trunk full of'm, right up there in my bedroom. Anyway, one
night me and your father got to drinking, and he told me about his
problem. Cried while he did it. Wanted a son more than anything. I
felt real sorry for him. So I told him to wait a minute, and I went and
retrieved one of my jars. I had your father unscrew the jar lid and
inhale. He was too drunk to ask what for and didn't even remember
doing it the next day. But he did tell me your mother was frisky that
night. And a month later they learned she was with child. She took
it as a miracle, her dreams coming true. Your father, well, as you
know by now, he always assumed she had another man."

Ellsworth followed Tanner up three more steps before the old
man stopped again. "That's my chapel. There ain't a soul who can
keep me from it." Tanner hurried from the house with the energy
of a man forty years younger. A man his real age.

Ellsworth stepped out of Tanner's house into a war zone.

Bullets whizzed, cleaving sod and spitting gravel, plucking
leaves from trees and blooms from flower beds. Bricks exploded and
wood splintered. Windows shattered. Everyone hunkered behind
whatever stronghold they could find, and Raphael led a line of children into Ellsworth's house. Tanner's ammunition and weapons
were quickly distributed, everyone eager to join the fight.

Donald Trapper and John Stone both held the punt gun, Donald at the trigger while John stood a few feet ahead holding the barrel on his shoulder. Donald fired. The entire gun shook. The blast took down a heavy bough at the edge of the woods. Retaliation came immediately from a machine gun, which tore the backside of Tanner's house apart and set a black Model T aflame. On the far side of the town hall parking lot, Omar stood in his white mask and dark suit, firing at the hillside, oblivious to the oncoming bullets.

A bullet whistled by, grazing Ellsworth's coat sleeve. He dropped to the ground, not bleeding, but stunned. He closed his eyes and listened—bullets, crying, fear. The sounds switched a trigger in his mind. He wasn't in Bellhaven anymore, but in France, and these were his comrades, his fellow soldiers.

Ellsworth opened his eyes and then opened fire—not aiming, just shooting toward the tree line and the yellow house on the hill. People on both sides fell in pain. He couldn't stop shooting. He'd been given a gun and a map as a teenager and trained to kill. He walked in clear view as others hid behind cars, buildings, house corners, trees, and hedgerows. He didn't hide, didn't flinch. He'd been born from a miracle, and he'd gather the people. They would win this fight.

Atop the hillside, Lou Eddington cantered on a horse behind his line of men, firing his rifle down the hillside. They locked eyes, and briefly time slowed. But then it caught back up in a flurry of bullets and pinging ricochets.

Uriel was right in the middle of the fight, firing a rifle like the rest of them, while Gabriel moved through the crowd, trying in vain to call a cease fire.

Up on the hill, Brother Bannerman stood behind a machine gun, letting loose a barrage of bullets. Redbirds circled, intermingling with the vultures, squawking and flapping as if in a sky fight of their own. Bullets cut blooms of every color from flowers and trees and bushes, and soon the air was littered with floating petals, the grass dotted with color.

Ellsworth saw visions of severed arms and legs from the war.

He kept firing anyway.

Frank Jessups stepped out from behind a purple crape myrtle and fired a pistol up the hillside. He'd once told Ellsworth he'd come to Bellhaven so he wouldn't be shunned for being different. And he'd found a home in Bellhaven, until Reverend Beaver kicked him out of the Methodist church he'd grown to love. Now his bullets had Reverend Beaver's name on them.

"Linda May! Linda May!" To Ellsworth's left, Alfred walked blindly toward the town hall, where dozens of town folk hid behind parked cars, firing over trunks and hoods. He carried a rifle and kept calling his wife's name. "Linda May! The dance is over, Linda May."

"Alfred, no!"

Alfred kept going, right into the no-man's-land between the town square and the woods. He raised his rifle. Fired. Fired again. Bullets whizzed. He didn't flinch. He reloaded, fired. "Dance is over Linda May. Time to come home."

Ellsworth ran toward his friend. Omar, too, still firing as he ran, his white mask askew and his hat off-kilter. A bullet whistled— *thunk*—and Alfred went down on his knees. Another bullet tore through the back of his beige suit coat and another four inches below.

Omar got there first. He picked up his fallen comrade and ran with him draped over his shoulder until they were safely behind the town hall. Ellsworth backpedaled to safety, then gave a man he didn't know an order to retrieve Raphael from the house.

Alfred lay bleeding in the gravel dust parking lot. "Did I get'm? Did I get'm?"

"Dem got'm," said Omar, crying. Tears dripped from the bottom of his mask.

"Linda May," said Alfred. "Is she coming back?"

Raphael arrived, slid next to Alfred's body, put his hands on the wounds. But there were too many. Alfred's eyelids fluttered, his face ashen.

"Is Linda May coming back?"

Raphael leaned to Alfred's ear. "She's come back, Mr. Dennison. She said to tell you she loves you. She always has and always will."

Alfred smiled, coughed blood, then gripped Raphael's hand. "Tell her I'm sorry."

"For what, Mr. Dennison?"

"For not . . . coming back . . . whole . . ."

Alfred stopped breathing. Ellsworth reached over and closed his eyes.

Omar sat like a masked statue for one minute, two. Then he jumped up, screaming, and turned his anger back toward the woods, firing with reckless abandon.

Gabriel ran after him. She'd been too busy trying to keep the rest of the town from killing each other to fire a shot of her own. But after watching Alfred take his last breath, she stormed over toward Donald Trapper and John Stone and bullied the punt gun from them. What had taken two men to carry was now maneuvered like a rifle by one woman. She leveled the punt gun toward the trees and fired, felling a live oak behind the line of men and forcing them to scatter. She fired again and toppled another tree, this one landing on the legs of a man who might have been the town's tanner.

Ellsworth surveyed the carnage. Anna Belle now fired her rifle from behind Jake Wagner's market wagon. Someone had removed the horse but left the wagon filled with produce, so shreds of shot-up cabbage littered the ground around Anna Belle's feet. Glass shattered and wood splintered from the town hall, the place where the town folk had broken bread and shared drinks and music and laughter for decades.

"*Gather the people.*" A bullet hummed. Ellsworth ducked.

"*Show them.*"

"*Show them what?*"

"*Show them normalcy. Gather the people.*" It was his father's voice.

Raphael still sat emotionless next to Alfred's body. "*Show them normalcy.*" He and the boy locked eyes. "Go get my gloves," Ellsworth said.

"What? Now? Mr. Newberry?"

"The baseball. And the gloves. Go get them. Go on now."

Raphael hesitated, then took off toward the house. He returned a minute later with a baseball and two gloves, the same ones Ellsworth had used during his Sunday games of catch with his father.

"You afraid to die?" Ellsworth asked the boy.

"No, sir."

"Didn't think so. Come on then. There's nothing more normal than baseball." Ellsworth walked out from behind the parked cars, and the boy followed him into the no-man's-land.

"Raphael, no!" Anna Belle had stopped firing. "Ellsworth, what are you doing?"

*I'm gonna remind them, Anna Belle.*

He'd made it out to the middle of the clearing. He and Raphael stood about fifteen yards apart. The firing had decreased already. Whispers permeated the lines on both sides. "What are they doing?"

"They're playing a game of catch."

Ellsworth rotated the ball in his grip, felt the stitches against his palm and fingers. He tossed the ball across the field to Raphael, who caught it and looked surprised that he'd done so. He surveyed both sides and flinched as another bullet scuttled through the air. "Toss it back," said Ellsworth. "Don't pay them attention. Just you and me out here."

Raphael nodded and concentrated, the tip of his tongue jutted from the corner of his mouth. A bullet whizzed by, but this time he didn't jump. He reared back and hurled the ball as hard as he could.

Ellsworth's glove popped from the impact. He shook his hand just like his father used to do, pretending the throw had hurt his palm. He plucked the ball from his glove, located the seams, and threw again. Raphael caught it. Ellsworth's eyes blurred from tears. First time he'd thrown a ball since Eliza's death.

The fighting and the shooting had all but stopped. Someone fired, and it echoed, but there was no return fire. Both sides watched as Ellsworth played catch with Raphael.

The only sound now was the pop every time a pitch hit its mark inside the glove. Ellsworth tossed another one, harder this time, and Raphael caught it. The boy stepped back a few paces before returning the throw. Sunlight beamed from a bright blue sky, and Ellsworth welcomed the warmth on his face.

Guns lowered on both sides as Ellsworth threw another strike. Pop.

Raphael laughed, went into a windup, and fired the ball right back.

Ellsworth caught the ball and watched the woods.

A distant rumble resonated, grew louder, like a pack of animals trampling across a tundra. Eddington's men turned toward the woods behind them, the approaching sound. The men and women in the town square who'd been using the cars for shelter now walked in front of them to watch the woods.

First, birds flew out, red and blue birds, sparrows and egrets. Then came the smaller animals—chipmunks, squirrels, and mice, followed by raccoons and woodchucks and a few skunks. A deer darted from the shadows, and then another.

The rumbling came now as a wall, as dozens of deer scampered, ran, and zigzagged from the tree line. All running from something, running in waves into Bellhaven proper as Eddington's line of soldiers parted for them.

A cow from down the road walked into town and barreled headfirst into Gary Henshaw's grain silo, then backed up and did it again. The side of the silo gonged, and the cow backed up for more. Two horses ran in circles in front of the avenue of oaks, both of them leaping up to rub their heads in the draping moss.

On the hill, Lou Eddington's horse bucked and reared, flipping him to the ground.

The rumble grew louder. More deer poured from the woods.

Ellsworth recalled Old Man Tanner's story from decades earlier, his description of strange animals hurrying from the woods as he was going in with his gun and lantern. He found Tanner in the crowd beside the town hall. The old man stared at the sky, concerned, and then looked at his arm—in particular, at the hairs that were now standing on end.

"Main quake," Ellsworth said.

And then the earth started shaking.

# CHAPTER 27

The ground shook and roared for thirty-five seconds.

Ellsworth dropped to the grass after five and began counting as he crawled toward Raphael. "... Twenty-five, twenty-six, twenty-seven . . ." He reached the boy and held him. They counted out the rest together as trees uprooted, cleaving waves of soil around slanted trunks. Birds fled boughs and took flight, blotting sun and sky as shadows flashed across the ground and the screaming intensified. People held on to whatever they could. Two narrow fissures opened, ran jagged up the hillside. Eddington's men dropped to the ground. Another tree uprooted, bringing with it a ten foot wall of the dirt-clotted root. Birds filled the sky with shrill, hysterical panic.

Raphael covered his ears. "... Thirty, thirty-one . . ."

Behind the town hall, Anna Belle was on the ground with her head covered.

Ellsworth and Raphael started crawling toward her as colorful flower blooms floated through the air. Sand mounds spouted over the grounds like small volcanoes, spewing water and dust into the air. One formed next to Anna Belle. She rolled away from the blast and tucked into the fetal position. Another erupted right beneath Gus Cheevers and bucked him a foot from the ground.

". . . Thirty-two, thirty-three . . ."

A loud crack echoed from atop the hillside. Eddington's yellow house swayed while Lou Eddington walked toward it.

*No,* thought Ellsworth. *Back away!*

Shingles popped from the roof and the chimney bricks crumbled. The foundation moaned and creaked like an ocean liner splitting at sea.

". . . Thirty-four, thirty-five . . ."

And then everything settled with as little warning as it had started.

Silence crept across Bellhaven. One by one the citizens stood from their crouches, surveying damage in every direction. Chimneys had collapsed. Foundations had cracked. Verandas had separated from facades, many of the roofs collapsing to the porch boards in heaps and splinters.

The animals lingered. Deer nosed the spewing sand volcanoes. Horses trotted and neighed. The cow by the silo walked in a tight backward circle. A squirrel on its hind legs stared at the blue sky where thousands of birds soared.

Old Man Tanner surveyed the sand blows, studied the sky and trees, smelled the air, watched the animals. "It's not finished."

Rabbi Blumenthal staggered from the jailhouse, which miraculously had not collapsed in the quake. Plaster and brick dust billowed from the hole in the back of the building. He'd been locked inside the cell during the gunfight, but apparently the shaking had loosened the lock. A raccoon and three chipmunks skittered by the rabbi's feet. The smell of sulfur permeated the air.

Ellsworth and Raphael made it to their feet and hobbled toward Anna Belle. But the earth shook again, and the screaming began anew. Ellsworth put his arms around Anna Belle and Raphael, held them tight, and began counting.

". . . Four, five, six . . ."

Everything settled again. *The first aftershock.* A quick burst, but enough to shift what had been on the brink moments before.

The yellow house was the oldest in Bellhaven. It had survived the '86 quake, but although many of the structures in Charleston and even surrounding towns like Bellhaven had added earthquake bolts to reinforce unstable masonry, the old plantation house had added none. Now it cracked and splintered, shifted near the roof-line, and then crumbled inward—slowly at first, bricks at a time, then faster. Then the walls collapsed altogether, and puffs of dark dust spun out like tornado smoke.

Captured in all the smoke and debris was Lou Eddington, who'd never stopped his approach toward the house after the main quake. Ellsworth could hear him screaming as the dust settled. He was still alive, though surely his limbs would be smashed paste-board thin.

The three of them hustled up the hillside, dodging sand cones and fissures. They covered their mouths from the dust and squinted through haze, following Eddington's screams. The man's lower half was pinned under a pile of debris. They tossed it aside piece by piece—the arm of a chair, the cracked porcelain of a bath-tub, shingles from the roof, multiple bricks. Then half of a wooden chessboard, shredded trousers, a lone shoe.

Linda May appeared on the backside of the hill between the old slave quarters and the house, her face blackened by dust and smeared with tear trails. "Is he dead? Where's Alfred?"

Anna Belle ran to her, and Linda May fell into her arms.

Raphael knelt beside Eddington's head, gripped his hand. As soon as they got to the wound he would heal him. Eddington stared up at the boy, confused, while Ellsworth tossed and shoved the bricks away as if trying to rescue a long lost friend.

Eddington's men approached from the tree line with caution, joined by a group of town folk coming to help free Eddington from the rubble. Within minutes, two dozen men and women from both sides were working together to remove the debris, Gabriel and Uriel among them. Gabriel lifted armfuls of bricks at a time. She hurled away splintered wood like spears.

Five minutes later they pulled Eddington and his mangled legs free. They were bloodied and oddly contorted. His shoes were missing and his pants were darkened and torn. His eyes bulged red, but he'd stopped screaming. Shock dampened pain, but that was only temporary. Raphael closed his eyes, put his hands on the leg wounds.

Eddington relaxed, found a steady breathing rhythm, and then offered his hand to Ellsworth. "Is it too late to sit down and make sense of all this?"

"Focus on the living. Then we'll talk." Ellsworth patted Lou's shoulder and stood. Down below, most people were either injured or tending to the injured. But a dozen men and women now skirted the tree line, testing it like some of the deer were doing. But while the animals wanted to return to their homes, the people felt the pull toward the chapel.

The ground shook again, this time for only three seconds. When it was over, the relief sighs everywhere were palpable. The worst was over. Fear turned tears joyful.

Berny the mail carrier took a step into the woods. Dooby Klinsmatter followed him. Then someone else, and then another. Their walks became jogs, then sprints as they disappeared into the trees.

Four more people entered. Linda May tried to follow, but Anna

Belle wouldn't let her go, even as she slapped at her arms and clawed at Anna Belle's cheek. Eventually Anna Belle wrestled her to the ground, and Linda May stopped resisting.

Ellsworth ordered Gabriel and Uriel to follow the town people into the woods. "Don't let them into the chapel. Don't even let them into the clearing."

They sprinted at an angle that would allow them to cut off the mail carrier's path before he even hit the yellow trees.

"Sometimes they slip through."

It was Eddington talking. Ellsworth focused his attention back on him. "Who?"

"They come up through the magma." Eddington winced. The shock was wearing off, the adrenaline slowing. "Like gas and steam. The angels cast them deep into the fires, but sometimes they slip through. Come back up from the pits." Eddington was sweaty and pale, delirious. His eyelids fluttered, and he motioned for Raphael to scoot aside. His lips pressed together firmly, like he was accepting of his fate.

Ellsworth gently shook him. "Eddington. Lou?"

Lou's eyes popped open. "Real name's Lucius, but I always hated that name. Thought it sounded too much like the devil's namesake."

"A name is just a name," Ellsworth told him. "Now hang in there."

Father Timothy hovered over Ellsworth's shoulder. "The name Lucius—it's a Roman name derived from the Latin for light. So's the name Lucifer, for that matter."

"Ain't that a hoot, Father?" Eddington grinned, winced as pain surged. "There's cracks everywhere, but none bigger than here in Bellhaven." He was on the verge of passing out again, but then his eyes shot open, alert and wide. He gripped Ellsworth's forearm and pulled him closer. "It got me the day I first visited that house. Entered my body like a disease and got right down into my bones. But I visited that chapel. I heard the voice of my wife and kids, and I wept. You know why?"

Ellsworth shook his head.

"Because they told me I was forgiven." Tears welled in the sockets. "They told me they still loved me."

# CHAPTER 28

Including Alfred, five had died in the shoot-out.

By late afternoon they'd lined up the bodies on the gravel out-side the town hall and covered them with blankets for the locals to claim, which three did, including Linda May, who hadn't left Alfred's side since they placed his body on the dust. She wore remorse like a cloak as tears gushed. Anna Belle sat with her, fear-ing she might make a run for the woods. Who could blame her? She'd abandoned her blind husband. He'd died trying to win her back. And forgiveness was only a quick jaunt through those woods. Alfred's voice was probably already in that chapel right now.

"Watch her," Ellsworth told Anna Belle. "She makes the first move, tackle her."

Gabriel and Uriel were still deep in the woods, blocking passage to the chapel. So far everyone who'd attempted to enter the woods had returned back into town, dejected. To channel their unease, Ellsworth ordered them to clean up the mess the earthquake and shoot-out had caused. Two of the five bodies under the blankets had yet to be claimed. Probably out-of-towners who'd been lured in by the same presence that had inhabited Lou Eddington.

Hopefully that being had exited his body when the house

collapsed. So far the man showed no signs of being under any kind of foreign influence other than delirium.

The injured rested in the churches, some on makeshift cots and others on the floor. Two had been clipped by bullets; the rest had minor injuries from the earthquake. Eddington was the worst off. Dr. Philpot said he was lucky to be alive and, without saying it aloud, attributed the man's survival to what Raphael's hands had done when they'd pulled him out of the rubble. The doc had splinted Lou's legs and injected him with morphine Ellsworth pilfered from Alfred's stash at the bottom of his footlocker.

It was a town custom to lay out the recently deceased in their homes before burial so the town folk could pay their respects and gather for food. But Ellsworth didn't like the idea of spreading out from the town square, where everyone had now congregated. They needed to stay in a group. Omar and his men had already gone door to door to make sure no one was unaccounted for or unknowingly injured or dead.

As the sun began its final swoop toward the woods, Ellsworth stood atop the town hall's rubbled façade and announced his plan to honor the five dead inside the town hall, then hold the burials all at once. That way they could all stay together and watch one another. The chapel wasn't what they thought, and many were hearing of its evil for the first time. "If anyone feels the pull toward the woods, then it is everyone's duty to stop them." The town folk agreed, some with reluctance. Many looked drawn and weary, as if they could barely keep their eyes open.

"We'll feed the urge with good food," he told them as Anna Belle stepped beside him. "And comaraderie." More nods of reluctant agreement. "We've taken down names of all the survivors, and even those who've felt the need to join us in recent days." He eyed a man across the room, who only hours before had worn white Klan robes but now was outfitted in a white button-down, suspenders, and trousers. His eyes were red-rimmed, his face unshaven and spent. "You're welcome to stay, but just know that at the first sign of malcontent you will be sent on your way, and it won't be by soft hands."

The Klansman jerked a nod. "I can put names to the two unclaimed then. Butch Monroe is the one on the left there. And beside him is Elmer Cantain. May God give them both peace in the hereafter, since they couldn't fine none in the here." He settled his eyes on Omar across the parking lot, who stood smoking his pipe. The Klansman continued. "Bein' as they were unfairly slain by the wicked evildoers and some jumpy blacks."

The crowd grumbled.

Omar stepped forward, armed. "Who dat dem coward hide b'hind coward mask?"

The Klansman spat at the ground. "I wear no mask at the current."

Ellsworth held up his hand to quiet the crowd, then faced the Klansman. "That will be the last word of hatred spoken in my town. See this as your first and only warning before I send you on your way with your newly claimed in tow."

The man looked around, outnumbered, and nodded reluctantly. "What's your name?" said Ellsworth.

"Bo Blythe."

"Consider this your official welcome to Bellhaven, Bo Blythe. Now make yourself of some use and start cleaning up your dead."

\\\\////

They spent the next hour readying the bodies, displaying them in clean clothes and on tables placed in a row along the side wall of the town hall, which two dozen of the locals had taken upon themselves to clean. Cobwebs no longer hung from the rafters. The animals, birds, and rodents had been chased outside, their droppings swept out with the dust. The windows that weren't broken now shone clean, and the floorboards smelled of fresh cedar oil.

Night swooped in without incident as they worked. Occasionally some would pause to look out the windows toward the woods, but another would remind them of their task and work would resume. At one point Reverend Cane dropped his broom and walked out the busted front of the town hall toward the woods, but Rabbi Blumenthal hurried to stop him.

The two men shared a look and escorted each other back inside.

The electricity had been blown in the fire, and the incandescent light didn't work. So they hung lanterns on wall hooks and placed dozens of candles about the hall. The light cast nimbuses of fuzzy glow around the vast room—a calming tone for the joint wakes.

Outside the hall, Anna Belle led a team of a dozen others to cook up enough food to feed the town, which numbered just over a couple hundred. First, they'd gone out in groups to the homes and the damaged market to collect ingredients, deciding to cook it all in the kitchens of Anna Belle, Ellsworth, and Old Man Tanner, whose homes had held up against the quake. Despite the earthquake bolts added after '86, many of the other homes and structures had shifted, including the jailhouse. After Linda May prepared her husband's body, she joined Anna Belle in the kitchen to help take her mind off things. She'd dressed Alfred in his favorite Sunday suit and even placed pieces of that "darn radio" at his side.

Anna Belle put Linda May to work chopping celery for the gumbo Reverend Beaver was fixing over a kettle fire in Ellsworth's driveway. Minister Beaver seemed chastened and was spotted humming a song as he stirred the gumbo and eyed Frank Jessups across the way with what looked like an inkling of remorse.

No more scuffles or verbal altercations broke out, but the tension remained as people worked. Glances flashed as some passed. Jaws clenched at the sight of others. Few words were spoken, and most people kept to themselves. Whatever had seeped into their minds at the chapel and the yellow house would not be quickly erased, so Ellsworth kept them on task.

The sky outside was clear and scattered with stars. An occasional gust of wind whistled from the trees, and everyone paused and listened when it did. Ellsworth encouraged them to ignore the sound, to keep their minds on work and try not to think about the woods. But that was difficult with so many woodland creatures—deer, raccoons, woodchucks, and even several foxes—remaining around town as if afraid to reenter their homes.

A threesome of skittish deer lapped water from a birdbath in Beverly Adams's backyard. A half dozen more stood in front of the Pentecostal church, sniffing the air. Brother Bannerman eyed them all, but not as closely as he did the dozens of snakes slithering across the grounds. He picked up two copperheads, one for each hand, and began speaking in tongues. He'd already started to rally some of his Pentecostals toward his house and away from their work.

Ellsworth watched Bannerman from the parking lot, where he and Raphael were helping set up tables and chairs, expecting overflow from the town hall. They'd rolled in three empty whiskey barrels from Tommy Tankersly's shed and filled two of them with sweet tea, one with water.

The only near skirmish that evening happened between one of Bo's Klansmen and a member of Omar's congregation. But just before their words came to blows, the earth shook with another aftershock—just long enough to remind all that they were insignificant pieces in comparison.

Ten minutes later Dr. Philpot parted the crowd, pushing Lou

Eddington in a wheelchair. Mayor Bellhaven walked beside them, still red-eyed from weeping over his family's plantation home. They stopped in front of Ellsworth, who offered his hand, and Lou shook it. Ellsworth and three other men helped lift Eddington's chair up the stairs into the town hall, and then a line began to form to honor the dead.

An hour later everyone had paid their respects. Then a cluster of clergy led a solemn procession to the Bellhaven cemetery, with grieving townspeople close behind. When the prayers had been said and the bodies buried, they made their way back to the square, ready to move from solemnity to food.

They eagerly filled their plates with corn bread, fried ham and chicken, cheesy grits, green beans, and Anna Belle's famous hoppin' John. For dessert they had an assortment of pies and cobblers—blueberry, blackberry, pumpkin, and apple. The chatter increased while they ate, but only to a steady murmur—most people were focused on their food and too busy eyeing the woods.

After surveying the tables both in and outside the hall, Ellsworth noted a change in the division of people. Hours ago it had been those on the hillside in a gunfight with those below. Now, as they gathered to eat, the two sides intermingled again, albeit cautiously, but the people had more or less divided themselves according to religion and race. Pentecostals sat with Pentecostals, Protestants with their various Protestant groups, Catholics with Catholics, blacks with the blacks, and on down the line. Instead of two sides, the town seemed to be separating in numerous subgroups.

Ellsworth didn't like the look of that, either. He didn't like the looks each table gave the other, either, especially since almost everyone was still heeled. Rifles leaned against chairs, and pistols rested next to plates, all within arm's reach and still loaded.

The only one not eating was Brother Bannerman, who had

ventured closer to the outdoor tables with his two new pet snakes. But these two, unlike the placid Adam and Eve, looked angry. Everyone stopped eating to watch as the snakes coiled restlessly around Bannerman's forearms and wrists. He held the snakes up high and started tapping his right foot in the dust, calling out to his Savior and condemning everyone to eternal damnation and hellfire, to which three of the Mormons and two of Bo Blythe's Protestant unhooded Klansmen took offense and stood from their chairs.

The snake coiled around Bannerman's right arm and sank its fangs down into the meat of the preacher's hand. He screamed but didn't stop preaching. The snake in his left hand then lurched out and bit Bannerman's neck just below the jawline. Bannerman stumbled backward, arms swooping, and crashed to the gravel. Both snakes slithered away as Bannerman writhed on the ground.

Ellsworth had seen copperhead bites before. Though rarely deadly unless the one bitten was allergic to the venom, they were painful. But Bannerman was laughing. The men who'd been ready to attack him moments ago stood down, their faces confused.

Raphael hurried to the preacher and put his hands on the two wounds simultaneously. Bannerman fought him, screaming for the Lord Jesus Christ to cast that boy devil away. He made it to his feet, and three of his brethren escorted him to his house. All the way there he kept shouting that the good Lord would save him if it was his will.

Ellsworth let Bannerman go. He had bigger problems to worry about. A mysterious commotion sounded from the woods, and the crowd grew alarmed. Deer scampered at the tree line, and redbirds flew in and out of the shadows. Gabriel and Uriel emerged from the woods, walking side by side, hurrying at first and then slowing as they noticed the gathered crowd.

Ellsworth gestured for everyone to remain calm and then met

Gabriel and Uriel beside the town hall, out of earshot from the others.

Gabriel was out of breath, but spoke calmly. "It's growing, Ellsworth."

"What's growing?"

Uriel said, "The clearing around the chapel."

"It's not gradual anymore," Gabriel added. "The leaves are withering. Trees are dying one by one. The clearing is expanding outward."

"Spreading like water across a table," said Uriel.

Ellsworth hadn't noticed it initially. But now, as Uriel stepped into the moonlight, he did. "Your hair!"

Uriel touched his hair. "What of it?"

"It's white."

"I warned you." Gabriel looked down at Uriel. "You stood in one place too long."

# CHAPTER 29

While everyone was still in the town hall, Ellsworth decided to call a meeting.

He connected three tables on one end of the hall and gathered the leaders from each church, along with Lou, Anna Belle, Tanner, Gabriel, Uriel, and—out of respect for the office—Mayor Bellhaven. In a show of solidarity he invited the Klansman Bo Blythe as well. He wanted all parties represented at this head table.

Raphael had declined a seat, claiming he had something else he had to do.

Gabriel brought three cases of Old Sam from Ellsworth's shed, and she wasn't stingy with the pours. No one objected, even the ardent drys in the hall. Bo Blythe stared at his shot, contemplating, then held it up as if toasting the table and downed it in one gulp. He poured more, swirled it, and stared to his side, where Omar sat positioning a wax straw through the slit of his mask. He sucked bourbon and swallowed it like water.

Blythe scooted his chair another inch away from Omar, as if he actually believed what he'd said when he'd sat down beside the man on Ellsworth's order—that he couldn't get too close in fear of "catching a colored disease." To which Omar had exhaled pipe smoke in his direction and the Klansman had been too stubborn to move from the cloud.

Ellsworth carefully watched both men, glad that neither of them was heeled. Before the meeting he'd requested as sheriff that all weapons be left outside the hall. He'd gotten pushback from several, including both Bo and Omar, but ultimately they'd agreed to disarm and parlay peacefully.

Ellsworth offered a toast to those who had died and called the meeting to order. He reiterated what Uriel and Gabriel had told them about the woods surrounding the chapel. The clearing around the structure was growing outward, killing trees as it moved.

"As what moves?" asked Anna Belle. "What exactly are we dealing with here?"

"Whatever is inside that chapel. It's coming up from the ground."

Tanner retold the story of the '86 earthquake, when he'd initially found the chapel hidden in the brush. "Everyone here now knows what it did to me, how it aged me and jingled my brain. That didn't stop me from going in, anymore than it stopped you. But once I realized what it was doing to me, I started clearing out the woods around it."

"Why?" asked Anna Belle.

"So that I could share it with the rest of the town." Tanner chewed his lip. "But not in the good way, Anna Belle. And I'm sorry about that. But it had its claws so deep into my brain that my intent was to take the entire town down the same hellish road I'd been on."

Uriel patted Old Man Tanner's shoulder. "Don't blame yourself."

"Ain't got nobody else *to* blame," Tanner said in a huff. "If I'd been stronger, I would've stopped. It maybe slipped me the thoughts, but I still had free will. It's just that the line was blurred.

And I didn't know whatever it was would gain steam. But it did. The more people visited, the stronger that chapel became." He gulped his bourbon. "I gotta say, I didn't see that coming."

"But what *is* it?" asked Anne Belle.

"The devil is what it is." All eyes shot to Lou Eddington in his wheelchair. "That's what everyone's thinking but not saying. It's in there dangling that apple and daring us to pull it from the tree." He slurred his speech slightly—he'd mixed bourbon with morphine—but was coherent enough to make sense. "I believe I was pulled here because of my intense need to be forgiven. I was vulnerable. Weak. A simple artist seeking answers."

"An easy host," said Ellsworth.

Lou agreed. "The day I visited that house, I went up to the third-floor attic. Something didn't feel right up there. There was a window—a little round dormer that turned in its frame like a globe, and it was open just a smidge. About two-dozen flies buzzed around it, so I crossed over to close it. But when I got within a couple of feet of the window, chill bumps covered my body, then I got so hot I nearly fainted. I dropped to one knee. And then I had this feeling that something was trying to squeeze into my body. I tell you, it was strange.

"After that, one by one, those flies died right in front of me—just dropped out of the air to the floorboards. There was one left, buzzing and tapping against the window glass like it was trying to get out, but then it died like the others. That dormer started spinning in and out, in and out, and then it closed with a snap, airtight. Bam. I blew at the dead flies, and they scattered like dry leaves would. I left the house in a hurry and swore never to return."

Mayor Bellhaven said, "But you did."

Lou nodded. "Bought it the very next day. But by that time it already owned me. It also gave me bad ideas I knew were wrong."

He looked directly at Ellsworth. "I stayed up night after night carving those chess pieces of the town. And I moved your piece right to the middle of the board along with Tanner's."

"I heard a voice," Tanner said. "That's when I walked across the street and stabbed you."

"Except the voice referred to him as Michael, right?" Tanner blinked, nodded, as Lou glanced around the table. "At the end of the big 'quake yesterday, I walked toward the house, even as I saw it tilting. It was still pulling me, like it wanted to take me down with it, and I didn't have the know-how to resist. But then something happened, just as I reached the sunporch. My knees started wobbling, my skin tingled like pinpricks, and then suddenly I felt . . . lighter, like a shucked corncob. I felt that thing leave me, just as noticeably as I'd felt it arrive inside the attic weeks before. Then the house collapsed. I was sure I was going to die, and I'm still not quite certain why I didn't, but I'm grateful."

His story finished, Lou gave Ellsworth a little nod and pulled out his tobacco pouch. He concentrated on the ritual of stuffing his pipe and lighting it while conversation buzzed around the table and more bourbon was poured.

Bo Blythe said, "So what are we doing here? Sitting around telling campfire tales?"

Omar leaned back in his chair, sipped more Old Sam through his straw. "Tell dem what story you got now, cracker. Killin' and beatin' up dem blacks."

Bo stood, knocking his chair to the floor.

Omar was out of his seat in a flash, toe to toe with the Klansman, his mask inches away from Blythe's face.

Ellsworth pounded the table and stood. "Stand down. Both of you."

Blythe kept his eyes on Omar but spoke to Ellsworth. "Remind me again why we're takin' orders from a one-legged man with a chump badge."

Ellsworth said, "'Cause this one-legged man is the one now doin' the talkin'. And he's tellin' you to either sit down or leave town. Nobody here's stopping you."

"Maybe I will." Blythe downed the rest of his bourbon and slammed the glass down hard on the tabletop. "Maybe I will."

Anna Belle said, "Only cowards hide behind hoods."

Blythe said, "I wear no hood at the current, woman."

Anna Belle pointed at Ellsworth. "Because *he* ordered you not to. Just as he ordered you to leave your weapon at the door." Blythe scoffed at the notion. Anna Belle went on, raised her voice. "How many times have you been stabbed in the chest and lived? How many times did you have your leg blown off and come back to tell about it? How many train derailments have you lived through? How many times did you live through disease or knock on death's door and still come out fighting? Huh?"

Blythe chewed the inside of his mouth but didn't answer.

Gabriel said, "Ellsworth is the only one here equipped to lead us against an enemy none of us can see. The other side's been trying to kill him since the day he first took breath." Whispers turned into head nods and affirmation. Gabriel glared at Blythe. "You ain't left yet because you're scared. And you're listening to that one-legged man because that's just what we do around here."

Blythe said, "So what do we do now? I'm not one to run from a fight. And whatever's out there is responsible for the deaths of two of my brethren."

Ellsworth said, "Two of *our* comrades. There is no more 'me' in this town. It's 'us'—" He pointed out the town-hall window. "—against them. And by the looks of things it's them who's winning right now."

Omar stood there for just a second before scooting his chair back and facing forward. Blythe stood there for another awkward moment, clearly trying to save face. Then he nodded, picked his chair back up, and sat in it.

Omar scooted his chair back in and faced forward.

Ellsworth took his seat. "I was born and raised Catholic, as was Father Timothy here. My friend Omar is a Muslim. Reverends Cane, Beaver, Yarney, and Hofhamm are Protestant. Rabbi Blumenthal is Jewish. I could go on but I won't, and I'm not telling you anything you don't already know. But what we are as individuals don't mean a hill of beans in a hog house. If the devil is what we're facing, he'll only succeed if we let'm."

"Hear, hear," said Lou.

"He's turned us against one another," said Reverend Cane.

"Segregated a town we once swore would never be segregated," Ellsworth added. "The town I was born into valued inclusion. What thoughts of hate or disdain we may have had for one another was bottled and buried, our temptations churned into camaraderie and laughter, dancing, and music." Heads nodded around the table. "Our enemy might be invisible, but we allowed that invisible evil to manifest when we made the choice to turn against our brethren."

Ellsworth downed a gulp of Old Sam and his voice picked up steam. "But I say, no more of that."

"No more," echoed Moses Yarney, staring across the table at Reverend Beaver.

"We each have our own places of worship," said Ellsworth. "Our own denominations and what-not, but this here town hall has always been *our* church—the Bellhaven church. The one place where one and all were welcome at the table." Gabriel nodded emphatically from her place next to Uriel.

Ellsworth poured more bourbon and stood. "My father built

317

this town hall for a reason. I remember the wise words he said before he left this earth. Church is people. Church is art. Church is music." He held up his glass. "Church is the gathering, ladies and gentlemen. And sometimes that's all that's needed." He tipped his head back and swallowed, and everyone around the table did likewise.

Ellsworth wiped his mouth with a shirtsleeve. "Our town gathering place was burned down three years ago because of hatred. Then we got muddled up with the war and its repercussions. It's long past time now that we find a way to gather again. Our beliefs may be different. Some may not believe at all. But we have the same questions, the same needs, the same desire for good to prevail. And it's time to focus again on what brings us together instead of what could tear us apart."

He turned toward Bo Blythe. "You asked what we're going to do. Well, I'll tell you. In the morning we will formulate a plan and enter the woods *together*. And *together* we'll defeat whatever this is that's been tearing our town and our lives apart. Are you with me?"

A roar of approval filled the hall. Everyone stood, energized, swelling with pride, shaking hands and patting shoulders. The energy spread outward to the rest of the hall. Heads turned toward the entrance as Raphael backed into the hall. He guided four men who carefully carried Anna Belle's piano inside. They placed it under the window, and a fifth man situated the bench just where Raphael pointed.

Then the boy sat and played.

Ellsworth couldn't quite place what it was he played—Eliza would have known; she had an ear for such things—but the sound was warm bathwater, the chords a soothing ointment for all their wounds. All eyes settled on Raphael as his healing fingers danced across the keyboard. And when he finished, the town hall applauded.

Ellsworth, with Anna Belle's help, stood atop his chair and shouted over the throng. "There's plenty of food left over and bellies yet to be filled." He held up his bottle. "And there's plenty more of these left in my shed. May the roof above us never fall in, and may we friends beneath it never fall out!"

Now Raphael was playing Mozart—or was it Beethoven? It didn't matter. Three couples had already joined hands and begun dancing.

Omar walked past Ellsworth in a hurry for the door. "Dat music need more. Time to blow dem dust off dat ol' bass o' mine and make dis rooftop go pop."

"And tell Trapper to get his violin!"

Anna Belle helped Ellsworth from the chair and whispered in his ear. "Thank you."

"For what?"

She shrugged, then took his hand and pulled him to the middle of the hall.

"Anna Belle, what are you doing?"

"We're dancing."

"I don't dance anymore."

"Eliza always thought you were a graceful dancer."

"When I had two legs."

She gripped his left hand and placed her other on his shoulder. "How about this?"

"How 'bout what?"

"Shut your head, Ellsworth, and just follow my lead."

They soon found a steady cadence. Omar returned with his double bass and the town barber with his violin. Soon after that Beverly Adams started singing, and moments later Gabriel joined her. Soon the town hall was full to the rafters with music and noise and laughter. "Turn Your Light Off, Mister Moon Man." "Swing

Low, Sweet Chariot." "Oh, Johnny, Oh Johnny, Oh!" "Joshua Fit the Battle of Jericho." The entire hall joined in the singing.

The music was so loud that no one could hear outside, where the sound of leaves in the trees slowly died, the chapel's clearing grew outward from the heart of the Bellhaven woods, and the whispers grew so constant that the woods now had a musical drone of its own.

Something akin to a swarm of bees.

# CHAPTER 30

The town hall had some magic left in it after all.

All it needed was reminding.

By three in the morning half the bourbon had been consumed. Everyone was relaxed and fighting tiredness, but they didn't want the night to end. Lou drunkenly sang Irving Berlin's "Oh! How I Hate to Get Up in the Morning." Reverend Cane played cards with Father Timothy, who was laughing because he'd made Anna Belle Roper blush moments ago—telling her she was pretty and if he wasn't a priest he'd marry her. Reverend Cane was laughing because Beverly Adams had just brought him a piece of apple pie, saying she'd run out of dead crickets. At one point Reverend Beaver left his Methodist cluster and tottered over unsteadily to shake hands with Moses Yarney. The AME pastor and his friends responded warily, but the two men spoke enough civil words to be considered a conversation. Reverend Beaver then approached Frank Jessups and invited him back into the church. He even embraced Jessups in a long hug that drew an odd look from Beaver's wife.

Across the room, Gabriel arm wrestled Gus Cheevers and Reverend Hofhamm at the same time. And after she slammed both their arms to the table, she danced with jingle-brained Timmy

Tankersly, who didn't seem to know what he was doing but loved every minute of it.

Omar plucked his double bass to accompany Raphael on the piano and Dr. Philpot on his clarinet. And when that song was over, he leaned his instrument against the wall and went full throttle into the fastest hambone the town hall had ever seen, stomping his feet and patting his hands on his legs, sides, chest, the top of his head, and even his mouth slit like this night would be his last. "If dem diamond ring don't shine, Momma's gonna buy you dem bottle of wine. If dat bottle of wine gets broke, Momma's gonna buy dem a billy goat . . ." His rhythmic gyrations and deep bass voice must have thawed whatever tension remained with Bo Blythe, because two minutes later Bo was in a chair beside Omar taking a hambone lesson and singing "Home Sweet Home" in a reedy tenor.

At just past four in the morning, Ellsworth spotted Anna Belle leaning against the piano while Raphael played. The boy never seemed to tire, and neither did the town folk on the dance floor, shuffling and stepping through the lantern glow and smiling like the old days.

Ellsworth leaned in close to Anna Belle's ear. "I reckon I still owe you that walk."

"Thought you'd never ask." She offered her elbow, and together they strolled outside, where more people partied and danced in the parking lot. They toasted Ellsworth as he passed, but he shied away from the attention, guiding Anna Belle in the opposite direction.

The air was balmy for this early in the spring, more like steamy Charleston air after summer rain. The clear sky was full of stars and circling birds, all black under the moonlight. Ellsworth led Anna Belle toward the avenue of oaks, where he and Eliza used to take their daily walk. Still choked with cars, the road was passable on foot.

After a while, Ellsworth let go of her elbow and cupped her

hand palm to palm. The night they'd spent together on the jail-house floor had connected them, placed a bridge over their playful bickering and brought them to terms with what it had been in the first place—flirting. They both knew they carried a torch for one another, but neither of them needed to verbalize it. They'd known each other since they were kids. Now they were both grown, both widowed. And both knew just how fragile life could be.

"This is nice, Ellsworth."

"Can't argue with that, Anna Belle."

They swayed together as they strolled beneath the vaulted ceiling of limbs. His arm tingled from her touch, and his heart sped in a way he'd doubted it ever would again. She'd been his first kiss at age twelve, and he reckoned it wouldn't be the worst thing in the world if she was the last. He stopped, faced her, and then leaned in until their lips touched. Hers were as soft as he'd remembered, with a pinch of bourbon on her breath. She laughed and he did, too, and they stood for a moment with their foreheads touching.

"What's funny?" he asked.

"I don't know."

He looked over Anna Belle's shoulder. "We have company though." Omar had followed them outdoors with his rifle and watched from a distance. He'd sworn to protect Ellsworth, and he wasn't backing down from that promise. "I don't think Omar likes us being out here alone."

Anna Belle tiptoed and kissed him again, this time with a finality that said it was all he was getting tonight. "I suppose we are breaking your own rules. No straying from the pack."

"I reckon so. Do you hear that?"

She nodded. Away from the music, the noises from the woods were more noticeable. It sounded like an army of cicadas was at war with a swarm of bees.

"This party, as much as we all needed it, is just a bandage," said Ellsworth. "Come morning, there will be blood."

"Do you have a plan?"

"No. Figured I'd sleep on it."

"Only have a couple hours left to sleep."

"I don't need much."

"Well, whatever you decide, I'm going with you tomorrow."

He gripped her hand again. "Figured as much."

She squeezed his palm, and they started back toward the town hall. "Heaven has no rage like love to hatred turned," she quoted. "Nor hell a fury like a woman scorned."

"Shakespeare?"

"William Congreve."

"Never heard of him."

"Doesn't make it untrue, Ellsworth."

They walked the next two minutes in silence, until the piano and violin and laughter again began to drown out the ominous buzz from the woods. Omar tipped his hat as they passed, and Ellsworth returned the gesture. But instead of returning to the town hall, Anna Belle pulled Ellsworth to the other side of the road and toward his house.

She said, "Omar, we'll be in for the night."

Omar laughed. "All right den, Mrs. Roper."

Anna Belle led Ellsworth to his front door. Her pace quickened at the stairs. He did his best to keep up as she climbed each one, even as his heart threatened to jump from his chest.

# CHAPTER 31

Ellsworth opened his eyes once more to sunlight and birdsong.

Shadows flashed past the window. Wings fluttered. But beyond the high-pitched bird chatter, the drone from the woods still loomed, louder now than it had last night. He reached across the bed, found that side empty, and then startled when he heard another voice in the room.

"She went home to get ready."

Ellsworth sat up, clunked the headboard. "Gabriel? What are you doing in here?"

Gabriel sat on a wooden chair in overalls and dusty boots. A four-foot-long wooden box rested across her lap. Her sandy hair was long enough now for a small ponytail that she wore tied up atop her head like the curved handle of a teacup. "You know, this doesn't surprise me none."

"What doesn't surprise you?"

"You and Anna Belle." She said it with a half smile, but Ellsworth sensed hurt. And then the smile grew full. "When we were kids, I used to imagine being married to you."

"You did?"

"All the girls in Bellhaven did. We all carried a torch, and you know it. Don't be so coy."

"Not trying to. Just didn't think I was that much to set eyes upon."

"It was the way you carried yourself—with a confidence that was contagious. And a kindness you wore on your sleeve."

He furrowed his brow. "Did we have kids?"

"Pardon?"

"You said you imagined marrying me. Did we have any imaginary kids with this union?"

"Oh." She blushed, tried to hide it, then nodded. "Twelve."

"Twelve kids?"

She laughed. "Twelve kids."

"You're holding up fairly well then, Gabriel. Twelve kids. Wow."

"You always were so unassuming." She stroked her hand across the woodgrain of the box on her lap like it was a pet. "But you were the leader we all looked up to. Still do."

"What's that on your lap?"

She flipped a metal latch, and the wooden box opened from a central seam. "I've been working on it for days now." He caught a flash of sunlight off steel. "Maybe you should get out of bed first."

He swung his leg from the covers not bothering to hide his cotton underdrawers and white undershirt. Gabriel didn't look away as he strapped on his prosthesis, slid on a pair of tan britches, and cinched them with a belt. It wasn't like she'd never seen him half clothed, with all the times they'd gone swimming in the Atlantic or scrounging the salt ponds for blue crab.

Ellsworth crossed the room to her but stopped cold when he got close enough to see inside the narrow box.

"Go ahead," she said. "Just don't cut me with it."

Inside the box, a sword rested on a bed of red velvet. He gripped the hilt and lifted it from the box. The steel shone so brilliantly it was nearly blue.

*Blue Fire.* The knight sword he'd dreamed of as a kid.

Gabriel stood beside him. "It's double-edged. With a blood groove down the center."

"To lighten the blade, yes."

"And there's gold blended inside the cross guard and the pommel."

"For balance." Ellsworth touched the rounded pommel, gripped the hilt with both hands, slowly navigated the blade through the air, and then ran his finger down the beveled grove that the fuller had carved into the steel.

"I smelted down some slave shackles and whatever old iron I could find."

Ellsworth studied the blade, then looked at her. "Why the sword?"

"Brother Bannerman is dead," she said, ignoring the question. "They found him in the woods this morning, along the tree line. Half his hair had turned white. He was on his way back out instead of in. Dr. Philpot thinks he died of an attack of the heart, coupled with the copperhead bites."

Then she eyed the sword in his hands. "That's for today, when we go into battle." He started to contradict her, but a battle was exactly what loomed. "Michael the Archangel," she said. "He's always been depicted with a sword when he fights the dragon. He's the protector and leader of God's army. And he was the conqueror of Satan during the war in heaven when Satan and the fallen angels were cast down to earth." She shrugged. "If you believe in such a thing."

She patted Ellsworth's shoulder. "There's a scabbard downstairs that goes along with it."

Ellsworth fought tears. "Thank you."

She leaned down, kissed his cheek. She smelled of oven dust and forging tools, of safety. "Say, Ellsworth, I was . . . I mean, I've been wanting to . . ." She wiped her brow and sighed. "When you went into that slave house, back when we were nine . . ." She shook her head.

He knew what she wanted to ask. But answering it now would put too much finality on things, such as they were. So instead he put his hand around the back of her neck and kissed her mouth. When he pulled away, her cheeks were red and her eyes glowed. "You were saying?"

She blushed even deeper. "Oh, nothing. Never mind. Just lost my head there for a moment." She laughed and wiped her mouth. "Always hoped you'd be my first kiss. I just never imagined it would take this long." She pointed to the closet, where a beige suit pinstriped in red hung on the outside of the door along with a matching fedora.

"I set that out for you." She flashed that half smile again. "Always thought you looked fetching in it."

\\\///

Ellsworth limped down the street with his fedora slanted against the morning sun, the sword in its scabbard around his waist, and a shotgun propped against his shoulder.

Anna Belle walked beside him wearing a white blouse, brown vest, and trousers that looked like Calvin's, rolled up at the ankles and cinched with one of his belts. She had a rifle in her left hand and extra ammunition draped over her right shoulder. *Will bullets even work?* Who knew, but it made sense to have *something.*

Following Rabbi Blumenthal's advice from a few days ago—"*I don't think the chapel likes fire, Ellsworth.*"—Gabriel hefted two flaming torches. Hopefully they'd stay lit when they got close. *If* they got close.

Uriel was with them too, striding with a pistol on each hip, a coiled rope around his neck, and the mayor's flamethrower in both hands.

And Raphael stuck close by Ellsworth's side, carrying a medical kit inside a satchel he'd propped over his shoulder.

The street seemed strangely deserted, and Ellsworth wondered briefly if it would be just the four of them going to battle in the woods. *If that's the way it is, we're ready.* But then they skirted the town hall to find the whole town gathered in the field on the edge of the woods. At least it looked like the whole town. Every religious leader stood with his flock—not in huddled clusters, but as one collective line with no breaks, one congregation blending in with the next.

Rabbi Blumenthal stood armed with the Talmud. Reverend Beaver carried a Bible and a candle. Reverend Cane carried an open Bible and recited verse. Omar, heeled with a couple of pistols under his jacket, held the Koran outstretched in both hands. Father Timothy carried a gold cross; Reverend Hofhamm a cross and a German Bible. Reverend Moses Yarney stood side by side with Bo Blythe's unhooded Klansmen, the lot of them whispering prayers as they gazed out toward the woods. The Watchtower people stood toe to toe with the Latter-day Saints. Even Lou Eddington had been prepared for battle, propped atop a brown mare with his legs fastened in stirrups and his lower back braced by wood across the saddle.

Ellsworth looked up and down the line and spotted Father Radkin twenty yards to his left, dressed in deep purple and holding a thurible of smoking incense.

"He came after all," he whispered to Anna Belle.

"I heard he arrived just after sunup," she whispered back. "Now what's the plan?"

"Just what I said last night," he said. "We all go in *together*." He took a step toward the woods, and the rest of Bellhaven followed.

It was beautiful in the woods this early in the morning. Dew dappled the colorful blooms of every tree, flower, and bush. Butterflies danced and fluttered through patches of sunlight. Hummingbirds twittered and darted. But twenty yards in they saw the first dead deer. Raphael insisted they stop to bury it with deadfall.

Over the next quarter mile they found a dozen more deer lying stiff, all in positions that suggested retreat. *Brave animals. Frontline soldiers.* They left them where they'd died. It was too risky to stand still for the amount of time it would take to cover them. Even in the five minutes it had taken Raphael to bury the first deer, everyone had grown panicked. The antsy feeling of being watched had overwhelmed them. They'd had to move on.

Once they were past the yellow trees, everything in the woods seemed to bloom more vibrantly—violet azaleas and white oleander, pink and red camellias, sun-bright goldenrod. *Don't be fooled by the beauty.* They pushed their line onward, separating only to navigate trees or cross gurgling streams lined with colorful foliage and berries. They sang and recited verse in defiance of the increasingly loud, buzzing drone of the unseen.

Lou cantered his horse up next to Ellsworth. "I had a dream last night of a great fire. And I dreamed I died today in these woods." They walked silent for a minute. "I think I'm ready," said Lou.

"You don't go into battle unless you are," said Ellsworth. *But am I now?* Memories of last night with Anna Belle still resonated. Her shoulder nestled in the crook of his arm. The smell of her hair and the beating of her heart against his palm. He stole a glance and found her eyes on him as she moved through the woods with rifle in hand and that belt of ammo over her shoulder.

Lou rubbed the horse's neck. "My wife and two kids, they were dying from the Spanish flu. It hit them so fast—they were fine one day and the next day they were at death's door, literally gasping for air. Deborah begged me to do what the doctor would not. Nobody ever recovered after being that far gone, and she couldn't stand to see our boys suffer like that, even for another night. She begged me to let her go at the same time they did, all of them together. She feared that if they died at different times, they'd be separated somehow in the afterlife."

Lou paused, swallowed, and looked down at Ellsworth with anguish in his eyes. "So I liquored up and injected them one-by-one, lay with them until the end. I thought I was doing the right thing, but I've wondered ever since."

Ellsworth clenched his jaw, patted Lou's leg. "What you heard in the chapel . . . you're forgiven."

"But am I? We both know now that it wasn't really them talking."

Ellsworth didn't have an answer to that. Lou was right. Everything they'd heard there was fool's gold. But he touched Lou's boot again, and they continued on together.

Birds flew both above and below the canopy of dark gnarled boughs and flowering magnolias, twittering and whistling as they fluttered in and out of sunlight and shadow, surface and sky—cardinal birds everywhere, plus blue jays and sparrows, warblers and hummingbirds. A woodpecker tapped against a nearby tree. Donald Trapper stopped to watch, and Gus Cheevers grabbed his arm to keep him moving. Heads turned at every sound. Eyes flicked with every gust of wind.

Ellsworth warned them to ignore it all. When the woods got denser, he used his sword to strike down vines and clear deadfall. As the droning intensified, he walked with both hands on the hilt, the blade poised in front of him, ready to strike, just as he'd been ready to cut the imaginary slave masters had they come out of those slave houses years ago.

"The air's getting thicker," said Gabriel. "Harder to breathe."

Father Timothy shifted his cross to one arm so he could loosen the collar around his neck. Others had begun to scratch at their hairlines and arms. Lou's horse neighed and bucked and dug its hooves into the ground. Raphael coaxed her into moving forward again.

The cardinal birds flew low, dipping more than they had previously, fluttering over shoulders and between legs as if trying to communicate. And then roughly two dozen clustered to form a ball in the air before scattering, spinning away like wind-tossed rose petals, diving low to the ground again and kicking up loose leaves.

"They're trying to slow us down," said Tanner, whose pace had quickened as they ventured more deeply into the woods. He was now only steps behind Ellsworth and Gabriel, holding a torch and a jar of gasoline. "They're trying to distract us."

The drone grew louder, painful, forcing many in the line to slow and hold their ears. A yellow warbler flew directly into a tree trunk and dropped to the ground. A sparrow did the same against another tree five yards away.

Gus Cheevers slowed, then stopped. He watched the birds and scratched at his neck, his breathing labored. His eyes glazed, and his hand rose toward his head, pointing the barrel of his revolver toward his temple. His grip shook, but just as his finger twitched against the trigger, Anna Belle grabbed his arm and pulled him from his trance. He gulped, sweat dripping, and thanked Anna Belle with a nod.

It was that way up and down the line, but they pressed on, helping each other. Father Radkin clinked the thurible with small, controlled swings, pushing incense and smoke across the path, reciting Latin prayers as he shuffled along.

Another cardinal bird flew into a tree and dropped dead to the ground.

They neared the clearing, which had indeed grown outward to a hundred-yard radius of dead trees and black, ashy leaves, shriveling so fast now it was visible to the naked eye. The smell of burnt leaves was so thick it made the air even harder to breathe.

Their torches rippled. The flames whooshed, grew weak, then whooshed again.

Reverend Hofhamm dropped to his knees, coughing and grabbing his throat, as did dozens on down the line, ripping at their collars. The buzzing drone pulsed with the wind, and with it came the screams. Reverend Cane and Reverend Yarney held their Bibles high and walked deeper into the charred clearing where moss burned like wicks and leaves crumbled black.

Bo Blythe fired toward the chapel in the distance, the broken door swaying as light flickered inside, casting prisms through colored glass. More drew their weapons and fired as Bo clutched his neck and dropped to the ground, choking and gagging.

Father Radkin's voice grew louder, spitting out Latin verse, sifting incense, his posture wavering. Father Timothy helped him along, the two of them walking deeper into the unknown, where unseen voices cut through the wind and echoed so loudly that ears began to bleed.

The blade of Ellsworth's sword moved as if tugged. Pressure against his legs made walking almost impossible. The air was quicksand. He cut his sword in a swath, and it moved in slow motion.

Dooby Klinsmatter suddenly screamed, stopped cold, and then began methodically walking backward, firing his rifle into the air. Linda May Dennison ran full steam into a tree trunk and dropped in a bundle. She got up slowly and did it again before Raphael could get hold of her resisting arms.

Omar gripped the Koran in his left hand and fired with his right. One of his men clawed at his throat, dropped to the ground, choking. Seconds later two more men dropped.

The chapel door rattled, then flung open and slammed against the façade.

Ellsworth felt more pressure against his sword. "Something's coming through."

*How can we fight what we can't see?*

Thousands of cardinal birds circled. *They're here for a reason.* Then a massive cluster flew toward Ellsworth, spinning and fluttering until they formed what looked to be the contour of a man standing seven feet tall and approaching unimpeded.

The birds had outlined the unseen shape, made the invisible visible.

*Was this what Raphael saw on the outskirts of the woods when he got to Bellhaven? The man made of cardinal birds?*

Omar fired as the figure stepped forward. The birds scattered from the bullet but formed again a few feet away—around another approaching figure. Omar fired again with the same result. Across the clearing, both in the open space and the area between the charred tree trunks, birds swooped from the sky with a purpose, clustering together to form the contours of whatever was emerging from the chapel's door.

Tanner had called them demons. There were dozens of them now, all coming toward their line. All made visible by the clustering birds.

Shots fired, birds scattered, reformed. The forms charged, blowing their line back. Many of the town folk hit the ground, coughing and clutching their throats.

One of the cardinal-bird forms approached Ellsworth. He swung the sword in an arc and cut a path through the birds, clipping feathers and beaks before the birds scattered and reformed three paces back. Another figure approached, and another. Ellsworth cut the first with his sword, a parallel swipe to the ground that severed the form at the waist, but the second was upon him, reaching with arms of flapping wings, clicking beaks, and beady eyes.

A yellow warbler flew in the clot of cardinal birds, as well as a green hummingbird. A shot rang out, but unlike the sword, the bullet did little to scatter the form. More birds hurried in, mostly cardinals, but also birds feathered white, yellow, blue, and black.

Two dozen forms now attacked their line in a flurry of feathers. Bullets cleaved but passed through, taking chunks from the chapel and trees and plunking into the stream. *Are the bullets doing anything?* Ellsworth hacked with his sword and scattered another form.

*We have to get to the chapel somehow. Have to burn it down.* But so many of the cardinal figures now stood in their way, and all the torches were flickering low as if they were choking too. Gabriel fought off form after form with the torches in her swinging hands, her fists colliding in puffs of red feathers as more of her brethren dropped around her. Uriel fired the flamethrower in bursts of orange light, daring them closer, and they seemed to be afraid of the fire.

*But is it too late? Had we all been in the woods too long?*

*Has the evil grown past our ability to fight it?*

Old Man Tanner burst into the clearing and ran toward the chapel. Three forms swarmed him. He hunkered down, swung the torch as he moved, but they smothered him, so many birds twittering and shrieking around his flame. Choking and gasping for air, he unscrewed the lid to his gasoline jar and doused himself with the pungent liquid.

"No!" yelled Ellsworth. But Tanner hugged his torch and his body ignited, scattering the birds and giving him enough space to stagger toward the chapel door, diving in just as more forms of redbirds emerged into the clearing. One of them leaped at Eddington's horse, knocked him to the ground. Lou fired twice but then clutched his throat as he gagged and writhed on the ground. The mare backed up with a terrified neigh.

Twenty yards down the line, Donald Trapper and two others carried buckets of pitch, tar, and gasoline. Ellsworth ran toward them, slaying bird forms left and right. In the background he saw Anna Belle firing her revolver and swinging someone's torch. They were holding their own for now, but they were all quickly becoming overwhelmed.

Trapper dropped his buckets to the ground, fired his pistol, and screamed like a maniac. Ellsworth closed his eyes, gathered himself, and then plunged his sword into Tanner's buckets, then ran the coated blade through one of Gabriel's torches. Flame burst forth from the blade, licking orange-blue fire.

He corralled Eddington's horse, climbed atop, and kicked it forth into the clearing, slashing the flaming sword through cluster after cluster of cardinal figures. They backed away from his swinging blade. And then Gabriel stepped into the clearing with her two torches upraised. To Anna Belle's dismay, Raphael did the same, tiny compared to the rest but unafraid.

Uriel hung back, fiddling with the flamethrower, which had stopped working. Finally he threw it down, secured the ten-foot rope he'd had draped over his shoulder, and ignited the tip of it until it flamed orange-red.

The roof of the chapel was burning. Tanner had accomplished that much. But bird forms continued to pump from the open door, some larger than the ones before.

Ellsworth urged his horse forward. His cohorts had formed a small circle with him, swinging their fiery weapons. Ellsworth rode through the clearing, slashing his flaming sword from side to side. Uriel swung his flaming rope in controlled arcs, cutting through the birds as efficiently as Gabriel and Raphael did with their torches—she swinging above while the boy swung low.

The chapel rumbled, and the earth shook through another aftershock. Ellsworth counted four seconds of movement before the chapel door popped off as if pulled. The threshold around the door cracked, then crumbled as if something huge was forcing its way through.

Birds swarmed toward the door, clustering, churning, and finally forming the contour of a beast that stood ten feet tall, with a tail that scraped like a brush across the ground. It flailed its arms as if trying to deter the birds, but the cardinals kept coming, thickening the mass, slowing any progress. The giant form thrust a hand toward the outer edge of the clearing, blowing back those who remained standing, clearing them out like a scythe through a field. On the ground they choked and grabbed their throats. Hands tightened against revolver grips, and the barrels moved toward their heads.

Ellsworth charged, thrashing and swinging Blue Fire, but the fire was growing weak around the blade. The giant form knocked him from his horse. He rolled but held on to his sword.

The beast raised another arm of flapping birds and swung it in an arc. They ducked. Torches flaming, Gabriel charged directly into the body of the beast. The birds dispersed, then reformed. Uriel swung his rope, which burned shorter with every swing. He was tiring. They all were, and their fires were weakening. Raphael attacked the beast's tail with his torch, but every swing held less force.

Ellsworth went for the head and thought he'd severed it. Cardinal birds scattered and reformed like wind knifing through fog. And then a voice sounded from the woods.

*"Push'm back, Michael. Push'm back to the deep and burn this place down."*

*America Ma.*

Latin cadences sounded behind him. Father Radkin had pushed in closer to the chapel with Reverends Cane, Beaver, and Yarney, his voice booming as if performing the largest-scale exorcism ever administered. Radkin flicked holy water from a bottle he'd pulled from his purple robes. The smaller bird forms cowered. Reverend Hofhamm had found his feet and held a cross up high, singing loudly in German. Rabbi Blumenthal approached with his Talmud, Omar with his Koran.

Gradually Ellsworth and his three angels pushed the beast back, all of them swinging their fire at once. The beast broke apart, hissing, reforming, beaks and talons and broken red feathers scattering like dust, then gathering again. But they were making headway. They were backing the beast down. They were almost to the burning chapel.

Voices sounded from the open door. Raphael's parents. Uriel's mother. Old Man Tanner. Gabriel's father. Ellsworth's parents. Eliza. All inviting them to come in and kneel upon the healing floor one last time.

"They're not real," Ellsworth screamed, swinging at the beast. "Not real. Don't listen!"

The beast broke apart, arms and legs and head, but then fluttered back together, chirping and clacking against the chapel's exterior. The chapel's stained-glass windows shattered, and fire shot through. The roof buckled. Ellsworth swung with everything he had, blinded by flapping red wings.

"Hold," he screamed to the others as he took another step toward the chapel. "Stay back. I'm going in alone!"

He swung another violent cut with his sword. Bird wings scattered, singed, as he staggered across the threshold.

Beams burned all around him. Statues stood charred. Tiles from the mosaic floor popped and blackened. The figures in the bas-relief turned gray, then black, then orange as the walls were engulfed.

*Push'm back, Michael.*

Ellsworth gave one last plunge into the cardinal birds that remained, and then the roof caved in. Heat charged. Suffocating smoke and flames licking orange and red consumed him.

He heard Eliza's voice. *Michael . . .*

Blinding light. He walked toward it willingly.

\|||//

The buzzing drone was over.

The woods basked in silence. The cardinals had returned to the sky.

Ellsworth blinked heavy eyelids. Butterflies flashed across his vision. They'd pulled him from the chapel, which was a smoldering heap now, a tarred black mound of wood and stone spiraling dark smoke into an azure sky. The people, his people, crowded around, watching him as he lay on the deadfall. He couldn't move. Their voices were whispers.

*He can't die. He won't die. You watch and see. He fought back the beast. He saved us from the woods. He defeated the dragon.*

"Michael?" Gabriel hovered above him, her face angelic in the coppery white glow.

Ellsworth smiled. "Gabriel."

She wiped her eyes. "Michael, stay with us now."

Raphael stood next to her, eyes darting across Ellsworth's burned body as if unsure how to proceed.

"Don't," Ellsworth said to the boy. "Don't try. Not this time."

Raphael knelt and put his hands on Ellsworth's arm anyway. "But Mr. Newberry . . ."

"Keep throwing that baseball," he said to the boy. "Promise me."

Raphael nodded.

Ellsworth located Gabriel again. They locked eyes, and he grinned. "There's a door in the floor, Gabriel."

"Michael . . . what?"

His heart plodded, thumped intermittently now as Anna Belle's face came into view. Her beautiful face. He felt pressure against his hand. Felt her palm there, her interlocked fingers, and somehow he could hear her heartbeat.

"Don't you dare," she said. "Don't you dare die on me now, Michael Ellsworth Newberry."

He didn't mean to laugh. But it was odd how sometimes things came full circle. "Oh, Anna Belle. Reckon it's as good a day to die as any."

# AFTER

Bellhaven wept, but not for long.

As the new sheriff, Gabriel didn't let them. Ellsworth wouldn't have approved. He'd died to save the town, and he'd done so willingly, knowingly. So they put his body in a casket Omar built and buried him in the Bellhaven cemetery next to Eliza and Erik.

Gabriel announced Anna Belle Roper as her new deputy, and together the women breathed fresh air into a town reeling from another tragedy. Star badges pinned to their uniforms, they were the first to test the woods after the chapel burned. Blooms still painted the landscape like magic, but the air was different—a good different, just air plain and simple. They passed the yellow trees with no event and even took several long breaks to test what standing still would feel like. Again, nothing. At the clearing, the dying trees had stopped their march outward. Birds sang and twittered, but most of the cardinals had gone. The chapel was a mound of sooty black; not as high as Gabriel would have thought. But then, Anna Belle reasoned, the debris could have sunk deeper to fill the holes underneath.

"Probably plugged it up good too."

They sat on a log inside the clearing, sharing a canteen of water and listening to creek water spill over rocks. The sun beat down with hints of summer. A deer scampered in the distance, and a yellow warbler sang from a nearby bough. Just a pleasant spring day. They sat for ten minutes before moving on. Gabriel wondering if Anna Belle had been waiting for the same thing she'd been waiting for—Ellsworth's voice to come forth from that tarry heap of burned chapel. But that was jingle-brained thinking that needed to be unthought.

Before leaving the clearing, Gabriel approached the heap and spotted a blue tile somehow spared from the mosaic floor. She pocketed it, and the women returned back to town.

When it came time for the yellow trees to be splashed with fresh paint—an annual chore—Gabriel ordered them all cut down instead. She told them there was no need to fear the woods any more. So they felled all the yellow trees in two weeks and chopped them into firewood.

By the end of summer all the earthquake-damaged houses had been repaired. Lou Eddington had the top of the hill cleared, and the framing of his new house began soon afterward. He was proud of his new design, which included only one story and ramps for his wheelchair. He gave Anna Belle his bright red Silver Ghost and made her promise not to dent the fenders. He also asked if she would ever consider courting a man who'd never walk again, and she said, "I reckon anything is possible."

Omar took charge of building the new town hall. They'd leveled the old one, and the new one was finished before the fall leaves turned. The first party held there was a big one. They named the town hall after Ellsworth—Newberry Hall—and hung his sword horizontally above the front entrance. It became custom to touch the blade on the way out.

Raphael did what Ellsworth had asked of him and kept pitching. His fastball picked up speed every month, according to Omar, who'd assumed the role of playing catch with him. It was a Sunday thing they'd do, and Anna Belle would watch them throw and bring sweet tea when they were parched. She officially adopted Raphael a week before Christmas.

The next year the flowers bloomed in their typical seasonal patterns, and Ned Gleeson was back to making his birdhouses again.

Gabriel awoke on the one-year anniversary of Ellsworth's death with an idea to finally tear down the slave houses behind the hill. But first she and Anna Belle and Raphael placed flowers at Ellsworth's grave, and everyone in town paid their respects. They held a nondenominational service in the town hall and then partied most of the day away.

That evening as the sun went down, Gabriel told Anna Belle she was going to the slave houses and asked if she wanted to come along. It was time for them to be leveled once and for all, but first she figured she'd case them out.

She had gone in there a handful of times over the years to see if she'd see anything like what had happened when she and Ellsworth were nine. But it had been several years since she last ducked inside that cold threshold, and she hoped this time would be different. Some questions needed answers, and this one had all but burned a hole in her gut.

Sheriff and deputy approached the first slave house together, with Raphael a few yards behind them holding a lantern.

Anna Belle said, "Remember the time we were all set to go in and kill all the masters? Ellsworth had that stick you'd carved and pretended it was a sword."

"And everyone turned tail—"

"Except you and Ellsworth."

"I've never told anyone this, but he went in. By himself." Gabriel eyed the doorless opening. "Wait here."

"Gabriel? What happened? Did something happen when he went in?"

*Something happened all right.* She took the lamp from Raphael. Then she stepped up the concrete stoop, felt the rotted wood around the doorframe, and ducked inside. Cobwebs festooned the ceiling, blackened by years of candle smoke. A bird's nest took up half the tiny broken window. Leaves, dirt, and bird droppings covered the floor. She stood, hands on hips, surveying the dank interior. Wind entered behind her and nudged a thicket of wet leaves, exposing an uneven floorboard. She squatted down, brushed away dust and leafy filth. The boards were warped and splintered, rotted in parts, but something else caught her eye. The boards in the middle of the floor looked different than those around the edge—not only their color but the way they cut into the other boards. There was a three-foot-by-three-foot square where the gap in between the boards was wider.

Gabriel took the pocketknife from her trousers, stuck the blade between the boards, and pulled. The old wood creaked, and one board cracked, but then the square of boards came up in one piece.

*A door in the floor.*

Gabriel fell back on her rump and laughed until her voice echoed.

Anna Belle appeared in the doorway with Raphael. "What is it? Can we come in?"

"Watch your step." Gabriel pointed to the opening at her feet and smirked. "There's a door in the floor. Ellsworth's last words to me. I assumed he was talking about the chapel."

Anna Belle stepped closer and peered into the dark void. "I don't understand."

"I'll explain in a minute. Hand me the lantern."

Raphael picked it up and handed it over.

Gabriel stuck her head down into the hole, and in the lantern glow she saw a ladder and a muddy floor—and dark openings leading both north and south. "Well, I'll be . . ."

Anna Belle knelt beside her. "What is it?"

Blue Fire, the original sword she'd carved for Ellsworth from a tree branch, rested in a pocket of mud and slanted grip-up against the cold wall.

"Blue Fire," whispered Anna Belle.

"He left it down there." Gabriel shook her head knowingly. "The slaves built a tunnel connecting their houses, Anna Belle. That's how he ended up in the third one."

"Who?"

"Michael. Ellsworth. I thought he'd vanished. He played it off like he did."

"Gabriel, what are you talking about?"

Gabriel shone the lantern in the opposite direction, and the tunnel, supported by a network of brick and stone, extended at least twenty yards under the hillside. "Toward the river. They were preparing to escape one day." She came back up for air, feeling lightheaded, and sat back on her heels to catch her breath. Then she told Anna Belle and Raphael the story of Michael disappearing from the first slave house that day and emerging in a daze from slave house three.

"So he was only play-acting?" asked Anna Belle.

"Suppose so. I'd always assumed it was another thing unexplained from the woods. Another thing unexplained about him."

Raphael clapped and whistled, staring down into the door in the floor. "He got you good, Miss Fanderbink."

"Don't call me that anymore. Please. What a stupid name. I always wanted to change it."

"Name is just a name, Gabriel," said Anna Belle, reminiscing.

"So what should I call you?" asked Raphael.

"Gabriel will do. Just Gabriel. Reckon I don't need a middle or last."

They laughed about it—about her name, about the door in the floor—and the laughter turned to tears. Felt good to let those clean tears drip down their cheeks and remember.

Gabriel was about to stand when a cardinal bird showed up in the window. The arrival brought with it a palpable silence, aside from the fluttering of wings.

The three of them watched the bird in awe, how it eased into the nest and stared at them, head darting side to side and up and down as if it had just jerked them a nod.

Gabriel nodded back.

And then the cardinal flew away.

# DISCUSSION QUESTIONS

1.  Ellsworth Newberry was never able to have a son of his own. Describe different ways that Raphael helps fill the void, and compare his relationship with Ellsworth to Ellsworth's relationship with his own father.

2.  The novel ends with the same basic line with which it begins: *It was as good a day to die as any.* Although the words are the same, discuss the difference in meaning as it pertains to Ellsworth's mind-set at the beginning and end of the story. How does Ellsworth change throughout?

3.  How do hope and redemption play a role in the novel, specifically regarding Ellsworth and his past?

4.  Eliza, despite not being alive for the entirety of the novel, is a driving force for the narrative. Discuss her relationships and how they change the story.

5.  Throughout the novel, the theme of good versus evil permeates the narrative. With Lou Eddington's chess sets as one example, discuss others that could also fit the bill.

6.  For 1920, and even today, fictional Bellhaven is a very tolerant town. Explain how tolerance and intolerance are portrayed as catalysts throughout the novel.

7. Discuss how the topics of religion and gun violence in the story are similar or different than in today's environment.

8. After tragedy and the repercussions of the Great War, Bellhaven is a town in need of healing. From the old parties in the town hall to the daily gathering of war vets inside Ellsworth's living room, how do food, music, and togetherness play parts in this healing process?

9. Throughout the novel, even though the town hall is dilapidated, how is it more than just a building? What does the town hall really stand for?

10. Birds—cardinals, in particular—play a large role throughout the story. Discuss various ways the cardinal birds affect the narrative.

11. How is the chapel, and the discovery of it, a catalyst for everything that happens in the novel, in both good ways and bad?

12. The concepts of archangels and guardian angels are major themes in *All Things Bright and Strange*. Discuss any times when you may have felt someone was looking out for you in a similar way.

# ACKNOWLEDGMENTS

*All Things Bright and Strange* has a great deal to do with birds. I thought I'd kill two with one stone here and combine a few author notes with my thank-yous! Like my previous novel, *The Angels' Share*, this one is set back in history yet takes place in a fictional town. While being as historically accurate as I can to the time period, this gives me more freedom to create a bit of my own world and allow some of that supernatural in. In other words, this is one of those books that may not fit into a particular genre. Is it historical fiction? In a sense. Southern fiction? Sure. Commercial fiction? You bet'cha. Southern gothic? That sounds cool too! But basically, it's just a story I wanted to tell, and hopefully, if you made it this far, you liked it.

While the earthquake that takes place during the story is fictional, the great quake that leveled Charleston in 1886 was, unfortunately, quite real. At the time, as mentioned in the novel, no one had any idea how it could have happened—they thought earthquakes could happen only *between* tectonic plates and not also *inside* them. I read about this devastating Charleston earthquake, and the story started to evolve. I thought it would be fun to make up a new reason altogether for that earthquake, a supernatural reason, and that's where the idea of the chapel came into play. I've always been fascinated by the live oaks in Charleston and Savannah, and how they're almost magical in the way their branches twist and turn and grow every which way amid all that clinging moss. The mystically haunted Hoia Baciu Forest in Romania helped to inspire what would eventually become the Bellhaven woods. If you haven't heard of that Romanian forest, google it—it's fascinating! So I had these seeds growing for a story, and one morning I was driving and noticed a tree with, I kid you not, at least fifty cardinals in it. It was winter, and so the tree had no leaves, yet it was bursting with red color. Equally as unbelievable, about fifty yards away from the tree of cardinals stood a tree that held about a dozen big black vultures. I nearly drove off the road I was so shocked, but by the time I made it home, I was already formulating this story about magical woods and birds and bright colors, and *All Things Bright and Strange* soon came to life.

As usual, I may be two-finger typing these books by myself, but in the complete production process, an author is never alone. However, any mistakes are, of course, my own. I always get paranoid that I'll leave someone out, so for all those I'm accidently forgetting, thank you! Instead of saving the best until last, what say we flip that trend and go ahead and thank my wife, Tracy, from the get-go! Thank you for eighteen years of paying for stuff I can't afford to pay for—because I'm a writer. Hopefully, as the books continue to mount, that role will soon flip—because I'm a writer. And with a writer, you just never know what you're going to get, so thank you for being so flexible and understanding of all the oddities of this soon-to-be lucrative business. ☺ Thank you to my parents for raising my siblings and me in such a loving and creative household. Your shout-out is on the dedication page, in case you missed it. Thank you to my siblings—David, Joseph, and Michelle—your names just might be showing up on the dedication page of my next book! So beware! Thank you to my cousin John

Markert for supporting me from day one, from that very first terrible page I wrote twenty-plus years ago, and acting like there was hope for me. Craig Kremer, the perfect idea bouncer. To Gill Holland for reading that earliest draft, and for your constant support of my career. To Charlie Shircliff for letting me proof this book at your desk with that Michael the Archangel statue looking right at me. To my kids, Ryan and Molly, thank you for being interested in what I do—and keep reading! Speaking of reading, thank you to the following for reading all or parts of the book before publication: Tim Burke, Emma Markert, D'Ann Markert, Alex Markert, Rhonda Bunch, Phil Hoskins, Alden Homrich, Holly McArthur, Frances Ashbrook, Lee Ashbrook, Jeff Bunch, and Kathy Hoskins.

Thank you to Anne Buchanan for the line edit and expert advice. And thank you to all my friends at HarperCollins and Thomas Nelson, especially to my editor, Karli Jackson, for championing my work—your advice is always right on target. Thank you—from editing to production to marketing and beyond—I'd name you all, but I'd have nightmares that I left someone out! You know who you are, and you know I know, so thank you again!

And finally, you know the saying, "My dad can beat up your dad"? Well Dan Lazar isn't my dad, but he is my agent, and I bet he could beat up any agent I put in front of him, figuratively speaking of course. As far as agents go, he is the best, of that I am certain; and I'm still wondering to this day how I got him to sign me! But thanks Dan! And Torie! And everyone at Writers House for believing in me!

Now, back to writing.

Until next time, dear readers . . .

James Markert
Louisville, Kentucky
May 2017

DISCOVER THE MAGIC OF
UNEXPECTED KINDNESS . . .

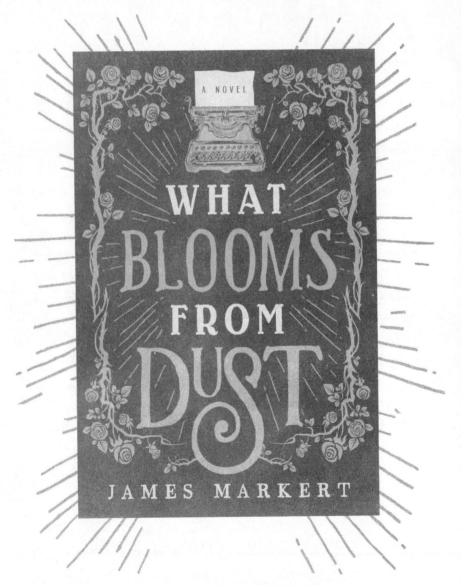

A NOVEL

WHAT
BLOOMS
FROM
DUST

JAMES MARKERT

AVAILABLE JUNE 2018

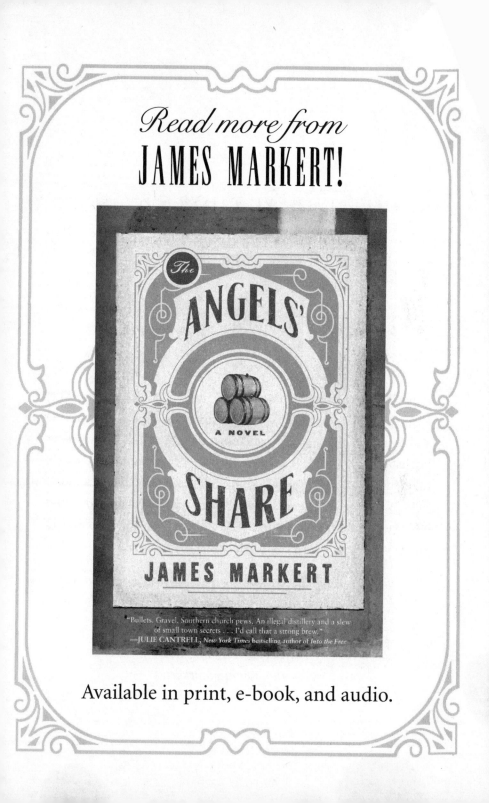

# ABOUT THE AUTHOR

James Markert lives with his wife and two children in Louisville, Kentucky. He has a history degree from the University of Louisville and won an IPPY Award for *The Requiem Rose*, which was later published as *A White Wind Blew*, a story of redemption in a 1929 tuberculosis sanatorium, where a faith-tested doctor uses music therapy to heal the patients. James is also a USPTA tennis pro, and has coached dozens of kids who've gone on to play college tennis in top conferences like the Big 10, the Big East, and the ACC.

\|\|//

*Learn more at jamesmarkert.com*
*Facebook: James Markert*
*Twitter: @JamesMarkert*